Finch Books by Carryn W. Kerr

Single Book
The Renascent World

I0662035

THE RENASCENT WORLD

CARRYN W. KERR

The Renascent World
ISBN # 978-1-83943-902-5
©Copyright Carryn W. Kerr 2020
Cover Art by Louisa Maggio ©Copyright July 2020
Interior text design by Claire Siemaszkiewicz
Finch Books

THE
RENASCENT
WORLD

Dedication

For Mom and Dad.
If I had a thousand words to thank you, they
wouldn't be enough to express my eternal
gratitude for your unconditional love and
encouragement.

At five years old, Cassidy had outlived almost Earth's entire population. Now, at sixteen, she's in a forbidden relationship with an unworthy Earth boy.

Prologue

I stood outside our home virtual experience slash living room, trying to summon the courage to enter, but my stomach was clenching so hard that it threatened to double me over. I hugged myself, rocking back and forth, and a soft moan seeped through my lips. When footsteps approached, I looked up. My eighteen-year-old brother strode across the dark wood flooring of our hallway toward me then leaned against the door frame and crossed his feet.

Although his stance was relaxed, he was not. His dense blond brows were as knotted as his fists, and his knuckles were turning white. His speech betrayed nothing when he spoke in his usual rapid-fire way. "Don't you want to wait until Mom and Dad get home from work before you go in, Cassidy? You might need them when you come out of the VE." Then he wrapped his arms around my head and shoulders. "Damn, little sister, I wish you didn't have to do this."

I loved how Liam cared for me, but his concern didn't ease my tension. I bit my lip, not exactly answering his question. "Were they here when you went in, Li?"

"On *my* 'Age of Understanding' birthday? No. You were at school, if you recall, and I went in while they were at work. Call it pride or whatever, but I hardly wanted Mom and Dad to see me break."

"And did you?" I met his bright green eyes. "Break, I mean?"

"Not to scare you, Cassidy, but everyone does."

I fixed on my leather sandals. "I know I'm supposed to go in alone, Li, but I really wish you could go with me."

He puffed a smile. "Honestly, Cass, I'd prefer that. Plus, I don't really care what Gina thinks."

Liam dropped his arms from my shoulders. He looked around as if we'd be caught and stopped or he or I would change our minds and back away. He jerked open the door to our home virtual experience room and held his hand, palm up, toward the center. I wanted to flop into the corner of the L-shaped leather couches, but I knew we weren't using them today.

Liam took my hand as the door sealed behind us. I sucked in a sharp breath and Liam gulped. The ceiling-mounted VE cube whirred, throwing a triangular light to the floor. The light expanded, sliding over our feet, up our legs, bodies and heads. A gravitational pull sucked us to the middle of the room, and a thick mist swirled around.

A light shone from out of the eye, and I grimaced. The stumpy body of Gina Petri, Petriville's founder, emerged through the mist. Horn-rimmed spectacles magnified her steel-gray eyes, and a toothy smile grew beneath her parrot nose.

Liam squeezed my hand as if to calm or comfort me.

Gina's oh-too-sweet melody reminded me a little of a snake. "Miss Jones, I hope you do not take too much stock in what you observe today. You must understand that I wiped this memory from our children only to protect you when you were young. At sixteen, I believe you will comprehend the miracle of the occurrence. This incident is now, after all, mankind's history. You may resent that I did not save your grandparents, Aunt Susan and her daughter Sarah, but only you were of the caliber I desired." She paused, and I wondered if she gave personalized messages to every sixteen-year-old in Petriville. I was about to ask Liam when Gina held her palm out toward something just past us. "Now, bear in mind what I have said as you visit your virtual experience."

The thick mist again swirled around and consumed Gina. Some seconds later it dispersed, leaving us in another time, just a short distance from where we now stood, right outside our front door.

I drew in the fragrance of spring flowers and freshly cut lawn. The soft early-evening breeze brushed my skin and tiny recording drones floated around spectators like silent flies, recording the events. As sunset's orange glow deepened, a three-dimensional version of Dad exited our home, looking all of the eleven years younger than he was now. The drones took in every facet of Dad's tall, fair, sculpted physique. The image of Mom stretched out on our front lawn. An incredulous expression lit her olive-toned face, her dark hair haloing around her head, her jeans never quite long enough to reach her ankles. *My beautiful, elegant mother.*

At seven and five years old, Liam and I buzzed around our parents. The breeze fluttered Liam's soft blond curls as he clasped my tiny hand in his and pointed to the sky. I recalled none of it but noted how, even then, we were tall for our ages and my deep blue eyes contrasted with my olive skin and straight, dark hair. And the knobby knees Liam had so often teased me about protruded below the hem of a pale blue dress that I could almost remember.

The scene was so lifelike that it drew me into the moment. All the way up and down our block, neighbors stood. They lined the cobbled walkway, stood on their front lawns or in the park. No eyes left the darkening sky as the myriad of tiny recording drones floated around families, capturing what would become our history.

Petriville's launch into space should have left me with a thousand vivid memories, but mine were like broken shards of glass—shimmering or shattered. To an onlooker, Petriville's launch must have seemed unnatural—a town within an indestructible dome, a transparent kaleidoscope of rainbow colors. The dome had ballooned into a sphere that had grown and grown until thrusters had propelled it into Earth's exosphere. Complete with houses, gardens, trees, conveyor streets, schools and shops, Petriville seemed to magically hover at the sphere's center. It was pure science, of course.

My focus drifted back to the VE, my gaze drifting upward. The most magnificent scene materialized, laced in tones of the softest blues to the deepest greens. Draped over it all, clouds floated in languid majesty — crisp white to deep, dark gray. It was as though we were Earth, and Earth was our enormous moon.

I stood, a spectator in the scene, and turned to Liam. "This is not new, though, Li. Earth isn't much different now from how it was then."

Although he'd seen this all before, he wore an incredulous expression. "Wait, Cassidy. This is so *you*

12

can see how it was back then. Plus, you know Earth wasn't like this for most of our lives."

Almost as soon as Liam had spoken, a swirling mist once more stole the scene. From its depths, a new visual experience emerged. Liam firmed his grip on my hand, clenching his jaw.

Again, we were outside our home, this time in the park over the curved, cobbled walkway. Everyone was outside on this dark night, ignoring the drones, which were skimming the standing crowds. All eyes were locked on the night sky. Whimpers escaped men, women and children. I followed their skyward stares, and my chest constricted.

Dad pulled Mom back against him as tears flooded her deep blue eyes and cascaded down her cheeks. All around, deathly silence fell.

The asteroid hurtled through space, its trajectory placing Earth in its direct path. It drew nearer, so much nearer.

Even though I knew the outcome, I found myself wishing things would turn out differently — that the meteorite would incinerate in Earth's atmosphere or the asteroid would glide past and miss our home planet entirely.

As the asteroid entered Earth's atmosphere, flame enveloped the monstrous bulk, turning it to a fiery meteor.

The fireball and tail shot across the sky, its speed impossible, incomprehensible, as it burned its way through the atmosphere toward Earth. And it barely lost any of its immense bulk as it neared. Then an ethereal brightening seared the dark sky. A shimmering mushroom of debris, light and dust shot into the air before raining back toward Earth.

Screams shattered the night, an echo in a chorus of onlookers' grief. But all I heard was Mom as my young parents collapsed to the ground, comprehension slamming into them. They had just lost almost everyone they loved. Searing pain tore into my gut. I clenched my fists until my fingernails bit into my palms. I barely noticed that I was clinging to Liam, that he held me against him, his arms as tight as the vise gripping my heart, that I shook, sobbed and that tears slid down his cheeks too. My parents' continued screams cut a burning, stabbing pain through my chest, constricting my throat. But I couldn't drag my eyes from them or escape the suffocating VE. My body numbed. A weighted, nauseated, distant dream took hold. I tried to lift my hand to wipe at the tears burning my cheeks, but my hand wouldn't move.

The VE faded into the swirling mist then slid away. We were back in the room with the familiar leather couches. After the longest time, Liam loosened his grip and I stepped away, wiping my cheeks. Liam kept his eyes on me. "Are you all right, Cass?"

A choked "Why would they make us—?" was all I managed as my tears gushed. Some fell onto my wrist, splashing Grandma's antique, white-gold wrap-around bracelet pen and the sixteen silver sparkle bangles Mom and Dad had given me that morning. My 'Age of Understanding' gift. Sixteen. The old maxim really applied to me. But it felt back-to-front, like the soft sensation of a boy's lips on mine should have preceded what I'd just witnessed.

And it wasn't for lack of wanting. I yearned to be in the arms of a boy, tasting his sweet lips. But I hadn't yet met the boy who had recently begun starring in my dreams—the boy with eyes the color of a tropical ocean, dimples etched into his cheeks and the body of an athletic Greek god. He most likely didn't exist, but he had ruined me for anyone else. A single, soft word made its way through my lips. "Why?"

Liam absorbed my gaze. "Not witnessing this doesn't erase nor diminish what happened. Don't you think this a fair way to honor the people who lost their lives?"

The words scraped through my throat. "I thought that was what our annual 'Extinction Day' commemoration was for." I hated the crass term. It didn't sound at all like an honor. Instead, I added, "I hate Gina for terming it something so cold."

Liam took my hand. "You shouldn't worry about her, Cassidy. She's just a crazy old bat."

Although it wasn't his fault, I glared up at him. "Are you sure that's all she is, Liam? Because I'm not."

* * * *

I was to learn from Dad that over the weeks following the meteor strike, live images of Earth had flashed across Petriville's digital billboards. Although the impact had flung rubble far out into space, the encasing compound had deflected any that floated too near to us. The hazy, red firestorm blur had steadily expanded from the impact site, consuming massive areas before finally burning out. What had remained of Earth had no longer been visible — no oceans, no land masses, no distinctions at all. A dense, solid gray cloud had shrouded the planet. As dust had blocked the sun, plants had withered and died — and life had dwindled and ceased.

Scientists had estimated that more than a hundred years might pass before we could return to Earth or that an ice age might follow.

Neither happened.

By three years post-impact, the haze had become significantly clearer, the shroud less dense. Some variations had appeared through the fog. Europe and parts of Asia, the hardest hit, were blackened, stagnant wasteland. But, in the southern Americas, forests and rivers appeared — for lack of a better term — *less dead.*

Many years before, world-renowned geologist Dr. Graham Porter had researched the Eltanin Impact Crater in the Southern Pacific Ocean. He had discovered a remarkable compound and had named it Kaleidotonium.

Gina Petri had gotten her hands on the Kaleidotonium and had had a dome constructed. It was permeable to water and the unique breathable-gas concoction required by organic life. While it had kept the cold out, inside, the town of Petriville had been built and populated.

Deep in Petriville's core, power was generated, and the high-speed rotation of the Kaleidotonium shell kept our town at its center. Like on Earth, our sky was blue. Ice and water particles that we encountered in space permeated the shell and fell in the form of raindrops. Artificially stimulated, our seasons and weather patterns matched Earth's Northern Hemisphere.

But as fascinating as it all was, to us — the youth of Petriville — it was just home.

Chapter One

A few months later

The playground equipment lay still, the night calm. A nearby sprinkler system *whoosh-whooshed* a fine spray over the park's flower beds. My friend Harriet and I dropped to adjacent sectors of the roundabout, and the familiar rough, cold metal scratched my back—but not irritating enough to make me leave. It never was. We tolerated nearly anything for our favorite nighttime activity—even the unexpected, fine rain that was sure to shower us in a mist at any moment.

We kicked off from the ground, and the silver roundabout glided into a slow rotation.

Harriet raised her blonde head, a smile dimpling her cheeks. As usual, in her diluted Scottish accent, she announced every sentence as if it were an exclamation. "Still amazing, hey, Cass? Earth-gazing!"

"Mm-m." I shrugged. "It's a beautiful planet."

She changed the subject. "Why are Liam and Jonas still training? They should kick back for a while!"

I shrugged. "There's always next year. Anyway, what does it matter how the boys spend their holidays?"

Harriet giggled. "They make me feel guilty for relaxing."

I laughed, rolling my head in her direction. "Forget them." A strand of hair fell over my eyes. I attempted to thrust the heavy tresses back inside the confines of my red beret.

Harriet gaped at me, arching a blonde brow over her bright blue eyes. She sat up. "Hey, lanky, let me help you with that. Half your hair has fallen out."

"I'm not lanky," I groaned, sitting and sidling over to her.

She rearranged my hair. "Uh, I think you are. And these"—she reached up and held my hair in one hand then tugged at my jeans belt loop with the other—"ankle coolers only accentuate your long legs. What are you complaining about, anyway? I'd swap my height and hips for your athletic frame in a heartbeat." She tucked my hair back inside my beret. "There! Much better."

"Oh please, Harriet. Boys love your curves."

"Yeah? Boys might, but my clothes don't." Then she yelped, "What the—? What is *that*?"

For the briefest moment, I considered her weak attempt to divert my attention. But, in my visual periphery, I had caught a flash too. As I jerked my gaze skyward, the flashes withdrew. I jolted upright, and my heart thumped. Harriet was on her feet beside me, both of us gaping at the sky. For long minutes, we stared upward, but the flashes were gone.

Although we retreated to the roundabout, my eyes did not leave Earth—a beacon against her star-flecked backdrop. Still, no repeated pulsing light materialized.

Concluding the flashes had been the result of something striking Petriville's outer dome, we fell back into casual conversation — that was, until a quick motion made me swivel my head toward the conveyor street that fringed the park.

"Why is my mom in such a rush?"

She was walking in long strides, almost running. Her upper body was visible over the top of the park's surrounding hedge. The conveyor gave her the appearance of someone floating.

Harriet raised her head and I answered my own question — my voice a squeak. "She saw the flashes!"

We leaped up.

Harriet gestured toward the corner. "That way, Cass!"

I needed no encouragement. We raced toward the intersection where the walkway passing our home met the dual conveyor street.

As Mom caught sight of us running, she slowed her stride for a few seconds. We made it to the corner, just as she stepped off. The conveyor continued its revolving journey beneath the transparent, glowing intersection footbridge.

Mom did not break pace as she sped along the walkway toward our house, her voice flat and dry. "Come with me."

After passing the garden-path entrances of two homes, we turned into ours. I looked into Mom's deep blue eyes, a mirror of my own. She pursed her lips, glancing back over her shoulder then around.

"What's up, Mom?"

"Indoors, Cassidy. Please wait to speak until we're indoors. Dad is waiting."

That did not explain her agitation but I didn't pursue it further. Not then.

We strode along the garden path between rows of flowers and our perfectly manicured lawn, vaulting all three patio stairs as one.

A moment after we burst through the front door, Dad and our third-generation Dobermans, Achilles and Yvon, came running from the kitchen. All their eyes rested on Mom's strained expression.

Dad frowned. "Hey, Emily, tell me what happened."

"Dare we hope, Peter? But I think Graham might be alive!" she exclaimed, still looking around as if someone might have followed us inside.

I sometimes considered how at-odds my mother's pompous-sounding speech was with her soft, gentle nature.

Mom turned to me. "Please, girls, go upstairs. Cass, your father and I need to talk. We'll tell you what we need from you in a moment."

I mouthed at Harriet, my heart still thumping. "Need from *me*?"

Harriet silently met my gaze as she and I ascended the stairs to my bedroom, closing the door behind us.

Without pausing for a break, Harriet fired the questions as a statement. "What was that? Will your mom tell us? It must be about the flashes!"

"Well, I'm sure I don't know, Harri. It's bizarre."

A short while later, a soft *rap-rap* fluttered my bedroom door. I leaped up and jerked it open. Mom and Dad stood on the landing.

"Come in," I said quickly. "Is this about the flashes?" Their eyes widened as they entered, and Dad closed the door.

"I thought you girls might have seen it." Mom's voice was tight.

I took in her ashen face. "Why would that bother you, Mom?" I turned to my father. "Dad?"

Harriet stood in uncharacteristic silence beside my pale mint-draped four-poster bed.

Dad glanced at Mom. I focused on her as she drew a deep breath, placing both hands over mine. Her intense eyes shimmered with a desperate plea. "I will explain in time, Cass. But since you have enrolled to study environmental sciences after summer vacation, I can justify offering you an internship. I'd like you to start tomorrow. You may not tell anybody what you're doing there. Understand? Not *anybody*!"

My temples throbbed as I considered her offer, but before I could speak, Dad took over in a stern voice, finally involving Harriet in the conversation. "Harriet, Emily and I will discuss this with your parents, but please" — he paused, darting his eyes between Harriet and me — "please," he repeated," do not mention a word to anybody. We'll tell you everything once we've made sense of it ourselves."

"What was the light, though, Dad?" I shot out. "And who were you talking about, Mom? Did you mean Graham Porter? The same Graham who discovered Kaleidotonium?"

Dad's tone sharpened. "As I told you, Cassidy, *we* need to make sense of this. What we think, however" — he hesitated, then added in a grating whisper — "is that many lives will be at stake if this gets out!"

I opened my mouth to say more but closed it again. Although I wanted to know what was going on, it was clear that whatever the truth of the matter was, it *terrified* my parents.

Chapter Two

After breakfast the following morning, Mom and I prepared to leave. The sound of Liam's favorite visual experience show blared through the house. The door stood ajar and the triangle of light descended to the floor, this time filling only half the room with animated sound-producing images. My brother was draped over the leather couch with one muscled leg on the center table. He wore sweat-dampened running clothes and had tossed his socks and shoes onto the wooden floor near the front door.

Achilles and Yvon were melting onto the throw rug beside him. As Yvon heard my footsteps, she leaped up and darted across the room, her sharp claws clattering on the wood flooring. I feinted her charge, and a giggle burst from my chest. She very narrowly missed knocking me flat as she skidded by then spun back.

Kneeling, I stroked her sleek, black head. "Hey, crazy!" She pushed upward into my hand.

In contrast, Achilles appeared exhausted from the early morning run with Dad and Liam and remained flat on the throw rug beside his favorite person. He did, however, raise his head and twitch his pointy black nose in the air. Then he resettled and, as though deciding that I deserved only the attention of his sad brown eyes, continued gazing up at me.

Liam made no effort to leave the comfort of the couch and merely twisted his head toward me. He shoved his sweat-disheveled blond hair from his high forehead, which protruded as if the frontal lobes were engaged in an escape attempt from the confinement of his skull. Using his wrist, he rubbed an itch on the bridge of his nose before acknowledging my presence, "Hello, little sister." How could he appear, and even sound so calm while words flew from his lips in rapid fire?

I shook my head and rolled my eyes at the cereal bowl balancing precariously on his thigh. Still stroking the bump on Yvon's head, I shrugged my brows at his balancing act. "One day, you're going to spill that all over yourself."

He shrugged. "Maybe," he agreed and turned back to his VE Show.

I left the room and headed toward the front door where Mom was tapping her foot a little less than patiently.

Liam yelled after us, curiosity tingeing his voice, "Where are you going?"

Leaving the question hanging in the air, I followed Mom out onto the porch and closed the front door.

After crossing the ever-glowing intersection footbridge, we stepped to the conveyor's edge. Passing commuters opened a space for us. We hopped aboard, riding the gentle upward slope. On each sidewalk of the dual-conveyors, a row of lollipop trees and Victorian street lanterns ushered us to town. They abandoned their posts only beneath glowing, transparent footbridges and for the huge, strategically placed, neon digital billboards. Before long, we were approaching the large shiny black number two, marking the conveyor's end. Hundreds of pedestrians were dismounting the twelve conveyors, cutting wedges between each of Petriville's dozen sectors and converging in the circular town square, like the hands of a clock.

In the square, six even-more-prominent digital billboards stood. They switched between two scenes. In the first, the bright orange Petrician Enterprises banner wafted in a breeze. In the second, Gina Petri's bespectacled face and parrot nose shadowed her broad mouth as it stretched into a proud, toothy smile. Three cherubs punctuated the midpoint of the 'clock', spewing water into a surrounding fountain pond. In the park, Petrician Enterprises' employees milled about on aspen-shaded park benches or bustled along the square's cobbled paving as they headed to work.

Mom led me across the square toward the Environmental Sciences building in sector five. After passing the shiny black four and dual-conveyor, I glanced down at a manhole cover. "Do you know what I think the manhole is for, Mom?" Before she could respond, I led her down the path of my overactive imagination. "I'll bet tunnels connect the town in some sort of underground maze."

She laughed and raised her eyebrows but without comment, and led me across her office park's entrance tiles. In front of the building, circular cutouts in the paving imprisoned maple trees as they shaded pretty park benches.

The prospect of entering Mom's two-story building unnerved me. The old-style stone construction felt acutely eerie. Hairs prickled the nape of my neck as we mounted the entrance stairs. I paid little attention to the few who exchanged greetings with Mom or the robot janitor as he mopped the shiny silver lobby floor. This was as far as I'd ever been inside Mom's office building.

At the end of a long corridor, thick double doors halted our progress. A label on the door read *Environmental Scientist – Emily Jones*. Mom placed her finger on the red biometric access indicator.

Instantly the door clicked open, revealing a large, circular room with a raised silver platform at its center. Surrounding the platform, three evenly spaced, arched silver arms narrowed and curved up toward each other, almost meeting at the top. It reminded me of a three-fingered claw.

A long, tiled screen arced along the circular wall above a curved desktop. Various pieces of unfamiliar equipment stood atop the desk. I found the soft blue lights soothing to my eyes, but Mom flicked on bright lights before beginning to work.

"I'll go through the equipment, but it is sensitive, so please do be careful, Cass."

"Of course, Mom…absolutely." But what I had really wanted to say was, *'If you're so damned worried about the stuff, why ask me to work with it?'*

Unaware of my internal dialogue, she added, "Interpreting the returned data will keep you busy while you are waiting."

I screwed up my eyes and cocked my head. "Waiting for what, Mom?"

"Bear with me, will you, Cass? I am getting there."

She proceeded, explaining that many years before leaving Earth, Petrician Enterprises had placed five thousand pods across the continents and in the ocean. The meteor strike had destroyed many – those nearest the impact point. But most had survived, due to their titanium composition and octagonal structure. She went on to tell me that claws, attached to these pods' outer walls, took weekly soil, water and air samples. An automated process then transmitted that data to the machines on her desktop.

She sat and gestured to the wheeled office chair beside her. I dropped to the proffered seat and pulled it to the desk.

Mom then explained which machines analyzed the collected samples and graphed this information. She concluded by showing me which screen-tiles displayed the interpreted data. Each tile served a different purpose.

After a short while, I had grasped the first few basic concepts. "You're a good teacher, Mom."

She gave me a half-smile. But my curiosity niggled over something she had not yet mentioned. "What's that silver platform? The one in the center." *As if she needs the clarification.*

Looking down, she drew a deep breath, not speaking before expelling the air. "That, Cass, would have found value" — she paused then quietly added — "had anyone on Earth survived." She raised her deep blue eyes to meet mine. "It's a virtual communication pod. It links with and works through the pods I was just talking about."

"Wow, Mom. So, if anybody *did* survive..." I trailed off as the sad comprehension dawned. If anyone had survived, why hadn't they used these pods?

Mom nodded slowly in answer to my silent question, casting her gaze downward.

My curiosity had not waned, and soft words slipped through my lips. "How does it work, though, Mom?"

Biting her lip, she smiled, as though recollecting. "Dad and I tested it once. The technology is incredible." She looked up at me. "Quite amazing. Along with standard audio feeds, the technology encompasses a series of electrical currents — an air displacement and concentration formula." She brow-gestured at the three silver protrusions. "Those arms generate both, and the result is rather more than a mere three-dimensional image." She sighed, smiled and, with a dismissive wave of her hand, added, "It's rather difficult to explain the effect. We could try it out when we're back on Earth, you and I."

Her use of 'when' distracted me. Reality set in. No longer would we talk about '*if*' we could return to Earth. It was now only a matter of time.

My mind drifted to the possibility of survivors. "But, Mom, what about the flashes?"

She sighed, adding resignedly, "They may not mean a thing, Cass. Truthfully, I'd rather not discuss this until we have something conclusive."

"But I can help, Mom. I'm assuming you think there might be survivors on Earth? I can search for them."

She sighed as if that were impossible. "My dearest daughter, as bright as you are, do you honestly think *you'll* find something I haven't, when I've worked with this for more than eleven years and the technology for way longer than that?"

After a brief silence, Mom went on, explaining the printed data — what to look for and why. She told me only things concerning Earth's recovery — not as I had hoped, to do with possible survivors.

With this new understanding, though, a warm tinge of hope welled in me.

Mom pulled me back from my musings, "I'll arrange for your biometric access, as we'll need you to do evening collections."

I pressed again. "So why can't I talk about my work here, Mom?"

"Because you'll be working with incredibly sensitive information." She widened her eyes, and her tone added, '*Of course*'.

Her reasoning did not ring true, but she sighed. "I suppose the truth is that Gina is unaware of our search for survivors."

"I don't understand, Mom. Why would you need to *hide* survivors from Gina?"

"We are just not sure." Her voice cracked, and as a single tear slipped down her cheek, she turned away, swiping at it.

She hadn't answered my question at all, but I went on anyway, "Who's this 'we' you keep referring to?"

She dipped her eyes. "Never you mind that. Anyway, the signal is line-of-sight dependent, and we need you to monitor video feeds from the external pod cameras."

My frustration overflowed. "Why must I help you if you insist on keeping things from me?"

"Cassidy! I'd have thought your sense of moral obligation would be motivation enough to *want* to help us. These questions are of no concern to you." She sighed, softening her voice, "I am sorry, Cass, but this is important."

She was wrong, though. These questions greatly concerned me. But she was right, too. I *did* want to locate survivors if anybody had lived...desperately! So, I diligently engaged myself in my evening internship.

* * * *

As the days dragged on, the data and video footage continued to reveal an Earth devoid of life. I all but lost optimism, shrinking inside myself as reality dawned. The chance of anything existing down there *was* near zero. A hundred unrelated causes might have triggered the flashes.

For three weeks I plodded on before anything changed.

After routinely drawing the data, I strolled down the hall for coffee. When I returned, I rested my feet on the desk with the mug on my thigh, enjoying the warmth of the hot ceramic filtering through my jeans. Settling in to wait, I flipped through video footage around Earth's pods, while the various instruments whirred and beeped, completing their data analyses. Most scenes looked like dull stills. I flipped past those and focused on the pods nesting in recovering or thriving plant life.

I expected to see nothing. There was never anything to see. I had turned away for just a second, but movement in my peripheral vision made me snap my head around.

I almost fell off my chair. *What was that?* I jerked bolt upright, nearly spilling the coffee in my lap.

Setting the mug on the desk, I drew myself nearer the motion-triggered, now-flashing video tile. I held my breath while three-hundred-and sixty degrees rotated slowly past the camera.

It appeared again at the edge of the lens. Something *was* moving out there.

I attempted to zoom, retract, tilt and raise the lens to see more — attain more clarity in the images. Fidgeting with the classic white-gold wrap-around pen on my wrist, I waited nervously. The camera made another slow three-hundred-and-sixty-degree rotation —

scanning its surroundings. I found myself gritting my teeth as it neared its end. Another short flash smudged the same screen-tile, but only as it skittered past the spot.

Again, a full rotation passed before I got a brief glimpse of the activity.

Feeling frustrated, I lifted the office handset and dialed home.

Mom answered on the second ring. "Hi, sweetheart, are you in the office?"

"No," I replied without thinking, before deciding that sarcasm was probably not conducive to a productive conversation, "Sorry... I mean, yes. I think there's something you should see. I've made a copy. I'm sure there's movement at one point in the camera's rotation."

"Really?" Mom's voice rose in pitch. "Which pod is that?"

"PQ316T." The alphanumeric system made sense to her. She would know the exact location of this particular pod. "But it's in the middle of nowhere," I added, pouting.

"Transmit the clip to me, would you? I'll let you know shortly." She had spoken in a brisk tone, though she'd kept her voice level.

After assuring Mom I'd do as she'd asked, I pressed the disconnect button and transmitted the clip to her. While waiting for her to return my call, I tapped my fingers on the desk — absently following the camera's slow rotation.

Even though I expected it, the sudden beeping of the phonepad's earpiece made my heart leap. The camera had reached the spot again and I had almost missed its revelation!

My stomach pitched and fell as I considered what the reality had just become. My hands shook as I scrabbled for the phonepad's answer button. I needed to calm myself.

Mom spoke before I could tell her about my most recent observation, "I don't see anything, Cassidy."

"There's something else, Mom —" I began.

She cut me off again. "I'm certain that you think you saw something," she continued, "but your mind is playing tricks on you."

She disconnected the call before I could tell her she was wrong, because I had absolutely no doubts now — none at all — because what had passed over the camera's lens was a hand.

Chapter Three

I fell into a surreal wide-eyed trance.

Selecting the video clip, I replayed it and paused. It *was* a hand — a real human hand. I hovered over the clip, pondering.

What I did next made no sense. I wasn't even sure what compelled me. Without really considering my actions, I lifted the small laser, clicked it at the screen tile, activating the relevant virtual keyboard and mouse. As both materialized beneath my hands, I selected and deleted the clip. Then I moved to the next screen-tile and the next, repeating the process and erasing every bit of related data.

After the fact, I began comprehending my deed. "Cassidy!" I chided, "Are you insa — "

A voice cut me off — male, smooth, cadenced, languid and barely audible. "Hello?"

A sharp shiver tingled down my spine. I jumped — grateful I'd finished my coffee. Otherwise, I would surely have tipped the contents onto my lap. The voice had come from behind me — inside Mom's office.

I spun my chair and launched up in one motion. Had somebody entered without my noticing? *How rude…sneaking up on a person like that.*

But nobody was in there.

Then again, "Anybody there?"

I refocused on the pod's outer camera footage. Although, I shouldn't have bothered. Those transmitted no audio feeds.

Only then did the raised silver platform draw my attention.

I gasped and stood frozen, my jaw dropping as I gaped at the alluring figure there. He graced the platform like a celestial being. Short, sun-flecked waves crowned the masculine head. He stood poised — his well-toned physique a golden bronze. But his aquamarine eyes shimmered with all the same anguish that was racing through my veins.

My heart thumped. He looked a lot like the boy from my dreams!

He was a hologram, of course — a simulation. I was sure of that fact but equally sure that he was as real and alive as me. And he was on *Earth. He* was the owner of the hand!

I walked toward the platform and stepped up warily, twisting my bangles around my wrist.

The apparition jumped back…startled.

My heart skipped a beat. I gulped.

He circled the edge of the platform, flexing and clenching his fists — like a predator circling its prey.

I did, too, but my mouth was dry. I couldn't stop swallowing.

"Who are you?" My voice emerged as a ragged croak.

"Eric Morgan. And you are...?" His measured response made my heart lurch. A faint Texan accent rounded his words.

I gasped and "Cassidy" was all I managed to choke out while admiring the hard chest and shoulder muscles beneath the T-shirt and his smooth, bronze skin. A wide leather belt held his jeans low over his tight, flat abdomen.

He stood tall. I would surely fit beneath his chin. His high forehead softened the heavy, troubled brow beneath it. Vigorous physical labor had built this body, these calloused hands and strong fingers. When he pulled his soft, full lips into a grimace, the change in expression dragged long, crevassed dimples down his cheeks, deepening as the scowl grew.

As he laid his hands over his hips, the edges of his toned shoulders tipped forward. I dragged my eyes away—mortified by my lengthy observation.

Chagrin warmed my cheeks. I humiliated myself further by stating the obvious. "You're on Earth, Eric!"

He said nothing but kept his eyes on me and frowned.

I stopped circling and gestured dramatically with my palms up. "What exactly is confusing you?"

He glanced around then said, "Your statement was a bit strange. Where else would we be?"

"So, you *are* real!" That was more for me than for him.

"Seriously?" He threw a sarcastic half-laugh, again frowning and flashing his dimples. Still, he circled me. "What did you expect? Some kind of illusion?"

My responses were running from bad to worse. "I mean, you really are on Earth."

Before he could comment, I quickly followed my ludicrous statement with the only question that mattered — the one that had been swirling through my mind since laying eyes on him. It made my mouth parched, my breathing too labored. I enunciated each word. "How...did...you...survive?"

Now he just looked horrified. "What do you mean, how did we survive? Are you kidding me?" He narrowed his eyes. "It's sure not clear what you're about, but it sounds like you're *not* on Earth! That kind of begs the question... Where are *you*?"

When I didn't answer, he looked around. A contemplative, distressed frown pulled his brow low.

He broke the silence as though speaking to himself rather than to me. "And since I'm standing inside some communication pod and you're obviously in a control center, I'm guessing you know where I am." He grimaced and carried on as if he had drawn his own conclusion. "Well that's just fantastic! This must be the place Graham mentioned."

"Graham?" I inquired.

Again, he ignored my question but turned his askance gaze on me, voice catching. "Where exactly are you" — he paused and swallowed — "Cassidy?"

"I'm in my mom's office." Then I repeated, "Graham who?"

Still, he offered no response.

"What is Graham's surname?" I urged more loudly.

He shook his head as if to clear it then raised his aquamarine eyes. He tugged his face into a sneer and hissed through clamped teeth, "Why are you so interested?"

I fired the words back. "Tell me, Eric! It's important!"

He cocked his head, seeming unsure whether to reveal the information, then he sighed. "Graham Porter."

I gasped, my throat constricting. A hoarse whisper escaped my lips. "Graham *Porter*?"

Did he know that we owed our lives to Graham? That we lived due to his discovery? But, wasn't Graham in Petriville with us? I'd never seen him, though Joshua Carter, our parents' astrophysicist friend, spoke of him often enough. Photographs of the two men receiving awards adorned walls in his and his wife Caroline's home.

Since Joshua, the man who had discovered the asteroid, lived here with his family, I'd always assumed that Graham, the man who had unearthed Kaleidotonium, lived here too. Nobody had ever implied the contrary.

"That's what I said, isn't it?" he snarled, squaring off into a defensive posture.

My voice faltered. "Why are you still on Earth? Why is Graham still on Earth?"

He steeled his jaw more before he half-repeated my question. "Why are *we* still on Earth? *Why?*" he emphasized in a near shout. "Let me ask you this. Why are you *not* here? How did you escape? And where in this damned universe are you?"

Twice I had asked him direct questions and twice, he had deliberately avoided answering me.

Although he had not answered my questions, he seemed surprised by *my* unwillingness to reply. Regardless, he continued as if he had gained sufficient comprehension. Immeasurable horror froze him in place.

He fisted his hands. "You're working for Gina Petri. So, this was how she betrayed Graham and left us to die!"

Again, he looked around at his surroundings. "And now you know our location." He gave a sarcastic half-laugh as he again circled me. "That's exactly the information you needed."

He swiveled as though to leave.

"Wait, Eric. Please let me explain."

He turned back. "Okay then. Confirmation of your location will be a good start."

I sighed then conceded, "I am in Petriville. We are not on Earth. We are in her orbit, though," and quickly added, "but I am *not* working for Gina. I'm working for my mother." I looked down then raised my eyes, only a whisper escaping my lips. "What do you know about Gina?"

The hologram started fading in and out.

"I'm losing you, Eric. I'm losing transmission."

"Wait, Cassidy. Are you —?"

His final words were lost. In a flash, he evaporated. Sharp emptiness replaced him.

My mind was still spinning as the biometric access indicator beeped. I leaped from the platform toward my chair just as Mom raced through the office door. She looked around suspiciously, heading directly toward me.

"So you did see it!" I blurted.

She said nothing, but hardened her face into a grimace. She gripped my upper arm and dragged me from her office down the corridor. My bangles jingled as she jerked me outside behind her. "Tell me, Cassidy. What exactly did you see? Tell me everything."

She was hurting my arm.

I pulled away. "No, Mom, No! It was nothing."

Mom fixed her eyes on mine, reached up and tucked a stray strand of hair behind my ear, "If there is anything, anything at all, Cass, you must tell me. *Please!*" she emphasized. "We'll only maintain this alignment for a few months." Then, with a sigh, she threaded her arm through mine. Still looking around furtively, she whispered, "Let's get home before we discuss this any further."

* * * *

For the next two weeks, I continued my evening job, searching video feeds for another flash of light—or another sign of Eric. Neither appeared.

Chapter Four

As was customary on the last day of summer vacation, Petrician Enterprises invited all youth on a zoo outing. This holiday was no exception.

Darkness still blanketed Petriville when Liam and I left home. I snuggled into my cream turtleneck and sucked in a sharp breath of fresh, crisp air, a subtle burn tingling my airways.

As if I would somehow miss her in her jeans and bright pink jacket standing at the intersection bridge with Jonas, Harriet waved both arms in the air. "Over here, guys!"

Eyeing his sister, Jonas shrugged and pulled his puffy lips into a *'Seriously?'* pout.

We crossed the bridge to the far side of the dual-conveyor. The neon digital noticeboards now looped garish propaganda about Gina Petri's remarkable achievements.

Weight-activated, both conveyors lay still. Liam and Jonas brought the conveyor to life, and Harriet and I followed. We stayed a little behind them.

Harriet lowered her voice as we sailed past the park. "I've not seen you, not once, since you started working for your mom!"

Ignoring her taunt, I glanced at the glowing, transparent underside of an intersection bridge as we drifted beneath it. Harriet turned, gauging my expression—or giving me the chance to explain. I didn't.

She lowered her voice even further. "Have you heard anything more? About the light, I mean!"

I half-centered on Harriet, and half-glanced at the school from which we had just graduated, the school Liam and Jonas had left two years before.

Harriet put her hands on her hips, arching one brow and throwing me a side-glance.

I finally responded as we glided beneath the next bridge. "I'm not supposed to talk about my work."

Harriet met my apprehension with an empathetic frown.

I added in a defeated whisper, "I'm not even sure I want to discuss this, Harri."

"This is *me*, Cass! And what do you mean you're not sure you want to discuss this? We've never kept anything from each other before. Not *ever*!"

"It's complicated." I sighed without elaborating. We journeyed beneath the next few intersections in irritated silence.

Mama Candy's drifted into view, its ever-changing display twirling across the sidewalk. Still, I kept my lips together. A robot cleaner walked toward us, vacuuming the sidewalk, low curb and conveyor borders. It wore a short black dress, a white apron and cap. In a perfectly smooth feminine voice, it announced, "Good morning, fellow Petrivillians."

I shook my head, muttering to Harriet, "At least it keeps our streets clean."

It looked pretty — our town, not the robot. Pretty and perfect. *Too perfect.*

We hopped off before the shiny black number two, skirting the town square behind Liam and Jonas, where we exited into sector four. While jogging up the wide, stone staircase, the dark glass doors to Petriville's only train station glided open before us.

A high-tech silver bullet train waited at the platform. Harriet scowled, gesturing at the lively crowd, exclaiming more than asking, "Seriously? This place is already packed!"

Liam responded in his usual rush of words — contrasting his casual demeanor. "Did you expect something different?"

"Here we go again." Jonas shook his head as we moved to board the train — his Scottish accent not as strong as Roger's or even Megan's, but somewhat more pronounced than Harriet's.

A group of girls, seated on each side of the aisle, started singing some old Earth song. Harriet swayed her hips to the imagined beat, making her way to the back and plopping onto the black leather bench.

As Liam and Jonas whumped down opposite us, I caught an exchanged smile between Liam and Harriet — one I wasn't meant to witness. Something twisted in my stomach as I considered how the three were keeping something from me — and how, with their wavy fair hair, they looked more like siblings than Liam and me. I felt, suddenly, like an outsider.

Liam leaned forward and rested his toned forearms on his knees, wrist-rubbing the bridge of his nose. He fastened his bright green eyes on mine, lowering his quick-fire voice. "Hey, sis. We sort of miss you hanging out with us."

A dry chuckle escaped my mouth. "Thanks for the 'sort of'. It makes me feel so loved."

Liam continued, "So have you seen anything interesting while working for Mom?"

I cocked my head, squinting. "What makes you think I've seen something, Li?"

I threw a glare at Harriet.

"Nothing." He paused. "Just curious."

"Oh, no, you're not. You're looking for information."

He didn't skip a beat. "Not for anything that I wouldn't tell you, if our roles were reversed."

I scowled at Harriet again.

She turned away then back. "What? I haven't said a thing! Seriously, Cass." Then, rolling her eyes, she added, "So yes, I told them. I'm sorry, okay? But I don't see why they shouldn't know." She didn't sound one bit sorry, though—not at all.

Liam urged Harriet to change seats with him and he dropped beside me.

A resigned sigh broke from my chest. "I suppose they'd have found out eventually."

Liam threw his arm around my shoulder and pulled me to him, whispering into my hair, "I do miss you, though, little sister. And you know I love you, right?" With a sincere smile, he pulled back to observe my face. Manipulation was really not Liam's thing.

"Fine. Just don't try exploiting my trust again." I grunted and went back to gazing out of the window. The train slithered silently through Petriville's outskirts and the automated ecological factories. The slow, continuous descent found us coasting through the first crop-farming ring then the domestic-animal circle.

I shivered from a sudden drop in temperature as we descended deeper into the valley, before the bright orange hue of sunrise peered over the horizon, bringing warmth with the light.

Outside the window, Petriville's two hundred mares took flight across the green paddock, their heads and tails high—manes flowing from their sleek, muscular necks. Stallions were housed on the far side of Petriville. Otherwise, they would have fought over the mares.

This was a ring that we knew well. If we weren't riding for sheer pleasure, we were training for the MAC—or Mounted Archery, Climbing and Combat Challenge.

My mind drifted to Petriville's three-phase sporting event, held near the end of each year. During the first stage, seventy-two horses galloped from a starting-line while riders fired arrows through three red balloons on each of three lined-up posts. As Team Paladin, we never shot fewer than twelve balloons. Last year, we had totaled fifteen between us. Only when a full team had completed stage one, untacked and released their horses, did the turnstile permit anyone entrance to the next staging area.

Stage two consisted of team members climbing up a sheer rock-face to a broad shelf. Once on top, stage three began. Here, twelve zip-line handles were spread out across the shelf. Everyone who made the summit fought and scrambled for these. But even after obtaining a handle, the fight wasn't over. Other players tried wresting handles away while we made for the zip lines, which were attached to sturdy posts. After hooking the handles on the zip lines and lifting our feet, momentum took over. Only when moving too fast for anyone to keep up were we safe from other teams. Players could have run down the slope, but riding the zip line was a much quicker option.

Dropping into the pool near the end of the un-braked zip line took no small amount of courage. The alternative, though, was to slam into enormous air-pockets, which protruded like thousands of huge, air-filled fingers from the zip-line bumper-wall. Anyway, that resulted in disqualification.

The winning team was calculated by the time taken to have all four team members in the pool plus ten seconds per balloon remaining on the team's posts. We, as Team Paladin, had won the MAC Challenge for the last three years running.

I returned to the present, gazing longingly through the window at Zenobia, who was, as usual, leading the group of mares.

The train glided on, passing through the next ring—more crops—and finally the outer ring—the valley's nadir. Veering left, we continued our journey alongside the zoo habitats—their boundaries invisible to the eye.

As we passed a group of animal clinics, a guide who stood at the front of the carriage spoke into a mouthpiece.

As usual, Jonas aped the guide's rehearsed speech, along with cues and nods—identical every year.

"As you can see, vegetation changes from habitat to habitat. This is to cater to each species' environmental requirements." Jonas mouthed along. "But, 'Where is the boundary between habitats and the train line—or even between each habitat? The animals could walk across from one to the next,' you might say." The guide—and Jonas—paused and looked around smiling and nodding, as if about to reveal something startling and unusual, though we had heard the speech countless times.

He—and Jonas—continued, "Well, if you look very carefully, you will notice a soap-bubble-like appearance—the way habitats reflect light in rainbow colors. This is because the same invisible compound that surrounds our world of Petriville encases each one." Again, they both paused, smiling and nodding.

"We might be lucky enough to see some animals today, but the habitats are huge, and the environments are designed to camouflage them, so it is quite unlikely. If you get real close, you'll see a faint purple glow outlining each habitat's entrance."

When the guide—and Jonas—finished the monologue, my sides were aching from suppressing my laughter. Harriet hugged herself and her body shook with laughter as tears poured down her cheeks.

The train continued its route—a companion to the donut-shaped habitat ring—and followed the undulating wave of environmental changes. We streamed past large grassland tracts furnished with thorn-trees, jungles, wetlands, sandy deserts with sparse, low brush, solid ice stretches, snow-capped peaks and even rocky mountain-like terrain—though not mountainous at all.

Mostly, the environments flowed, one into the next. But occasionally, sharp changes gouged distinct boundaries—a harsh desert breaking a territory of the greenest forestry or a solid ice habitat neighboring a swamp.

The enormous habitats joined each other in a single, continuous circle around our town, like the moat of a castle.

"I always wondered whether the habitats are designed this way to keep something out," Jonas muttered drily.

"Or in, for that matter," Liam concluded without skipping a beat.

Finally, in the late afternoon, the train ended back at the circle's starting point, and we began our homeward journey out of the valley.

Chapter Five

The new academic year brought new beginnings for Harriet and me—the start of our undergraduate studies. Although the virtual men and women presenting the lectures were once Earth's most exceptional professors, they had, almost undeniably, died along with the rest of Earth's population.

Although Harriet and I had been there before, Liam and Jonas seemed compelled to usher us on our first day. So, together, we walked to the vast lecture halls that fringed the town square in sector eight and paced the white Roman staircase.

When we entered the first-year lecture hall, a middle-aged woman handed us each a rolled digipar. As though we were receiving some esteemed invitation, our digitally embossed and gilded names glowed against the stark, glossy-white digital parchment.

Harriet glanced over her shoulder at me. "Party!" she sang, fluttering the rolled digipar in the air as she headed for the back row. "Don't you think, Cass?"

When she pulled a chair from behind the long desk, I shrugged. "You don't know that, Harri."

Even before sitting, she tapped her fingerprint on her digipar's seal. It unfurled before her, and, slowly, the gilded writing materialized against the stark white.

My hands flew over my mouth then I said, "You're not reading yours now, are you? *Here*...in the lecture hall?"

She dropped to the seat. "Why not? It's probably something nice."

I slumped beside her, ambivalent shivers filtering through me. "I can't say I share your enthusiasm." And dread sharpened my senses even more when the overseer dropped tissue packs onto our desks.

Rather than opening my digipar, I observed Harriet as she silently read the contents of hers.

Her face paled, her eyes glazing over. Then gooseflesh speckled her arms and tears slid down her cheeks.

She snatched the tissue pack from her desk. Without looking at me, she ran from the lecture hall, along with every other student who had immediately opened their digipar, leaving the rest of us gaping at one another.

Now I raised my rolled digipar and stared at my gilded name for the longest time. *Cassidy Jones*. Finally I sighed, muttering beneath my breath, "I may as well get it over with," and I tapped the seal. When it lay open in my hands, the gold writing emerged. My stomach contracted into knots. I understood Harriet's reaction.

Dear Cassidy,

It is after much research and consideration that you are receiving this letter.

You will have noticed that every one of Petriville's twenty-five thousand sets of parents has one son and one daughter and that all our youth are above-average in every respect, that you all have a minimal range of common genetic flaws and are above-average in athletic ability, IQ, facial and physical anatomy. This is no mere coincidence.

Among their other attributes, your parents were selected for their particular skill sets, all necessary for Petriville's successful launch into space and operations thereafter, as well as our eventual, successful return to Earth. Prior to selection, all children were genetically tested to confirm a match with your parents. A second test was also conducted. As young as you were at the time, our advanced equipment could evaluate and determine your ultimate procreation potential.

As our scientists have recently discovered, it will not be long before we may return to Earth – a year at most.

You'll soon understand what a great honor this is. Once we are home, it will be your privilege and duty to begin the repopulation process.

Congratulations!

You, Cassidy Jones, have a ninety-eight point five-nine-percent match with Jonas Winters. We expect you to begin the mating process within the maximum period of one year from receipt of this letter.

Signed,
Gina Petri

Tears streamed down my face before I had even concluded the letter. I quickly resealed the digipar.

Horror and resistance burned through me like a hot iron—but not just horror and resistance... The denial came with flaring, searing anger—so much anger!

I had never in my wildest dreams even considered this possibility. This was our home—our safe-haven. It had been for as long as I could remember. Another thought slammed into my chest. *Mom knows about the letters.* It made sense. She had, without explanation, excused me from work tonight—of all nights.

"We're a breeding program—just like our pets and the zoo animals!" I seethed through my tears.

As my remaining classmates' tear-laced faces rotated toward me, I continued ranting. "How could our parents do this to us?"

I stood, lifting the re-rolled digipar between my thumb and forefinger. "I will *not* do this!" I raged and strode resolutely from the lecture hall toward the bathrooms to find Harriet.

Students filled the corridors. Most sobbed, shouted, crooned and slumped to the floor, boiling with betrayal. Many stood with those they dated, though nobody wanted this supposed forced mating. No one was ready for that. And surely I desired neither Jonas nor anyone else who lived in Petriville.

As I reached the lockers, the scene playing out at the far end of the corridor made me shudder. Liam stood with Harriet facing him. *Too close.* She was laying her hands flat against his chest while he was cupping her cheeks in his. Tears streamed down both their faces. Unaware of my presence, Liam leaned forward and kissed her forehead.

I gaped at them. The burning in my chest intensified. As I stormed forward, they saw me. Their arms fell away. They stood apart—obvious guilt tugging their mouths and faces down.

"What the—?" I gestured between them. "How long has *this* been going on?"

Liam did not face me but closed his eyes. He spoke then—not to me, but to Harriet. "Didn't I warn you this was a bad idea?"

Harriet dropped her gaze, whispering, "I'm sorry, Cass."

I ignored her and, sure he would side with me on the matter, I snapped, "Where's Jonas?"

Liam locked his bright green eyes on mine and bit his lip, his voice gentle. "I don't know, sis. We haven't seen—" He broke off. "Oh."

Jonas was striding toward us.

"I thought you two would be out here," he growled as he cast his eyes on our siblings.

Without pause, he turned to me. "I want to talk to you, Cass. I should have done this a long time ago."

He was scowling, his face red. After making one sneering backward glance at our siblings, he gripped my hand and dragged me toward the exit.

Chapter Six

Jonas burst through the front doors and paced down the wide, white staircase—towing me into the square. He headed for a shady wooden park bench, where he dropped my hand and gestured for me to sit. I did not but almost glared at him as he set his jaw and tilted his head back.

While his rage seemed to simmer and slowly fade, I sustained my glower.

The words flew out of my mouth in a fiery storm. "I can't believe those two. Did you know about this?"

He slumped to the bench, lowering his head into his hands.

I flopped down beside him and he turned to me with a deep frown. "About *them*?" He half-laughed, shaking his head. "They've been together for weeks."

"Well, why am I the last to know about it? Are they trying to hide it from me? Why?"

Jonas didn't immediately answer but raised his eyes as sarcasm trimmed his voice. "Well now, let's see…

Maybe this is why…" He paused, holding his palms up toward me. He met my eyes and softened. "Look, Cass… Liam was sure you wouldn't be happy about them dating. He had Harriet so convinced you'd freak out that she was scared to tell you."

I laughed. "Scared of *me*?"

He chuckled. "What? You don't think you can be intimidating?"

I sighed, ignoring his jibe as my temper cooled. "I suppose, in a way, I did know. I'm still not forgiving them. They're not getting off that easily… Anyway, Jonas, you didn't bring me out here to discuss Liam and Harriet's newfound romance, so you obviously want to discuss the letter contents, right?"

He dropped forward again. "So, I am sorry, Cass. I mean…for dragging you out here, but seriously, how do you feel about this whole thing?"

I glanced at him and replied noncommittally. "I'm sure nobody is happy."

He shook his head sharply. "Well, some are, but we're not talking about them." He met my eyes and spoke so softly, so gently. "Would you feel differently if you were paired with somebody else?"

I frowned. "You're so far ahead of me, Jonas. I've barely had time to comprehend the letter, and here you are talking about a future based on them." I steadied my breathing and slowed my speech. "What exactly are you trying to say?"

His face flushed as he took a breath before he spoke. "You have no idea then, do you?"

Before I could evade his impending declaration, Jonas continued, "Surely you know how I feel about you, Cass."

I breathed in to suppress another burst of anger rising in my throat. "It's not as if we have to jump into this right now. Plus, they can't force us to do this *ever*, if that's not what we want."

Jonas' green eyes searched mine. "It's not that I disagree with you on that, but at least tell me if there is somebody else — if I'm wasting my time."

"Damn it, Jonas, *no!*" I paused. "Well…not really." I closed my eyes, not wanting to see if his face showed any signs of hurt. Whispering, I added in consolation, "A year is a long time. We can't possibly know how we'll feel by then."

"That's true," he sang, a mischievous smile twisting his lips.

I met his gaze. "And we've been friends since we were kids. I need time to comprehend these letters, you know?"

When Jonas fell silent, I closed my eyes, my heart tearing from my chest. I sensed his eyes boring into me and finally opened mine to his soft green stare.

He pulled his mouth into a faint grimace, but he said nothing more and laid his arm around my shoulder, drawing me to him.

We sat in silence until two familiar figures emerged from the lecture hall. I scowled as Liam and Harriet descended the broad staircase and walked toward us. As I looked at their joined hands, Harriet tried to jerk away, but Liam firmed his grip around hers.

I wanted to leave, but Jonas touched my arm, his warm breath breezing my hair. "Wait, Cass," he said quietly. "Let Liam explain. I know he wants to. Give him a chance, yeah?"

As they neared, Jonas stood. Harriet bit her lip nervously as she threaded her arm through her brother's. Without another word the siblings headed toward the homeward-bound conveyor.

Liam took Jonas' place on the bench and I moved away, widening the gap between us. I shot the words at him. "You lied to me, Liam. You and Harriet."

He leaned forward, resting his forearms on his thighs. After a pause, he rotated his head toward me, speaking barely above a whisper. "Listen, Cass. I am sorry. Neither Harriet nor I *expected* to fall in love."

I shifted farther away. "How can you say that, Liam? These things don't just fling themselves on you. You must have had some idea—some sign that you were about to."

He studied the cobbled paving. "Of course there were signs, Cass." He twisted toward me again. "You noticed them too. Harriet said you did." He sighed then continued, "You were always at Mom's office. And Harriet was spending more time with Jonas and me. You knew that already. We rode the horses together, trained in archery, climbing and combat and just talked. Things just happened from there."

He fell silent, his eyes on the cobbled paving again, giving me time to absorb his words.

I broke the silence, blinking back the tears clouding my vision. "It feels like I have lost my brother and best friend in one instant."

He turned to me again and swallowed hard, his speedy voice so soft. "Why though, Cass? You'll always be my little sister and I love you more than you can imagine. That won't change." He paused for a beat. "Plus, you're Harriet's best friend. You have no idea how this was worrying her."

"But what if it doesn't work out, Li? Whose side do I take? Who do I betray?"

He sat upright then reached for me and, wrapping his arm around my shoulder, pulled me toward him. A soft smile formed on his lips as, uncharacteristically slowly, he added, "My sweet sister, in that unlikely event, neither Harriet nor I would put you in a position where you had to choose."

I lay against his shoulder, enjoying the warmth of his arms holding me to him. "Do you know if everyone got a digipar, even the younger kids?"

He raised his brows. "Some dude was walking up the stairs just now, ranting about his fourteen-year-old sister having received one."

I cocked my head. "Why now, though? Is the timing significant?"

He shrugged. "It may be. I'm sure we'll find out soon enough."

A hush fell over us as we contemplated possibilities.

In silence, we stood and walked the conveyor home, his arm strung around my shoulder. And in silence, we stepped through the familiar white front door into our home's warm interior.

As the mouth-watering aroma of roast beef and potatoes wafted through the air, Achilles and Yvon slammed into our legs in greeting.

"Hi, guys," Mom and Dad echoed from the kitchen as Liam and I stroked Achilles' and Yvon's hard black heads. My parents' voices had sounded strained.

Liam met my gaze and our words came out simultaneously. "They know about the letters."

Chapter Seven

After laying colorful serving mats, silver cutlery and white crockery on the dining room table, Liam and I brought the serving dishes. While we placed them in the center, Mom and Dad pulled out four chairs.

Dad wasted no time.

As we sat, he laced his fingers and raised the subject. "Well, Liam and Cassidy, is there anything you'd like to ask about the letters?"

Liam stiffened as his gaze darted between our parents. He wrist-rubbed the bridge of his nose, his words emerging in the usual rapid-fire. "Don't you think this is unethical, Mom? Dad?"

"Oh, Liam," Mom sighed, her high English voice subdued, "you just don't understand, my son." She seemed to appraise him. "You couldn't possibly." A single tear slipped down her cheek. She batted it away.

I slipped in. "But Liam's right, Mom. It's not ethical. It's archaic. How can it be okay to demand that your children have sex when and with whom you have chosen?" Because I was now sure that our parents had put forward the names — their personal preferences for our *mates*.

Mom shot her eyes open as wide as saucers. She spluttered on a sip of water. Dad unlaced his fingers and clenched his fists, gasping, "Cassidy Jones! This is nothing of the sort."

Tears streamed down Mom's cheeks. "You must understand, Liam and Cass. We truly had no choice. You cannot possibly think that this is what we wanted for you. Anyway, we thought you liked Jonas."

I swallowed. "That's exactly it, Mom. I *like* him. Why would you do this to us?"

Dad deflated, the steam leaving his voice. "This was one of the many conditions of our employment with Petrician Enterprises."

Liam put it together. "Gina made you sign" — he air-quoted — "*acceptance*, so she wouldn't leave our family on Earth to die."

"Precisely, son," Dad whispered. "Precisely. Mom and I had to leave our parents, Mom's sister, Aunt Susan and your cousin Sarah back in Cape Town. We could tell them nothing of what was to happen, nothing about the impending meteor strike. Gina's chosen people from all over the world left their families to seek refuge in Petriville." He met Liam's then my gaze. "Petrician Enterprises offered our children — you — life, on the condition that we kept silent. On top of that, they required that all fathers were vasectomized. They made the offer to fifty thousand parents — twenty-five thousand families. And do you know what?"

Liam speedily concluded Dad's thoughts. "Not one declined."

Dad locked eyes on Liam and nodded. "Not a single one."

Mom cut in softly, "They had somehow obtained tissue samples from your birthplace facilities." Then she added, her voice catching mid-sentence, "And as tiny children, they observed you without our knowledge."

Without thinking, I blurted, "I would rather have let my children die with dignity, like everybody else's."

Liam shot me a glare.

I looked at my lap as my brother rasped, "That's not fair, Cassidy. You can only speak for that fact when you *are* a parent."

He shoved his chair back, stood and strode upstairs.

As I raised my head, my eyes met Mom's tear-streaked face and Dad's intense frown.

I stood much more sheepishly than Liam and headed to my bedroom, muttering under my breath, "Well, that couldn't have gone any worse."

Chapter Eight

A few evenings later, Mom seemed distracted as we worked at her office desk discussing graph data. When she fixed her deep blue eyes on me, I knew why. She frowned with such intensity that the skin between her brows made a sharp wedge. "Are you sure you have nothing else to tell me, Cassidy? Should I be concerned?"

"Look, Mom" — I pleaded, committing only to a half-truth — "something may have shown up, but I need to be sure. Please, give me some time. It only happened once and that was weeks ago." My next sentence was a blatant lie. "I'm not even sure if it was anything. I would have told you if I was."

With a frown, she acceded, but disappointment tinged her voice. "Very well, Cassidy. I'll see you at home later."

She swiveled toward her desk and reached for the brown leather handbag lying on top. Instead of lifting it, she returned her gaze to me. "She will find out, you know? So, if you think it's nothing and even if it's something you feel you should hide, trust me when I tell you not to keep it from Dad or myself. Okay?"

I tried to hide the grimace tugging at my lips and the confusion gripping my face as guilt raked through me. My attempt was less than successful and all I could choke out was a feeble "Thanks, Mom."

She looked back at the wall-mounted analog clock, still wearing a worried frown. But without pursuing her point, she stood, lifted her handbag and headed for the door. Halfway through, she rotated again but our eyes met only briefly as she allowed it to close softly behind her.

With a deep, shuddering breath, I turned my focus back on the graphs.

Nothing stuck out as unusual. I moved to the video feeds.

"You there, Cassidy?" I spun my chair around, stunned. I hadn't seen him in over three weeks. The mere whisper of his smooth voice made my pulse race.

Uncertainty twisted his face — perhaps even fear — as he stood on the silver platform, the three shiny metallic claws caging him into his own dimension.

My throat constricted. I had scrutinized the mesmerizing apparition for way too long. My cheeks grew hot as I took in the pale gray T-shirt hanging loosely over his bronzed, athletic frame — a complement to the stark platform. He looked around and frowned.

"Eric." I swallowed, half-tripping as I stepped up to join him.

He sighed, not seeming to notice my flounder. "That you're here is kind of unexpected."

"And that's why you haven't returned in what...almost a month?"

He laughed a sonorous, smooth river of sound, the fissured dimples drawing deep lines down his cheeks.

"It's not funny, Eric. I don't know what it's like down there. Something may have happened..." I trailed off.

He was much more relaxed than before. That was instantly apparent in his demeanor — the casual stance, hands lying loosely over his perfectly spaced hips.

Dropping his chin, he shuffled his faded hiking boots before easing his aquamarine eyes upward until they met mine. "Things were a little complicated. You mention this to your mom? Or anybody *else*?" He accentuated the last word, stiffening slightly.

"This?" I gasped, though I knew what he had meant. I wasn't deliberately being difficult. His intense examination had made my heart leap — throwing me. A long, thin strand of yellowed grass was in his hand and he was rolling it between his thumb and forefinger.

I shook my head. "I haven't yet, Eric. But I am doing this at my mother's request, so I should." I gestured at his hand, screwing up my face. "Is that a piece of straw you're holding?"

He raised the hard-knuckled limb as if noticing the long strand for the first time. "Uh-huh." A soft memory seemed to touch his lips and a gentle smoothing crept over his cheek dimples.

With Eric seeming more compliant, I continued my questioning. "Did Graham tell you about Gina? Is that how you knew?"

"Mm-m... So you figured that I avoided answering some questions last time. But trust is something people earn."

I blew out a snort. "Well, do you trust me now?"

Eric shrugged. "It's not that simple. It isn't exactly you that we don't trust."

"You're being very cryptic, Eric. Who's 'we'? In addition to you and Graham, I mean. How many of you are there?"

"Ah-h." He raised his brow as if that was precisely the question he had expected me to ask. "Now we arrive at the crux of the matter."

I rolled my eyes, but he didn't seem to notice and raised the straw – using it as a pointer. "That is information I will surely die to stop Gina from getting her hands on." He moved his gaze upward then right, as if weighing possible outcomes in his mind, then he grinned. "That could be arranged, I guess. Ah well, some of your questions don't pose a threat. They are things Gina can't use against us. One thing's for sure, Graham is the only reason anyone's alive out here." He swallowed – his voice straining through gritted teeth. "And he never followed some sick selection criteria." He sighed, softening. "Hey, it's not your fault you're there" – he faltered – "but you'll forgive me for not entirely trusting you, not after what we've been through out here. For all I know, you may be colluding with Gina, gathering information. Then you'll betray me – uh, I mean us – in deeper ways than you can probably imagine."

I turned our prior conversation over in my mind. "Graham Porter played a significant role in Petriville's existence – our survival. It makes no sense that Gina would have abandoned him."

Eric raised his brows, bitterness twisting his beautiful features as he clenched his fists, crushing the straw. "You seriously don't believe she left Graham to die?"

"It isn't that I don't believe you, Eric. And" — sarcasm snuck into my voice — "I don't expect you to believe me either, but I am *not* working for Gina." I shook my head. "Plus, you still haven't actually told me *how* you survived."

He looked around again and in a low voice, murmured, "Graham figured she'd desert him. He built the facilities years before the strike, not far from some of her pods."

"Why would Gina have done that, Eric? It doesn't make any sense. Her mission was to save humanity."

"Pah!" he blurted.

Confusion swept over me. Why was I so drawn to Eric? Even now. Even with all this uncertainty and anger swirling around us.

"This may seem condescending, Cassidy, but you're being incredibly naive." He locked his eyes on mine. "You should know that those who survived the impact — those of us still on Earth — will be in danger when you return."

I growled, "Why are you so stubbornly refusing to believe that I won't mention anything to Gina?"

He steeled his expression, his words measured. "That's not what I'm saying, Cassidy. We knew making contact was a risk — is a risk, every time — whether you tell her or not."

I shifted. "How will Gina learn of our communication, though?"

"Nobody said it would be through your doing. But you may be right, and we get lucky. Maybe Gina won't find out." He frowned, a doubtful half-grimace.

"Eric" — I paused, waiting for him to meet my eyes — "you asked me if I've mentioned our meeting to anybody. I'd like to know the same from you. And why should I believe you or trust Graham — especially if Gina left him on purpose?"

He threw a sardonic laugh. "You're just going to have to figure out for yourself what's really going on."

Eric dropped his shoulders forward as a sigh slipped from his full lips. Appearing drained by our exchange, he slid to the floor against the invisible inner-pod wall. Drawing his broad knees up, he settled his forearms over them. He rolled the remaining tattered blade of straw between his thumb and forefinger, observing the floor with a vacant expression.

I sat too — opposite the seemingly tangible three-dimensional image and struggling against the urge to reach out to touch his fingers.

As I twirled the bangles around my wrist, we merged in mutual silent contemplation. I gulped. Eric twisted his face with an unspoken torment. He crossed his feet and inspected his hands — forearms flexing and softening as he clenched and unclenched his fists. The long straw was in shreds now. He eyed it then turned it over in his fingers before flicking it aside.

For a moment he appeared to form something of a resolution as he shifted and straightened, but then he dropped back against the wall and resumed his musings.

"Eric?" I murmured, drawing him back to me.

He raised his eyes — but not his face — locking them on mine. My throat closed at the intensity of his gaze. I swallowed the thick lump that had formed.

"So, if Gina could only learn of your survival through our communication, why are you talking to me? Why did you come here in the first place?"

He straightened, his voice low. "There are things you don't know and that I won't discuss." He slowly shook his head. "Not yet." Then his voice caught. "There are children out here with us. Think of them, if not Graham or me."

I wrapped my arms around my knees and pulled them to my chest. As I considered Eric's words, my eyes blurred.

Slowly, I murmured, "Even if I believe you about Gina, there's no way I can help."

As empathy tingled my skin, I added in a whisper, "Did nobody else in your family survive?"

I bit my lip, waiting for his answer.

Eric drifted his gaze up to me. He opened his mouth to speak then closed it and swallowed.

He didn't offer to share his own torment. "Younger kids lived with us, some as little as two years. In the beginning, they screamed for their mothers and fathers, especially at night. Often, we held them until they fell asleep, but we were kids ourselves. Sometimes, just surviving was difficult." He sucked in a sharp breath and a single tear slipped from his eye, running down his cheek. He quickly swiped at it.

My heart ached for him. "I'm so sorry about everything you have lost, Eric. You must think our lives pampered."

He didn't answer but again locked his unusual eyes on me. "Eric, the last time you were here, you waved your hand over the outer camera."

He dipped his eyes for a moment then raised his brows. "That's because I figured it wasn't active. Did anybody else see?"

"I doubt it." I cocked my head, a half-smile stretching my lips. "I deleted the footage."

A soft laugh accentuated his dimples. "There may be more to you than meets the eye, after all." Slowly he shook his head, opening and raising his hands.

When they fell back to his knees, a slight breeze touched my skin—as though the air displacement had moved through space. Excitement scorched its way through my belly. "I felt that!"

Eric shot his eyes open. "You did?"

I hit my leg. "Did you feel it too?"

"For sure." He grinned. "What about touch?"

My pulse quickened at the prospect of Eric touching me—his skin against mine. "I didn't think there would be any sensations, but now I'm not sure."

A mischievous smile curled his lip, the dimples sliding down his cheeks. "How about we run an experiment of our own?"

Again, biting my lip, I dropped my head, cringing from the flirtatious smile that found its way onto my mouth. But I wasn't alone. A definite glow had reddened his cheeks too.

He ventured, "What if it causes some kind of time-space explosion?"

"Is that the best you can offer?" I murmured coolly, but my heart was thumping.

He threw his head back and laughed. The resonant reverberation surged through my body—a sharp, undeniable yearning.

Although I barely knew Eric, my entire being reveled in the warm comfort of his presence. It was as

if I belonged to whatever moment he owned —
whatever space he occupied. In that instant, I knew I
always would.

He reached out so suddenly that I jerked back,
startled. When he laughed again, I relaxed.

More slowly, this time, he reached his fingertips
toward me. A moment later, I mirrored his movement.

Even over this vast expanse of space — this chasm
that separated us — our gazes locked on our hands as
our fingertips drew nearer. The intensity of the static
electricity exchange grew exponentially with each
nearing fraction of distance.

When our fingertips merged, the severity of the
power rocked me backward. An electrical charge
surged back and forth between us — flooding every
connecting nerve fiber in tingling rapture.

I rotated my hands, facing my palms upward.

Responsively, Eric turned his over mine.

I slipped my eyes closed, believing he probably did
as well.

If our fingers merging had rocked me, I could neither
bear the electric shockwaves coursing through my body
as our hands touched, nor articulate the emotional flood
overwhelming me and making my eyes burn.

It was more intimate than touch — more haunting —
as if Eric's energy tingled through my veins. Gooseflesh
flooded, not just my hands, but my core — as though the
full length of every nerve fiber stretching through my
body shuddered in anticipation.

I gasped and finally raised my eyes. Eric riveted his
focus on me, but no smile remained on his full lips.

His chest muscles were heaving, his breathing
ragged, his jaw contracted — exaggerating the sharp
outline.

"Wow!" he exclaimed, biting his lower lip. "That was unexpected."

My cheeks warmed. A wild, ragged gasp escaped my mouth.

Eric withdrew. Again, his features hardened. "This doesn't mean I believe you're not working for Gina."

I drew back too, gazing down as I blinked, my voice a sarcastic croak. "No of course you don't. I mean, why would you?"

When I looked up again, the apparition of Eric shimmered in the dimly lit surroundings. A moment later, he vaporized.

Frustrated tears filled my eyes. I leaned against a protruding silver arm, lowered my head to my knees and wrapped my arms around my legs.

After some time, I stood, turning once to look at the platform as I left Mom's office. I wasn't angry—not exactly, but as I rode the conveyor home, a sense of hollowness gnawed at the pit of my stomach. *Is Eric so insensitive to my complete honesty? Or has life handed him such a raw deal that he has come to suspect everyone?*

When I reached home, I slipped past the kitchen and headed upstairs just as Liam came out of his room.

Mom called from the kitchen, "Cassidy, aren't you going to join us for dinner?"

I closed my eyes, scrunched my face up and shook my head then opened my eyes to see Liam stopped on the landing and squinting at me. "Is this something I can help with, Cass?"

I shook my head again and he murmured, "I'll tell Mom and Dad you're not feeling well."

"Thanks, Li," I choked and stepped into my bedroom, closing the door behind me.

Chapter Nine

Two individually addressed party invitations arrived for Liam and me the following day—posted through the slot in our front door. Every Petrivillian youth received the same glossy white, gilded digipar.

While gliding along the conveyor toward college that morning, Harriet voiced my thoughts. "Well, we all know what this party is. It's hardly a meet and greet. At the very least, it's a sanctioned date and mate."

Jonas' brows arched upward. He shot a glance at Liam before turning to his sister—his voice grating. "I don't see you protesting, Harriet. You and half of Petriville." He sighed, conceding, "I guess it's better Liam than some jerk. I'd flatten anyone else who came near you."

I glared at him, gritting my teeth. "It's still not okay, Jonas. Who has ever heard of kids being encouraged in that direction?"

Liam smiled but didn't slow his speech. "Light up, little sis. Look at the bright side. You guys get to go shopping."

I rolled my eyes. "Don't be patronizing, Liam. Also, why should a party diminish my resentment? I do not like being forced into this and I don't think I'm going."

Liam frowned as he wrapped his arm around my shoulder, his voice softening but not slowing. "What picture would that send, Cass? If Gina has such control over Mom and Dad and you put yourself on the radar as a rebel, don't you think you'll make trouble for them?"

I sighed, my anger subsiding. Liam was right, as always. And I did quite like the idea of dress shopping.

Harriet latched onto the thread. "Let's go after college today, Cass. It will be fun. We haven't been shopping in ages."

* * * *

That afternoon, Harriet and I crossed the town square to sidewalk four and Madame Belle's Boutique. The store's twirling musical display dazzled spectators — all gathered inside and out for the pre-party shopping experience. Virtual mannequins danced into and out of the shop's window, their eclectic range of outfits flitting and fading between Earth's old brand names and top boutique attire. Hundreds of sparkly colored balloons floated just above street level, as if invisible strings held them in place.

Despite the swarm of party invitees, a robot-assistant sized us both in minutes.

Harriet chose a long, light-metallic-silver dress with a leg-slit up one side. Ties in the same fabric crossed the low-cut back. She completed the outfit with long, glossy, black gloves and a matching, contoured collar — accentuating her pale, delicate neck. The stilettos would make her tall enough to bring her petite, blonde head almost to Liam's jawline. The high shoes glimmered and danced between two shades — the dress's light-metallic-silver and the glossy black of the gloves.

I chose a rebel statement in my dress — to my mind, anyway.

It was the same aquamarine as Eric's eyes and brought out the green flecks in mine, complementing my sleek, dark-walnut hair. A daring slit slithered up one leg of the fitted dress. The air flowing through the fabric felt silky cool against my skin. A thousand silver strands crisscrossed the low-cut back. Myriads of tiny manufactured diamonds snaked up from the bust and joined into patterns of silver thread on the glowing, stark-white contoured collar. The long gloves matched the neck adornment, color for color and pattern for pattern. My stilettos shimmered and changed between all three colors. I was as tall as Jonas in these — not that I was going *with* him. *Not at all.*

Less than an hour later, we left the store, swinging the cotton bags holding our purchases.

* * * *

In the three weeks since receiving the invitations, Eric had still not returned.

But party night arrived. For tonight I'd forget. For tonight I'd have fun.

Mom had braided and decorated my hair with the same snaking diamond rows as those adorning my dress. After slipping the sixteen bangles from my wrist, I packed them in a jewelry box on my dresser then fastened a light silver wrist-chain in their place. I jiggled my slim, olive-toned wrist, the delicate piece shimmering in the dresser's light as it fluttered against Great-Grandmother's stylish, white-gold wrap-around pen.

Watching my reflection in the full-length mirror, I twirled. My makeup and dress looked perfect. After misting perfume on my wrists and neck, I stepped from my bedroom.

From the top stair, my eyes fell on my parents, who were gaping up at me from the bottom.

"Cass!" they both gasped. Dad slipped his arm around Mom's waist as she dropped her head to his shoulder. I descended, holding onto the wooden railing for balance.

Out of my comfort zone in stilettos, I tripped and stumbled. But, judging by the open-mouthed looks on my parents' faces, they hadn't noticed.

Liam emerged from the VE room.

I gaped. "Wow, brother."

He wore sleek, body-hugging pants, in the same glossy black as Harriet's gloves and neck collar, accentuating his muscular thighs. The matching contoured neck collar extended into a shaped epaulet over his athletic shoulders. It tipped over onto his chest and arms, where it merged into his bodyshirt's light metallic-silver fabric.

He dropped his jaw as he stared up the stairs at me. "You don't look too bad yourself, Cass."

When he offered his arm, I accepted, and with a final good-bye to our parents, we left.

"'Not bad' was an understatement, Cass. You look seriously stunning this evening," Liam whispered as we turned onto the sidewalk toward Jonas and Harriet's home. "Beautiful, in fact." He chuckled. "I'll be flooring guys tonight."

Liam all but held me up as we passed the manicured front gardens then turned up the garden path to the Winters' home.

"Thanks, Li. You look really good yourself. Harriet's going to be blown away."

He smiled down at me. "You think so?"

I frowned then smiled. "Of course. Look at you. You're the hottest property in Petriville, for sure."

He laughed but straightened his face before we ascended the few stairs. Biting his lip, he glanced at me.

I nodded and smiled. "Don't be nervous, Li. You've been here a hundred times before."

He knocked tentatively.

Roger Winters swung the door wide, his Scottish voice booming with a perpetual half-laugh. "Agh, welcome, Joneses. Come in! Come in! Well, won't you look at this lass? Aren't you a sight for sore eyes, then?"

He stepped aside.

Megan gave us both a soft kiss on our cheeks, first Liam and then me. "I wouldn't want to sully that beautiful makeup, now would I?"

"Jonas! Harriet!" Roger boomed again. "Get down here, you two. You don't want to keep your friends waiting, do you, then?"

As they descended the stairs, I looked not at Jonas, nor Harriet, but at Liam. He gulped. His eyes glazed over as he dropped his gaze to his shoes then looked up again, blinking and swallowing. He opened his mouth as if to speak but closed it and coughed.

I dropped my arm.

Liam locked his bright green eyes on Harriet's bright blues. As he offered her his arm, he bit at the smile spreading across his face.

Jonas strode toward me with an air of confidence.

I grabbed his arm and smiled, revealing my stiletto-clad foot. "Thanks, Jonas. I'm likely to tumble out of these, otherwise."

He laughed as we waved goodbye to his parents and left for the party.

Harriet clung to Liam, who firmed his arm around her waist. They walked behind Jonas and me—out of our earshot, I suspected.

After crossing the footbridge, we stepped onto the conveyor. The digital displays along its expanse flashed bright images of couples and singles arriving at the venue—all dressed to kill. An interviewer sounded off names over Petriville's hidden speakers. Half the adults stood on walkways and sidewalks, watching the displays to catch a glimpse of their children.

Jonas glanced upward as we passed one. "You outshine them all, you do, Cass."

I smiled, mimicking Eric in a mock-Texan tone, "Why, thank you, Jonas."

He smiled, thankfully not cottoning onto my thread. Nevertheless, he mime-tipped a hat. "It's my pleasure, ma'am." It sounded funny—the Scottish-Texan mix.

I laughed, leaning more heavily on him as we stepped from the conveyor. When Liam and Harriet caught up, we crossed the square, passing grassed areas with benches and trees. Eerie amber lights splashed the old-style stone of the municipal building. My gaze drifted up the thick flagpole, rooted beside the wide Roman stairs, up, up, its apex high above the building. The self-lit bright orange Petrician Enterprises flag wafted in the breeze.

I drew a breath as we ascended the broad staircase into the foyer.

Crowds filled the elevator banks. Eventually, it was our turn to enter the large glass enclosures.

The doors automatically closed at capacity. Then the elevator glided downward for what seemed like an age. Finally, we slowed and came to a halt.

When the doors opened, I gaped. We stood at the entrance of a massive stadium. This stadium contained no ordinary seating. Encircling the field were at least fifty thousand, metallic-silver, luxury, leather recliners.

We did not head toward those.

Petrician Enterprises had decorated the entire center field with sweeping, overhead gold drapes and balloons. Matching gold overlays adorned three thousand tables, at the very least. And just above the center of each table, an embellishment rotated in mid-air — three ellipses, one gold, one silver and one black slid through each other, their orbits intersecting, somehow without clashing.

A robot waitron ushered us to our table, with a digipar displaying our names in embossed, gilded lettering on both sides.

Four teenagers already sat at the table, excitement illuminating their faces. I knew them — two very well. They were astrophysicist Joshua and Caroline Carter's children. "Hey, Samantha…Paul."

Harriet added in mock sarcasm, "Fancy seeing you two here. Why didn't you walk with us?"

Thirteen-year-old Paul's blue eyes glinted in striking contrast against his warm brown skin, his tightly curled hair having been neatly trimmed for the party. He shrugged shyly, glancing at his sister. "Dunno."

Samantha was older and beautiful—with her alluring, large dark eyes and long, wild black hair. She gave a confident smile. "Mom and Dad walked us here." She tugged her lips into a grimace as she rolled her eyes. "They say they're fetching us too."

The other two were Gina's grandchildren. Although knowing that they'd never chosen their grandmother, I could muster no warmth in my voice and muttered a dry "Hello" to the unremarkable, dark-haired Gregory and Amanda.

I drew my own chair before Jonas could, while Liam withdrew one for Harriet.

Relieved to take the pressure off my feet, I sat. Jonas fell into the remaining chair beside me.

When the crowd settled, some random Petrician Enterprises representative gave a thankfully short welcoming speech.

Then, dinner was served.

I wondered about the supply source of the meal—prawn-cocktail hors d'oeuvres with a lemon-marinated ocean fish main—but it did taste heavenly. By the time the robot-waitron served the chocolate mousse dessert, I had dismissed my casual observation. They likely bred fish and crustaceans in Petriville. The cacao plantations, among others, grew in the fourth quadrant—between sectors nine and twelve.

A robot waitron swept over to our table and slid her apron to the side—as though the frilly white cloth was attached to a sliding door that curled around her waist. She proceeded to shove our dirty plates onto dishwasher racks inside her rather slender body.

Once the tables had been cleared, silence fell. All eyes drifted to the central platform, which lit up like a Christmas tree. A collection of musical instruments decorated half the stage. Huge screens rose up beside it.

A spotlight illuminated two short women standing at the stadium entrance — one in advanced middle age and the other one younger.

Amanda clapped enthusiastically, while Gregory shoved his shoulders back and pulled himself upright. "That's my mother and grandmother."

Harriet tipped her head to the side. "I know your grandmother but not your mother. What's her name? And where is your father?" As if only just noticing it, she blushed at her candor.

Amanda didn't seem offended as she delivered her obviously rehearsed statement. "You must know *Susan* Petri. She's our mother. Our father wasn't a nice man. He didn't come with us."

A hundred silent photography drones followed the women's quick, short steps to the central stage. It tracked Gina as she left her daughter at the base and mounted the four stairs to the large platform. She turned toward the podium, clearing her throat and pushing a pair of horn-rimmed spectacles farther up her hooked nose. Thick lenses magnified her steel-gray eyes. Her parrot-like face and proudly erect posture accentuated her cold demeanor. I shivered. A collection of curious whispers sounded across the stadium. "Gina Petri?"

Forgetting that her grandchildren were at our table, I muttered, "What's *she* doing here?" My eyes moved up to meet their glaring faces.

As Gina leaned toward the microphone, it crackled to life. The thousands upon thousands of our peers instantly hushed.

Her voice emerged silky smooth—a slow, melodic rhythm. "Good evening, everyone." She paused, singling students out with her eyes. "Thank you for joining us tonight. For those who do not know me, I am Gina Petri."

A loud cheer erupted.

Gina smiled warmly then waited for silence before continuing, "The reason for this party, this magnificent event"—then she spread her arms wide over the stadium—"is two-fold. Firstly, I will tell you more about Petriville, but that begins with a question. Have you never wondered why you are safe out here in space? Or why no threat has ever penetrated Petriville? Well, this, I shall explain."

She raised her chin before continuing, "Of course, outside the Kaleidotonium, a force field constitutes our first line of defense. Thus, we repel large debris before it reaches our outer shell. Besides that, there is an early detection system. Petriville, as a mobile unit, skirts larger debris before it even nears. As you can see, every scenario was predicted and calculated with precautionary systems implemented to maximize your safety."

She went on, "The energy technology relating matter and antimatter moved forward in leaps and bounds over Earth's final years of exist...mm-m, not Earth's existence, man's existence, as we knew it. And Petriville was designed and built around that completed technology. In fact, our power cell was ready only months before our departure. Of course, we acquired this before anybody else. It was a relatively simple task that required not much more than slotting the mechanism in place. A few others obtained the technology — too late to be of any use to them, of course."

My mouth fell open. I barely noticed Gina's pause. But she had smiled so broadly while making the last statement that her mouth had almost pulled into a laugh.

Oblivious to the cold glares piercing her, she continued, "Regarding your salvation, I graciously accept your heartfelt gratitude. If not for me and the gift of my vision — to save and create a superior race of humans — you would no longer be alive. We touched on this in the letters, but I shall add detail to the subject. In the twenty years prior to Earth's destruction, gene identification advancement was exponential. For example, we identified things such as the potential to commit crimes — not foolproof yet, but reasonably accurately — the potential intellect and athleticism of a subject. In fact, along with facial attribute software, we even determined the specific adult facial features a baby would one day possess." She looked around at her subjects before adding, "I dare say, we are rather happy with the outcome."

Most of our idiotic peers applauded loudly, while Gina took a sip of water then proceeded dismissively, "Of course, your parents know all this. They always have. But neither their selection nor yours would have taken place were they among those few who objected to the communication chip removal, which was, by the way" — she rolled her eyes dramatically — "one of Earth's latest technological enhancements. We needed to keep you" — she air-quoted — "*off-the-grid*, so to speak. They would have told you none of this, though."

She smiled in full confidence of this fact. "I do, however, believe that the time has come for you to comprehend all the facts and, once back on Earth, to fulfill your responsibility to mankind."

"With this knowledge, you will understand how and why you were selected." She moved her eyes over the crowd, tipping her head almost imperceptibly. A self-satisfied expression crossed her features as she continued. "I shall not beat around the bush. You all know what is expected. Our intention for tonight is that you connect with your mate." With the iciest chill in her slow, melodic voice, she added, "Every one of you.

"Also, I have received notice of a rebellion, factions that for reasons unfathomable are against my cause. This will *not* be tolerated! Do not suppose, for a single second, that you will not be subjected to the severest of punishments if you refuse your role in our society. You received the gift of life, where others received death. You were chosen, thanks to your parents' superior breeding. It is your duty to repopulate Earth with a better generation of humans. If you refuse this simple requirement, you are of no value and shall be treated accordingly."

She smiled as though she had been idly bantering with us—not making a devastating declaration. Brusquely, she concluded, "In light of this fact, the next MAC Challenge has been canceled."

Amid a collection of jeers and boos, all eyes turned toward our table. We, Team Paladin, were, after all, Petriville's MAC idols. We had been for three years running. But, ignoring her subjects, she announced, "Let the festivities begin!"

Very lifelike virtual musicians materialized before the instruments. As they played, two virtual vocalists appeared — one male and one female. In dramatic over-animation, they harmonized into the microphone.

I turned to Harriet. "Do you think Gina included musicians in her grand ideas of a so-called superior race, or do you think she considers arts inferior to sciences?"

"What?" Harriet shouted back. I tried again, but the loud music made it impossible. She couldn't hear me, so I gave up.

Over the next few minutes, most appeared to thaw to Gina's revelation, their tension noticeably subsiding. Many took to the dancefloor.

As if an outsider, I cynically observed our species' budding mating rituals, but my eyes fell on Liam and Harriet more than others. Were they really okay with Gina making them pawns in her insane project?

But I, too, got caught up in the moment — swept along with the crowd. That was, after all, why Gina had arranged this party.

I met Jonas' bright green eyes as he turned toward me, smiling softly. He stood and ushered me from my stupefied state toward Liam, Harriet, Samantha and Paul — the young boy dancing up a moonwalk storm. Gregory and Amanda remained at the table, gorging on second then third helpings of dessert.

When a slow song found Liam and Harriet separating themselves, Jonas pulled me to his chest. He wrapped his arms around my waist, his warm, rough cheek lightly touching mine. It felt...nice. But I dreamed that it was Eric who was wrapping his arms around me — Eric who was holding me against his chest.

As the song ended, Jonas leaned forward and placed his mouth to my ear. "Stay for the next, won't you, Cass?"

I pulled away, frowning as I mouthed, "I am sorry, Jonas. You're a good person." I wasn't sure if he had read my lips, but I turned away, removed my shoes, lifted my dress and headed for the exit.

Jonas followed and caught my wrist a moment before I stepped into the elevator. "Are you okay, Cass?"

"Not really. I'm not sure how anybody can be. I can't do this—not yet, anyway."

I stepped into the elevator and turned toward him. As the doors closed, Jonas called, "You look amazing tonight, Cass."

Then the doors shut tight and the elevator ascended.

Chapter Ten

Rather than skimming the cobbled square toward conveyor two and home, I crossed toward Mom's office. Turning for a moment, I gazed up the municipal building's flagpole to the bright orange banner. With a shudder, I turned away.

Except for the robot janitor, the building seemed deserted. The pseudo-male, thankfully, never remarked on my late entrance or unusual attire. I hurried down the long corridor and entered the familiar circular chamber, allowing the door to slip closed behind me.

Without thinking, I found myself stepping onto the platform. There, I leaned against a protruding silver arm, my shoes dangling from one hand and the silver metal cooling my feet. Nothing but still, quiet air surrounded me.

I raised the dress and slid down the smooth metal protrusion to the platform base. Wrapping my arms around my legs, I pulled them to my chest and rested my chin on my knees.

As I pondered the evening's events, tears slid down my cheeks and over my lips, tickling my chin as they dropped away. My eyes grew heavy. Drowsiness washed over me. Before I knew it and without realizing I was about to, I slipped into unconsciousness.

* * * *

"Cassidy?" The familiar voice brought me back to the world.

My eyes fluttered into focus.

"Cassidy?" he repeated, "Are you okay?" He was crouched before me, bringing back the memory of the vision from my dreams. He reached forward and touched my cheek with the backs of his fingers — a piece of straw between his teeth.

The charge sent a surge of tingling waves through my body.

I blurted in confusion, "Eric! What? How? When — ?"

He laughed, the soft smile not leaving his lips as he plucked the piece of straw from his mouth. "Mm-m, you're not seriously looking for answers to those questions."

"But why now, Eric? And why so late?" I glanced at the wall clock. "I'm not normally here at this time."

"Fair questions." He shrugged. His casual manner relaxed me as he continued, "We don't exactly neighbor the pod. It's not as if you're normally here now either. And it made sense to wait until tomorrow evening, but on arriving I stuck my head inside, and there you were. At first, it looked like you were sleeping or hurt, so I figured I'd check."

I smiled, thankful that my high-tech makeup would show no tear-smudges, until Eric softened his voice to a gentle tone. "Why were you crying?"

My voice grated, a little rough from the earlier tears. "How would you know I was crying?"

"Making you uncomfortable was not my intention. Your eyes are red and a little puffy is all."

I sighed, relenting. "It's a crazy time. Gina Petri told us some things that are, to say the least, hard to swallow." I looked up and, meeting his eyes, whispered, "I suppose this makes no sense to you."

He cocked his head, his tone still soft. "I'm listening. What troubles the brooding Cassidy Jones?" He sat, pulling his legs up and draping his arms loosely around his knees as he rolled the long strand of straw between his fingers. "What made you this sad?"

I told him about the letters, recounting how irritated I was that Liam and Harriet were falling into her trap. When I explained my friendship with Jonas and how Gina had matched us as partners, Eric perceptibly stiffened. Finally, I answered his actual question and delved into the subject of Gina's huge revelation tonight—not missing a single disclosure, including her warning of certain death to rebels.

By the time I'd finished, Eric's mouth was agape. He sputtered then whispered, "How can your parents let her get away with this? How did she force their silence?"

My eyes fell to my hands. "I don't know. But Gina has a way of manipulating people into giving her what she wants."

I glowered, blinking back the tears collecting in my lids. "I don't want to be used like this, Eric. I don't understand how anyone can allow it. We're too young and it's not right. At least I want to love the man I'm forced to have children with."

He met my gaze and frowned, emphasizing his cheek dimples. "Nope, it's most definitely not right, Cassidy. You say they're proposing this for after you return to Earth?" He didn't seem to expect an answer to his question and continued, "It means we have time. We'll figure a way out of this."

I didn't miss his use of the plural. That thought led to another. I really knew very little about him or Graham.

"Eric…" I waited until his gaze rested on me before continuing, "What has it been like? I mean, life on Earth…since the meteor strike?"

His eyes twitched, jaw set. "That's not something I want to talk about."

I threw a blank stare, my voice sounding pained in my ears. "Oh…you don't trust me enough to answer my question?"

He sighed and dropped his eyes to the straw he was rolling between his thumb and calloused forefinger. "In some odious way, I guess you kind of have a right to know."

Eric slowly pushed himself back against what I assumed was the inner pod wall—invisible to me. Repositioning his arms loosely over his knees, he blinked a few times. When he lifted his face, he focused not on my eyes but on my hand—at the delicate silver chain looping over Great-Grandmother's wrap-around pen.

He appeared to hold his breath and sat in silence for a long while. Finally, he shuffled and sighed, "It's not like I know where to begin."

I helped, drawing the first word out. "Okay. Well, how did you meet Graham?"

He closed his eyes as if he were recollecting. "Mm-m… From what I recall, Southern Brazil was gripped in a heatwave." When he reopened them, a soft smile curled his lips. "Our daddy was playing ball with Caleb and me in the hotel swimming pool. Our mama was lying on a deck chair under an umbrella, keeping half an eye on us while holding a book in one hand and a cocktail in the other. Suddenly this wind flurry came up, blew the sunhat clean off her head and took it high, high up in the air."

Eric smiled. "This crazy-tall man with skin the deep rich of mahogany was exiting the hotel lobby onto the pool deck. He carried an air about him — stood out from the very first, wearing the crispest white cotton dress shirt you ever saw. He was near the pool when the hat came plummeting down. It plonked down right on top of his woolly, gray hair like it was planned."

Eric broke into a small laugh. "In a twisting sleight of hand, he had the hat off his head and spinning around one finger. Mama had barely reacted before he'd plopped it back on her head."

Eric swallowed, his smile fading. "I remember it like it happened just yesterday. It's one of the last happy memories I have of my family together."

He shook his head as if to clear it, his attention falling to the straw in his hand. "Anyway, my parents and Graham got to chatting about the hydroponic farm. He never mentioned that the place was a refuge, nor did he speak about the impending meteor strike." Eric grew more solemn. "Graham only told us after the impact that Joshua Carter was a close friend."

"I thought so," I inserted.

He cocked his head, frowning and lowering his voice into a growl. "He's there with you, isn't he!" Not a question – or at least, it didn't sound like one.

I replied in a soft, round-about attempt at justification, "He has stunning children. Samantha has these huge dark eyes and Paul is a sweet, innocent boy who just loves dancing."

Eric gulped. But as if expecting such an answer, he nodded. "Well, the last time they'd spoken, Joshua'd warned Graham that he predicted the meteor to impact Earth within a matter of months. Until now, Graham never mentioned *why* they stopped communicating. He used to shut down whenever we asked. So, we figured Joshua never made it to the facility and died in the impact." He narrowed his eyes as he shook his head then proceeded through gritted teeth, "Obviously, now it makes sense."

"I know, from your perspective, that it's not fair, Eric, but you can hardly blame Joshua for saving his family."

He opened his palm. "It makes it no less wrong – no matter how you try to justify it."

I couldn't argue with that. We dropped into silence as I watched the seconds ticking by on the wall clock before bringing Eric back to his story. "Was the facility nearby?"

The small respite had smoothed his emotions. He raised his eyes to me. "Yep...just a short distance into the mountain." He smiled softly. "It was incredible – seeing it that first time. Graham was sure proud to show our family how the entrance was hidden. He told us all about the particle energy-containment technology that they used to create artificial sunlight. One of the caverns contained this massive field of grazing cattle. Caleb plucked a piece of straw-grass from the field and cut his hand when he yanked it from the ground." Eric beamed before his smile fell away, his face straightened and his gaze distanced. "After that, he was never *not* chewing on some stray strand of straw."

Eric drew a deep, shuddering breath. "It was late when we were done. Graham invited us for a sleep-over in one of the dormitories. But our mama was getting a migraine and wanted to head back to town — to the hotel. They almost encouraged Caleb and me to stay. Of course, we never complained about that."

Eric pulled his hands into fists — buckling the straw as he flexed his forearms around his knees. A dark shadow clouded his face, his lips pressing into a flat line as if locking the words away — the sentence that was so unbearable to him. He closed his eyes and whispered, "Our parents left a short while later. On their way back to the hotel, their brakes failed in a mountain pass. We never saw them again."

He looked back at his clenching fists, regarding them like they belonged to someone else. "Graham brought word to us in the morning. Authorities had notified our Uncle Tom, Dad's brother, but the family was holidaying in Europe. They booked a flight for the following evening. That evening never arrived for them. It was the day the meteor struck."

Again, Eric raised his eyes. "We felt as if fate had dealt us such a cruel hand. At least we had each other. Graham lost all four grandchildren and both his sons. They refused to bring their families to the refuge — said he was raving. It was too late by the time they realized he was not. Graham had the cave exit sealed before dust and fires could reach us. That's where we remained for twelve years. Back in those early days, we had access to news channels — at least until not enough living souls remained on Earth to warrant broadcasting. Graham kept the detailed information away from us kids. He later said that back then, sealing the entrance — not reopening it to search for survivors — was the hardest decision he'd ever made. Toxic gasses and the fires made it impossible to go outside and nobody was exactly knocking on the door."

Long, silent seconds slipped by. Eric dropped his eyes back to the straw in his fingers.

When he finally met my gaze, he stood abruptly. "This place is stifling. I need to get out — be on my own for a bit."

I tilted my neck back and looked up at him. "I am sorry. I never meant — " I stopped. Never meant what? Didn't I mean to hear about Earth? The refuge? His parents? Caleb? But I did. I wanted to hear it all. My curiosity could keep, though, and I could wait for a better time for Eric…for me.

I moved to stand too. The simulation appeared so lifelike that Eric extended his hand to me. But, realizing his mistake, he withdrew it. I had almost accepted his help. Instead, I puffed a smile and stood, unaided. He shook his head, his eyes unyielding.

He locked on my dress and swallowed, raising his gaze to meet mine before dropping them to the shoes in my hand. Eric half-gestured with the straw. "I'll bet the shoes and dress look fine together."

I bit my lip. "They look okay." I glanced down at the silver floor beneath my bare feet then up again — a shy smile tugging at my lips as his gaze moved over my dress.

"Better than okay, I expect. Won't you put them on?" he whispered.

Bending and raising my dress, I slipped the shoes on then righted myself. My eyes were almost level with Eric's lips. I took in their soft, smooth, fullness then moved upward to his beautiful aquamarines. He widened his mouth into a smile then bit and released his lower lip. The rigid jawline and cheek fissures made my heart flutter. He stood back against the protruding arm and crossed one leg over the other. Loosely laying an arm across his solid abdominal muscles, he lightly feathered the straw in his hand. Making a twirling motion with his finger, he whispered, "Show me."

I twirled a little self-consciously, but my confidence grew with Eric's smile. I spun a second then a third time before I slowed and stopped — facing him.

"Wow!" he whispered. "You look like a goddess from" — his speech slowed, his voice fading as he concluded — "another world." The smile disappeared… from both our lips.

I tilted my head forward, my eyes on the floor. When I looked up, Eric shuddered before me and neither he nor I spoke before he again dissolved.

Chapter Eleven

As I entered the office the following day, Mom was still at her desk, speaking in no general direction. She was observing graphs on seven different screen-tiles, while the eighth seamlessly converted every word she uttered into perfectly punctuated and paragraphed text.

Seeming to lose her train of thought, she swung her head toward me, sounding irritated. "Cassidy... You startled me." She moved her gape to the clock "Aren't you early?" then lowered to my wrist and formed an intense frown. "Your bangles, Cass... Why did you not put them on after the party? Dad and I gave you those as a symbolic, 'Age of Understanding' gift."

I shrugged, answering her in reverse. "I felt like a change. Plus, Gina's latest revelations rendered their symbolism a little lost on me. But see" — I grinned in solace — "I'm still wearing Great-Grandmother's."

She arched a brow, but before she could raise another objection, I continued. "Anyway, aren't you late, rather than me being early?"

She gave a small laugh. "Ha! I suppose I am." She paused. My breath caught as she added, "I've been working through some data."

I stammered, "Are...are you looking for something specific, Mom?"

She refocused on the graphs and answered distractedly, "Mm-m, yes. Of late, I've identified several locations that are habitable. I'm verifying the data's accuracy."

My breathing eased. "Anything relevant?"

Mom squinted and cocked her head before slowly answering, "There is another reason for my search, Cass. Gina has requested I present my findings on habitable regions next week. I'd very much like you to be there."

She cocked her head, waiting for my response.

I hesitated for a moment and, turning toward the clock, absently acceded, "Sure, Mom. Of course."

When I re-centered on her, Mom shook her head slowly. Then, she lifted her handbag from the desk. "Anyway, sweetheart, I am done for tonight. We'll see you at home later."

I nodded as Mom stood, walked toward the door and released the lock. As she pulled it open, she twisted back—her voice tired, pleading, "You can't keep this from me, Cassidy. You *do* need to tell me what you've discovered."

I met her eyes. "I will, Mom. I love you."

A smile warmed her lips and her deep blue eyes twinkled. "As do I you, my beautiful daughter. More than you can imagine."

As the smile faded, she allowed the door to swing closed behind her.

Not two minutes after I had taken my place before the long, curved screen, his whispered voice sounded behind me. "You here, Cassidy?"

I stood but took my time mounting the single silver stair — observing him during the extra few seconds.

My breath caught. I bit my lip.

The faded T-shirt lay ironing-board flat against the steely outlines of his ripped torso — the well-toned muscles clear evidence he had suffered no malnutrition during his lengthy refuge. As always, he rolled that single strand of straw through, around and between his fingers.

I stepped up before him.

A broad dimpled smile brightened his face. "Hey," he intoned in the softest voice.

He looked at my wrist. "So you left those bangles off after the party. They were nice, but for my part, I like it better this way. Then I can see that smooth, olive skin on your wrist."

My breathing hitched, cheeks flooding with heat as I raised my arm to display the snaking white-gold pen — long-since empty of any form of ink. "I won't remove this one. It was my great-grandmother's. It's kind of sentimental."

Eric raised his brows, a warm smile forming on his full lips. "Maybe one day it will hold the same value to one of your great-grandchildren."

My pulse raced. It always did at the sound of Eric's cadenced voice. But over the next few days, things between us began to change.

Eric remained camped near the pod, entering at the same time each evening. Usually, he sat against the pod wall, with his knees up.

He revealed nothing more about Graham, the refuge, his parents or Caleb. As much as I burned to hear it all, I balked at the idea of raising the subject until Eric trusted me—which apparently, he did not. Over the passing days, he threw a thousand questions at me about Petriville. Where did we get our food? What were homes like? Had Gina traveled all over the world and personally selected each of our multicultural citizens? And every possible related inquiry. I openly answered every question I could until a prickling sensation crept up the nape of my neck, a dark thought filling my mind. *Is somebody prompting him with these questions?*

Finally, on the night before Mom's and my proposed meeting with Gina, I decided it was my turn to ask the questions.

So, when Eric began with his regular tirade, I cut him off. "Eric, this does not seem quite fair. For five days I have answered your questions, every one of them—without holding anything back. You know everything I know about Petriville now. The size. Our population. About the schools and shops. Our available resources. You know everything about the entire town's layout, and you have told me nothing—not even about the location of Graham's refuge. I understand that you don't trust me, but I'm beginning to think you're playing me for a fool—using me to gather information so that Graham can plan a strike. We have resources, after all. Is that not what men waged wars over in years gone by?"

He remained quiet for my entire onslaught. Then an amused smile stretched his lips. I wanted to reach over and slap it off. But as I considered, he burst into a relieved laugh. "Hold up, Cassidy, girl... I wondered why you'd asked no questions. Here I was thinking that your lack of interest implied you didn't care enough to know."

At his declaration, my eyes stretched wide. "I didn't want to be insensitive, Eric. You must have gone to hell-and-back out there. I didn't want to ask you to dredge up any painful memories."

His smile faded as our eyes met. "It wouldn't make sense to lie to you, Cassidy. Sure, some memories still hurt like crazy. But"—a soft smile crept back on his lips—"talking about my family is kind of cathartic, to be honest. It helps me to remember them. Plus, right now, there's no one I'd rather share those memories with than you." His last words trailed off and he fell silent.

Now that I had the floor, I stammered and asked the first stupid question that came to mind. "Is...is somebody at the pod with you, Eric? Sitting outside?"

He laughed, rolling the straw between his fingers. "Like some kind of chaperone?"

"Not a chaperone." I paused, then sighed—well, if he wanted my honesty—"I thought more along the lines of an interrogation aide."

He shot his eyebrows toward his thick hairline, curling his lip in mock-irritation. "Seriously? You think this is about information gathering?"

"So, what then, Eric? What *are* you about?"

He dropped his gaze and, as he slowly shook his head, allowed a smile to creep onto his lips. "It's sure not about that."

He paused before adding softly, "Finding out about your life was my intention, but not for the reason you're imagining." An intense spark glinted in his eyes. "I wanted to get to know you, is all...and" — his voice grew even softer — "open up to you, a little." He shrugged and broke off.

"Why, Eric? You don't even trust me."

He broke into a deep, resonant laugh. "Well, you know what they say... Keep your friends close and your enemies closer."

I rolled my eyes. "I was serious, Eric. If I had a pillow and you were any nearer than half a dozen...spheres away, I'd throw it at you."

He chuckled, but I cut him off. "Are you trying to distract me from asking questions?"

His smile faded. "Of course not, Cassidy. Ask anything you want."

Although aching to learn about Caleb, I couldn't, after the light-hearted banter, jump straight into that subject, so instead, I delved into an easier topic. "How many live at the refuge?"

"Originally, around two thousand, but families have started heading out on their own."

I gasped, "Two thousand! And the farm supplied enough food for everyone?"

"The farms are massive and supplied more than enough." He laughed. "There are caverns full of grain, even now."

"And what about illnesses? Didn't disease spread through the caves?"

Eric ground his lips together, deepening his dimples. "I could ask you the same thing, but I'm guessing Gina had that well covered. Anyway, it's not like we were without healers — mostly, they used plants with medicinal properties." He turned his eyes away for a second. "We still lost people. Surgery wasn't well enough equipped to save everyone. The strong survived, I guess. Sometimes, people just disappeared, always over New Year's. It was bizarre." His dark pupils contracted. "And after Graham opened the caves, a group went out in search of survivors and just never came back." He swallowed hard. "Have you lost people in Petriville?"

My eyes fell to the silver floor, before I raised my chin and met his gaze. "We have highly advanced robotic surgeons and medicines. A man died a few years back. A geologist, husband and father—in a bizarre kitchen accident. He slipped with a knife in his hand."

"One man?" He gasped, wrenching his brows down. "Only one death out of fifty thousand people? How's that possible? How did it happen?"

Empathy forced me to glance away because they had suffered so many losses out there. "The knife flew into the air and, in its downward arc, sliced into his carotid artery. His wife witnessed the incident and rammed a kitchen towel into the wound, but he had lost too much blood and never regained consciousness."

Eric shook his head. "Were children born in Petriville?"

"No babies were born, Eric. Gina coerced our fathers into having vasectomies when they came to Petriville."

"Well that's one thing we have in common. None were born out here either, but Graham would not have enforced it."

Eric's previous comment was still vexing my thoughts. I bit my lip and inquired in my most gentle tone, "Eric" —I waited for him to meet my eyes—"did someone that you cared for disappear with that group?"

His eyes glazed over then closed. A single tear pressed through each lid, his Adam's apple bouncing up and down. But as he wiped the saline fluid away, he answered so softly that I could barely hear him, "You've already figured the answer to that, I'm guessing, Cassidy."

With his elbows, he pushed his cross-legged knees to the floor then pressed the fleshy part of his palms into his eyes. He frowned and blinked away the shimmer. "Not three months ago." He choked out, "He survived all this time. But he just *had* to push the boundaries, take up every challenge, had to—" Eric gritted his teeth swiped at his eyes and straightened. "Caleb meant everything to me. He was my brother, my best friend, my family...everything."

Dropping his eyes, he considered, "It's not fair to exclude Graham, I guess. He was about as cut up as me when Caleb died. Graham is like a father to us. He taught us everything we knew."

As Eric's anguished memories resurfaced, his eyes glistened. "Now it's just Graham and me." He paused then carried on as though he hadn't. "Thing is, I was so insanely angry with Caleb when he left us. He was supposed to live. He was tougher than me. I'd have taken his place—no question." He fell silent and looked away.

"I don't know what to say, Eric. I'd never have pressed if I'd known you'd lost him so recently." As much as I wanted to know what had happened to Caleb, I couldn't again drag Eric into the torturous memory, and I sensed that he wasn't yet ready to tell me everything. I'd have to be patient.

"It's not your fault, Cassidy. You didn't know. And"—he hesitated—"and I wanted to tell you. There's no logic to this, but I wanted you to know." He broke for a longer time before finally speaking. "Nope. I do know why." His eyes glinted for a second before the light faded but he said no more.

He stood and, like before, moved toward me, holding his hand out palm flat—not an anchor, an invitation.

I gasped, my throat congesting. No part of Eric's body could give me purchase in this simulation of him. I longed to feel the rough warmth of his fingers. Would I ever know the porous canvas of that sun-gilded skin?

I stood to meet him.

When Eric dropped back, he frowned. I resented the astronomical distance in the small space between us—longed to close the gap and experience the nearness of his body.

My heart thudded. Eric fell silent—his face an expressionless mask as his beautiful eyes coasted over me.

"Eric," I ventured.

He lifted his chin.

The floor seized my attention. Groping through the shy apprehension taking hold, I rubbed my forearm. Finally, I summoned the courage and raised my eyes but stumbled through the words—part murmur and part whisper. "Why did you want me to know about Caleb?"

His aquamarine eyes, though soft and serene, glistened and yet pierced me to my core. He steeled his jaw, then sighed and phrased his question in a smooth, gentle cadence. "You haven't figured that out?" Then he added, "Sure you have. Or at least, you must know why I want to share the most important aspects of my life with you, why your company is more valuable to me now than almost anyone here on Earth. I do. I knew it the moment we met."

I swallowed the lump gripping my throat. Moisture sprang into my eyes.

Eric gave a low chuckle. "Bad as that, is it? You look nothing short of horrified." The smile stretching his lips fell away and his Adam's apple bounded as he swallowed.

He stepped closer, reaching his free hand up. I leaned into his virtual fingers as they brushed my cheek. The static airflow grew and grew, until the tingling heat beneath his fingers was too much, the ache ripping through my chest.

Eric blinked. "You're so far away, Cassidy. So far…"

I stared quietly into his eyes, into their depths—drawing in the intense earnestness of the strong, compassionate man I may never physically meet.

"One day"—I dreamed aloud—"one day we'll find each other back on Earth," then I added drily, "If we don't land on the far side of the planet."

Tracing his flexed jawline with my eyes, I ground my teeth. He rotated his hand to cup my cheek, scorching his aquamarine gaze down my body.

I closed my eyes. But for the sensation of Eric's skin, the hot, static tingle beneath his touch felt real. Where his fingers grazed my cheek, I ached for the rough, calloused ridges beneath his touch.

My eyes drifted open. I reached up, moving my finger over the outline of his hand. His chest muscles rose and fell in a ragged rhythm, his breathing strained.

Eric dipped his eyelids. When he dropped his hand away, the static diminished but didn't entirely dissipate. I laid my fingers lightly against my tingling skin as we fell into mutual silence. He opened his eyes — locking on mine.

I broke our shared moment, croaking the words out. "You should not come here tomorrow, Eric. My mom is presenting pod data to Gina."

The edge of his lip curled up, his voice guttural as he replied, "That's okay. The food has pretty much run out here, so I'll need to be getting back to the refuge." He took a moment then changed the subject. "Cassidy, you believe me about Gina, don't you?"

I nodded. "I wouldn't have told her, you know."

Eric smiled softly. "Sure. I know."

He turned away for a moment then back. "You think she knows about us?"

"I don't know, Eric, but" — I paused, desperately not wanting to say the words I knew I must — "it's safer for us both if you don't return. Plus, we'll be out of alignment in a few weeks anyway."

He squinted, confusion and something like pain tugging his brow down. "What? Ever? Why not wait until we have no choice?"

I was about to break my heart with my following sentence but keeping him away from Gina suddenly seemed the most important thing to do — the right thing to do. If what he had said was true — that Gina was a danger to them — we might not have a few weeks. Our time was up. "No, Eric. No. And I'll repeat it a thousand times. I don't want you to come back. Ever."

Eric gulped but didn't speak. He didn't move — a frozen statue.

I looked down to hide the tears rolling down my cheeks. Eric was safer this way. But my heart ached with every beat and my throat closed with every breath.

In my blurred periphery, Eric's virtual image shuddered. In a flash, I changed my mind. "Don't go, Eric," I pleaded, as if he had a choice. But my words fell on deaf ears. He had vanished from my world as quickly as he had appeared.

I slumped to the floor, rocking and groaning as tears spilled down my face.

His absence left a gaping hole in the room—a yawning cavity in my chest—as though he had ripped my heart from my body and taken it with him.

Now I desired nothing more than to return to Earth—to return to the same planet as Eric.

Chapter Twelve

I arrived home from college to find Mom pouring over a collection of digimaps and digigraphs she had laid out on the dining table. She glanced up. "Come here for a moment, Cass. I would like to go through this with you for the presentation tomorrow." She began outlining the less-affected regions — or, at least, those that had entered a healing process or were further along their path of recovery.

I tried to sound nonchalant. "Is it possible that survivors made it to any of the other pods, Mom?"

She sighed. "Someone we knew built five refuges across the world, all of them near pods." She closed her eyes briefly. "Over the years, I have checked the areas for signs of life. Two, I am sure, did not survive the initial impact." She paused for a second then asked the one question I had been dreading. "Don't you think it's time to tell me what you know?"

"Could it wait until after the presentation, please, Mom? I'll tell you everything then. I swear, I will."

She clenched her jaw, raising her eyes to the left. Then she sighed and nodded, giving me the ultimatum, "Tomorrow night then."

Mom returned to the graphs demonstrating the births of vast wastelands, deserts of prodigious proportions — hostile environments where nothing could survive, neither plant nor animal.

We stayed up late going over data. Finally, after I made a huge yawn, Mom sent me upstairs to bed. The series of emotional days had left me drained.

* * * *

The following morning Liam joined me at the breakfast counter. My hands shook with nervous anticipation of the upcoming presentation and I knocked my glass of orange juice over. The golden liquid spread across the marble, weaving its way among dishes and condiments before dripping over the edge to the floor.

Liam launched up and grabbed rags from the drainer. On returning, he tossed me one and lifted a cereal box by the flap.

He moved his eyes up — bright and teasing as we cleaned the mess. "You seriously look like you're heading to your execution."

"I think I might be, Li." I grimaced, blinking furiously at the sting in my eyes. "I'm just nervous. If you're here this evening, I'll tell you about it."

Liam took my rag, walked to the drainer and wrung both his and mine out then soaped, rinsed and re-wrung them before tossing one back to me.

While I wiped away the residual stickiness, he returned, pulling me into a side-hug. "For you, Cass" —

he pressed his cheek to my temple—"I'll be here." His face grew solemn, his tone so soft, so gentle. "What else is going on, baby sister? Please tell me."

After rinsing, wringing and folding the rag, I turned and gazed at him.

A tear slipped down my cheek. I bit the edge of my lip. "I will...after—" I broke off and turned away, readied myself and headed off to university.

But it was a wasted day of lectures. I couldn't stop brooding over the meeting. Whenever I tried concentrating, it goaded me into over-the-top imagined conversations with Gina. With something of ambivalence agitating my senses, Harriet and I finally exited through the high arches of the campus doorway, descending the wide staircase into the town square.

Liam waited on a shady park bench but not for me. He gestured Harriet over with his chin, feigning nonchalance. Only the corners of his mouth betrayed his cool look, twitching the tiniest bit.

In contrast, Harriet's expression radiated warmth as she waved her arms in wild abandon.

Before heading his way, she turned and lifted both my hands in hers. "Cassidy, I know something is going on with you... I mean, more than this presentation."

My temper flared. "Really, Harriet? You and Liam have taken to discussing me now! I can't deal with this at the moment."

She wasn't dissuaded and continued as if I had said nothing. "I know I've been a little unavailable—at least lately anyway. But that doesn't mean I care any less. Whatever is on your mind, don't let it distract your focus this evening. Get out there and show that woman what for!" The familiar broad, dimpled smile warmed her face. I couldn't help but respond. I gave her a tiny smile.

Harriet turned and, swaying her hips, she sashayed toward Liam. With an air of appreciation, he leaned against the backrest. Suppressing a grin, he raised his brows toward his thick hairline — studying her.

For a moment, he shifted his gaze to me. A concerned grimace twisted his mouth as he blinked once and crossed his fingers.

I waved and mouthed my thanks before crossing the town square toward Mom's office.

As soon as I entered the circular room, I froze. My heart jolted.

Mom was not alone. Leaning against the office desk with a smug grin contorting her haughty features stood Gina. My mind raced. For what possible reason had she moved the presentation two hours forward?

Something else caught my attention. My eyes floated to the silent video, looping across twelve tiles of the screen, curving around Mom's office.

The feed was centered on the silver platform and two familiar figures sitting cross-legged at its center. A chilled blade slithered down the nape of my neck.

Shivers engulfed my body. I struggled for air — gasping and heaving.

Gina cut into my horror — dramatically turning toward me with folded arms.

No melody rang out in her voice now, though she spoke in the same, calm, monotonous tone — her voice as cold as ice. It terrified me so much more than if she had yelled.

She pitched her eyebrows upward. "Would you care to elucidate this?"

I needed an escape. My eyes slipped closed, my mind speeding through different options — trying to concoct a plausible reason or at least a believable lie.

Not only had Gina's discovery torn through me, but seeing Eric displayed on the platform had brought a searing agony of emotions flooding to the surface.

I peered up at the poor-quality video, the lack of audio and grainy facial expressions.

After a long pause, I muttered, "It's a simulation game."

"A simulation *game*?" Gina sounded marginally amused, her brow arching even higher.

I met her stare, dead-on. "Yes. What else?"

Her voice remained flat, her mouth stretching into a sardonic smile. I wanted to gag. "Do you normally become so…intimate with simulations?"

She was enjoying herself, obviously exhilarated by how easily she could inflict torture on me.

Fury burned down to my bones. I barely managed to control my voice — to keep my tone from rising in pitch. "What does it matter to you if I play games in my free time?"

She maintained the dubious, amused expression on her flattened mouth. "What were you talking to this…*simulation game* about?"

Even before her accentuated use of the words, I knew she wasn't buying into my story. But she couldn't debunk my fabricated tale. "I was asking the simulation questions. Isn't that how these games are played?" I barely managed to suppress the sarcasm crusading for control of my voice.

Gina turned toward Mom with the beginnings of a sneer. Was I getting to her after all? "And I suppose you knew nothing of this."

She had caught Mom off guard — unable to prepare a defense for me. It was better that way, better that Mom didn't have to lie. She stammered before answering, "N...no, I knew nothing about the simulation."

Gina stopped her questions but she pierced me with optical daggers for the longest moment.

Neither her voice nor any other facial features betrayed her malice — though her rancor cut through the air like a sharp knife through butter. Without moving her gaze from mine, her blackened pupils pierced straight through me as she gestured at the screen. "I think we both know that this is no simulation."

I didn't know whether my next response would appease her or trigger a violent outburst, so I opted for silence.

She cocked her head. "Very well, Miss Jones. I won't need the presentation today. We have living proof" — she gestured toward the screen again — "that Earth is more than habitable, at least in one region."

She turned to Mom. "I see that Graham Porter implemented his hydroponic facilities, after all." Her eyes turned stony, boring through Mom as she added pointedly, "The strangest thing is that my technicians seem unable to locate data linking from which pod the transmissions came. I wonder if, perhaps, *you* know why that could be?" Without waiting for Mom to reply, she shook her head, dismissively. "Never mind. I have full confidence that they *will* find the information."

Gina gave a smug smile that oozed enjoyment, as did her overly erect shoulders which she had squared toward me. She felt no mercy for Graham, no compassion for his people. Her understanding that others had survived gave her the appearance of someone preparing for a sports match or battle—the excitement of the challenge, the thrill of the hunt.

My blood ran cold. A million terrifying thoughts surged through my mind.

Gina cut into them. "As I said, there is no place in Petriville for rebellious factions. Continue with this little charade of yours and I shall be inclined to abolish your family to the remotest corner of Earth. And don't you think that you will be able to run to Graham for aid. He and his little clan shall no longer inhabit their pathetic refuge once I've established its whereabouts"—she chuckled and continued—"or any other place, for that matter."

With that, Gina turned on her heel and stalked out of Mom's office.

I broke then and, through the tears that streamed down my cheeks, I burned. Enraged was not a big enough word for how I felt, a sense of acid clawing at my skin. Mom closed the gap and wrapped her arms around my shoulders. "Cassidy," she crooned, rocking me as if I were a young child. "Cassidy!" she said again then stood back and observed my dull expression. "It will be okay, my child." She seemed so sure that, as she tucked a thick strand of dark hair behind my ear, I almost believed her.

"I am sorry, Mom," I wailed. "I never intended—" I couldn't even finish my apology.

She clutched my hand and led me from the building, ignoring the robot janitor's "Good afternoon," as she tugged me toward the paved area outside her office. Then, gesturing for me to sit on a wooden park-bench, Mom collapsed beside me.

It was more than just the light breeze sending a crisp chill through me. Mom wrapped her arm lightly around my shivering shoulders and I hugged my legs up to my chest. Through the fog clouding my thoughts, I stared at my knees.

My lips twitched into a smile at the memory. When Liam and I were younger, he sometimes referred to me as *'Knobby Knees'*. It seemed so long ago.

My gaze drifted up from the lantern to the almost-barren tree. Autumn's last leaves dangled wistfully from the twigs — the fallen ones forgotten, vacuumed by Petriville's cleaning robots.

Lowering my chin, I considered my explanation.

When Mom pulled me around to face her, a light crease stretched across her forehead, her eyes searching mine. With a sigh, she slowly shook her head. "Oh, my daughter... You should have told me." She looked up, reconsidering. "No. You're not to blame. I should never have allowed you to become involved."

"But I *am* involved, Mom. I'm glad to be. I needed this."

Again, she shook her head, but neither anger nor irritation leveraged her voice, only concern. "Do you have any idea what you may have done, Cassidy?"

I turned toward her, new tears leaping into my eyes. "I've just as well lined them up against an execution wall. Will she really seek them out to harm them?"

She rubbed my shoulder gently, speaking as if to herself. "Dad and I vowed never to lie to our children again. We've kept so many secrets that I barely know what's true anymore. I suppose the time has arrived for me to test my resolve." She penetrated me with her deep blue eyes as she addressed me. "I don't know, my daughter, but if we're to go on what Gina just said in there—" She broke off, shaking her head as she slumped.

I drew myself back to the present, catching Mom's gaze. Since we were confessing—"Mom, did you know that I deleted the pods' outer video?"

"I considered that you might have, Cassidy, but you deleted the pod video. Cameras mounted around the platform in my office captured you." She glanced upward. "We can only thank the heavens that no audio was recorded."

I cocked my head. "How would *you* know that's cause for relief?"

Raising her eyebrows, she dropped her chin. "I know Graham, Cassidy. He may not have given the young man to whom you spoke many details, but he certainly originally sent him to gather information. Gina would have used that against you. What happened after the fact…only you and he know."

I pressed my cheek into my knee and rotated my face toward Mom. "What will Gina do to us? To our family?"

"I honestly do not know, Cass"—her face grew solemn—"but you need to level with me, with us. What exactly did he say about Graham and the refuge? Tell me everything you remember."

I relayed every detail about Eric and Graham, while Mom stroked my exposed cheek with her free fingers. When I told her about Caleb, she met my eyes with a shimmering glow in her own.

After I concluded, she heaved then spoke in her softest voice. "Contact was supposed to be once-off." She diverted. "You are in love with Eric. What is his surname?"

I didn't confirm her statement but lowered my chin before answering, "It doesn't matter now, Mom. I told him I didn't want him to come back."

She slid her teeth over her red lip. "I doubt very much that he'll listen. But tell me who he is, Cass. I'd like to know about my daughter's first love."

My face warmed as I voiced his name. "He's Eric Morgan." I half smiled. "How much did you see?"

She cocked her head, empathy softening her eyes. "Nothing that would cause you embarrassment — only enough to tell me how you both feel about each other."

I bit my lip then looked up again, half a question in my next statement. "So you knew they'd make contact, Mom?"

She nodded slowly. "If they survived and were able, yes. But only once and with minimal details."

Every few moments, Mom glanced into the shadows — scrutinizing every person who emerged from surrounding buildings, behind trees or around corners.

She murmured, "We must be careful when and where we discuss this, Cass. Gina may have put people onto us." And with a pause, she shook her head. "Liam, and now you, should never have become involved. It defeats everything that we have done."

"Huh?" My brow strained. "Liam's not involved in this, is he, Mom?"

"Sadly, my dear Cassidy, he is" — she sighed, defeat and exhaustion wrenching her forehead — "and I expect that so much danger lies ahead."

"What do you mean, Mom? How is he involved?"

"Well you know Liam has always been too observant for his own good. He started asking questions a long time ago. In fact, it was only a short time after we started asking ourselves questions. At first we diverted and perhaps gave him small falsehoods, but then his questions became more complex. It became impossible to avoid answering him truthfully. And as to how he's involved, he sits in on all our discussions and his ideas about how we should proceed are invaluable. He's quite the strategist."

After a long blink, she changed the subject. "Now, tell me about you and Eric."

"You know, Mom," I whispered, "I've never felt like this about anybody before." As soon as the words slipped out, I knew I should not have said them, because my resulting reaction was a complete, uncontrollable meltdown.

Mom firmed her arm around my shoulder, but she remained silent as my tears dripped down her neck, moistening her turtleneck fleece, while spasms from my unrelenting sobs shook both our bodies.

Eventually they dried out and I regained my composure.

Mom lifted my chin to meet her gaze. "Since you are involved, there is much that you ought to be aware of."

I shot open my eyes.

She changed her tone to something more resolute. "What you said confirms some of our suspicions." She sighed again. "We may be in for a battle upon our return, but we honestly do not know whom to trust in Petriville. It is difficult to acquire this information while we are still at Gina's mercy."

I grimaced. "Are you saying this fight is already underway, Mom? How many of us are involved?"

She said nothing about my deliberate use of 'us' as I included myself in their operation, nor did she answer my second question. "Only the beginnings, Cassidy… We have so much to do before our return to Earth."

We dropped into silence, watching the late-afternoon shadows lengthen as the sun dipped. The nearby horizon and small arc differed hugely from images of Earth's sunsets. I had to admit to myself that the idea of going back to Earth terrified me, not only for us but for Eric, Graham and who knew how many others.

Mom had drawn inward — reflective. She surprised me by standing abruptly, as though she had reached a decision. Gazing down at me, she smiled, holding her hand out. "Shall we go home?" I clasped her long, elegant fingers in my own — so similarly shaped — and stood.

Few remained in the office park now, most buried in news digipars, though this did not eliminate them as possible trackers.

I searched for stalkers on the conveyor. The late hour and relatively vacant surroundings counted in our favor.

When our well-lit garden path met us and a welcoming glow poured through our home's windows, contentment flowed through me for a moment. But that changed when the definite awareness slapped me back to reality. This life was soon to come crashing down around us.

Chapter Thirteen

As Mom twisted the front doorknob and pushed through, Dad's frown greeted us. "Hey, Emily, what's going on? We expected you home hours ago."

Liam, Harriet and Jonas had gathered in the entrance too. Mom and I stood for a moment, gazing at them in silence.

Dad pulled Mom to his shoulder. I could only just make out her strained whisper as she leaned in and cupped her hand around his ear. "We'll talk later, Peter."

Liam steeled his jaw and screwed up his eyes before mouthing at me. "What the hell is going on?"

Harriet pushed past Liam and grabbed me by the elbow. "Ease up on them, guys. Can't you see they've had a rough day?" With that, she ushered me through the back door to the wrought-iron table.

The aroma of lamb stew, rice and vegetables wafted through the cool night air. My stomach grumbled then twisted in resistance.

Harriet scooped a huge serving onto a plate and plonked it on the table in front of me, gesturing at it. "Eat!" she commanded.

After picking at the food for a while, I drifted back to the present and glanced at the concerned frowns on Dad, Liam, Harriet and Jonas' faces. Their eyes were neither on Mom nor I but on our almost-untouched meals.

While Liam and Jonas cleared up, Harriet served tea from a matching floral tea set and tray. A shiver swept over me and my eyes drooped. Harriet spooned honey into a steaming mug and set it down in front of me.

I met her eyes, shaking my head. "You should have seen that woman," I murmured, cupping the warm mug between my hands. Liam hung a jacket over my shoulders and rubbed my upper arms.

I glanced up at him. "You knew about the resistance?"

He nodded. Another shiver shot through me, but the constant soft breeze in Petriville never made me this cold.

Dad had wrapped a small blanket around Mom's shoulders. She curled her fingers around a mug of tea. Even now — even in the confines of our back garden — she kept glancing around nervously.

Leaning against the backrest of the wrought-iron chair, Dad opened his mouth to speak but closed it again as the back door opened. A familiar swarthy man pushed his square, bearded jaw through. Professor-like — an electric mop of black-and-gray curls topped his head. It was Joshua Carter, the renowned astrophysicist who had discovered the asteroid.

His wife, Caroline, followed, peeking her head of glossy black braids below his. "Ah, thought you all might be out here. We let ourselves in. Hope you don't mind."

Jonas and Harriet's parents, Roger and Megan Winters, followed a moment later, joining us at the table. They had just helped themselves to tea when, exuding excitement, Caroline explained how fiercely Samantha and Paul were training to follow in Team Paladin's footsteps.

Perhaps it was chance that Samantha and Paul were not here tonight, but I wondered if Caroline and Joshua had deliberately excluded them.

"Cassidy" — Mom summoned my attention — "would you like to tell everybody about Eric?"

I opened my mouth but got no further before my voice caught. Mom cupped her hand over my knee. "That's okay, Cass," she added quietly. "Do you mind if I tell them? They do need to know."

I offered a brief nod — only just containing my melting composure.

While Mom spoke, her audience listened — captivated. But when she mentioned Eric, Jonas' gaze dropped to his lap. I closed my eyes, not wanting to witness his discomfort.

Joshua slipped black-rimmed glasses from a breast pocket and wedged them into the groove above his tapered nose. He sighed, placing his forearms on the table and loosely interlacing his large, bony fingers. Gripped by emotion, the usually calm Mr. Carter blew his nose into a white dress handkerchief.

Finally, his rich Nigerian accent emerged. "You cannot imagine how relieved I am that my good friend Graham survived." Joshua shook his head slowly and bit at his soft smile.

Dad broke the short silence in a low voice, his eyes on me. "Now, Cassidy, since Gina has singled you out, she will make things difficult for you and, by extension"—he paused, his eyes moving to Liam, Harriet and Jonas before he continued—"you three. We, therefore, believe that you will be safer off the craft." Again, he paused, this time for longer. "If Gina does locate the pod, you can bet your bottom dollar that she will bring us down nearby. In that case, you will need to find Graham."

My heart raced at the thought that we might land near Eric, but I focused on my fidgeting hands and fingers.

I answered softly, "What if Gina is watching?"

"We have contacts who can help there. As for Gina finding the right pod... With help from a certain person in the technical department, that particular pod's feed may well have found itself permanently corrupted...or missing. He's been deleting evening feeds from that and other pods ever since the flashes. But Gina is growing suspicious. She has eyes on him now."

Dad turned to Mom then again to me. "Listen, guys, Emily and Cassidy look exhausted. They've had a tough day. It sounds like Cassidy has had a couple of tough months. Let's break for tonight."

I didn't protest. I was tired.

Harriet moved to my side, urging me to my feet. "Why didn't you speak to me, Cass? You're always so protective over me. For once, I would have liked to help you."

Fatigue gripped me, and as we walked toward the door, I was surprised by the amount of sarcasm in my voice. "You and Liam were so damned preoccupied with each other that I hardly wanted to bother either of you."

She gaped at me. "A simulation! Seriously? I'd have assured you he's a figment of your imagination! And anyway, what makes you think he's not?"

I swiped at my eyes, sighing in acquiescence. "I wanted to…to tell you about Eric, but—" I broke off when Jonas fell in beside us, cutting into our conversation.

"So this Eric is the one then?" His soft Scottish lilt sounded strained.

I closed my eyes. I did not want to discuss Eric with Jonas.

"What do you care, Jonas? I hear you have more than enough girls after you."

He sighed. "I'd hardly think that's true, Cass. Anyway, they're not you." He cocked his head and shrugged. "This won't affect our friendship, will it?"

Jonas deserved better than my insensitive reaction, but I didn't reply.

He softened the blow with a laugh. "Could I take your silence to mean we're good then?"

Nodding my head, I puffed out a laugh and slipped my arm around his waist. "Incorrigible!" We walked through the door together and I muttered, "You know, Jonas… Since Harriet doesn't need me anymore, I think maybe you're my new best friend."

Chapter Fourteen

Surprisingly, considering what had transpired, Gina had not blocked my access to Mom's office, so I continued with my evening data collections.

A few days later, I left work to meet Liam, Jonas and Harriet at the stables for an early dusk ride. Since they had gone ahead of me to feed and groom the horses, I headed to the train station on my own.

As I mounted the stairs, the glass sliding doors reflected the image of a brute of a man. He walked just a short way behind me. The nape of my neck tingled, gooseflesh rising on my arms. His twisted, scarred face didn't fit with Petriville's perfect specimens. Rigid muscles bulged through his tailored jacket.

He entered the train a few carriages down. My heart raced as I scanned the otherwise-empty car. A chill surged through me. Setting a brisk pace, I walked down the aisle in the opposite direction.

At the far end, I slid the door open and stepped through to the next carriage. As the door slid shut behind me, I glanced back over my shoulder and froze.

He was already pulling that carriage door open. As the train passed through the factory ring, I broke into a run. The wheat farms and domestic animal rings still lay ahead.

Twisting as I launched through the next carriage door, I tried to turn the lock. It wouldn't budge. I tried again, wasting precious seconds. Still, it wouldn't turn. I gave up, turned and sprinted. As the carriage doors glided open, I surged through then slammed them shut, glancing back as I did. He stayed the same distance behind me. No matter how hard I pushed... No matter how I sped through the train... He neither gained on me nor lagged.

The train whistle screeched as we entered the station near the stables. The huge machine came to a halt. When the doors opened, I rotated mid-air while leaping to the platform.

My glare shot to the gorilla-like form ducking behind a pillar near the building's exit. This man moved so much faster than me. I couldn't leave that way. The deserted station closed in on me.

Think. Think. Think. My heart thumped the words.

I spun away and sprinted for the ladies' room. Ripping the door open, I launched through, twisting back to slam and lock it behind me. Only mildly less tense, I slid down the sidewall, gasping for breath.

The door rattled violently, stopped then shook again. I leaped up and ran to the back windows, pulling myself up to see through. It was a waste of time. Frosting covered the panes of glass. As an escape, if I broke one, it would be too small to exit anyway.

The door rattled again...and again. It was splintering. My heart pounded through my body. Then, the rattling stopped. What sounded like a scuffle broke out. A long, long silence followed. I listened.

Loud voices sounded outside—loud, familiar voices. I slumped and left the cloakroom as Liam's, Harriet's and Jonas' magnificent forms rounded the corner into the station.

"Hey, sis," Liam called, "we thought you weren't coming." His face dropped when he took in my terrified expression. He sprinted toward me and gripped me to his chest, darting his eyes around the platform.

"What happened, Cassidy?" Laying his cheek against my temple, he held my trembling body.

Every moment we remained in the station, I anticipated that the gorilla would reappear and I jumped at every sound. "Let's just get out of here," I begged. "I don't know where he's gone."

While we paced the cobbled road behind the brick building, I relayed the details of what had happened in a rough whisper, my gaze unconsciously flashing back. After rounding the hedge, we ducked down behind it and scanned the road we had just left.

The gorilla was gone. After a few minutes, we stood and made our way through the field toward the horses' barn.

On hearing our footsteps, Zenobia thrust her liver chestnut head from her stable and nickered—her faint dusty scent somehow comforting, homely. Her white diamond brightened her face like a sparkling jewel.

I still trembled while fitting the leather bridle to her head. Finally, I got her saddled and led her from the stable to a raised concrete block. Only after I had mounted did my heart start slowing to a normal rhythm. I settled into the comfort of the leather saddle and placed my feet in the metal stirrups and on the rubber treads.

Drawing in the fresh, grassy scent from the cool afternoon air, we rode through the horses' grass-filled paddock. An open, narrow gate led us into the gold-tipped maize plantations. Unripe maize scented the air as the early dusk sun drifted toward the horizon.

Jonas trotted Boudicca up beside me. "I'm not making light, Cass, but are you sure he was following you? Have you not considered that he simply rode the same train?"

I threw him a glare. "Really, Jonas? Sometimes... That's all very well for you to say. You weren't the one he followed."

As he clamped his lips together, I considered whether my overactive imagination *had* gotten ahead of me.

"He *was* following, Jonas," I concluded, quietly, "but I don't think he intended to catch me."

As sunset's final moments spread an orange thread along the horizon, Zenobia abruptly slammed on her brakes. She threw her head high, snorting loudly through her flaring nostrils, her heart pounding against my legs. She was always the quickest to react, but I heard rather than saw that a split second later the other horses matched her reaction.

The sharp grind of screeching metal split the air like something from a horror movie. Just ahead, an expanding light shot upward above the tall plants — a projection from beneath the maize. As Zenobia spun, she dislodged me, but when she took off at a gallop then bucked and twisted, it was the final straw. I landed hard on the ground and lay winded for a minute before spitting soil from my mouth. It sounded as though others had met a similar fate. I got to my feet as the pounding hoofbeats retreated—kicking up dirt—and the four horses galloped toward their distant stables.

"What was that?" Liam shot out in a sharp whisper from nearby.

"Harriet. Jonas," I called in a whisper, unsure where they had fallen.

A soft groan sounded on my right— Harriet's voice. "Shh," came from my left. Jonas.

Leaves rustled behind me. I spun, but it was only Liam.

Half-crouching, Jonas broke through the maize line beside us. He shot his eyes around. "Where's Harriet?"

I gestured in the direction of her prior groan. "I heard her from somewhere over there."

Liam was already shoving maize plants aside, scrambling in that direction. Jonas and I followed, barely breathing. Long seconds ticked by before we finally came upon a seated Harriet, her knees tucked against her chest. Liam dropped beside her, cupping her face in his hands. He brushed away the soil matting her hair and stroked loose blonde strands from her face.

Harriet inspected our panicked faces before responding, "It's okay, you know? Don't look so alarmed. I just winded myself. Why *must* you guys always assume the worst has happened to me?"

Liam choked a jackhammer whisper. "We don't assume, babe. We worry. That's all. Take a moment to get your breath."

Jonas took advantage of the short silence. "This is too weird, guys, but"—he gestured toward the light, his forehead twitching into a confused frown—"it sounds like voices are coming from underground, with that light... Maybe through a trap door?" He phrased it more as a question.

"I want to check it out," Liam suggested then turned to me. "Cass, when Harriet is up to it, take her back to the stables. Jonas and I will see what's going on back there." He thrust a thumb over his shoulder.

I hesitated for only a second, but he was right. As I opened my mouth to agree, Harriet, still wheezing, objected, "Don't you go thinking...a little spasm...will get in my way. I'm going with you, Liam. Don't even consider...trying to stop me!"

With his palm up, he surrendered before jerking toward the light. I froze. Babbling voices stung the warm evening air.

Harriet instantly leaped to her feet and ducked behind Liam. Her diaphragm spasm lost significance.

We peered between the maize stalks toward the light, but the night-shadowed plants standing in rows and rows—green and ripe with corn—obscured our view.

The voices grew louder...and louder still. A sharp crack cut the air.

A rapid, gruff "Silence!" followed.

"What *is* going on then?" Jonas whispered, but I couldn't listen to him. My mind whirled through a hundred terrifying scenes.

Liam cut into my thoughts with a quick, low growl. "Cassidy, I'm going forward. Stay here with Harriet."

Without waiting for my response, he and Jonas dropped into a leopard-crawl.

"Uh, let me think," I snapped in a derisive whisper, cocking my head before concluding, "No!"

I glanced at Harriet, who rolled her eyes dramatically. I nodded and we dropped to the earth to stalk after our brothers.

The light grew brighter as we neared. But not *one* of my earlier considerations prepared me for what the beam illuminated.

Liam and Jonas stopped a little back from the source. We crept beside them as the late dusk shadows moved in on us. The light revealed four soldiers — kitted in full uniform — standing beside a large square opening in the ground. Jonas had been right. Two shiny silver trapdoors opened on either side of a descending silver staircase.

I started.

"Automatic rifles?" Jonas whispered with a questioning lilt.

Harriet seethed as loudly as she dared, "Why do we need soldiers in Petriville? Who's going to invade us? Aliens?"

That wasn't the worst of it. I peered through a gap in the plants at the bright opening before us. My stomach reeled and pitched.

Emaciated, ragged men and women crawled through the opening, chains binding them together in a long line. As if that were needed… Most were so weak that even standing unsupported seemed an arduous task for them.

When the last haggard woman clambered out, my heart stopped. The head of the 'gorilla' emerged behind her, rising from below ground like a scene from a nightmare. Although no possible hiding place loomed in the nearby landscape — no further concealment, I dropped my head, half burrowing it into the soil. With my face toward Jonas, I thrust a finger at the terrifying figure.

Jonas' eyes widened. Again, that hot irritation bubbled to the surface. He *did* think I had imagined the man following me.

He held his palm up, mouthing, "Okay, okay."

In slow, calm authority, the gorilla argued, "Well, if these people die of starvation, are you useless men going to do their jobs? Ms. Petri will have you strung up for this."

The largest of the bunch responded as the others cowered into the shadows, "They're getting their rations. Let's see *you* try force them to eat."

He replied with icy calmness, "You *can* force them to eat — and you *will*. Because if one of these workers dies, I have full authority to see that you take their place in these chains."

Anger gripped my throat. My chest compacted, my stomach clenching. The gorilla held no mercy toward these workers. He wanted them only sufficiently fed to serve their purpose — as slaves.

Raising myself to my forearms, I locked my eyes on Liam's shadowed face. He clamped his teeth together so firmly that his facial muscles visibly stiffened. I watched his eyes as he glared ahead, more dangerous than I'd ever thought possible. His pupils had retracted to pinheads and were now dark as ebony, his bright green irises hazed over. As he curled his lips into a snarl, his aquiline nose wrinkled. I had never seen this expression on my mild-natured brother's face before.

I swallowed, returning my gaze to the scene ahead. The gorilla was leaving — descending into the ground. But he paused, again turning to his men. "If you see four youngsters out here, be sure to notify me."

Sarcasm grated the same soldier's voice. "When you say 'youngsters', do you mean kids? Teenagers? What?"

The gorilla had already turned away, descending into the ground. He ignored his subordinate's impertinence, yelling over his shoulder, "Not kids, you idiot. Sixteen, seventeen, plus. If you see them, bring them to me. Do you hear?"

The soldiers followed the line of workers, who had moved off into the maize-fields — thankfully not in our direction.

Light still poured from the opening. "I'm going in," Liam whispered after the men moved out of earshot.

"Are you insane, Li?" I blurted as he stood. "The man could still be near."

He glared at me, whipping his words out. "Yes, he could Cassidy. But there are four of us."

Jonas and Harriet had remained quiet during our exchange, still lying flat on the ground. They stood now. Large tears rolled down Harriet's cheeks but Jonas looked every bit as enraged as Liam. He grated his words out and they caught in his throat. "Are we going after this psycho then or what?"

Liam cupped Harriet's dimpled cheek in one strong-fingered, venous hand, his eyes not leaving hers. With his thumb, he wiped her tears — his fast words, warm and soft. "Babe, you two don't have to, but we are going after him."

He bent forward, touching his lips to her forehead before turning and following Jonas' light footsteps toward the opening.

Harriet and I had no intention of staying behind or, for that matter, returning to the stables and un-tacking the horses. I had no doubt that on hearing the horses' return, Marissa, the resident veterinarian, would take care of them without much thought to our wellbeing.

We followed only a second later, taking the narrow, shiny, silver staircase, descending between mirror-like silver walls. Just our soft footsteps sounded in the reflective stairwell as it continued leading us down — away from everything we knew to be real.

Nearing the bottom, Liam held his hand high, his voice quieter than a whisper. "Back up a few meters." As we obeyed, loud voices carried through the tunnel below — rough, male voices.

My heart raced as they grew louder. I begged silently, *Please, don't come up the stairs. Please don't…*

In continued conversation they passed by, not seeming to sense our presence at all. Relief poured out with my expelled puff of air. Liam carried on moving downward.

Only feeling marginally less exposed, I trailed the others into a cross-tunnel, heading in the direction of the railway line. That same silver metal surrounded us, seamlessly joining floor, wall and ceiling. A chill ran through me — a bad omen.

Liam turned away from the voices. In a tiptoed jog, he advanced along the cross-tunnel's curved inner wall that mirrored the bend of Petriville's side-street walkways and the zoo habitats. Sealed doorways formed equidistant dents in both walls. A soft draft blew my hair back as though an exit lay ahead.

Liam whispered his logic, "Assuming that he'll return the way he came, we can follow him down this tunnel to get to the station after the stables."

Jonas half agreed, "Makes sense if he lives *in* town, but I doubt that he does." He threw a look at me, and I nodded.

"Well, we've got nothing to —" Harriet broke off as a large tunnel opened on either side, dotted with central ceiling lights.

A strong draft overflowed into the side tunnel.

Jonas boomed, "Not an exit then. Just more, even bigger tunnels — out of the frying pan and into the fire."

"Shush, Jonas," I whispered, glancing left and right. The flooring of this larger tunnel wasn't silver. "Conveyor streets? What —?" I fell short as a shadow in the smaller tunnel caught my peripheral vision.

Not a shadow. I froze. Standing erect with a weapon in his hand was the gorilla, and his icy, gruff growl cut through the air like a sharp dagger. "You lot should have known better than to follow me down here." As he spoke, he raised then steadied the gun.

Not a second before the shot rang out, Jonas jerked my arm. We thudded down onto the main tunnel's homeward-bound conveyor — landing in a heap on top of Liam and Harriet. I leaped up, sprinting with the others.

I ran up beside Liam, glancing over my shoulder. "He's fast, Li. He's very fast. He had no trouble sticking with me on the train." Liam knew how I could run, that I easily outran every girl and most boys in the MAC Challenge.

Liam gripped Harriet's hand — making sure she could match our pace, despite her shorter legs. The conveyor further increased our speed. We soon burst into another cross tunnel. The rotating belt spilled us off onto the silver flooring. Before fully comprehending our situation, momentum and the glossy finish propelled us forward. Then we were running along the far conveyor. "Was it just him? Or are others...

following too?" Harriet panted, her voice shuddering with fear and exertion.

"I think others…are back there," Liam panted back.

Many feet pounded the conveyor behind us. Another shot rang out. I ducked away from the showering glass as a ceiling light smashed overhead.

I threw a glance over my shoulder. In the dim light of the tunnel, I couldn't see anybody but the footsteps grew louder. Jonas glanced back too, voicing what I had observed, "They can't see much in this light. They're just shooting blind."

Just then, a doorway ahead slid open. A gnarled, leathery hand pushed through, the twisted, claw-like finger flexing and straightening. "This way," the accompanying voice rasped.

After only a second's hesitation, Jonas growled, "How much worse can this be than getting shot at then?"

Needing no further encouragement, we raced toward the door.

Chapter Fifteen

The moment we entered, the door sailed shut behind us, cutting off all light. Raw, ragged panting pierced the pitch-dark silence. As I caught my breath—as it slowed—other soft sounds attracted my attention. Heat radiated from more than a few nearby bodies. The overwhelming reek of sewerage stung my airways.

Abruptly, too many hands gripped my arms and legs, pinning me. But before the cry could escape my lips, a rough, calloused hand clamped against my mouth—firm enough to stop me from twisting away. I choked in the dusty, grimy coating. The smell of it was hardly better than the sewerage.

I couldn't breathe. I couldn't scream.

Nor did I want to. Our pursuer was surely near.

To my right, Liam or Jonas thrashed around and shoved my surrounding throng, almost knocking us over—almost freeing me. My own writhing body made muted scuffling sounds.

The hands hoisted me horizontally into the air above them, body facing upward. The one over my mouth pressed even harder. As shoulders supported me, hands gripped my arms and legs with so much force that I could feel bruises forming.

Feet shuffled as our captors transported us away from the entrance. The pitch-dark went on and on—a tunnel for sure.

For about ten minutes our captors lumbered forward, until a faint glow softened the darkness. As it brightened, the silver tunnel roof unfolded with broken lights spaced along its center. Nothing else came into view. With my head gripped in place, I couldn't move it to look around.

The feet slowed then stopped.

The same raspy, hoarse voice croaked out. I couldn't tell whether it was male or female. It was neither kind nor unkind, but hard. "We're going to set you down. Do not scream or try to run. You'll never make it."

The obvious unveiled threat startled me.

In silence, the hands lowered me to the floor—surprisingly gentle now.

I looked toward the voice but couldn't tell whether its owner was male or female. Weathered and twisted, the hooded, gaunt, pasty face appeared marginally amused. The form was hunching over a staff.

A raspy, gritted voice emerged, charged with measured authority. "Remember what I have said. Do not scream or run. You're in our world now."

They had placed us so that we stood back-to-back, gazing at the surrounding circle, more than forty strong—those who had carried us to this place. They appeared emaciated, drawn and sinewy from long hours of toiling—worse even than the first group we had seen in the maize.

Liam tumbled his words out even faster than usual. "Why are you holding us?"

Gravelly voice ignored his question. "And what brings you down here? Why were you chased?" The person answered his or her own question. "Clearly you witnessed something you should not have. What a pickle." The voice laughed, a rasping, hoarse cackle that ended in a fit of coughing before finally addressing Liam's question. "Should we have left you in the tunnel? Would that have been better? Or worse?" He or she held a forefinger to their lips. "A real conundrum." Another cackle and another fit of coughing ensued. "First, let's escape this"—the seemingly epicene individual gave an animal-like nose-twitch in the air—"sewer tunnel."

A door to our right slid open. A mixture of clean, chilled air with bright, white light flooded out to greet us.

Our captors herded us through. The door whizzed shut behind us.

We stood in the general center of a pristine, stark bright silver corridor. Windows lined the wall to the alley we had exited, making it look as bright as day. *Surprising*. Light flooded this passage, contrasting to the pitch-dark alley from which we emerged.

Evenly spaced double doors led off the long corridor. They stood ajar, revealing large, rectangular rooms. Beds lined both walls.

The old, staff-wielding leader swept ahead, closing some doors—obscuring their sleeping occupants from our prying eyes.

"Hey!" Liam demanded, refusing to take another step forward. "Tell us what you want from us."

"Want from *you*?" rasped the voice ahead with another cackle and cough. "Want from *you*?" it repeated, as though the thought was absurd.

Liam's captor shoved him forward. We followed, receding from our entry point along the bright silver corridor.

"There's no point in fighting," the old voice commanded, stopping at another set of doors. One of our captors stepped forward, thrusting both doors wide. He stood aside and, with a hand gesture, welcomed us through. As if there had been no pause, the old voice continued, "It'll just get you into more hot water."

We stepped into what looked like an old farmhouse kitchen from one of my childhood picture-books—warm and cozy. Floral motifs covered the pine-cabinet-lined walls. In the center stood a large table of the same wood.

After pressing Liam and Harriet into hard, wooden chairs on one side of the table, they moved Jonas and me to the other. The 'guards' stood back, surrounding us. The old leader touched the outline of a bright blue water droplet on the wall—out of place against the old-world furniture. A second later a gap appeared and a filled pitcher slid onto the counter.

After bringing the pitcher and glasses to the table, the leathery old person sat at the head, filled five glasses and placed one in front of each of us. "Well, well. It's been a long time since we've had this much fun." With another cackle and cough, he or she looked back at the silent, nodding guards then turned their concentrated attention on us.

The intense pale-blue eyes bore into me, pupils of black orbs.

His or her pitch rose as if declaring triumph in the announcement. "I am Jaya!"

"Great!" Jonas coughed under his breath. "So we still don't know if it's male or female." His declaration had shocked him as much as me and he widened his green eyes.

The old voice gave a cackle and cough that could claim a person's life. "Another conundrum. Bigger perhaps than the first? Not a mind. Time escapes us. We must conclude our dealings."

Liam slammed his forearms on the table and bunched his fists. "Enough! Enough of your games. Kill us — if that's what you're planning — or let us go."

Harriet shot him a glare.

I guessed Liam was calling Jaya's bluff and followed his lead, my words quiet and deliberate. "Tell us what you want. You didn't bring us here without cause. And," I added, "who was that brute following us?"

Jaya smiled. "Aren't you a fiery bunch?" The eyes and voice dropped. "You wouldn't be so arrogant were you seeing through these tired, old eyes. But regarding that brute, there's worse down here. Much, much worse. As for the rest, it is not complicated. You have guessed the truth already. We *are* slaves." Jaya waved the leathery arms around. "People in this bunch are ill. I am no leader — just older and seeking retribution for the young. All living quarters are similar — sewer corridors are our front lawns. We're the only group with access. They'd block us if they knew."

Horror glued me to my seat. "How... How many people live down here?"

Jaya lifted the pale eyes, the old voice sounding tired. "Not as many as up there — a ratio of one to eight, more-or-less. The young ones hate you — say you're selectively naive. I did too…once. But I know better. Now I advocate that we send our fury in the right direction."

Jaya paused, sighed deeply then cast tired old eyes upward. "None of you lot have been down here before." Looking up again, Jaya locked on Liam. "You know, though, don't you? Or suspected. Tell me about that."

Outrage gripped Liam's face, pulling it into hard lines. He cast his eyes down then around at us. After wrist-rubbing his nose, his speech emerged in measured tones. "I couldn't get my head around what they fed us at school. That machines harvested fields, processed crops, fed and watered animals, milked, slaughtered, collected eggs — that everything functioned automatically, with only our veterinarians and agricultural scientists as overseers. I didn't buy it."

Jaya's intense gaze didn't leave Liam, but a soft smile formed on the tired, wrinkled lips.

Jaya dropped into silence for a moment then clarified Liam's observations. "Many processes are automated — processing and packaging mostly. Grunt work is done by" — with arms spread wide, Jaya gestured around in a circular motion — "well, us. As I'm sure you know, human and animal waste-gasses are collected just inside the Kaleidotonium shell — an added power source for the machinery."

Harriet shifted in her chair. "But that still doesn't explain how they stock shelves. You know — in our supermarkets." She gestured upward with her eyes and index fingers. "Not even robots pack the shelves, yet they're always full." She frowned for a long moment. Then she continued as if she hadn't. "Speaking of which, I don't mean to disregard your worth but why don't they use robots to do your work?"

Jaya laughed. "So many questions." Jaya answered anyway, "No. We don't go up there." Jaya drew a small rectangular object from the ragged robe—a visual experience cube.

Laying it in the center of the table, Jaya waved an arm, summoning us on a virtual quest. "Come. Let us rather show you."

A bright beam shot out from the device—an upside-down triangle, beaming up and out. From out of the light, a darkened chamber appeared. It really did seem like we were following Jaya on a journey through the light, into a different place, though we never left our seats. "This is just one of the chambers down here."

Inside the glow, the room revealed thousands of small shafts leading upward. Narrow conveyors, each carrying a different packaged product, fed each duct. The image latched onto a packet of frozen peas, following it into and up the shaft. Finally, it escaped into a supermarket freezer, pushing forward against the backs of other frozen pea packets. A woman reached into the light, selecting a pack from the front.

As the device sucked the light back inside, Jaya said, "Well, now you know. Simple explanation."

I cocked my head, curiosity straining my brow as I pointed at the small device. "Where did you get that from?"

Jaya gave a small chuckle, crunching up the cheeks. "Another story for another time. Our bunch is a rather resourceful lot." Jaya's face sagged. "As you saw, that task is mostly automated. Answering your second question is somewhat more difficult. Without Gina's slave requirement, we wouldn't be alive. But the answer is simple economics. We cost a mere fraction of the expense of robots, even over these long years."

My eyes stretched wide as Jaya shrugged, seeming to move back to the previous conversation. "Your parents know," Jaya pressed, in some telepathic act between him or her and my brother.

Liam nodded, drifting his gaze down to his loosening fists. "For some time, they've suspected that she enslaved people down here." He looked up again. "They want to oppose Gina on this."

Jaya nodded, dragging out the first word. "Yes. We guessed as much. Good people don't usually enjoy thriving off others' slavery, once they realize that they are."

After a shrug, Jaya concluded, "But they must wait. They cannot do anything until we're back on Earth. Remember us down here. Help us when you can."

Liam swallowed, his voice cracking as he choked out, "We will."

I swallowed too, fidgeting with my hands as I ground my teeth together, blinking back the tears prickling in my eyes. Across the table, Harriet's face tugged into a mass of anguished lines. She swiped ineffectually at the tears flowing down her cheeks.

Liam wrapped his arm around her shoulders, pulling her head to his chest. "We'll find a solution, babe. We *will* stop this."

Harriet broke away from Liam, dabbing her angry tears. "I can't believe she's doing this. How did we never figure it out? How naive are we?"

Jaya observed the scene with sympathetic lines clawing even deeper into the tired forehead and mouth.

I drained my water in one then turned to Jonas. Hardening his jawline, he flexed his large forearm muscles. Jonas met Liam's eyes and in a low growl reacted to his earlier statement. "You'd better believe we will."

Jaya appeared satisfied and summoned a guard. Pulling the man down by his shoulder, Jaya leveled the leathery, old mouth to his ear and whispered a few commands. The guard nodded then stood erect.

Jaya again turned to us. "Now remember. You have given us your word. Aaron here will lead you home. We often tour tunnels at night. Fewer patrols move around then. You won't find us on the streets. There are cameras out there."

Jonas' brow furrowed as he contemplated a new idea. "Jaya...?" he lilted. "Do you know any way off the craft once we're back on Earth?"

Jaya met his eyes with a confused frown. "If I knew what you were planning" — then paused — "but no matter. Several, distantly spaced elevator shafts run down the craft's outer rim. They didn't take us up that way. Soldiers got to the top of the craft using that method. Us, they dragged in through a strange triangular doorway at the base, straight into these tunnels. You'd be better off using the elevators."

Jaya abruptly stood. "You be off now." Through an inner door, heading into a deeper chamber, Jaya left.

Without a moment's hesitation, Aaron waved his arm and summoned us to follow.

Chapter Sixteen

Harriet buried her hand in Liam's as we retraced our footsteps toward the dark sewer tunnel. As the outer door drifted open, Aaron opened his hand to reveal a flat, black object lying against his palm. A beam shot out, cutting a sharp rectangle into the blackness. We entered the inky passage, but as the door shut behind us, Aaron turned in the opposite direction.

Jonas beat me to the question. "Why are you taking us this way?"

Aaron only responded with a summoning hand over his unturned shoulder.

The back of my neck prickled as I caught up to Liam. "Do we trust this...Aaron, Li?'

Liam tucked a strand of hair behind my ear. "I don't see any reason Jaya would hold us."

"Besides" — Jonas cut in — "if it wanted to hurt us, it would have done it in there, while it had us."

I threw him a glare. "Don't be condescending, Jonas. Jaya is not an 'it'."

He shrugged off my dispute. "Terminology, Cassidy. Until *Jaya* tells us whether *Jaya* is a man or a woman, what are we supposed to call *Jaya*? Since, other than the word 'it', the English language never did cater to gender-neutrality."

Rolling my eyes, I dismissed his comments with a hand wave.

By the time we had concluded our disagreement, Aaron had slowed at another doorway — the tunnel's far end. He turned the light off and held up his hand, his palm facing forward. He extracted a small panel from his jacket and keyed in a series of numbers. The door slid open. But he didn't go through or even lean forward. Instead, he waited, looking intently at both conveyors. Both were still. Only then did he peer through, turning his head, first one way then the other.

Finally, he appeared convinced that nobody was lurking in the tunnel. He stepped out, indicating that we stay on the conveyor's safety rim.

A surprised frown stretched my forehead when, for the first time, he spoke. His voice broke free in soft, reedy gasps. "If we stay off the conveyor, it won't move. Then they might not look for you in this tunnel."

The words slipped out before I had fully considered my inquiry. "Do you think they're still searching for us?"

Aaron cocked his head and raised his brows. A sarcastic non-reply wheezed from his throat, in his own imitation of my voice. "Do you think the sky's still blue out there?"

I rolled my eyes. "Not if it's nighttime." Ignoring my retort, Aaron set off at a slow jog, surprising for one so emaciated. We followed along the corridor lip.

I gritted my teeth in the half-lit passage as we passed too many closed doors.

Abruptly, Aaron slowed then stopped. Holding his hand up, he cocked his head, listening. He edged forward but stopped again. The conveyor broke for a cross tunnel. Ducking down, he stuck his head out, peering first left, then right then at the two far conveyors. Both were still. He dropped his hand, darted over the gap and continued running along the next conveyor's rim. We followed. When we had reached nearly halfway through the next tunnel, the conveyor we edged along suddenly began moving. Moments later, the other belt fell into familiar motion.

Before I could react, Harriet broke the silence that had fallen over our small band in her diluted Scottish accent. "We're trapped! What are we supposed to do now?"

Aaron again held up his hand then extracted a small device from his jacket. He ran to a doorway, working on the small hand-held panel. Nothing. Without wasting time, he jogged to the next-door. Again nothing. Patiently he trotted forward to the next and the next. Voices reached us. Nearing voices. Aaron slammed into the fifth door, pressing a sequence of numbers into the pad. Finally, a sigh escaped him as the door shifted then thankfully opened. He urged us through, ducking inside and twisting with the panel raised. The voices sounded so close now — almost on us. The door slid shut, not a moment too soon. We stood in pitch-dark silence, hardly breathing, listening.

A moment later, louder voices cut through the silence as the two groups met.

"Guess they're not in this one either."

"Nope."

"See you guys in 5C."

I took in the surrounding blackness. No sewerage stench permeated the stuffy air, but the dank result was no less comforting.

Finally, Aaron reopened the sliding door.

As we slipped out, back into the tunnel, I ventured, "What was that place, Aaron?"

His reedy voice gasped out the words. "I'm not sure, not about that one. Most are storage rooms—of a sort, anyway."

Twice more during our long jog, pursuers drove us into storage rooms. Then something changed. A sudden draft stopped us in our tracks.

Aaron paused then edged forward.

I shivered, the chill breeze raising gooseflesh on my arm. When a hand landed on my shoulder, I leaped into the air. "Liam!"

"Stay behind me, Cass."

I shrugged off his request. A strange glow accompanied the draft, and as we crept forward behind Aaron, both light and breeze gained strength.

The arched tunnel exited into an enormous hollow vertical cylinder—a vast, gloomy chamber. Bisecting the exit, a ladder rose to—I assumed—a higher level.

A gridded walkway ran along the inner circumference with a guardrail protecting its open side. Aaron did not step onto this. Instead, he stopped at the verge of the tunnel. Gripping the ladder in one hand, he held up his free hand and cocked his head.

I looked into the chamber and upward—to the underside of what was undoubtedly the town square. Then I moved my head down, peering through the grid, toward the belly of the craft.

After some time, Aaron nodded, as if to himself. Then he summoned us, stepped forward and reached for the outer railing. "Come quickly. Come quietly."

I inched to the railing. My eyes were irrevocably drawn over the guardrail. *Down, down, down.* Vacant space lay beneath the grid — beneath my feet — dropping away into the vast chasm. The gloom inside it deepened until the pitch-dark depths swallowed all light.

My gaze floated around the immense cylinder, the hub or exit point of twelve equidistant tunnels. No, not twelve. Twenty-four. The lower tunnels exited at grid level, the smaller tunnels a level above — the two connected by the bisecting ladder.

Squinting through the dim light to my left, something piqued my curiosity. I kept my voice low. "Are those elevator shafts?"

Harriet, who had been silent for some time, finally found hers. "Those are the elevators from the municipal building to the stadium."

Aaron ignored our comments but flashed Harriet an exasperated glare, his voice a harsh whisper. "What part of 'quietly' don't you understand?"

Turning away from the grid, he addressed Liam. "Which street conveyor is nearest your home?"

Liam whispered a spontaneous reply, "Two."

We picked our way around the grid, hugging the chamber wall. I observed the numbers etched atop each tunnel to the one we had exited. *Tunnel four.*

Aaron crept nimbly toward tunnel two's silver ladder. "Go first, Harriet, then you, Cassidy."

I focused on the ladder ahead of me and followed Harriet's voluptuous, athletic form. When she neared the top, she twisted her head, looking over her shoulder—not at me, but past.

She grew her eyes into saucers. A suppressed "Eek!" escaped her lips.

She turned back, soon gaining the top rung. A moment later, she scrambled into the tunnel, thrusting herself away from the edge. When I neared its apex, the same involuntary gasp escaped my throat as, in my mind's eye, I watched my body sailing past the lower guardrail and plummeting into the depths below. I shuddered as Harriet called down in an anguished voice, "It's not very safe...that ladder. Will Liam and Jonas be okay?"

As I clambered off into the tunnel, Harriet made a vague grab for my hand while I pushed away from the edge. "They'll be fine, Harri. Most likely doing better than we did."

Seconds later, Jonas then Liam heaved themselves into the tunnel and stood beside us.

A harsh, deep shout echoed through the chamber.

I moved to the edge and peered over. Dressed in full military uniform, at least a dozen soldiers exited a lower tunnel at the shadowed, far side of the chamber. Without a pause, they raced around the cavern toward us, heavy boots pounding on the grid. From behind, Liam wrapped his arms around my waist, tugging me away from the edge. "What the hell are you thinking, Cassidy?"

Just then, Aaron scrambled over the lip. "Why are you waiting? Run, you idiots!"

Inside the capsule-like tunnel, a row of yellow half-moon lights dotted the top—turning the shiny silver into brilliant, bright, glinting gold.

Aaron's reedy gasp sounded even thinner as he sprinted forward. "Stop at the first door."

No conveyors lay on this floor. But, somehow, the glossy surface gave purchase.

"Here." Liam halted beside a kind of ship's door, with Jonas just behind. Panting, they twisted the wheel just as Harriet and I pulled up. But the door didn't open. Aaron drew alongside, cocking his ear toward the chasm. "Quiet."

He extracted a strange, angular device from his jacket and slotted it into two aligning wedges.

When Liam and Jonas again spun the wheel, the door eased open.

The soldiers had entered the tunnel. Heavy boot-falls pounded in the distance.

Without a pause, Liam tossed Harriet through. Then me.

Jonas shot him a glare. "Don't even think about it." And he stepped through, with Liam and Aaron hot on his heels.

Together, they swung the door shut then spun the wheel in a clockwise direction until it clicked.

Again, Aaron slotted the angular device into the aligning wedges. "All doors require these. They're intended to stop our kind getting onto the streets — as though we'd want to." A mischievous smile played across his lips. "Somebody got hold of a few and the powers-that-be never renewed them. But that's a story for another time." His smile faded. "Maybe."

He shoved the device into Jonas' hand. "Here… I sense you may need this in time to come."

Jonas cocked his head, squinting a little, but silently took the device and thrust it into his jeans' pocket.

Harriet looked around us as we stood, squashed in the tiny silver room. "Are you insane, Aaron? You've brought us nowhere at all."

Liam pressed his ear against the ship's door. "Shh, guys."

The door rattled and I jumped back suppressing a squeal. Once more, it shook.

Aaron's wheezing whisper barely reached my ears. "They'll try every door. No matter." When he moved his eyes upward, I saw it — the underside of a manhole cover.

I beamed, launching at him and wrapping my arms around his shoulders. "Aaron, you're the meteor!"

He depressed a lever against the silver wall. The utility cover sprang open. Then he turned to Liam, holding out his hand. "I guess this is goodbye."

"For now," Liam agreed.

Jonas gripped Aaron's smaller hand in both of his. "You'll be getting back okay, then?"

Aaron smiled, impishly. "Of course."

As he squeezed Harriet, tears sprang into her eyes. "How do we thank you, Aaron? You saved our lives. We won't forget, you know?"

Aaron chuckled. "Neither will I let you."

We emerged from the manhole onto the sidewalk that trimmed conveyor two. We were outside Mama Candy's usually tinkling front door — the last shop before the housing rows began. The walkway stood deserted now.

I looked back down the manhole, giving Aaron a small wave. He again pulled the lever, the soft smile never leaving his lips as the cover closed.

Harriet lightly punched my upper arm. "Imagine if you hadn't gotten rid of all those bangles, Cass. With their continuous jingling, we wouldn't have escaped."

The moon had already begun the downward slide of its arc as Liam and I entered our home.

Our parents were not waiting up. They had become used to not worrying about us. We had, after all, always been safe in Petriville—until now....

Chapter Seventeen

On Saturday morning I awoke to bright sunlight peeking through my pale lilac curtains and Roger Winters' booming Scottish accent resonating from downstairs.

"Morning, Joneses!"

I turned away. "Argh." I pulled my pillow over my head, clamping it against my ears.

Dad reciprocated Roger's greeting in a much quieter, "Well, morning back to you, Winters family."

I smiled to myself, uncertain about the plural of their surname. *Winterses* just didn't sound right.

"Hey!" Harriet sang, opening and peering through my bedroom door. Without waiting for my response, she swept in and flopped on my bed.

"Seriously, Harriet, what are you doing here so early?"

She arched her brows. "You honestly think our dad gave us the sleep-in option? Please. You know him better than that. Besides, our parents arranged this 'meeting'." She air-quoted the last word.

As I slipped from the covers, Harriet sidled to the end of the bed. I strolled past the dresser, grabbed a brush and hairband and, pulling my hair up into a simple knot, stepped into the bathroom. After a quick wash, I slipped into my favorite white lace underwear and pulled a light cotton dress over my head then wedged my feet into leather sandals.

When I pulled Harriet to her feet, she muttered, "Aren't you at least going to tell me what's been going on between you and this 'Eric' before we join the others?"

I rolled my eyes. "Later. It's a long story." We made our way downstairs.

Liam, with a fully laden coffee-tray, headed outdoors. I breathed in the rich aroma. Harriet and I emerged from the back door to find the entire ensemble seated at the wrought-iron table—Mom, Dad, Roger, Megan, Joshua, Caroline and Jonas.

As we all exchanged "Good mornings," Liam set the tray in the center then extracted three chairs, inviting Harriet to sit down beside him. I reached for coffee before falling into the only remaining chair, between Jonas and Harriet.

Mom laid her arm across Dad's shoulder, smoothing his disheveled hair with her fingers while Dad placed mugs on coasters before them.

As we relayed our story, our parents and the Carters sat in relative silence.

Liam concluded with, "You already knew she had brought slaves on board, didn't you, Dad?"

Dad leaned forward, resting his toned forearms in front of him and clasping his hands. "Well, for some time, we've assumed as much" — he paused — "but we received confirmation only recently."

Roger placed his elbows on the table and leaned forward, resting his chin on his large fisted hands. "If Gina hasn't heard about what happened down there, she soon will."

With a nod, Dad sighed, "Agreed."

Mom closed then opened her deep blue eyes. The strain forced crinkling lines around the edges. "Would she suspect our kids, though?"

Megan had already formed an opinion on this. "Oh, I'm sure I wouldn't doubt that for a second. I'll bet she has been watching them for some time. Cassidy's hardly been clandestine in her behavior."

My mouth fell open, but Mom leaped to my defense. "That's not fair, Megan. You must know that this was hardly my daughter's fault."

"No, no, you misunderstand me. I know kids shouldn't have to worry about these things. But Cassidy hasn't exactly stayed under the radar."

Jonas rested his forearms on the table. "That's neither here nor there, Mom. But what will Gina do when she finds out?"

"If she suspects you lot, son, she'll monitor you more closely." Megan studied her lap. "But she cannot watch each of you every minute of every day."

Liam appeared lost in thought then diverted the conversation. "What else do you suspect? Or know?"

Our father had never been loud or imposing. His calm, quiet demeanor heralded his strength. When he spoke, people listened, not because he commanded it, but because what he said was usually worth hearing.

He furrowed his broad, high forehead into deep lines — hardening his cheeks. "We expect that Gina will keep these slaves working for her once we're back on Earth. They will never gain their freedom. Gina laid her map for what she deems perfect human genes. For the time being, we fit that mold. But our sources claim that they chemically neutered most slaves and left only the strongest unsullied. She, most likely, intends to produce more slaves with these people, which means that their ancestors will never gain freedom." Dad paused then swallowed, drawing his thumb and forefinger from his temples over his eyes and closing them on the bridge of his nose.

He gritted his teeth, locking on me as he continued, "Now, we believe that this is not all Gina is planning, not since she found out that Graham survived." He faced me. "I'm sorry this is on you, Cass, but with the knowledge of their survival, she may intend to add them to her slave collection — or even kill them."

My heart sank to my feet. "Why, Dad? Why would she do that? They have no intention of harming anyone."

Harriet gripped my hand on my lap, while Jonas leaned back and laid his palm over my shoulder.

Dad continued, his tone soothing, "Don't you see, Cass? She doesn't want anybody affecting her breeding program. She has planned to populate Earth with her perfect humans. No others. According to our sources, she even calculated the ratio of slaves per elite. There is no space for a single outsider in her perfect new world."

Harriet withdrew her hand and threw herself against Liam's chest, sobbing while I furiously blinked back the prickle in my eyes.

As he closed his arms around Harriet's shoulders, Liam squinted, cocking his head. "But humans will never be perfect, Dad. No matter what she does, some personality flaws will creep in. Look at us, for example. Doesn't the fact that a rebellion is forming already expose a flaw in her perfect gene calculation?"

"Well, you're right about that, son. I don't believe humans can ever be perfect — or are meant to be."

Jonas slumped his broad shoulders beside me and shook his head. "Is she honestly that evil then?"

Roger answered, his voice unusually soft and tender, "Aye. We believe she is, son. We believe she is."

I yearned to see Eric — to talk to him. Even if I could, though, I couldn't tell him what Dad had just mentioned. Gina was sure to be listening in now. But didn't Eric already know this? I sat erect.

"Dad…" I waited for him to make eye contact. "Eric mentioned that they would be in danger if Gina found out they had survived."

Dad straightened, too. "He did?"

"Yes, I'm sure of it."

Everyone sat more erect — their eyes fixed on me.

As he clasped Caroline's hand, a small smile touched Joshua's lips. Slowly, he shook his head, threading his thick knuckled fingers into the black-and-gray-curls. "I should have expected as much from the wily old man. Always a step ahead of Gina, he was. Always anticipating her next action."

I glanced at Jonas and he at me, our eyes meeting for a second. He rubbed his nape, looking down. This talk about Graham and, by extension Eric, was apparently making him uncomfortable. "I'm sorry," I mouthed, reaching for his hand. He shrugged a shoulder.

As much as I cared for Jonas, I remembered the moment when Eric and I had first locked eyes with so fierce a craving. I quivered. The intense emotions that had coursed through me from his virtual touch were still vivid in my mind.

Jonas lifted my hand, covering it in both of his — his concerned gaze steadily observing my face. Liam stepped to my side and shared a brief nod with Jonas then, taking my hand, he raised me to my feet.

"Let's walk," he said quietly.

And we did. We walked along the park's winding brick paving, the low white lanterns — sentinels to the path — stood unlit in the day. We talked about all that had happened over the past months, between and to us. All the while Liam kept his arm slung loosely around my shoulder.

He turned to me then, clasping my upper arms. An earnest expression gripped his features, his bright green eyes boring into mine. He spoke no slower than usual, but sympathy smoothed his voice. "I hate to see how this has affected you, Cass. And I know we can do little to ensure Graham and Eric's safety. If I haven't been there for you, I'm sorry. But you always seem so independent these days. I didn't think you needed me anymore, you know?"

I wanted to tell him I would always need him — that there would never be a day in my life I wouldn't, but he was speaking again. "I want to help you now — if you'll let me. Jonas and Harriet do too. We'll do whatever it takes to help everyone out there."

I smiled up at him as he drew my head to his chest. "Thanks, Li." Another thought tugged a grimace onto my lips. "Liam, what do they all think about Eric and me? I mean…it's embarrassing — you know, since I've never actually met him."

My brother gave a warm smile and shook his head. "Oh, trust me, Cass. Nobody there is judging." He gestured toward our house with a wave of his arm. "Only you know how you feel about Eric, just as surely as it is only me who knows how I feel about Harriet."

I opened my mouth to ask if Jonas was okay but I already knew the answer. And if Liam was unaware of Jonas' feelings... I shut my lips and we headed home in contented silence.

Chapter Eighteen

It wasn't long afterward that things changed again. I should have known they would.

While Mom and I examined the latest graphs, I glanced over my shoulder. A vivid memory leaped into focus on the silver platform. It was so intense that I barely managed to keep the ache from tearing through my chest. Though my heart shuddered, adrenaline was not to blame, because nobody occupied the space. I turned away, back to my work.

"Greetings," came the voice from behind us a moment later. I hadn't heard anyone enter the office, but I recognized that voice. An involuntary snarl gripped my mouth.

Mom replied politely, "Good evening, Gina."

I turned away, blinking back my tears. I would not give Gina the satisfaction of witnessing my heartache.

Gina did not respond to Mom—a rebuff that neither she nor I missed.

"Miss Jones, you will do something for us." *Not a request.* "I expect that your friend will soon make contact. You will be available when he does. You will establish their exact location."

I couldn't help myself and flew into an uncontrolled rage, screaming my thoughts out without pausing to consider the consequences. "I haven't seen him in *weeks*!" I could no longer hide my disdain or tears from her. Both poured out ferociously. Mom drew nearer, placing a hand on my shoulder, but I wasn't done. "And what makes you think he'd tell me? Plus, he can't return because we're out of alignment. And even if he could, he *wouldn't*."

Her voice dripped with sardonicism, more confident than made me comfortable. "Oh, he'll come. You forget that I'm in control of our alignment." Then, she raised her voice a touch, her tone icier than ever. "The pod will supply their relative location. But you will be certain to get their exact coordinates."

She turned and, thrusting her shoulders back, walked briskly from Mom's office.

As the door shut behind her, I melted to the floor. Mom kneeled behind me, holding me against her while I sobbed. "He cannot come, Mom. He must not. She'll find them if he does."

Gina's confidence that Eric would return concerned me more than the confrontation itself.

Petriville was closing in on me. I desperately fought against my ever-increasing claustrophobia. But Gina had full control. We would never escape her clutches.

Until Gina had entered Mom's office, I was so sure Eric wouldn't return. I had told him not to. Now, silently, I pleaded to him through space — begging him to stay away.

* * * *

Gina's presence pervaded the office over the following weeks. I couldn't escape her. Each evening she sat beside Mom, waiting for Eric's return. But as each evening came and went without his arrival, relief left me with physical pain. Most nights ended with me clutching at my stomach as it twisted in agony.

As winter relinquished its hold and a new spring was born, Eric had still not returned. Although over this time, the brightly blinking stars in the night skies above Petriville remained unchanged, our perspective of Earth began to shift.

The ever-nearing vision became a constant reminder that we were relocating within her orbit—visual confirmation of our return. With Gina's motive clear, the prospect of going back overwhelmed me with terror.

As each night crept upon us, the daunting sight of Earth loomed nearer and nearer. She was too close now, too vast and terrible—claiming the entire night sky as her own.

Relief overpowered me as doubt clouded Gina's features. Her evening visits had somewhat diminished. Over the following days, the dwindling ceased entirely.

A matter of days or weeks remained now. A full year had passed since Gina's announcement in the stadium.

Chapter Nineteen

Although deeply conflicted, I returned to Mom's office after lectures each day to assist with data and video collections.

One evening, as I strolled down the corridor, unease washed over me. Something was different—wrong. Mom's office door stood ajar.

The phonepad on her desk began beeping. I raced through and pulled the door closed behind me, sprinting toward the sound. In a single motion, I clutched and swooped the loose earpiece to my ear. "Mom?" I held my breath.

"I'm home, Cassidy. You sound out of breath. Is everything all right?"

I sighed then blurted, "You really worried me, Mom. What happened?"

"Don't stress, my daughter. I'm just a little tired tonight. When the collection run completes, would you please sort the data that I was loading?"

"Of course, I will, Mom. Did you leave your office door open?"

"It was open? How strange. Maintenance must not have closed up when they left."

Still not entirely comfortable as we ended the call, I wheeled the chair to the far side of the long, curved desk then began the evening's data checks.

Our analysis had changed of late. No longer did we study water, air and soil data but focused on weather patterns around specific pods.

I leaned over these printed graphs, uncertain of what to find. It didn't matter. We just collected this data and forwarded it to a meteorologist. An hour later, I transferred the data, completing my work for the day. After packing, I stood, but a familiar voice broke the silence. "Cassidy, you there?"

I twisted around and half-jumped, half-fell backward.

In barely any time at all, I was on the silver platform facing Eric."

"Hey," he crooned, his voice smooth and languid, "I hardly meant to scare you."

"Eric," I gasped, my throat dry as I attempted to steady my voice.

My hands trembled. Oh, to reach out and touch Eric, to feel his warm skin on mine. My body ached — burned — for these impossible things. I dropped my head into my hands and slumped to the floor.

"Why are you here?" I finally poured out, our eyes meeting as he knelt before me. He sat back on his heels, his jeans pulling across his strong thigh muscles. It was too much — gazing on the face that had permeated my dreams these long months. "Why did you come back?

I told you I didn't want you to," I rasped again as he reached a hand toward me.

I couldn't help myself, couldn't stop my hands from reaching toward his hardened fingers, his calloused upward turning palms.

While he spoke, he pierced me with his striking eyes. "You'll be needing our coordinates, Cassidy, before it's no longer possible…" He trailed off. "Do you want me to go?" A pained expression filtered through his features.

"Eric," I flooded, "it's so dangerous for you to be here." I softened into a whisper and glanced around. "This is what Gina wants. She wants me to get your hideout's location. Don't give it to me, Eric." I sighed. "Even knowing the nearest pod is too much. And now, she will."

Barely any space separated our hands. The electricity pulsated in a steady flow of anguish.

"It's been hell…not seeing you." He closed his eyes and ground his teeth. His cheek dimples hardened. "When you told me not to come back, did you really think your objective escaped me? The only reason I complied was that I decided to do the same for you — keep *you* safe by staying away." He contemplated. "Well, that's not the entire truth. Guilt tortured me for the sake of the kids. I figured, if I had to, I'd travel Earth to find you once you returned. And Graham seemed sure you hadn't landed yet."

He raised his eyes and tilted his head back, gesturing upward with his thick, dark blond eyebrows. In a singsong voice, he added, "Clearly he wasn't wrong." Eric paused and shook his head. "Then a whole bunch of youngsters came down with whooping cough and needed looking after. Plant-based medicines are slow acting. Down here, I'm guessing, we don't have near the equivalent of your cures."

He swallowed, locking his eyes on mine. "It made no sense, all things considered, but as time passed" — his face tugged into a grimace, accentuating the dimples — "it was like nothing else mattered if it meant losing you."

Softening his voice, he drifted his eyes to the floor then up again. "In some strange way, I wanted Gina to find us, so she'd bring the craft down nearby. Everyone's lives are at risk by me coming here. It's going to kill me later, but I need you, Cassidy, like I need air to breathe. Plus" — his voice sharpened — "like you mentioned before, if you landed on the globe's diametric opposite — "

In that instant our palms fused — or felt as if they had. I absorbed every part of Eric through my tingling, burning skin. My eyes blurred and my chest drew tight.

He fixed his eyes on me, slowly moving over my body. "Oh, Cassidy," he murmured, reaching up and outlining my face with his fingers.

I raised my hands and flattened my palms, a hairsbreadth from his chest muscles. The static surge and dip pulsed through me as his chest rose and fell. I moved my fingers up along the line of his neck, his jaw.

As he cupped my face in his hands, gooseflesh exploded over my skin. He stepped closer, one hand sliding to the back of my neck, his defined mouth drawing nearer. Using his thumb as a marker, he lightly touched his virtual lips to mine. I couldn't bear any more. Intense, broken-hearted tears burst in rivers down my cheeks.

"Eric" — I breathed hard, backing away — "you should not have come."

His whisper cracked as the words escaped his lips. "Yup, I know." He gritted his teeth. "But what was I to do, when—"

I cut him off—the agony of his unspoken phrase ripping through me. Agony, because loving Eric made me endanger everyone. Now, he had done the same. "You need to go, Eric, before it's too late."

"Find a way to escape, Cassidy. Do that for me."

"How will I find you?" I grated through my tears. "How?" I repeated.

"Go to the pod. We'll find each other."

A sound wrenched my focus, my absorption of Eric, away. The biometric confirmation beep on Mom's office door stole my attention from him.

"Get out of here," I whispered sharply, turning back to Eric, but only a faint after-shadow remained. My suddenly twisting head had alerted him.

He was gone.

Chapter Twenty

I leaped from the platform and tugged a chair out from behind the desk.

The door swung open. "Just a courtesy visit." Gina circled me, predatorily. "Have you heard from your friend?"

I kept my gaze on the floor, hiding my anguished face from view. My voice was raw. "Still nothing."

She replied in the familiar slow, monotone. "Very well. Where is your mother?"

I spread my arms wide, throwing glances around the office. "Not here, obviously."

"You will pass on my message. Tomorrow's news will report it. Nevertheless, your mother will need the landing coordinates." She placed an open digipar on Mom's desk. "She will have the area thoroughly checked and report directly back to me. We will re-enter in three days."

The cruelty of the coincidence slammed into my chest like a wrecking ball. I couldn't breathe. *Fifteen minutes.* Just fifteen minutes earlier and I could have given these details to Eric.

Grabbing my backpack, I raced from the office. I had to escape this trap that was my hometown.

Despite having just seen Eric, anger gripped my chest, bitterness seeping through my pores.

When I reached the homeward-bound conveyor, I finally stopped running and slumped to the black matting.

I longed for the real Eric — the callused hands sliding down my arms, the power in his embrace, his lips…warm, soft and moist against mine.

I bit my lower lip at the thought, so hard that the metallic taste of blood tingled on my tongue.

In what seemed like moments, the conveyor reached our walkway. I stood then stepped off into the familiar intersection.

As I burst through the front door, Mom was settling on a sofa in the VE Room with a cup of tea. I summoned her. "Can we chat outside, Mom?"

She lifted from her half-seated position. "Of course, Cass." But she cocked her head curiously as she followed me through the back door to the wrought-iron table.

Setting her tea down, she pulled out a chair and sat. I took the seat beside her. She closed her hands around mine, her squinting eyes fixed on my anguished face.

My eyes burned. Furiously, I blinked. "He came back, Mom," I whispered. "Eric came."

There was nothing Mom needed to say. She closed her arms around me, crooning against my cheek. She paused, adding, "The same pod, I assume?"

A whisper escaped my lips. "PQ316T."

I handed her the digipar and conveyed Gina's message.

She glanced at the coordinates then browsed the digimap below. She sighed. "Gina is aware of your communication with Eric this evening."

My eyes slipped closed. The sensation of a bad dream flooded me—a nightmare. As my body numbed, my hearing piqued.

A far-off thud touched my ears as, in the distant dream, the front door closed. I tilted my head to a vague memory of dogs' claws clicking and scraping on wood. Dad and Liam's rubber-soled footfalls reached me through a thick mist. The opening back door whumped—a dark shroud falling at the closing of a dramatic scene.

I opened my eyes to Achilles and Yvon clambering through the door together, their tongues hanging out. They bee-lined to their water bowls, sloshing the cool liquid over the lip. When their exuberant greeting followed, I couldn't help but giggle as, still wet-mouthed, they slobber-dripped water all over Mom and me.

Dad joined us at the table, standing behind Mom with his hands on her shoulders. She silently held the digipar up to him.

Grasping it, he raised it and read the contents. "Well, well, I guess we can't really be surprised." He glanced down at Mom. "We're decidedly close already. We knew that it was a matter of weeks...but days—" He smacked his lips together and broke off with a shrug then leaned over and kissed her lightly on the cheek. "This woman insists on keeping us in the dark until she has no choice. We'll be working nonstop until then."

"I am not entirely certain that we have collected sufficient data for successful re-entry," Mom uttered, then added, "and the coordinates cannot be correct. We cannot possibly land in the ocean."

Dad carried on browsing the digimap. He frowned. With a slow, comprehending nod, the creases smoothed out. "Mm-m, I'm not so sure about the location being wrong, Emily."

He rubbed the back of his neck with one hand, ruffling his blond hairline in the process. "It's a gulf, right?" He lilted the implied question. He didn't wait for an answer before he continued, "The basin size and depth are probably consistent with the size of the craft's lower elliptic disk. It's really plausible when I think about it. Very clever, in fact."

He paused, then sighed. "Now, Emily, don't you worry. We have more than sufficient data. Everything will be fine." He folded the sheet and handed it back to Mom.

"I know, Peter. I know that you're right." Mom pondered for a short while. "I am frightened, though. For us all, you know?" She glanced up at him before continuing. "It feels the same as when we left Earth. I know everything ran smoothly then, but I am so terribly afraid for our return."

I squeezed Mom on her shoulder. "You and Dad must have carried the whole burden the last time, Mom. We'll share the load now. You'll see. It will be better."

Finally, Liam emerged through the back door, smiling. He jogged up and threw a sweaty, toned arm around me.

"Yuck," I groaned, pushing him away, "you're wet."

"Oh yeah?" He lowered his eyes to his sweat-dampened clothes as though just noticing. "You should have joined us. You know…for a run." His smile faded. "Are you okay, little sister?"

I glanced up at him. "We're going back to Earth in three days."

He pulled back with a frown. "Seriously? You're not kidding?"

I lowered my voice. "And Eric came back."

"What?" Dad and Liam chorused.

I told them about Eric's visit, leaving out the bits that really mattered to me.

As one of the many aeronautical engineers on board, Dad must have had a good understanding of the subject. But surely, he didn't know everything. "Should we be worried about re-entering Earth's atmosphere?"

"No. Not at all, Cass. That's all covered."

I considered our proposed landing in Eric's near vicinity. Even to live on the same planet was more than I ever dreamed. But knowing the danger descending on them, I shuddered. Against all the odds, Earth's rightful heirs had suffered through the transition, yet endured. After all this, Gina sadistically intended to snatch it away from them.

Chapter Twenty-One

It did not take the three days Gina had anticipated. She gave us no preparation time at all. Severe shuddering shook our home in the early hours of the next morning, jerking me from sleep. I screamed, half-falling from my bed as I raced for the door.

Pictures and trinkets crashed from my walls and bookshelf, bits of glass and debris spraying across the floor. I slipped my feet into running shoes and, without tying the laces, raced from my bedroom, almost bumping into Liam on the landing.

I looked to him for comfort but found none. His face mirrored my own terror. Real fear creased his forehead widened his eyes and strained his mouth. Seeing my unflappable brother this tormented served only to intensify my own anguish into sheer panic. I stopped and shrunk back from what was surely our doom. But Liam grabbed my arm, yelling, "Come on, Cassidy, run!" He dragged me forward.

Mom and Dad were waiting for us on the top stair. Together, we raced down. The dogs merged with us

and stuck to our sides while we ran from our home —
looking to us for protection as this unknown fear shook
their world.

No discussion edged on the possibility of our house
collapsing on us. That awareness was foremost in all
our minds.

Neighbors ran, screaming, pouring from their
homes, turning to watch the trembling buildings. Even
on the walkway, nobody escaped the violent tremors.

Shock flooded through the onlookers as they stood
frozen in place, gaping and wide-eyed — shock, fear
and dread.

In a numb stupor, I witnessed the walls of the corner
home caving in. Then, the roof came crashing to the
ground. Our neighbors crumpled onto the walkway.
Mom and Dad raced to their aid. But my feet had
turned to lead — too heavy to lift. Rooted.

I gaped around me at the unfolding devastation and
prayed fervently that nobody remained indoors. A
familiar scream drew my attention up the walkway
toward the Carter's home. Caroline was clutching on to
Joshua, wailing. A deep sigh slipped from my chest.
The family was at least gathered outside, Paul and
Samantha cradling their Siamese cats.

Another home along our walkway collapsed. More
shrieks accompanied the thunderous crash — more
devastation.

Get a grip of yourself, Cassidy, I chided internally.
These people need help.

The shuddering stopped. The screaming faded. A
long, deathly silence followed.

Before I managed to calm myself — and just as
suddenly — it began again. The shuddering wasn't
worse, but I stared helplessly as yet another house
collapsed. Then another.

Achilles and Yvon whined, pacing back and forth between Liam and me.

Still, the shuddering continued. Was the whole sphere breaking apart? Was this our end—our grand finale?

At least Eric will be safe was the last thought to pass through my mind before the second, sudden subsiding of the tremors. Another eerie silence fell. It was not truly quiet. As collapsed homes began to settle, the creaking and scraping of wood and metal permeated the night. But slowly, the buildings came to rest in their newly fallen states.

I waited for a long moment. Neither I nor anybody else moved, as though any activity would trigger another onslaught.

My breath caught. Spinning to Liam, I pleaded, "What's it like down in the tunnels? Do you think Jaya's people and Aaron are—?" I broke off. Liam wasn't listening to me.

His face paled, his eyes widening. "Harriet!" He gasped and started running—no, not running, sprinting—in the direction of the Winters' home. Leaving Mom and Dad with our dogs and stricken neighbors, I bolted after him.

Liam surged ahead, gaining a big lead—a quarter block ahead of me already—as I rounded the corner.

I scanned the sidewalk for my friends. Stark horror struck me with physical force when the reality sank in—when my eyes fell on nothing but emptiness. Not emptiness, exactly. A crumpled heap of rubble took the space their beautiful home had once occupied.

"Harriet! Jonas!" I screamed into the night, unable to see them in the milling crowd.

I drew up beside Liam, who was standing amid the smoking rubble, tears sliding down his cheeks.

I reached out to hug him. For the first time in our lives, he pushed me away, not wanting my comfort.

"Where are they, Cassidy? Where is Harriet?"

I grabbed his sweatshirt sleeve as warmth flooded through me. "There, Li. They're there. They're okay," I blurted, so relieved as I pointed at the Winters family. They stood on the sidewalk, huddled together. Their longhaired German Shepherds, Max and Lucy, lay panting at their sides.

I paused while Liam sprinted at and clung to Harriet, holding on to her as if he would never let her escape his grasp. As she sobbed into his shoulder, my heart sank at the thought of her agony. Her family had lost everything.

Neighbors surrounded Megan and Roger, but Jonas stood alone—numb shock marring his handsome features. Shock held him in torpor. He gazed around like he had lost something but couldn't remember what. Slowly, I walked toward him and pulled him into a hug.

"I am so, so sorry, Jonas. You don't deserve this." I was unsure of what more to say and fell silent.

He firmed his arms around me as he buried his face into my neck, shaking as I held him. His tears awoke a horror inside me. I couldn't help myself and silent tears slid down my cheeks—for Jonas, for my friend.

When Roger and Megan returned, Jonas stepped away, wiping his eyes on his dark hoodie's sleeve.

Roger gestured to a nearby digital display, addressing us numbly. "They're advising everyone to move to the town square."

I glanced up. Beneath the bright orange 'Petrician Enterprises' a red message flashed across every digital display along the main conveyor.

So, in a collectively traumatized state, Petriville's citizens and our pets trudged the motionless conveyors.

When we neared the town square, increasing confusion tugged at my brow. "Jonas" — I cocked my head toward him — "none of the public buildings or the square have suffered the slightest damage."

Jonas' voice emerged in a numbed monotone. "Well, that's because they're not brick and mortar, but molded metal structures, colored like old-style stone."

I gaped at him but he was right. These buildings could withstand a force that most homes couldn't.

Liam never left Harriet's side for a moment — even clutching her to him as he collected blankets and pillows from the pile beside the fountain.

I led Jonas to a park bench. "Wait here for a minute. I'll get us blankets and pillows."

He didn't protest but slumped down. When I returned, he was huddled over with his head in his hands.

"Jonas." I approached, gently holding out my free hand.

He didn't respond but lifted his chin and gazed wordlessly up at me, the furrow not leaving his brow.

"Can I do anything, Jonas?" I asked softly. "Anything at all?"

He didn't answer but lowered his head back into his hands.

When Liam and Harriet joined us, Jonas finally raised his head to Liam's gently humming voice. "They're giving nicer blankets out in the stadium for those who want to sleep there. Do you guys want to go down?"

"I can't face crowds tonight," Jonas finally muttered, "not even for those luxury recliners," but his half-attempt at a joke fell flat since no smile lit his face.

"There's a nice patch of grass under some trees over there." I gestured.

Jonas nodded and stood. He removed the pile from under my arm and followed as I made for the spot.

We laid the blankets in a row on the grass. Harriet and Jonas lay between Liam and me. Wrapping myself up, I shivered at the surprising chill nipping my cheeks — though our four dogs lying on and around us added their body warmth to the mix.

Joshua and Caroline, with the Siamese cats in small canvas crates, joined our parents on a group of park benches nearby, while Samantha and Paul made their way to us, blankets in hand.

Samantha flicked her wild, black hair over her shoulder. "Do you mind if we join you?"

Liam gestured to his near side. "There's plenty of space here."

As Samantha spread the blankets out, Paul flopped down on them before she had finished.

She groaned, "Paul, what are you doing? Wait until I'm done, won't you?"

Ignoring her, he tossed a pillow at his older sister. "Catch!"

Unsure whether their house had survived the severe shuddering, I broached the subject tentatively. "Are you guys okay?"

"Our house didn't fall," Paul said honestly, a moment before comprehending his insensitivity, "Sorry, Harriet. Sorry, Jonas. I didn't mean..." He trailed off.

"It's not your fault, Paul." Jonas sighed.

As we fell silent, I lay contemplating. Over the weeks and days before this horror, I had the sensation that we would crash into the enormous planet. Now, I was sure we had.

* * * *

The following day, Petriville's safety inspectors began stringent checks on those homes still standing. But for Jonas, Harriet and all the others who had lost their homes, not only had their houses come crashing down that night but every tangible memory and worldly possession also lay crushed beneath the heavy rubble. It was a weight that diminished their existence.

They cleared our house for our return late the following morning. Dad welcomed the Winters family. *"Mi casa es su casa,"* he told them—until their home could be rebuilt.

Although our home stood, photographs and other memorabilia lay smashed on our floors and staircase.

We spent the remainder of the day cleaning and salvaging. By the end of it, our home was relatively habitable.

While dusk settled, fatigue leaving me melancholy, I gazed through the back door at our four dogs. They tore around the garden in oblivious, rough play. It made me consider our own ignorance of the actual occurrences.

When the slow process of rubble removal began, we spent many hours at the site of the Winters' home, searching for and salvaging their belongings.

All over town, Petrivillians did their utmost to assist stricken friends and neighbors.

Huge robotic cranes rose from below the sidewalks and walkways, their humanoid counterparts aiding with lighter tasks. In programmed productivity, they lifted large chunks of walls and roofing onto dumpsters, conveying them to waste processing plants in Petriville's outskirts.

Over the following weeks, the proverbial dust settled. Humanoid robots began rebuilding fallen homes.

With scavenging no longer our primary focus, I took in our changed perspective.

The disappearance of Earth from the night sky had a similar effect on me, as would the sudden vanishing of the Moon. It left me with the sense that something was wrong or missing or lost. In the dark of night, silent angst wrenched at the upward-turning faces of conveyor commuters. Through the trepidation, the comprehension dawned. We were finally on Earth. *Home.* We had landed in Gina's intended location. But she had been quiet since our return.

Chapter Twenty-Two

While planning our departure over the following two weeks, the Winters family resettled in their rebuilt and refurnished home. Mom and Megan oversaw our food. They crammed dehydrated meals into four backpacks — not the most palatable offerings, but when considering taste versus weight, they sufficed.

I thought packing my belongings would be a simple task — until I looked at the massive pile laid out on my bed. I flopped on my back in the middle of it, contemplating what to leave behind and equally convinced that I needed everything.

In the end, I squished my barest essentials into my biggest backpack. Each day we took full bags to the stables and added them to our cache in a curtained alcove at the back of the tack room.

Finally, with our plans in place and our luggage at the stables, we sat around the meeting table on the most beautiful spring evening I could remember — a real Earth-born twilight.

While we waited for the adults, Jonas breathed an enormous sigh, tilted his head back and studied the night sky. I smiled. His wavy blond hair was a few shades darker than when we had first met so many years ago. He still pouted those plump boyish lips in precisely the same way, though. "We may not be able to see Earth above us anymore, but doesn't this feel right?" he muttered.

"That's because it *is* right, just like what we're about to do." My voice came out harsher than I had intended. I threw him a glance. "Thanks for doing this, Jonas." I sighed. "I mean that."

"I'm not doing this for you, Cassidy." He lanced his green eyes straight through me then softened. "I would. You know I'd do anything for you. It's just that this is so much bigger than just one boy and one girl."

I rolled my eyes. "Of course I know that, Jonas. That's not what I'm saying. I mean, you don't have to do this and" — I paused, afraid of making things even worse, then choked — "I...I'm glad you're coming. That's all."

Harriet and Liam had remained quiet during our exchange. She lay over two chairs, leaning back against his chest, while he draped his arms around her and buried his cheek in her luxurious blonde hair.

Envy knotted my stomach as I observed them. I yearned to lean into Eric's warm body, to feel his arms locking around me.

Just then, the adults emerged through the door, holding steaming cups of coffee. As Mom handed me one of the mugs she carried, I drew in the strong aroma.

Joshua set a brown leather satchel beside the table. Still pulling his chair out, he spoke in his familiar rich, clipped tones. "Now, we need to discuss a few things before you leave." He sat and moved his chair in, resting his forearms on the table and cupping his hands around the mug. "I'm guessing Gina believes she still needs you for her endgame. That does *not* mean you'll be free from danger, however. Be careful. Keep your eyes open."

He sat back in his chair and reached into the brown leather satchel, extracting a rolled digipar. This, he handed to me — as if considering me the most driven to meet our objective.

"You'll need to give this letter to Graham." Then he emphasized, "Only his fingerprint will grant access to the contents."

I nodded and tentatively closed my hand around the digipar then laid it on the table before me. Joshua again rummaged through the satchel. This time he withdrew two large folded digital parchments. Sliding his mug out of the way, he unfolded one atop and to the side of the other. Once he had wriggled them flat, he jabbed his forefinger to the top left corner of each. "All your fingerprints will grant you access to these."

As the digital parchment came to life, he edged forward and, resting both forearms on top, softened his voice, "These are digimaps of the area" — he glanced at Mom then laid his finger over an already-circled spot on the digital parchment. As if made from water, the area around it rippled — "and this is the pod's location."

Appearing to address only me, Joshua squinted his intense brown eyes. "We don't know exactly where the hydroponic facility is but must assume it is not far from the pod." He paused and drew a breath before glancing around at the four of us. "Once you escape the craft, you will need to split into two groups. Both will have digimaps. Group one should follow the river westward. The terrain looks tricky, so cross the river at the mouth before going north. You can turn inland when it levels out a bit. Group two should go in from the southwest. Again, follow the lay of the land."

A thick strand of my dark hair had fallen forward and clouded my view of the map. I shoved it behind my ear then glanced at Liam. He arched his brows and widened his eyes, drifting from adult to adult. "You have absolutely no idea where the facility is?" he lilted questioningly.

Again, Dad and Liam's matching bright green eyes connected. "Well, no. Sorry, son. We agreed with Graham that it was best nobody knew. That way, the information couldn't be forced out of us."

"Mom," I rotated my head in her direction. More loose hair strands floated over my eyes. I puffed them out my way. "Do you know what the pod looks like from the outside?"

She sighed. "You won't miss it, not this one. Trust me." After meeting each of our gazes, she added, "Please be careful. Now that Gina knows which pod you're aiming to reach, she may very well set a trap." She shook her head and made a deep frown.

In unison we nodded, but nobody spoke.

Jonas leaned forward on his elbows. Lacing his hands, he steepled his index fingers and laid them against his lips. "So, we're hoping to intercept them on one of our routes. Isn't that a bit of a long shot then?"

"Well" — Joshua opened his palms — "our meteorologist contact seems to think that this" — he paused and rippled an area southeast of the pod with his finger — "is the most likely place."

Harriet had been unusually quiet...until now. "So, what you're giving us is some vague task and no real idea where to go."

Megan laid her hand over her daughter's. "You don't have to leave, Harri. It would be better if you didn't. You should stay here with me."

Harriet rolled her eyes. "Well, thanks for your positive energy, Mom. Great pep talk! Besides, Liam is going." She cocked her head as though the decision was a no-brainer.

Megan flashed her a sharp look. "Really, Harriet! You give off so much self-assured certainty yourself that I can't but help it."

Joshua cut back in, ignoring the mother-daughter clash, "One more thing..." He gestured toward two enormous black backpacks, propped against the wall beside the back door. "I got those from Graham many years ago. They contain wafer-thin sheets of Kaleidotonium." He observed our horrified faces. How did he expect the horses to lug the huge bags?

Joshua smiled, reading our expressions. He had, most likely, reacted similarly during his introduction to them. In answer he silently moved his chair out, stood and strolled over to the two bags. As he lifted one with his little finger, his smile broadened. "Don't worry. They'll be your lightest luggage."

He still appeared amused when he continued, "The sheets are extremely light and strong. They slide out and interlock into a large dome. One of these will easily accommodate you and the horses."

His smile broadened as he observed our impressed nods. "Please don't forget... The sheets are rigid and sharp, so don't cut yourselves. Because of that, they wouldn't be much good as armor, but they could shield you if needed. They provide some amazing camouflage. You'll see." He seemed so dazzled with his addition to our luggage that I found myself beaming too as he continued, "Unlike the craft, the inside of these sheets is coated with a breathable waterproof film — to keep you dry."

Harriet still didn't appear appeased. "Why aren't you going with us? Why do you all get to stay here while we plunge into untold dangers?"

Liam squeezed her shoulders. "You know their colleagues would report them missing, Harri. We can get away relatively unnoticed. Our parents can't manage that. You know this already."

"They're sending us into the lion's den, Liam. Why must we even go? It makes no sense."

Roger drooped his eyes, his usual jovial manner crumbling. He landed a tired glare on Dad. "I must agree with my daughter, Peter. Why are we sending them out there? There has to be another way."

Jonas shook his head. "No, Dad. We're a part of this resistance and more than capable. We've been stuck in this place for years." He dropped his voice. "Let us do this. We owe it to those people in the tunnels — Jaya's people — if nobody else. We have to win their freedom."

Dad sighed. "Now as much as I hate the idea, your son is right, Roger. We must grow this resistance if we are to stand a chance against Gina. For that, we may need Graham's help. I'm sure he'll have resources."

Roger nodded, slumping in defeat.

Jonas turned to Harriet. "You don't need to go, Harri. In fact, I agree with Mom. I'd feel better if you didn't. But I need to fight for these people — this cause — the first worthwhile movement we've encountered."

Harriet turned to Liam. He stroked her hair back, kissing her lightly on the forehead. It always stunned me how he spoke so fast, yet his voice flowed out so soothing, so full of compassion. "Maybe Jonas is right, babe. You should stay here."

Also feeling the gooseflesh-like need to protect Harriet, I was inclined to agree with them, however unjustified. She was more than capable of taking care of herself.

Thankfully, I kept my opinion to myself. But Harriet's cocky manner returned with vehemence. "What? And give you guys the glory? Not a chance!"

Nobody smiled, but I knew Harriet carried more resilience in her small frame than they credited her with.

Joshua cleared his throat, his eyes glazing over as he scrutinized our faces. "You four may be in for the greatest challenge of your lives. When this ends, not only Graham and Jaya's people will thank you. Everyone will know your names. You'll earn a place in the New World History books. In fact, I do believe that your fame from the telling and retelling of this adventure will outshine your MAC stardom." He handed us each a digipar. "Study these code words and sentences. Graham's letter has them too. They will react to your fingerprints and fade after a minute of inactivity."

Dad handed Liam another sealed digipar, addressed to Marissa—the resident stable veterinarian. "This consent letter is from Gina's office. It states that Petrician Enterprises permits you to take the horses on a weeklong trip around the zoo. Only give it to her if she requests it, as it will expose our inside contact to Gina. He's aware of the risk, though."

Liam nodded in understanding and hesitantly grasped Marissa's letter.

The dark cloud embracing me didn't lift but eased when Dad laid two compasses on the table. "Gina has landed the craft so that if the railway line was extended through the zoo, you'd end up at the beach."

The ordinarily silent Caroline interrupted in her intoning Nigerian accent. "The train circles Petriville alongside the habitats four times per day. It leaves the station at eight, ten, twelve and two. It takes twenty minutes to reach the zoo then another five or so to reach the deer enclosure. Make sure you keep hidden within that window of time. A contact will open the entrance for you, but you'll have to locate the far exit yourselves."

Roger began a lengthy scientific explanation of how Petrician Enterprises' engineers had, during landing, collapsed the domes above and below the disk.

I zoned out. It was enough to know that a solid orb no longer surrounded the craft, as that would have made our escape somewhat more complicated — impossible, really.

Roger gave an anguished frown and glanced down at his large, clenched fists. Before speaking, he uncurled and forced his thick fingers to flatten, "You kids will be okay then? Are your bows in good nick and your arrows sharp?"

As Jonas and Harriet's gazes fixed on their father, Dad's shifted between Liam and me. Slowly we nodded in agreement.

Megan hugged herself, her sparkling blue eyes glistening with tears as she added to the tension. "By the way, nobody knows where Gina is. She hasn't been at work since our landing. Not even Susan, her own daughter, knows where she's gone. What if she's out there and you come across her?" Her tears then ran down her cheeks.

The words left my mouth unconsidered. "It's a big world. I doubt that will happen."

Now that it was real — now that we were ready — intense fear clamped my airways. When had Petriville turned into a prison? Not for those who accepted their roles, but for those who denied Gina, no place existed for us here.

Chapter Twenty-Three

The others drift away into the night. I am alone. Darkness surrounds me as I lose myself in contemplation.

Through the haze, I hear a voice – gentle, soothing. He is behind me. "Cassidy," he says. I know that voice. I always will. A hand touches me. I shiver to the calloused fingers curling around my shoulder, but it is not unpleasant. I reach up and lay my hand over the hard ridges of his knuckles.

As I twist my head around, my gaze washes over the smooth bronzed forearm that I expect. My view floats upward, to his brow, furrowed and heavy over the familiar aquamarine eyes – the shallows of a calm, tropical ocean island on a sunny day. Compassion is filling them in shimmering silver sparkles.

He speaks, but his words are my thoughts. "We are doing this for us, but more than that, we're doing this for others." He breaks off. How does he know my mind?

I stand, turning as I gaze up at him and he moves his arms around my body. He pulls me against him as I slide my arms around his waist, run my hands over the smooth muscled ridge along his spine. I lie against him, feeling his chest rise and fall as he breathes. My head fits easily beneath his chin. As his hot skin warms mine, I tremble. I want to tell him how I miss him — how I yearn for him, but words won't come. He pulls back, smiles down at me and opens his mouth to speak. But it is not his voice that reaches my ears — that softly calls my name. I hear it again — my name — and drift toward the voice that is pulling me away from Eric.

Mom sat at the edge of my bed, gently rocking me awake. She held a cup of tea in her hand. I followed her line of sight to a steaming mug on my bedside table. Righting myself in bed, I crossed my legs beneath the sheets and reached for my coffee.

As I raised the mug to my lips, she whispered, "I know it's early, Cassidy, but I would like to talk before you leave. Just a moment with my daughter…"

A smile filtered onto my lips. "Is Liam awake?"

"He is. Dad is with him."

I took in Mom's glistening deep blue eyes — red lines crisscrossing the whites — and blinked. "I take it you didn't sleep well last night?"

Mom shook her head. "You don't have to do this, my daughter. We'll find another way to reach Graham."

I leaned toward her. "I know, Mom, but I'm ready. I *need* to do this. And it's not only for Eric — " I swallowed the lump in my throat, my words soft. "You didn't see those people in the tunnels."

Mom laid her hand on my forearm and gave it a squeeze. "I understand. But watch out for Gina's men out there. Don't take chances."

"If you hide our absence for as long as possible, Mom, we'll have time to escape the craft before Gina notices. At least that way we can gain some distance."

Tremors engulfed her body and she shuddered a sigh.

My chest jolted. "I need you now, Mom. I'm scared too."

She must have heard the desperation in my voice because she closed her eyes and took a deep breath. When she drew me close, I melted into her arms and allowed myself to forget, to enjoy my mother's warm embrace.

Mom waited on my bed while I readied myself then we descended the stairs.

Dad and Liam were already at the dining room table. At the center stood a large bowl filled with scrambled eggs and a plate piled high with toast.

I stared at our last warm meal for who knew how long. Although the rich aroma wafted over to greet us, my mouth felt too dry to eat.

"Hey, Dad," I half-whispered and, draping myself over his shoulders from behind, kissed his cheek. When he reached up, he blanketed the entire side of my face with his long fingers.

The whites of Dad's eyes also exhibited the telltale red lines of too-little sleep. For the longest moment, he held my face against his rough, fair skin.

While we picked at breakfast, Mom and I joined in their muted musings. I stood and stacked up the plates.

Mom stopped me with a raised hand. "Don't, Cassidy," she murmured. "Dad and I will clean after —" She broke off then ducked and dabbed at her eye with the sleeve of her night-robe.

We couldn't drag this out any longer. It was time to leave.

From its resting place beside the front door, Liam lifted and slung one of the black backpacks that Joshua had given us over his shoulder, Jonas having the other. We had stashed our bows and arrows inside. We would pick up the backpacks containing our clothes and food at the stables, where we'd left them. As an added precaution, Liam had included his hunting dagger.

This was the parting nobody wanted. For a long while, we clung onto our parents. At least I wouldn't be alone—at least I would have my brother.

Achilles and Yvon, sensing that something was up, hovered around our feet. I broke from Mom and Dad's embrace and dropped to a knee. I shifted my eyes between their soft brown gazes then threw an arm around each of their necks. "I am really going to miss you two."

Liam crouched to meet their eyes, rubbing their ears as they pushed against his hands.

Finally, I stood. Then Liam and I turned and headed through the front door. I didn't look back as we closed it behind us and marched down the garden path.

Harriet and Jonas waited at the intersection bridge, also dressed in Jeans, T-shirts and trainers. Feigning the nonchalance none of us felt, we made our way to the stables.

When we arrived, Marissa, the resident veterinarian, emerged from behind the barn and helped us retrieve our bags from the alcove in the tack room.

Not appearing alarmed by the number of bags, she still added, "Have you packed enough concentrates for them? And water buckets?"

"We have collapsible buckets and Jonas is packing their food now." I grinned.

Without any acknowledgment, she turned away and headed toward her office, calling over her shoulder, "Look after the horses."

"You know we will," Harriet called back.

A few minutes later, she re-emerged from her office with a small pack in her hand and directed her instructions to Liam. He had assisted her with inoculations in the past. "I've packed some emergency supplies. Some, you'll need to administer as intramuscular injections and others as oral pastes, but everything is labeled. I've also included bandages, salves and sprays for wounds or other minor injuries."

As he thanked her, Marissa winked. The broad smile she broke into brightened her usually expressionless face.

We moved toward the brick-built stables. The eight horses, including Zenobia, were in their stalls and tacked. As I rounded the corner, her eyes were fixed on it as if waiting for me — or the carrots I usually carried. She nickered and, as always, a broad smile found its way onto my lips. "Hey, girl."

I inspected both the packhorse and Zenobia's tack for areas that might rub or pinch during the long haul. Afterward, I led them outside to a three-stair-block and mounted my mare.

While waiting for the others, my gaze drifted up to the hazy blue, morning sky and the splattering of fluffy white clouds — clouds that could only belong on Earth.

Chapter Twenty-Four

Leaving the concealment of the stables, we brushed through the lush, tall grass of the mares' enormous paddock and entered the maize fields.

Their billowing green stems and gold-flecked tips soon swallowed the surrounding lands from view. Without thinking, we found ourselves detouring around the area where we'd encountered the slaves.

It was still early morning when the habitats began rising before us. Our timing was perfect to miss both train tours. We emerged from the maize fields, not to face a tract of grasslands, jungle, wetlands, desert, ice, snow or even the rocky, mountain-like terrain. The habitat before us was filled with tall, dense, darkened pine forests.

After dismounting, we led the horses over the railway line and on toward the habitat. But as I walked ahead of Zenobia and my packhorse, my feet slowed, stomach twisting. It wasn't because of the habitat exactly—invisible as it was—but the towering trees within.

A lean man in a white lab coat emerged from the animal clinic and half-jogged down the gravel path toward the habitat entrance. Glancing back at us, he called softly, "This way. Hurry."

He stopped at the end of the path and pressed his hand up against what appeared to be thin air then stepped through that 'air' and held the invisible doorway open. "I've sent everyone to a breeding lecture at one of the larger clinics but still… Get deep into the forest as soon as you can."

Jonas was first to reach the entrance and quickly led Boudicca and his packhorse through.

As he passed by, the man held the door with one hand while extracting a suction handle from his lab coat with the other. He thrust the suction handle toward Jonas while giving instructions. "From inside the habitat, you can barely see the doorways, but the exits are against the neighboring habitats. Since the door opens inward, you'll need to press this suction handle against it and pull."

As we led our horses through, we each muttered our 'thanks' and received a curt nod in exchange.

The man glanced around uneasily, seeming desperate to be rid of us. "Hurry off now before someone comes."

He sealed the entrance, closing us inside.

Acute claustrophobia gripped my chest as I turned to face the doorway — now a solid cliff face of gray rock. The way it curved inward above us made me want to fall backward.

Although it was just an image engrained into the Kaleidotonium, it looked so real. I turned a full circle and took in the cliffs caging us into this enormous valley. Against both neighboring habitats, the walls were flat. The rear and front of the dome arched toward each other in a subtle rainbow, curving high above the treetops. The vast, blue sky, backdropped the brush and trees, breaking the cliff summits — the accumulated elevation of cliff and trees made only a quarter of the dome's height.

As much as we couldn't see out, the awareness that we were visible to passersby made my stomach knot. Turning away, I jogged with my horses into the tree line.

After we had mounted, Liam pulled his mare up beside Zenobia. He reached for my hand, pressing softly as he heaved, "Well, this is it, little sister. Are you ready?"

I nodded and drew a deep, shuddering breath. "As ready as I'll ever be."

The forest closed in on us. We began our journey into the unknown.

As Liam moved to ride with Harriet, Jonas trotted up beside me, puffing up his already puffy lips as he observed the habitat perimeter.

He spoke as if we were in the middle of a conversation. "So, we'll use the boundary as our guide then."

I glanced through the trees toward the neighboring habitat and took in the towering gray cliff face blocking it from view. Many times, while passing the habitats by train, we had commented on the vast differences between environments. Dense brush and trees flourished in this lush green habitat. Although sparse dry vegetation and the red rock typical of a barren desert filled the adjacent one, we could see nothing through the enclosure boundary.

Holding the packhorse's lead rein, I urged Zenobia into an easy trot beneath the canopy of trees. The spongy carpet of pine needles stretched away into the distance, cushioning her bouncy gait. I found a certain peace in our surroundings and drew in the thick fresh scent of pine when a small deer silently and suddenly broke through the trees ahead. Zenobia slid to a halt and I nearly toppled over her shoulder. Then Jonas' mare, Boudicca, rammed into Zenobia's rump, causing her to leap into the air.

The equally frightened, though much smaller deer froze, batting its long eyelashes at the horses.

Eventually, the little doe concluded she was not quarry and slowly vanished into her surroundings.

After many more encounters with the large variety of deer species, the horses became desensitized to the strange animals.

That was, at least, until we emerged from a copse of particularly dense trees into the midst of a very large herd of huge buck — aiming their long, pointed horns at us. Zenobia's muscles tensed beneath me, her heart pounding against my legs.

"Oryx," Liam suggested.

"Huh?" It was furthest thing from my mind. Then I responded with "Mm-m" as my gaze drifted over the herd. I wasn't at all sure how knowing the name of the species made them any less intimidating. But we retreated and skirted the gathering animals.

The remaining journey unfolded without incident. We reached the outer extremity in the late afternoon, stopping beside a stream inside the tree line — the towering gray cliff looming over us.

Liam and Jonas extracted one of the domes. Placing his hand on an outer panel, Liam muttered, "So let's see if we can figure this out."

As he slid the panel away from the others, his eager laugh burst out. "This is incredible."

The interlocking panels seamlessly slid up and around him, expanding and bumping into us. We moved back and back again. Liam disappeared behind…well…nothing.

Harriet held her palms out toward the obscure ballooning dome's mirror-and-rainbow effect. "This is insane. It's like magic, don't you think, Cass? Magic! I think I'm in love all over again."

"Thanks," Liam muttered behind the invisible barrier.

Jonas chuckled. "Not sound-proof then?"

"Nope," Liam's voice sounded again, "and from this side, you're all clearly visible."

In moments, the dome had erected itself, the outer edge covering the stream. Liam emerged through a large doorway, beaming and outlined in a purple glow. "Well, nobody expected that."

I moved back and scanned the clearing where the dome stood but did a double take. If I didn't know better, I would have thought nothing was there — at least not until I looked carefully at the way it reflected light and mirrored its surroundings. That wasn't exact, either. Rather, it absorbed its environment — became it. Nothing was visible through the translucent panels or even the panels themselves — different to the habitats, which appeared transparent from the outside.

After leading the horses into the dome and untacking them, we fed a divider rope through hooks (part of the structure) to separate horses from the baggage—and us.

"So, let's go see what lies beyond this valley." Jonas dug in a pack, extracting the suction handle and a small pair of binoculars.

Liam and Harriet remained at the camp to feed and water the horses then prepare a late lunch. We had not stopped during our ride but had sipped on water from our hip flasks and eaten dried fruit and nuts.

Jonas and I crept to the forest edge, the gray rock cliff just beyond.

We stood behind a tree, my stomach again clenching. "How do we know if someone is out there looking into the habitat or not?"

Jonas grimaced. "We don't, so cross your fingers and stay low."

Dropping into the brush, we leopard-crawled the short distance to the habitat's edge. A faint purple glow marked the doorway. Jonas drew a deep breath then rose into a crouch and pressed the handle against the rock.

As he pulled inward, the door opened. I slunk to my knees, a gasp escaping me. We stood and stepped through. Jonas allowed the habitat doorway to slip closed behind us.

An expanse of grasslands spread out beyond the dome—terrain from which you might expect a pride of lions to emerge at any moment.

In the distance, what ran along the craft's perimeter made my heart sink—an almost continuous row of single-story buildings. It was not the cluster of buildings that sent a shiver through me and made my heart pound in my chest, not at all. At least a thousand men mingled there, dressed in full military gear.

Jonas turned to me, his face filled with grave lines. "Military barracks?" He paused, lifting my chin with his finger. "You're as pale as a ghost, Cass."

My heart shuddered. "Why would she need a military out here, Jonas? What is she planning?"

He didn't answer, but his eyes filled with compassion.

Anger tore through me. Gina had only one reason to place her military out here — at the edge of the craft. Eric was right. She *had* expected survivors on Earth. And now that she knew of their existence, their safety was questionable.

A sharp metallic glint in my peripheral vision made me wrench my head back toward the buildings. It had only lasted a second.

I gripped Jonas' wrist in my hand and dove behind a cluster of boulders. With no other choice, he fell beside me.

"What did you see, then?" he whispered harshly, knowing I had pulled him down with good reason.

"I don't know" — I began doubting myself — "but it may have been a reflection."

I propped onto my forearms, peering over the boulder. "Over there!" I adjusted my balance and directed his gaze.

He gasped as he glimpsed the subject of my horror and he angled his body toward me.

"This is not great." He shook his head, flashing a glance back at the closed dome doorway. "We won't make it back into the habitat before they spot us — not dressed in these." He tugged on the belt-loop of his jeans.

A group of armed soldiers was marching through the long grass directly toward the habitat — our habitat.

A soft, tender glow reflected in Jonas' eyes as they locked on mine.

"They couldn't have seen us, could they, Jonas?"

He turned, looking over his shoulder. "There's nowhere to go. Keep flat behind the rocks, Cassidy. Don't move. Don't even breathe."

I didn't need more encouragement than that and ground my body into the gravelly, grass-covered soil.

The soldiers approached. Pounding footsteps made the ground tremble, getting harder and harder as they neared. They were nearly on us — meters away — when suddenly they veered and continued their march along the habitat perimeter.

After a long moment of holding our breaths, an audible sigh escaped us both. Still, we remained behind the boulders.

"I guess we can be reasonably sure that no lions live out there." I turned to Jonas, who was staring my face. "What?" I snapped.

He didn't reply.

"I'm sorry, Jonas, I don't... You don't deserve — " I tilted my head and squinched my eyes, my heart pounding like a bass drum. "What are her real intentions?" I erupted, furiously blinking back tears.

Jonas said nothing. There was nothing he could have said. But he gently slid his arm around my shoulder and drew me against him as we lay in the grass.

I didn't immediately retract but lingered against his warm body while the soldiers disappeared around the curve.

"Let's wait a little while, to make sure they don't return," Jonas encouraged.

After some time, we crept toward and pushed the dome entrance open. Jonas released and removed the suction handle before we headed back to Liam and Harriet.

After our arrival and over our very late lunch, Jonas relayed our scouting mission details to Liam and Harriet.

"Well then, obviously we move at night," Liam rationalized, "so, we sleep until…say…midnight?"

Nobody objected.

Chapter Twenty-Five

I lay in my sleeping bag as sunset's orange glow filtered into the dome. I tossed and turned, pondering where we were and what we were doing. But as dusk descended, I finally drifted off to the sound of chirruping night-beetles.

"Eric!" I cry out in unbearable agony, reaching out of my dream toward his outstretched hand, longing to grasp his strong fingers.

"Cassidy!" he replies, but he is too far and the scenery changes.

We are standing on opposite apexes of a snowy mountain. The immense chasm separating us is unimaginable – impossibly vast. There is no way to reach him – no way to touch.

The backdrop flips past again. We are on the bows of passing ships and lean over the railing, stretching toward each other. Desperation fills my heart and anguished lines wrench his face. I yearn to touch him and sheer despair bites into the pit of my stomach when our fingers slip past. I gaze after his tall, athletic frame as he dissolves into the distance.

I crave the warmth of his skin, long to run my fingers through his hair, to taste his lips, smell his scent.

"Cassidy!" I hear him cry.

"Eric!" I respond with a moan.

I woke to the same moan sounding in my ears as my connection to Eric shattered — this link that I sensed had *always* bound me to him — and once again, he was ripped away from me.

When Jonas crept to my side, I turned my face away, blinking back the burn in my eyes. He wasn't deterred, but a hardness tinged his voice. "How can I help, Cass? You were calling for Eric."

I brushed him off. "You can't help, Jonas. It was just a stupid dream, that's all." I sniffled. "Anyway, I'm sure it's time to go."

He replied with justifiable curtness. "Around about time."

Liam and Harriet slept, his arm draped over her small, inert body. As I gently shook his shoulder, the rocking motion woke them both. He sat bolt upright, appearing startled as he wrist-rubbed his nose. "Are we late?"

"No." I chuckled at his startled reaction. "Relax, Li. We're perfectly on time."

Under dim, downward-facing headlamp light, we broke camp and slid the dome into its compact form, packing it, along with our bows and arrows, into the huge bag. After preparing the horses, Liam and Jonas threaded the daggers onto their belts, securing them around their waists.

When we reached the tree line, I balked. "You guys know this is our last place of safety?"

Liam poked his head out from behind his horse, his voice rushing out in soothing tones. "We will be okay, Cass. I'm sure of it."

He added, "Turn your headlamps off. We'll use the moon as our guide."

After our eyes adjusted to the diminished light, we stepped from our fir shelter. Jonas placed the suction handle within the glowing purple outline of the habitat's rocky exit. He pulled and held it open. After we had led our horses through, Liam handed his horses' reins to Harriet. Returning, he held the door open so Jonas could lead his mares through. The moonlight glowed overhead as we stood in the open grass plains.

Clutching my packhorse's lead rein in one hand, I mounted Zenobia and recoiled as a rush of vulnerability washed through me. I sucked in a deep breath and straightened, fixing my attention on the not-far-enough-away barracks' lights.

Stars twinkled in the night sky above us, the moon shining too brightly — throwing a golden, glowing path across the grasslands. The effect was eerily mesmerizing and momentarily diverted my attention from our outrageous journey.

Our ride was uneventful. Some hours later we rode into a darkened area — a large gap between the low buildings where the grasslands ended.

Jonas chuckled. "I can smell the ocean."

Harriet rolled her eyes. "You don't remember what the ocean smells like, Jonas."

He chuckled again. "Well then,, how do I know that's the ocean I can smell?"

I shook my head. "How can you be so relaxed when we might die at any moment?" I focused on a noise I thought I could hear, unfamiliar sights I thought I could see. On top of that, my pounding heart was distracting — thumping in my ears.

My chiding response didn't appear to bother Jonas. "I don't see any danger, do you then?"

"That doesn't mean we're safe," Harriet whispered sharply, her reaction just as tense. "Guards might be just around the corner of those buildings."

Liam made a concerned frown as he dismounted. "Could we keep the chatting down, guys. I'm trying to listen."

Following his lead, we dismounted too and, holding the horses' reins, proceeded on foot.

Although Liam's concern made my adrenaline spike and may typically have seen me darting to the nearest hideout, my desire to escape Petriville kept me moving forward.

The edge of my world brought me back, suddenly and sharply. A simple, waist-high metal railing separated us from the mountainous drop to the white sand below.

Struck with awe, I peered at the ominous beach. Moonlight and an eerie yellow glow emanating from the craft's edge washed over the white sand.

Fear forced my words out before I thought to stop them. "Our world hasn't been too bad, has it? We've always been safe here."

Liam moved beside me, taking his horses' reins in one hand.

He reached the other arm around my shoulder, his voice soothing. "That is true, Cassidy, but at what cost? Yes, we've fared well. And yes, we've been educated. But for which world? The world our parents knew no longer exists and it shouldn't only be us..." He trailed off as his voice cracked.

Swallowing, he glanced down toward the pebbles he rolled beneath his shoe.

After a moment, he lifted his shimmering gaze to meet mine. "It shouldn't only be our responsibility to repopulate Earth. The option should have been available to everyone. There was enough time."

He paused and sighed. "That's something we cannot change, but" — he gestured outward with his hand — "Graham's people who survived out there" — then he turned and gestured toward the tunnels — "and Jaya's people down there? It is our responsibility to make sure they have a chance."

In a flash, his involvement in this was apparent. He was so much more dedicated to this cause than I had realized. My amazing brother the revolutionary?

I dropped both my horses' reins and threw my arms around his neck. "I love you so much, Liam."

"I love you too, baby sister." He gave me a squeeze. "Now, let's go find Graham" — he smiled — "and Eric."

I turned to Jonas and Harriet. "Are you sure you want to do this? This is the turnaround point."

Harriet rolled her eyes and reached for Liam's hand. "I'm not answering that question again."

When I shifted my attention to Jonas, Liam's arching brows caught my peripheral vision, so I rotated back to him instead.

"Do you seriously think I've been doing this on my own, Cass?"

A wary smile tugged my lips. "So, we're all in then."

In a less tense situation, I might have chanted the Musketeer motto, but I did not. Not then.

I gazed out from the craft's edge. As my eyes grew accustomed to the dim light, I took in the many different asymmetric shapes looming through the darkness.

Liam looked around, but not at the beach. He was focusing at the top of the craft.

He frowned. "We're too exposed out here. We need to move."

Jonas stretched his body out over the railing.

I grabbed at his clothes.

"What were you doing?" I whispered harshly as he dropped back to terra firma.

Harriet growled at him, "You could have fallen!"

"I didn't lean far," he drawled. "I just wanted to find one of those elevators Jaya mentioned."

"And?" Liam held a palm up.

"It looks like Jaya was right. A shaft runs down the side of the craft, just a short way to the south." Jonas gestured in that direction.

"How far? We only have a few hours before sunrise." Liam was shifting his eyes uneasily.

"Ten-minute walk, I think." Jonas turned toward his horses. "They're tired. They need to rest."

As we led the horses on the short walk, my anguish grew, worsening with each passing minute. "Why aren't there any guards around? It feels like we're walking into a trap."

Liam held his hand up. Moving his finger to his lips, he cocked his ear in the direction of the elevator. "I can hear voices," he whispered.

Slowly, we approached the shaft entrance. Gears clanked into motion. I glanced through the gates and down the shaft at the rising elevator.

Harriet slit her eyes. "I thought this was too easy."

Liam nodded. "Get behind the shaft."

We needed no more prompting than that and quickly ducked the horses to the back of the elevator housing. Jonas tossed his horses' reins at me. Harriet took Liam's. Unsheathing their daggers, they slipped around the corner—one on either side. I peered after Jonas as the elevator clunked to a halt.

Men's muffled voices came from inside. The elevator gate clanged loudly, as if somebody had pulled it back. I tensed. But Jonas launched around the corner with lightning-speed.

I dropped the horses' reins and leaped forward behind Jonas as he brought the butt end of his dagger down. It landed hard behind the soldier's ear. The man slumped to the ground.

Liam's target spun away a second before his dagger had struck. The blow landed with a sharp crack on the soldier's collarbone. The tall, powerful, exceedingly fast man twisted. He launched his entire, muscled body at my brother. Although almost his height, the soldier outmatched Liam in brute strength. Ramming Liam backward, he pinned him against the elevator's back wall, gripping Liam's throat in his large hand. Harriet half sucked back the scream threatening to escape her. Liam fought back, squeezing the man's jugular in his hand, but his strength was waning. His grip on the man's throat grew noticeably weaker. As Jonas launched through the door, I followed. I side-vaulted, slamming my heels into the sides of the man's knees. As he buckled and collapsed, Jonas brought his dagger down behind the soldier's ear. The elevator reverberated as his body struck the floor.

"Liam, Liam!" Harriet ran to his side, supporting him as he doubled over.

A rough, hoarse cough broke from his throat as he rasped, "I'm okay, babe. I'm okay."

Jonas dug two ropes from his pack and tossed one to me.

While binding the taller soldier, he instructed, "Tie his wrists, Cass. Then pull the rope down to his ankles, so he's in a backward curve." In a growl, he added, "We're taking no chances."

As I finished, Jonas gagged them both then dragged the smaller man into the elevator.

The horses had not drifted far, despite the loud fight but had plunged their noses into the long grass a short distance off. Jonas and I caught then led them into the elevator that was enormous enough to hold a tank.

As soon as the gate closed behind us, the elevator began its slow descent.

Liam's breathing finally steadied. I moved to him, wrapping my arms around his neck. "Are you okay, Li? I'm so sorry I didn't react sooner."

He smiled softly, nodding as his voice grated, "You did okay, Cass." He broadened his smile. "I can't believe you probably broke his knee. Did you even see how big he was?"

Jonas shook his head slowly. "This is it then — if we do actually make it to safety, I mean." Leaning down, Jonas untied the ropes and stripped uniforms and boots from the soldiers. Harriet cleared her throat and Jonas responded mechanically, "You never know. We might need these outfits. These are no ordinary soldiers. Look... This one is a major and that's a colonel."

He tossed both uniforms and boots to Liam, who shoved them in a pack on his horse. Jonas re-bound the soldiers' ankles and wrists, but this time, without adding the backward arching rope.

I peered through the bars as the land slowly rose to meet us. "What are we going to do with them?"

Harriet scowled. "I think we should kill them. I mean, look what this idiot did to Liam." She kicked the taller, now-underwear-clad major for emphasis.

Liam wrapped his arm around Harriet's shoulders, a gentle smile curling his lips. "We're not going to kill anybody, babe. We'll tie them up somewhere safely out of the way. We'll have time to escape."

The moonlight disappeared behind the craft's arc. Only the eerie glow edging the monstrosity lit the beach below.

With the ascending landscape, dread rose to meet us. I swallowed more than once at the dryness in my throat then gasped from holding my breath for too long.

Zenobia grew restless, feeding off the anxiety gripping me.

I buried my face into the silky, liver-red hair of her neck. "it's all good, Z," I lied, "all good, sweet girl."

Although overwhelmed, I wasn't alone.

The elevator jolted and stopped. I peered through the bars. Various shapes and sizes of darkened driftwood littered the alabaster-white beach sand. Little else was visible through the limited space.

My heart pounded as I slid the gate open. It creaked too loudly and I cringed.

Liam dragged the taller soldier through the exit and dropped him to the ground. My horses and I followed close behind. In the half-dark glow, an empty, desolate beach stretched away before us.

It was in a daze that I stood on the white sand — something I couldn't remember ever having done.

Jonas shut the elevator gates with a soft clang.

There was no turning back now.

And that was when the voice that would always catch me off guard penetrated the night. "Greetings!"

A chill shiver ran through my spine. Numb with exhaustion, defeat and horror, I crumpled to the beach.

Chapter Twenty-Six

Strong arms slipped beneath my armpits, raising me to my feet. My eyelids drooped as Jonas' soothing voice reached my ears. "The gate triggered the elevator's automated recording, Cass. Gina's not here."

Harriet moved beside me, encouraging, "Come on, girlfriend. We made it. We're off the craft."

My gaze found her cheeky, dimpled smile.

I bit my lip. "I know that. Of course, I do. It was just that hearing Gina's voice just freaked me out, you know? I'm fine now."

While Harriet and I held the horses, our brothers tossed the smaller soldier onto Boudicca's back. They bound his wrists and ankles to the girth rings on either side of the saddle.

When they attempted to lift the tall, defined major, Jonas gasped, "Nuts! The deadweight of this dude is as heavy as lead." And they dropped him back to the ground.

Finally, they succeeded in heaving him onto Liam's mare.

After fastening his ankles and wrists to the saddle, we moved off—angling southwest across dunes and ridges.

Astonishment swept through me when I glimpsed the forest ahead. So many taller trees still stood.

Towering trunks bordered the beach. Way, way to the south, the soft glow of the craft's ellipse jutted over the white sand. As it reached into the forest beyond, its immense weight crushed the trees in its path. The size and eerie glow of the craft stirred more fear in me than the prospect of Gina capturing us.

Jonas, his eyes also on the astronomical shell, sucked in a sharp breath. "It's taller than most of Earth's old cities, I'm sure. And it must be broader than two hundred following ships."

It stood black in the night—an enormous bright silver disc with the softly curving top, while rows and rows of the strangest yellow lights lined the solid, flat, coin-like sides.

A daunting sense threatened to cripple me. "How can we possibly stand against this thing?" I paused, gesturing at the monstrosity. "Its very existence seems to suck us in with almost-magnetic pull."

Jonas shook his head. "It doesn't matter how inconsequential we are, Cass. Smaller people than us have conquered great tyrants in times gone by."

As we moved into the fringes of the forest, the trees seemed to absorb us into them—barricade us from the dreaded shape.

A little farther in, Liam and Jonas untied and lowered the men to the ground, binding them to separate trees.

Afterward, Liam dropped to a log and, meeting my gaze, tapped his palm on the natural wooden bench beside him.

I collapsed to the log. My eyes followed Jonas and Harriet as they moved away.

Liam shook his head. "This is where Joshua said we must split. But how can I — ?" He trailed off and, resting his elbows on his knees, steepled his fingers.

I side-glanced him. "Honestly, Li. I'll be okay. You're the strongest among us and you need to take care of Harriet. That means you follow one route with her and Jonas and I will take the other." I angled toward him.

He fell silent, flexing and straightening his steepled fingers — pondering.

"I know it's the only option, Cass. Harriet is such a fragile little thing. But how do I let you go on without me? I don't think I can." He again fell silent. Then he shook his head. "No! It's not an option. We'll find another way."

"Listen to me, Liam. You know Joshua wouldn't have advised us to split without good cause. In two groups, we're less conspicuous. It's only for a few days. We'll soon join up. Plus, we already have two domes, so we can use one each."

He sighed. "I'd never forgive myself if anything happened to you."

"Nothing will happen, Liam. There is no other way of doing this, is there?" I paused and swung my arm back toward Jonas and Harriet. "I'm sure they're having the same conversation over there."

We drifted into silence and Liam frowned with deep, conflicted lines while he pondered my suggestion.

I waited, gazing north of the craft and over the ocean. Moonlight reflected off the rippling surface. The massive structure jutted far into the sea and broke the larger waves—leaving the water between it and the shore shimmering in a lake-like appearance.

Finally, Liam laid his arm around my shoulder. I rested my head against his temple. A smile found its way onto my lips. I knew his decision.

"Okay, Cass. But you must know I'm far from happy about this. Despite that, I do trust Jonas to take care of you. And you're probably right"—his voice cracked—"about being inconspicuous."

He gripped me more firmly around my shoulders and pulled me to his chest. "I love you so much, my beautiful little sister. Please come back safely to me."

"I'll be fine, Li," I murmured, "but the same goes for you." It was my turn to shudder. "I can't imagine my life without you in it. I don't want to."

A single tear escaped my eye.

Liam lightly dusted it with his thumb, a soft smile forming on his lips. "Then it's best that we both survive this thing."

I turned back to Jonas and Harriet, who appeared to have reached a similar decision.

Before leaving, and again using the butt end of his dagger, Liam made sure both soldiers would remain unconscious for some hours.

Dawn approached and humidity hung heavily over the early spring morning as the sparkle of dew on plants brought our world to life. Blended scents of fresh tropical forest, ocean brine, citrus and the sweet aromas of flowers filled the air. Birds chirped and insects hummed their entrance into the morning—few compared to Petrivillian spring dawns. The thick undergrowth was formed by thousands of baby trees, ferns, brightly colored flowering plants, moss-covered rocks and fallen, bare trunks. Tall, sparse trees made the bulk of the forest—towering smooth gray pillars. The pale light already burned heat into the forest. But the beauty of Earth radiated around us—the splendor so graphically displayed across nature's canvas.

Under the morning sky, Liam clung to me.

I searched his bright green eyes for strength, during one of the toughest moments of my life—the moment of our divide.

My voice caught. "I'm not saying anything will happen, but, promise me you won't blame Harriet if...if—" I couldn't complete the sentence—couldn't say what Liam wouldn't want to hear. "Take care of each other. Do that for Jonas and me, okay?"

Liam screwed his eyes closed, fine lines feathering the skin at the edges, his voice hoarse with emotion when he again opened them and he met my gaze. "Please stay safe. Mom and Dad will never forgive me—hell, I'll never forgive myself—if something happens to you." He shook his head, gritting his teeth as he handed my bow and arrows to me and strung his over his back.

Harriet didn't release Jonas while hugging me and wailing, "Please don't tell me you don't share my bad feeling about this."

"Everything will be fine, Harri," I consoled, patting her on the back.

Jonas gave her a squeeze. "Don't worry so much, sis. We'll see you in a few days, then."

Still, it was with reluctance that we extricated ourselves and mounted our horses, the pack animals following.

I didn't look back when Liam and Harriet's mares retraced their steps to the beach, or as they crossed the shallows of the river mouth to follow the beach due north or as they rounded the curve that would have hidden them from view, anyway. But every beat of my heart followed as they disappeared.

In silence, Jonas and I moved deeper into the forest.

Chapter Twenty-Seven

I paid close attention to the passing days. "Day Six," I muttered to Jonas — or possibly to myself. Was he even listening? His frown — and the fact that he was gazing at the haze between the mountain and the sky — suggested his mind had drifted a million miles away.

Two days before, after emerging from the forest, we had crossed a river and traipsed the plains. The mountains, initially a distant shadow, now loomed with ominous foreboding.

Finally, he voiced in a flat monotone, "If Gina has returned but hasn't yet found out we've gone, she soon will."

As the foothills slowly closed in on us, claustrophobia seized my chest. "Should we go around the hills?"

"Yup. Anyway, the horses are too tired to go over the —" Jonas stopped.

I followed his line of sight toward the nearest peak. In jerky movements, a head rose over the top — and not just one head. More and more came into view, rising until their horses' ears and heads appeared then finally their hooves. As they stopped atop the ridge, I surrendered to our doom. At least a hundred uniformed soldiers surrounded us, spread over the tops of the expansive foothills.

I turned to Jonas as he shook his head and frowned. A flood of nausea washed through me. "All this for nothing."

Jonas peeked over his shoulder—seeking an escape. There was none. "Surrounded!" he stormed. "Is this how it ends, then? Is this it?"

I fixed on the closing gap of soldiers. "How long until they reach us? If we let the horses go, maybe they'll seek out their friends—and alert Liam and Harriet in the process. I don't think they'll get through the gap with us on them."

Without a pause, he dismounted. "That's our best bet, I'm sure. There's no escape for us. But at least if the horses are free, they might alert somebody to help us."

Loosening the packhorses' girths, we dropped their loads to the grassy earth. I moved to Zenobia and worked at her tack, though my fingers shook while trying to undo the buckles. Jonas unfastened Boudicca's bridle—her saddle already on the ground.

"Zenobia," I whispered in her ear, "find your friends. Find Liam."

Shoving my hand and her bridle into the air, I shook them both. As the soldiers closed in on us, through a choke, I yelled, "Go, girl! Run!"

She responded to my desperate plea, galloping with all the grace and speed she possessed.

A second later, the other three spun and followed. While the horses made for small remaining spaces between the soldiers, we cheered them on. The soldiers did not give chase, though. The mares swept between them and galloped northward. My heart shuddered as the men closed the gap between them and us.

Jonas threw his arms around me, covering as much of my body as he could—his body, my shield. His defensive posture melted my heart.

I froze, clinging to him as the surrounding circle contracted. They raised their weapons. Long guns…rifles. As if we could threaten them… No matter how Jonas tried, he couldn't protect me—unable to cover me from all sides.

I turned and met twin dark holes leveled too close to my face—the barrel of a long gun.

My focus drifted down to the sharp sting in my side, to the protruding fletching of a dart.

I had expected more pain, more agony to accompany my death. But my inquiry met only the burning sensation above my hip and the ache of my knees on the stony ground as I landed. I toppled forward, my hands moving in slow motion as I reached up to cover my face. Not quick enough, I hit the ground hard. Grit scraped into the skin of my chin, my nose, my cheek—embedding into my flesh.

I fell to the side.

Then, nothing.

* * * *

Vague movements slowly brought me back to the world. *Where are we?* Crude knots cut into my wrists and ankles. My belly ached from bouncing on the front of a saddle.

A sneering voice from above cut through the air. "A-ha, this one's awake."

As the reek of foul breath hit my airways, I retched.

I glanced around, as much as the limited range allowed past the horse's body. Jonas lay limply over the front of another soldier's saddle.

"Jonas," I cried. "Jonas, are you okay?"

"Jonas, Jonas," came the same sneering voice above me.

Jonas didn't answer. I gritted my teeth to the acidic tears filling my eyes and finally passed out again.

I woke what seemed like hours later as the soldier tossed me onto a hard, flat surface. Pain lanced through my stomach—bruised from the bouncing while I had lain over the saddle's pommel. I winced. I opened my eyes and, without lifting my cheek, scanned the area to my side.

Where was Jonas? Panic rose up in my throat, a mist fogging my brain.

I lifted my cheek and turned the other way. A sharp stab of pain shot through my skull. My head almost collided with Jonas' limp face and closed eyes. Through the grime and dried blood coating his skin, many small cuts scarred his face, his neck bruised and swollen.

"Jonas," I whispered.

When his eyes fluttered open, warm relief washed over me. "What did they do to you?"

He slipped his eyes closed. "They didn't use darts on me. Let's just say their boots were harder than my head."

We were still outdoors. Night had fallen and the full moon glistened. Torches lined the sandstone walls, lighting the rough stone courtyard of some ancient castle or fort.

Jonas' gaze locked on mine, his eyes searching. Booted footfalls approached. The soldier kicked Jonas, dragging him to his feet.

Rough hands gripped my upper arms, wrenching my body upright.

As my stomach heaved, bile rose in my throat. The stench of old alcohol stung my nose as the grimy hands dragged me, my feet scraping across the stone floor.

After hauling us through an arch and down several staircases, they stopped at the end of a long corridor. We faced a solid, riveted metal door. Rattling filled my ears as a soldier turned a huge metal key in the thick lock. The door squealed as he pushed it inward before it clanked to a stop and revealed an old stone-walled cell. The putrid hands shoved me to the jagged floor inside. Jonas winced as he thudded to the ground beside me. Our water flasks just missed, skidding and clattering across the uneven floor. The door clanged shut. Keys again rattled at the lock.

My gut churned. I pulled myself to my knees — dry heaving against my empty stomach.

"You okay?" Jonas groaned.

I never answered but gripped the water flask between my tied hands, drained it and lay back down.

Jonas tossed his empty bottle aside then stood and turned his back on me. "Get my ropes then, will you?"

I drew myself up, knelt and tugged at his bindings with my teeth. After a few hard jerks, they finally came loose, falling to the stone floor. He worked at the knots that bound my wrists. When the ropes dropped away, I experienced no release of pressure. As blood rushed into my hands, pure agony burned through them.

My gaze shot to my wrists. The light silver chain was gone, but Great-Grandmother's pen still clung. My eyes dipped. I expelled a puff of air.

Aching, my fingers trembled as I tugged at the knots around my ankles. The same pain shot through my feet as those ropes fell away.

I lay back down and only attempted to stand after a long while had passed. When I did, tremors rendered my legs weak and ineffective. Hot poker irons shot through every part of my throbbing body.

These were not the aches I tended first. I threw my arms around Jonas' neck and melted into his shoulder.

He held me against his own trembling body, his face and breath warm against my skin.

Finally, he stood back, holding me at arm's length. He slowly shook his head, his voice hoarse. "Liam is going to totally kill me. I am so sorry I couldn't protect you, Cassidy."

I met his eyes. "You have nothing to be sorry for, Jonas. No one could have predicted this."

I scanned our meager surroundings. A high-ceilinged rectangular cell made our abode, with a large pile of straw in one corner. A small, barred window broke the longer outer wall, high in the center. A latrine cubicle and washbasin were half-concealed behind a low sidewall, which trimmed one, small side off the rectangle—giving little privacy.

"Do you have a clue what or where this place is?" I asked, though how would Jonas know?

He answered anyway. "I woke at one point and heard some soldiers speaking. They mentioned that Gina had visited here, so she *is* responsible"—he paused—"but don't worry, Cass. We *will* find a way to escape this place."

I searched his eyes. "Do you think she realizes how near Graham's hideout is?"

"I don't know." He slowly shook his head, his brows rising in defeat as he enunciated the words. "But I really wish we had *some* information."

As my little remaining optimism escaped me, I slumped in response.

"Hey," Jonas soothed, "we're alive, Cass." He raised my chin with his index finger, meeting my eyes. "Let's keep it that way, then. Don't give up on me now. You know how tough you are. We can survive this."

He lowered his chin and touched his plump boyish lips lightly to mine. Seemingly knowing how I felt about Eric, he didn't linger but pulled back and laid his cheek against my temple.

A short while later, we flattened the pile of straw into some semblance of a bed as best we could.

Sore, tired, hungry and frustrated that we had stupidly let ourselves get caught, I lay down. Jonas wedged himself in behind me, threading one arm beneath my head and with the other over my waist, he drew me to his chest.

Against his warm body and wrapped in his arms, I relaxed, almost forgetting our ordeal.

Sleep claimed me quickly.

Chapter Twenty-Eight

I woke to light streaming through the high window. As I stretched my aching limbs and body, a groan escaped me. Jonas was already pacing back and forth across the cell. He had washed yesterday's blood and grime away, but small cuts and bruises covered his face and arms.

Barely giving me a chance to resurface, he lifted me to my feet. "We've got work to do. There's fresh water in the basin, and surprisingly, they've left us soap, a cloth and toothpaste. You won't have much privacy behind the wall, but I swear I won't look."

When he grinned, I glowered, "You'd better not, Jonas. You don't need any more cuts and bruises."

He chuckled, "I won't... I won't."

Filling my flask with water from the basin, I gulped it down. My hollow stomach gurgled as it hit, and it did little to ease the hunger pangs.

Jonas wasted no time. As soon as I had finished washing, he summoned me. "Climb on my shoulders, will you?" he instructed. "I think I can get you high enough to see through the window."

He set me on the floor, one foot on top of his and the other just above the knee. Crossing his arms at the wrists, he gripped my outstretched hands. "Brace your arms."

Without warning, he pulled me into a thigh climb to his hip, waist then shoulders. In moments I stood upright, his arms firmly above him as he steadied me with his hands.

"Where did you learn to do that?" I looked down at him, gaping with incredulity.

He slowly shuffled an about-turn. "My dad was always teaching Harriet and me these crazy things when we were kids."

One at a time, I extracted my hands from his and leaned against the wall. Then, grabbing at two upright bars that framed the window, I pulled upward while Jonas pushed my feet from beneath. I took in the sights through the narrow passage of visibility between the bars and window frame.

A solid rock wall cut us off from the scrublands beyond. Inside the wall, a railway line with a bordering row of trees lay parallel to the prison. The track was empty. I tilted my ear toward the opening. "There's fast-flowing water somewhere nearby – a waterfall, perhaps. I can't hear or see much else, though."

"Let's get you down then," Jonas urged, allowing me to slide slowly through his arms to the ground.

A few minutes later a slot near the base of the door lifted. A tray slid through, holding two bowls of unidentifiable mush and two cups of coffee.

Although even our lost packed rations seemed preferable, my hollow stomach growled in anticipation. I devoured the semi-warm, soggy mass, scraping into the depths of the bowl with my fingers. The beginnings of a sardonic smile stretched my lips as I considered asking for more—like in the *Oliver Twist* theater play I'd seen a lifetime ago with Mom and Dad.

As for the coffee…At home I would have thrown the awful, washed-out beverage down the drain, but now the hot liquid was sweet nectar to my deprived taste buds—soothing my rough palate and parched throat.

When the door rattled, my heart started racing. A key turned in the lock. Jonas grabbed my arm and tugged me toward the back of the cell.

I planted my heels. "Don't do that again. I can take care of myself."

As I turned to stand at his side, the surge of bravery abandoned me.

Soldiers jerked the door open and tossed a tall, elderly man with skin of rich mahogany. My hand flew to my mouth as he skidded across the uneven floor.

My eyes blurred. I brushed the moisture away. I knew this man.

Bruises and fresh blood covered the swollen, weathered face. Red lines crisscrossed the whites surrounding the deep brown irises. Although aged, his unmistakable woolly gray hair drew me to the photos in Joshua's home.

Of course, not only his hair tugged me into recognition. Every feature distinguished this man's face—the high cheekbones with a splattering of a few even darker freckles, the straight jawline that his smile would soften, the defined brow ridges and high forehead.

"Graham?" I whispered.

He shied away — holding his bony hands up in front of his face. "Who…? Who are you? Who sent you?"

He cowered — dazed. Life's devastations had engraved deep lines into his umber skin, but some strength remained — filling his broad, lean shoulders.

Jonas offered Graham his flask. "We won't harm you, sir."

His soothing voice appeared to calm the man, though Graham's gaze bounced between us, his thick gray brows tugging together.

I took him in for a moment, considering Eric's complete devotion to the old man.

Finally, he slumped against the wall, dejected and broken.

After some time, he lifted his eyes and stared — I mean, really *looked* at me. The skin between his bushy brows squished into deep vertical lines then softened completely as his eyes widened. In a trembling almost-whisper he surmised, "You're Cassidy Jones."

He flashed his eyes to Jonas.

"This is my friend, Jonas Winters." I smiled.

A moment later, a new consideration gripped my chest.

Thick anxious words choked my voice as the questions tumbled out. "What are you doing here, Graham? Is Eric okay? Did Liam and Harriet reach you?"

Seemingly oblivious to my anguish, Graham replied in a slow, raspy whisper. "My own simple miscalculation got me caught. Eric is safe enough, young lady, but I'm afraid I don't know any Liam or Harriet."

My eyes slipped closed. "Liam is my brother and Harriet is Jonas' sister. Maybe they just haven't found the refuge yet."

Graham nodded. "Very likely. It's not easy to find."

He changed the subject. "You know, young lady, that you caused quite a stir in our peaceful camp." He expelled a deep breath then proceeded in the slow poetic cadence, a skewed smile curling the corners of his mouth. "Of course, I'm sure you didn't mean to do that."

I bit my lip and dropped my chin, clenching my teeth and fists. How could Eric allow me to meet Graham on my own—this man who was like a father to him? But rolling my eyes at my flawed reaction—this was hardly Eric's choice—I loosened my grip.

Graham didn't appear to notice my internal conflict and continued. "I won't lie. 'Tis a pity that Gina knows about us." He sighed and dropped into the quietest whisper. "Be very careful of her. Dangerous woman, that one."

My legs turned to jelly. I allowed myself to slip down the wall, hugging my knees to my chest. "Graham—" I waited until he squinted at me and the words cracked from my throat. "If you had been in Petriville with us, the meteor strike would have killed Eric and the others in your refuge."

He smiled gently. "If I had been there, Eric would have been too. But yes, in a sad way, I owe Gina some gratitude on behalf of the others. In suspecting she'd abandon my family, she gave me the foresight to save many people and many children." He paused then murmured, "Not that I could help my own kids or grandkids."

Graham's first statement was still playing on my mind. "What do you mean, Eric would have been there if you had been?"

Graham gave a small smile. Slowly, he shook his head. "Oh, oh, no. Of course not. My mistake. I met his family only later, when they were holidaying not far from the refuge. They visited the caves and I invited Eric and Caleb to stay over. That night, their parents were killed in a motoring accident, but I'm guessing he's already told you the story."

Jonas bunched his brow. "What's this facility of yours like?"

Graham chuckled. "Oh, I have no doubt that soon enough you'll find that out for yourself."

"So, it is nearby then?" Jonas cocked his head.

Graham lowered his gaze to the floor. "It is…too close for comfort." He sighed. "Don't you worry, young man. Eric will help us escape."

From the corner of my eye, I caught Jonas bristling at the mention of Eric's name.

Still, elation tingled in my gut. Elation…and at the same time, dread. "What if Gina catches him while he's trying to rescue us?"

Graham dipped his eyes. He sucked in a breath. "He'll plan it well. I think he'll be okay. 'Tis a pity Caleb is not with him to help. Those two together—" He broke off, shaking his head and blinking furiously. He went on, "Eric and Caleb shed blood, sweat and tears helping to run that facility. Invaluable, those boys were—always up at dawn and working late into the night. When smaller kids used to cry in their sleep, who do you think comforted them? Nothing was ever too much effort." He paused when his voice cracked then continued. "I miss that damned boy like my heart will never heal, but his brother…? I don't know how he gets through each day. Identical twins in every way, impossible to distinguish — if a person didn't know them so well." A sad smile curled one lip. "To me they were chalk and cheese, more like my own sons than my boys ever were — much as I miss them. Now Eric is all I have left."

Jonas shifted uncomfortably on the stone floor, but listening to Graham talk about Eric like this increased my yearning.

Graham had seemed so confident that Eric would help us break out. But he didn't know that the guards had different plans for us. How would he?

Chapter Twenty-Nine

On the fourth morning, the rich, dusty scent of rain hung thick in the air. While thunder rumbled through the cell, short, sharp cracks of lightning had me cowering beneath my hands.

Even within these strong walls, terror gripped my chest with each blast. Academia aside, nobody had prepared us for living with Earth's weather. I had never experienced anything so shatteringly powerful.

"I know it's just a storm, Graham, but is it always this loud and scary?"

Graham raised his brows and slowly shook his head. "Don't you worry now. You'll get used to it."

Jonas gave a nervous chuckle. "I think my stomach is competing, Cass, so it might not entirely be the thunder that's terrifying you."

He was right, though. Since a serving of mush the previous morning, our only sustenance had been water from the tap over the basin.

After ducking away from yet another bolt of lightning, I glanced down at my own growling stomach. "Do you think they're trying to starve us to death?"

Neither Jonas nor Graham answered. Because at that moment, they jerked their heads toward the cell door — to the many thudding boot-falls and loud, raised voices.

I froze.

The door rattled and jangling keys turned in the metal lock. The flash of a warning gripped my stomach as the cell door clanged open. Four soldiers pushed through — their faces in a near death-scowl.

When they grabbed Jonas and pinned his arms, a shriek escaped my throat. "No!" I grabbed for his waist, clinging as they tugged him toward the door. "Leave him," I begged, gripping his body with every ounce of strength I had. "I'm the one —" I broke off.

The kick landed hard against my side. As I grunted, the voice mocked, "Oh, you'll get your turn."

"Leave me, Cassidy!" Jonas shouted. "Let me go! I'll be okay. I'll come back."

"You don't know that, Jonas!" I screamed. But my hold was weakening.

The four men yanked Jonas from my grasp and dragged him through the doorway. I dropped to the floor. The clang when the door slammed shut reverberated through the cell, shuddering in my head.

I slumped to the floor. "No, Jonas, no, no, no." The pain of the kick shot through my side like a thousand needles. But what did that matter if they hurt Jonas? Or worse?

I yelled at Graham—wailed at him, "What will they do to him? How will I tell Harriet that I let her brother die?"

Graham shut his eyes. "Ai, Cassidy. He'll be okay. I'm sure."

A short while later, through the door—or perhaps the walls or window—Jonas' grunts of agony split me in two.

I squeezed my eyes shut and clamped my fists to my ears, groaning as I rocked back and forth, flinching at every resounding thud, every ensuing gut-wrenching moan.

Then Graham was beside me, covering my head with his arms and my ears with his hands.

The burning in the pit of my stomach grew hotter and I growled through gritted teeth. "If we survive this… If we get out of here, Gina will pay. Jonas is the one person who deserves none of this."

As the beatings continued, I withdrew into something of a trance—barely aware of the key turning in the lock.

As the soldiers tossed Jonas back into the cell and slammed the door behind him, I dove to his side. "Jonas, Jonas, Jonas," I crooned over his unconscious, broken, bloodied body as my tears finally flowed—dripping onto his torn clothes. I lifted his head into my lap and stroked his forehead. "What have they done to you, Jonas?" I murmured. "What have I done?" I whispered to myself.

Graham dampened a cloth at the basin then leaned down and held it out to me. Without speaking, I took the worn fabric and met Graham's eyes for a second before dabbing at Jonas' face.

He woke after some time, peering through the slits his swollen lids allowed. When he looked up at me, tears slid down the sides of his cheeks. "I am so sorry, Jonas," I whispered, leaning over him. "You know I love you in my own way. You're my best friend. Please be okay. Please."

I didn't ask what he had told them. None of that mattered. I continued stroking his forehead, dabbing his face with the damp cloth and humming softly over his inert form.

"Cassidy," Graham whispered, "let's get him onto the straw."

He gathered and patted the bed down beside Jonas.

My leg muscles ached from lack of motion.

"*Argh,*" Jonas groaned as we moved him. My forehead tensed at the agony escaping his lips.

Eventually, we got him onto the straw bed. I repositioned my legs then continued caressing him — silently willing him to survive.

Sometime later, he woke again and tried to move. "Stay there, Jonas."

I tilted the flask and dripped water slowly between his swollen and cut lips. He winced at first, but then he parted them for more.

Late that afternoon, hateful hands pushed the tray through the gap in the door. It carried three bowls of the same off-white mush and three mugs of washed-out coffee.

A strong desire swept over me to shove it back at them, but logic won out in the end. We needed every bit of sustenance the unidentifiable food could provide.

Jonas' eyes had swollen half shut — his puffy lids now shiny, dark purple. Large bruises and swollen bulges covered his face and arms — these new, much more severe injuries camouflaging those from the day of our capture.

He groaned as Graham helped me raise him into a sitting position, sliding him back until he leaned against the wall.

After giving him time to catch his breath, I held the bowl to his mouth and spooned small amounts of food through his parted lips — devouring my own between his painstaking gulps.

But Jonas kept at the arduous task until he had swallowed the last bite. He slumped back down to the straw. My heart warmed to the fact that he managed to eat at all.

Graham moved to his side. "Let me take a look at your injuries, young man."

Jonas didn't protest but shifted his arm. When Graham raised the torn T-shirt and inspected the damage hidden beneath the fabric, he sucked in a sharp breath.

Black bruises covered Jonas' ribcage.

Raw heat burned through my gut. I gasped, "Jonas, how do I even begin to apologize for dragging you into this?" My voice trembled on the last words.

"Cassidy," Jonas croaked, "it's not your fault. This is all on Gina. Coming was my choice, remember? But more importantly, I don't think they know who we are yet. They wanted me to give up fellow survivors."

The exchange seemed to exhaust Jonas, because he again closed his eyes and, a few minutes later, drifted to sleep.

That night, I comforted him through his nightmares, stroking his forehead when he cried out and holding his hand as we slept. My constant awareness helped me avoid touching his broken, swollen body.

The following morning was a near repeat of the day before. But the soldiers didn't drag Jonas from the cell this time. His broken body wouldn't have survived another beating.

Chapter Thirty

As the four soldiers hauled me from the cell, an alien screech scraped through my chest. Jonas managed only to groan his objection, while Graham tugged feebly at my legs. Neither of them was in any state to give real resistance. Both men's depleted strength and damaged bodies made their attempts ineffective against the soldiers.

As they dragged me farther down the corridor, I kicked wildly, twisting and writhing without pause. Desperately, I tried to break free and lost both shoes on the way.

Another cell door clanged open. When the men launched me inside, I whimpered, bouncing and skidding across the hard, stone floor.

They closed and locked the door behind me. The boot steps retreated.

It wasn't long before the door opened again. Four different soldiers entered.

I didn't notice his rank but quickly determined who their leader was — the big soldier who had attempted to intimidate me with his scowl alone.

I wouldn't falter. I must not. But Jonas...his condition... How long could my bravado last when the beatings began?

My heart sank as the leader lanced his first words through me. "Where is your brother?"

Comprehension slammed into my chest. My forehead strained as I clenched my fists. They knew who we were.

He sneered, aware of how he had surprised me. "And what about his little girlfriend, Harriet Winters? That's it, isn't it, Cassidy Jones?"

He smirked and scowled at the same time — if that was even possible — seeming impressed with himself that he could recite my name.

I was about to say as much then changed my mind. I should save my energy for the physical assault.

In the end, the words blurted from my lips with undisguised loathing. "I see our outstanding reputation has preceded us."

Sneering with disparaging intent, I wondered if my insolent response would make the resulting attack worthwhile. "I'm quite sure that if I did know where Liam and Harriet were, you never would."

The truth was that I really didn't know. I didn't know if the horses had found them, were even seeking them or if either were safe.

The soldiers didn't beat me with their fists, though they could have. My strength was no comparison to these hardened men.

Instead, they threw me to the hard, stone floor and stood back. The leader came in first, kicking me in the ribs…once. I grunted.

He pulled his mouth into a mocking growl. "Do you want to talk now?"

"I don't think so. Thank you, though," I offered with taunting politeness.

I couldn't tell where the next kick came from but groaned as pain shot through my stomach.

I curled up to protect my abdomen. Blinding agony shot through my skull as the next two hit my head. Wrapping my arms around it, I whimpered, trying to cover my face with my elbows.

The blows connected with my arms instead.

The intensities differed, though. Some boots inflicted more pain. Twisting and bending, I tried to block the worst ones as their kicks landed against my weakening body over and over.

No longer could I feel which blow came from which boot. Everything merged into the same numbing agony.

At the edge of consciousness, the pounding ceased.

The big soldier laughed sardonically, "So do you think you'd like to tell us now?"

My voice croaked in a hoarse, broken whisper, "I told you. I don't know where Liam and Harriet are."

"No more sarcasm, Miss Jones?" He thrust his face close to my head, spraying spittle over my cuts and bruises as he sneered his words. "Never mind… Tomorrow's another day."

I could bear no further assault and descended into a fog—unaware whether the beating resumed.

Then Jonas was leaning over me. I was sure my head lay on something filled with rocks. But no, he was cradling it in his lap, tears running down his swollen, bruised, cut cheeks.

"How bad is it?" I croaked.

He tightened his jaw. "Don't speak, Cassidy. They didn't touch your face, but your body and head—" He broke off.

"How are you feeling, though?" I whispered, knowing how every movement must still be torturing him.

"Don't worry about me now, Cassidy. Let's get you better, then?" The sweat gathering on his brow told me that he was far from all right.

When I tried to move, needles of agony shot through me. Some degree of pain connected every moving part of my body.

I gazed up at Jonas. "Your eyes are a little less swollen today," I choked, as the familiar green irises peered through slits.

I blinked. Moisture slid down the side of my face. "How long have I been out?"

As Jonas dabbed at my face, the fabric of the cloth burned my skin. "A couple of hours, Cass." He paused. "I thought you wouldn't—" He turned his face away.

"You'll be okay," Graham reported softly, "but you may have some fractured ribs."

Twice a day over the following week, they thrust the tray through the slot at the base of the door that always contained the same mush and coffee. Over this time, our bruises turned into a concoction of less dark purple and sickly yellow. Jonas began looking more like himself, too.

My ribs still ached with every breath. Pain lanced through me when I coughed. As for sneezing, it sent flaming daggers into my sides.

They had acquired no information from us. Perhaps they had never expected any.

Three weeks of incarceration found me sleeping more easily. But one night as I was drifting off, something…almost familiar sparked my recognition. I froze, twisting my ear toward the distant rumble.

Before I had reached out to nudge Jonas, his eyes flew open. "Did you hear that, then?"

I leaped up. "Lift me."

He was ready in seconds but winced as I climbed his body.

"Am I hurting you, Jonas?" I cringed and quickly grabbed onto the window bars, hoping to alleviate the pressure.

Jonas grunted then pushed my feet up in his palms. "Not so much, now."

Graham woke and instantly sprang to Jonas' aid, helping him to lift me higher.

The far-off din grew louder.

"It sounds like a train but I can't see it yet."

I clung to the bars, half-standing in Jonas' and Graham's palms until the massive locomotive came into view. "It's ancient," I concluded.

"I hear it now!" Jonas exclaimed. "How ancient?"

I didn't answer as, at that moment, the grinding screech of brakes reverberated deafeningly through the cell. The din continued until the giant machine eventually came to a halt just outside the window.

I pulled myself higher for a better view then ducked back again, whispering down to my spellbound interactive audience, "Some soldiers are boarding the train. But a lot more are arriving."

Jonas directed his question to Graham. "Do you know where they're coming from then?"

"Perhaps," he answered, cocking his head. "There's a camp of soldiers that settled not too far east of here."

After a short stop the train departed, going back the way it had come.

Three times the following day the cell door clanged open. Each time we dove behind the latrine wall. The soldiers had not come for us. On each occasion they threw a new inmate to the ground—one woman and two men.

The first two had come from the refuge and greeted Graham with cordial deference. He didn't appear particularly close with either of them, but he knelt to attend to their wounds. The last man wasn't familiar to Graham.

The fourth time the soldiers charged through the door, we didn't duck away, expecting another addition to our cell.

Before I had even comprehended what was happening, they gripped my arms and pinned them behind my back.

Through something of a fog, I heard my own voice wailing, shrieking, "Why me again? Why?"

Jonas and Graham tried to stop them—kicking and punching to break their grip. But more soldiers raced in, grossly outnumbering them.

When they dragged me backward, across the stone floor and through the stone doorway, tears surged hot and furiously down my cheeks.

I shouted the words back to Jonas. "Tell Liam that I love him. Tell my mom and dad... Tell them I'm sorry! Tell Eric—"

Jonas' voice broke, thick with tears. "No, Cassidy, you damn survive this. Please! I can't do this on my own. I—"

The deafening clang of the closing cell door cut his words short—reverberating through the long corridor.

Numb horror gripped me. Feebly, I kicked at my attackers as they hauled me toward the torture chamber and threw me to the stone floor.

Six pairs of boots surrounded me. *Six!*

I wrapped my head in my arms and curled my knees to my chest.

The door clanged shut.

"Stand up," one soldier yelled, kicking at my still-fragile ribs.

I scrambled to the back corner—cowering, not daring to look at them.

Another voice raised my senses, causing adrenaline to pulse through my veins.

"Leave us!" this voice commanded, but, for the first time, something tugged me back from my terror.

Chapter Thirty-One

"Leave us!" he commanded again—crisper, sharper this time. The five soldiers obeyed, leaving me alone with this man and my pounding heart. It wasn't fear that sped it, though—not this time.

He followed them to the door as they left. Closing it, he turned the key in the lock. He rotated toward me, glancing down at the brown military boots he wore. Before peering up again, he swallowed and ruffled the back of his thick, dark-blond hairline.

The outlines appeared harder and jawline steelier— more definite. He frowned in etched, anguished lines. They were the same, but different. Beautiful and perfect. My gaze danced over the high cheekbones and forehead, the familiar heavy brow, the tranquil aquamarine eyes.

"Cassidy!" he grated, closing the gap between us and sliding his arms around my body.

"Eric!" My heart pounded as I threw my arms around his neck, burying my face into his warm skin.

Words escaped me. I blinked back the unexpected tears of relief and exultation — relief that I was evading another beating and exultation that Eric stood here — in front of me.

Something didn't feel right. I pulled back, cocking my head as I squinted. "How come you know these soldiers so well? And why did they just listen to your command without question?"

He looked at the door and puffed out a breath of air, "We don't have much time, Cassidy, but if you must know. I made some" — he raised his eyes — "*friends*. They brought me in on the train." He tugged at his lapel, the edge of his lip curling into a mischievous smile. "This… I got this from Liam."

"Liam?" I blurted, trying to keep my voice steady. "Liam's with *you*?"

"Not so loud, Cassidy. Yes, Liam and Harriet reached us just shy of three weeks ago. Your horses had found them a few days before that. They're at the refuge — fretting like crazy about you and Jonas."

I squinched my eyes. "You still haven't explained about the soldiers."

He widened his aquamarines, his thick, dark blond brows arching as he shuffled his feet.

As he shot a glance at the closed door, he spoke in slow, measured tones. "This is wasting time. But it turns out that not every one of Petriville's five thousand soldiers is happy about following Gina."

I gasped, "Five thousand? Where are you getting your figures from?"

He ignored my blatant cynicism and continued. "These *friends* I mentioned lived in the craft's barracks, so I'm pretty sure they'd know. Plus, by the way" — he gestured at the closed door with his forehead — "they are helping with my cover. Gina's higher-ranking officers were mercenaries before on Earth. Most soldiers never encountered them on-board. In short, I can command these men standing outside that door because these pips" — he pointed to the stripes on his shoulder — "say I outrank them."

He paused, his voice and eyes softening. He stepped closer and raised my chin with the edge of his index finger, his words soft, gentle. "Hey now, Cassidy, you know me."

With his thumb, he stroked at the faded bruises along my collarbone.

He seethed, "Don't go thinking it's not straining every bit of my self-control not to go out there" — he gestured at the door — "and slaughter every one of the pigs who gave you these."

His eyes drooped. He moved his arms around my shoulders, pulling me against his chest."

I had never actually been this close to him — never absorbed him in this way.

His scent reached into me, drawing pure yearning from my depths — every bit as intoxicating as my dreams — so much more than his simulated self, because this was real.

His body warmth flooded me with...hope? A strange reaction. But in the seconds he had held me, the most definite sense of real expectation trickled through my veins.

He spoke in the familiar, smooth, cadenced voice, thick with emotion. "That they did this to you makes me sick." He shook his head and choked on his words, speaking half as if to himself. "You should never have left home. Yet it feels like I've waited a lifetime to walk into a room and see you standing there, waiting for me.

Well, it's not as if the scene in my dreams exactly portrayed a prison cell as the backdrop."

His pained smile pulled the same deep crevasses down his cheeks that I had grown to expect.

The smile lasted for only a second then dropped again.

My forehead tensed. I met his eyes. "What, Eric? What?" I repeated.

He shook his head. "And now I have to leave you here, Cassidy, no matter how I want to take you with me." He squeezed his full lips together. "It's played over and over in my mind, but I can't seem to validate taking you and the others with me. Gina has already sent signed orders with her plans for you all."

He looked down, shifting dirt beneath his shoe. Again, he met my gaze but left those orders unexplained. My imagination conjured a hundred outlandish scenes. Lurid mages of Jonas popped into my head, then Graham. Tears blurred my eyes.

I ducked my head. "Eric, you must tell me. What is she planning? I need to warn the others."

Eric pulled me back to his chest, a rigid arm around my body and the other around my head. He let out a deep, shuddering sigh and my chest heaved as his breath flickered against my skin and dusted my hair. He held me so hard that I thought he would never let me go. Neither did I want him to — to release his grasp and leave me here.

"Cassidy" — he leaned back to regard me, shaking his head slowly — "how do I walk away and let you go back in there?" His voice caught on the last word.

"You do not, Eric — not without first answering my question."

He bit his lip and, releasing it, lowered to mine. I reached up to meet his kiss. The touch was an explosion — warm, moist and full of longing. I parted my lips to his taste. He gripped me against him with one hand, the other on my neck, in my hair, clamping my mouth to his.

The ache was too much. "Eric," I moaned against his mouth.

He pressed his lips harder. His every labored breath heaved against my chest as I drew in his beautiful scent and twisted my fingers into his coarse hair.

His physical touch hit me with so much more intensity, so much more life than I had expected. The static electricity of the hologram paled in comparison to the sensation of his real hands, the taste of his soft, moist lips.

He drew back from me, catching his lower lip with his teeth, but his taste lingered.

Every part of me craved more of him — more of his body, his warmth, his scent, his taste. More of the tingle still surging through my body.

"Cassidy," his hoarse whisper sputtered, his expression hard, "much as I hate to leave you here, there's not much time."

Time stood still while Eric's warmth surrounded me.

He kept glancing at the door. "All I can give you is information and" — he locked his eyes on mine, ensuring that he had my full attention — "all I can leave with you is the tool you will use to escape. Well...not with you but hidden where you can find it."

He gripped me against him then dropped his arms and stepped back, as if he couldn't properly concentrate on the task at hand while he stood so near me.

I shared the sentiment. Standing so near him *was* distracting.

Of course, this was why he had come — why he had risked capture.

There was so much more I wanted to ask him, but time was not available — not here and not now.

He seemed unable to stay away, though. Again, he stepped forward, interlacing his fingers around the nape of my neck, his thumbs up the side of my face. "Cassidy," he spoke in a quick, urgent whisper, his aquamarine gaze locked on mine, pleading, "listen carefully. The handcuffs they will use have no key slot." He accentuated each of his next words to enhance his emphasis. "You. Cannot. Unlock. Them. You'll find a bolt cutter on the floor of the train or within reach, near the back of the last carriage. Graham is too old, so make sure that either you or Jonas get to the back end of the rear car."

"What are you talking about, Eric? You're scaring me."

"You need to be scared, Cassidy, because if you're not scared enough, you'll all die." As he moved one hand, opening it over his eyes and drawing his thumb and middle finger together, his voice was thick. "I'm not kidding. You've got to know I'd never do that to you."

He returned his hand to the nape of my neck. "Tomorrow, they will put you on some kind of high-tech coal shunt — all of you. They will chain you to rocks." He closed his eyes for a second, the muscles on his jawline hard. He drew a deep breath. "They are not taking you to Gina or anywhere." His voice cracked.

"It's up to you and Jonas. Graham is not strong enough for this anymore. Also, they've placed a spy in your cell. Speak only when you're real sure no one can hear."

He paused then continued, "Approximately ten minutes after the train leaves, the railway line will cross a ravine. The water is deep, but not the ravine itself. The floor of the train will slide away when you're over the drop."

I was listening, but my shock must have been blatant as I absorbed his words. "Are you trying to terrify me, Eric? Because if you are, rest assured that you're succeeding."

He observed his shifting boots, his voice soft. "It's not that I'm trying to scare you, Cassidy — or maybe it is." He looked up again, shaking his head. "You have to understand how important this is. The life of everyone in there depends on you."

"As though I'm not aware of *that*, Eric — or need the extra pressure."

A pained expression crossed his brow. "You need to know."

"Yes," I conceded, "and I want to. Please carry on."

With my face still between his hands, he swallowed hard and continued. "And I don't need to tell you what happens when the rocks drop to the bottom of the lake. Get those chains cut as soon as you've left the fort. Once you reach the ravine, it's too late."

He rapidly blinked his tropical ocean eyes. "The train is unmanned, but from the fort, they will use binoculars to watch you drop. The minutes between the fort and the lake crossing are hidden from their view. They won't see you moving around then."

My stomach twisted at the harrowing thought of this duty. "I'll do it, Eric, at least for those locked up in there." I gestured toward our cell.

"I'll be waiting for you." He touched his lips lightly to my forehead and moved his arms around my shoulders, closing me away from the world against his chest. "If there was any other way" — he paused — "but too many soldiers live in this place. Most of our people have moved away with their families, to settle farms, to start a new life on Earth. Plus, it's impossible to get into this place without the train, unless you come in through the main gate. But that only happens if you're captured."

Absorbing his warmth, I tilted my face and met his gaze. As he laid his finger lightly beneath my chin, he lowered and touched his lips to mine, warm and moist. Pangs of electricity flooded through me, covering my skin in gooseflesh.

Physical pain slammed into my chest when he pulled away again. "Taking you back to the cell" — he gritted his teeth, his brows drawing low — "I'll need to be rough." He blinked. "Be safe, Cassidy. Please, survive for me!"

Turning me around and pinning my arms behind my back, Eric opened the door with one hand and shoved me into the corridor, staying close behind.

"Doesn't look like she got much of a beating," one soldier muttered as we passed.

"Oh," Eric shot with a callous sneer, "there's more than one way to get information," and he shoved me through our cell door to the floor, while the other soldiers looked on approvingly.

I landed on the jagged floor. Jonas appeared ready to launch to my side, but Graham, with subtle prowess, held him back. Not turning his face toward Jonas, he murmured something unintelligible beneath his breath — most likely that it was Eric who had tossed me back into the cell.

Eric's kiss still scented my mouth, his fragrant aroma glazing my clothes. I bit my lip and closed my eyes, savoring the memory for one final moment.

I allowed reality to set in then caught Jonas' gaze and gestured him over.

At first, he remained stubbornly in place. Finally, he puffed out a breath and shook his head but sidled up to me. I wrapped my arms around his neck and leaned into him to hide my mouth from the others.

I whispered, "You and I must speak when we get a chance, but Harriet is safe. Liam too. They're at Graham's refuge."

Tears instantly slid down his face, our shared relief making our embrace seem more natural.

Graham squinted and frowned questioningly. With only my eyes, I gave one, small half-nod before allowing them to slip closed.

Finally, I turned back to Jonas and began my muffled explanation.

Chapter Thirty-Two

The burden weighed heavily — these people's lives in Jonas' and my hands.

He and I slept in the manner now familiar to us both since living in this cell — with me wrapped in his arms, but I turned to face him. Sleep did not come that night. We lay awake covering possible scenarios. Neither Jonas nor I knew what the morning would hold, in what formation they would lead us to the train, whether we should aim for the front of the line or the back, in which direction the train would take us, whether the soldiers would find the bolt cutter or worse, capture Eric. We couldn't predict those things. They distracted us from our purpose. Finally, we agreed on the obvious choice — one of us leading and the other trailing the group.

An unusually smooth-sounding train whispered up behind our cell during the early hours of the morning. My heart thundered in my chest and attempting to slow my breathing I chanted — *in and out, in and out.*

As I considered the others in our cell, my heart just resumed its frantic racing.

In the end, it was anger that strengthened my resolve—anger that Gina had given the order for our execution.

The sun had barely tipped the horizon when they came for us.

Fifteen soldiers entered the cell and cuffed us individually for escort. When I met Jonas' wide-eyed, panicked gaze, tremors gripped my body. I considered that we might all die today, under these bright blue morning skies—forever forgotten, a sad memory.

I drew a breath and, pulling myself upright, shot a glance at Jonas. If we were to succeed, we needed to summon the best versions of ourselves. He caught my eye and drew a short breath. He straightened and made for the door before anyone else could.

They didn't cuff the last man who, the day before yesterday, had arrived in the cell. I was sorely tempted to kick him as I passed by but chose to rather secure my spot at the back of the line.

They prodded us down the long corridor toward a solid outer door, which the lead soldier then unlocked. The early morning light drifted through the exit as they shoved us forward and outside.

We u-turned around a solid wall at the end of the walkway. The half-tubular train lay straight ahead— facing away. It was much nearer the fort than the main train-line—the angle too steep to have been seen from our cell window. 'High-tech coal shunt' was an understatement. These carts were much lower and had no wheels—and neither did tracks lie beneath. Instead, long, shiny silver tubes slid through deep, continuous grooves along the sides of the mirror-like train—just below the lip of the low, streamlined carts. The train — or was it even a train? — appeared to glide between these parallel tubes, and the tubes continued through a closed, chromed grid and on into the distance.

Jonas twisted his head to me, shaking it slowly.

My confidence melted. Under my breath, I muttered, "Get a grip, Cassidy. It's up to you now." I should have been a little relieved. I was standing in the right place at the back of the line and beside the rear of the last car.

As the soldiers coerced us with the butts of their guns to climb into the low carts, I shot a look around. A single boulder lay in the center of each waist-high carriage and a thick metal loop was deeply embedded into the top of each one.

As they padlocked our cuff chains to the loops, panic spread through my veins like needles of ice. Not that it held relevance now, but Eric had been right. No key slots were set in either the cuffs or the padlocks.

I lost the battle against my trembling hands. With that came the uncertainty and the fear. Jonas, Graham, the terrified woman, the little man… The task was mine to save them. I gasped for air and scanned the floor for the bolt cutter. Nothing! Heaving a deep, shuddering breath, my eyes dipped again. Still nothing. The train was presently stationary. But with no bolt cutter… My determination disintegrated. I began to accept our inevitable fate. Death by drowning.

Seconds later, the train slowly started gliding forward, but it quickly gained speed. Just as the front cart appeared to touch the silver bars, they shot upward into the wall above. Moments later, we passed beneath and between the fortress walls.

My heart pounded as if it would launch through my chest. Somehow, the adrenaline seemed to refuel my will to live. My determination reignited.

Frantically, I groped with my feet. I bent down, searching cracks and nooks on the floor.

Was everything switched around? Had Eric put the bolt cutter at the other end?

I was about to call out to Jonas at the front of the train when I paused. My gaze had fallen on something protruding from a groove on the inner edge. Eric had placed the bolt cutter so I could grab it with my chained hand. It was almost invisible to the unsuspecting eye — almost *too* well hidden.

Wrenching it free from the tight space, it nearly fell from my grasp. I had lost a full minute. In seconds, I had cut the chain from one cuff. The remaining length slid through the padlock and out. As soon as I was free, I made my way forward.

The small man was next. Without thinking to ask his name, I explained, "Don't pull your chain free of the padlock yet. They'll be watching. We need to let the rocks pull us from the train. And don't let the chain slide through the padlock until you hit the water."

He widened his eyes in terror, so I added, "Your instinct will take over. You'll be fine."

I moved forward and climbed the lip of his carriage. Balancing on the joiner, I clung onto and scrambled into the second low tube. I cut the young woman's chain, giving her the same instructions. But she was trembling so badly that I couldn't leave her. Hoping she knew who Eric was, I said, "Eric and others will be waiting in the lake to help us."

That seemed to ease her and, despite still shivering, she nodded.

Time was moving too quickly.

I leaped over her cart's front lip onto the joiner.

Grabbing onto Graham's cart, I dove into it. "Don't stop, Cassidy," he yelled. "Get to Jonas. He'll free me while you make your way to the back."

I hesitated only a second. I did have to return to my cart for the watchers. What he said had made sense. I leaped over the lip.

But, when I reached for Jonas' cart, clinging to the bolt cutter, I slipped on the joiner. Launching forward, I only just grabbed the lip of his cart. The bolt cutter slid from my sweaty palms.

A shriek burst from my mouth. But the bolt cutter was over the lip and fell, with a clang, to the floor inside his cart.

I looked up. The ravine was already in sight. *Too close*.

Sheer panic washed over me as I vaulted into Jonas' cart. I grasped the bolt cutter from the floor and jerked it up, but my hands wouldn't stop shaking. As I tried to cut Jonas' chains, it almost slipped from my fingers again.

"Easy, Cassidy," Jonas soothed. "Take your time. Breathe."

Then he was free.

I plunged the bolt cutters into his hands. "Please cut Graham's?"

Jonas moved into action before I had even retreated over the lip of his cart.

With nothing in my hand, I quickly made my way to the back.

I threaded my chain through the padlock and clung to the loose end. I looked to the front of the silver half-tubular train. Graham was free and Jonas had climbed back into his cart. As he clutched his chain in both hands, I sighed.

Seconds later, the train reached the gorge. There was nothing more to do. I drew a breath.

Everyone was ready. I had done my part. I'd succeeded.

Then the floor disappeared. I was in the air. Dropping. *No!* This was so much faster than just dropping. I was plummeting. The suddenness caught me off guard, the vacant space beneath me and the black ominous water inviting us to sink into its depths.

Chapter Thirty-Three

No moment of suspended time preceded the fall. There was no reflecting on my life. It was instant. As the rocks plunged, they yanked us down. I flailed through the air, clutching the chain with both hands. The drop lasted no more than a couple of seconds, but I hit the water hard, winding myself. The air was sucked from my lungs.

How little control I had over my body as I sank into the tepid lake.

I opened my eyes underwater, observing the rocks' continued descent. They soon faded into the dark, murkiness—their termination-point lost in the black depths. I shuddered then turned my face upward and rose.

When I broke the surface, gentle hands reached for me, guiding me backward through the water—downriver, away from the bridge.

I gasped the first words that came to mind. "Is Jonas okay? And Graham? Did he make it? The woman was so scared."

A gentle voice shot out behind me. "Everyone seems fine, Cass. Everyone, that is, except Harriet. She's pacing somewhere in the caves." He gave an emotion-filled chuckle.

"Liam!" I swallowed the sudden lump in my throat.

"You all made it, my beautiful baby sister—"

As we floated downriver, other hands nurtured Graham, Jonas, the small man and young woman.

Liam spoke again. "Sorry, Cass, but we need to submerge again—quite deep, but just for a second."

My every instinct repelled going underwater ever again.

Liam sensed my apprehension. "I'll help you, Cass. I've got you now."

He clung onto my hand, encouraging me as we dove straight down—deep into the water. After swimming a short distance, he pulled me upward. Moments later, we resurfaced. I sucked in a sharp gulp of air.

Wiping the water from his face, he murmured, "You see? Not so bad, hey?"

I wiped my eyes too, then gave him a cynical glare.

Liam chuckled more easily as he towed me toward the shore. "Glad to see you're already getting back to yourself."

As we neared, soft shouts echoed across the rocky beach. "Everyone survived! Survived! Survived!"

After the water shallowed and, despite my leaning heavily on Liam, my legs were trembling so severely that they could barely carry me. "I don't think I kept hold of my rock for long enough. Won't the soldiers have seen us separating from them?"

Strong arms moved in from behind and swept me clean off my feet. "Angle is too steep for them to have seen any distance into the ravine." Eric's voice was soothing now—calm again. He carried me from the water and lowered me to the edge of a boulder. Dropping behind me, he settled his legs on either side of mine.

I lay back against his bare, heaving chest. It was warm and cool, firm against my back.

He pushed my waterlogged hair to the side, his skin rough as he pressed his lips to the nape of my neck. As he firmed his arms, I melted into his grasp. "You made it, Cassidy," he choked, a deep sigh shuddering from his chest. "You saved everyone."

"I couldn't have done it without you, Eric," I whispered.

I twisted to meet his glimmering aquamarines. "How did you know what they would do? And what made you even consider the idea of making friends with *any* of Gina's soldiers."

He laughed softly. "Coincidence more than anything. We'll talk later. You rest now."

After touching his lips to mine, he pulled me back against his chest once more. He tightened his arms around me as he pressed his mouth to my ear, adding in the softest whisper, "Now that I've got you"—he sighed—"now you're with me..." His voice caught as he concluded, "I'm never going to let you go."

For a moment, I warmed, but then something else clamped my chest. "Eric, won't the soldiers be able to see us out here? We're so exposed."

He chuckled. "Look up, Cassidy. Tell me what you see."

I followed his hand as he gestured skyward. "Uh...blue sky."

But shimmering rainbow colors joined the cliff face in an expansive, arcing bubble. It curved down into the ground and along the rocky beach then out toward the middle of the lake. I gasped, "Wow, Kaleidotonium! So, that's why we had to dive. We're beneath a dome. Is this whole area part of the refuge?"

He nodded, his expression solemn. "Caleb and I used to sit under the bubble out here when the cave got too stifling. Though neither sky nor sun was visible in the early days, it was nice to be outside, I guess."

While we dried, Eric indicated the community's key members. All were gathered on the rocky beach under the concealment of the large dome.

Ethan and Craig were almost interchangeable to look at, though not family. Like their noses, they were long, lean and pale, with white hair and beards to match. I learned that Ethan was involved in weapons development while Craig trained crows to carry messages to and from the refuge — mostly to those who had settled farms elsewhere.

Eric went on to point out their veterinarian, horticulturist, medicine woman, chef and assistant chef. "Let's not bog you down with too many names. You'll get to know them all soon enough."

He referred to their head chef, merely as 'Chef'. That was, at least, one less name to remember.

I turned back to Eric, grinning. "And you, Eric... What do you do here?"

"Me?" He laughed. "Why, I just roam the plains on my horse and make friends with passing soldiers."

He bit at the edge of his lip, as if trying to hide a smile, his aquamarines twinkling mischievously.

I rolled my eyes. Eric's resounding laugh raised gooseflesh on my arms—his voice slamming the fact home that I was finally with him.

As a wave of exhaustion crept over me, Liam returned. "You know you took ten years off my life," he complained, rubbing his nose.

Eric stood, closed his hand over Liam's shoulder and gave him a curt nod. "Excuse me for a bit?" Without waiting for an answer, he moved toward Graham.

Liam dropped to the rock beside me and wrapped his arm around my shoulder.

He sat quietly for a while as I leaned into him. Then, slowly, he shook his head. "When we realized you were in there—" He broke off, gesturing toward the fort. He cleared his throat and added, "Harriet was a wreck. She's going to take some time to get over this." He paused again, his voice choked as he met my eyes. "Tell me what happened, little sister."

As I relayed Jonas' and my experiences over the past weeks, he kept shaking his head. "I should never have let you go, Cassidy. No matter what Joshua said, I should have—"

I cut him off. "Li, Jonas did everything you could have done, everything you would have done. He was amazing."

Liam quietly considered my words. I mused over how he cared. Of course, he loved me every bit as much as I loved him. I knew that.

I turned, surveying the small lake. "It's beautiful here," I murmured, "so different to the world we grew up in."

My eyes shifted to Jonas and Harriet, her arms so firm around him as they huddled together on a boulder a short distance away.

I closed my eyes. "Does Harriet blame me for what happened to Jonas?"

"No, Cass. Trust me. She was so worried about you both. She blamed Gina — only Gina."

I followed Harriet's eyes, her attention fixed on Jonas.

He wore only his boxers and had one leg pulled to his chest. His wet shoes and clothes were draped over the hot rock beside him. He was too lean from our weeks of improper nutrition. The skin covering his ribs was still a sickly, pale shade of yellow.

I grimaced at the memory of his beating — and mine.

Jonas caught my gaze. "Thank you," he mouthed, a soft smile on his thick, boyish lips. "You did it."

Maybe it was because I knew him so well, but I easily read his lips. Tears pricked my eyes and, biting my lip, I blinked then returned his smile. I wasn't sure if he would as fluently read my lips, but I mouthed the words anyway. "Thank you, Jonas. You were the meteor." I closed my fist and smiled to emphasize the last word. He must have understood, because he immediately nodded.

Chapter Thirty-Four

Eric stood as tall as Graham, though decidedly more defined — chiseled. They were near the cave entrance, conversing with the super-skinny, almost-as-tall, Ethan and Craig. The men's posture, with their hands fisted on their hips and squared stance, implied they were not discussing Sunday dinner.

Eric still wore no T-shirt. He had thrust it down the front of his jeans near the hip. A brown leather belt held the faded denim jeans across his taut abdomen.

While he was half-turned away from me, I took the opportunity to examine the bronzed skin that smoothly enveloped his lean muscles. When he met my gaze, he bit the faint smile stretching his lips and looked down at his shifting feet. He rubbed the nape of his neck and flashed another glance in my direction. My heart pitched as the dimpled fissures stretched down his cheeks. He raised his head and turned back to his conversation, now with a definite glow to his cheeks.

Scanning the gathered crowd, my scrutiny landed on a red-haired beauty, who, having witnessed my exchange with Eric, shot me a less-than-happy glare.

Although I rolled my eyes, I wondered — *Am I just one of many?*

I refocused on Liam, who was still sitting beside me on the boulder. "I see I have competition."

Liam raised his brows at the redhead. "What, her? She's not the hottest girl here." He chuckled. "Harriet is."

I ignored his bias. "What? Do you mean others here are *more* beautiful?"

"Cool it, Cassidy. Eric doesn't seem to respond to these girls' efforts."

"Seem to?" I spat. "And girls? How many of them are there?"

"Get used to it. It's not going to change just because you've arrived."

I changed the subject. "How did you and Harriet find Eric?"

"We didn't. Eric found us when we rode up the mountain pass." He broke off and shook his head before continuing, "When the horses returned a few days before that, we thought we'd lost you guys. Harriet and I were tracking their prints, but Eric told us it was a bad idea. He said Gina's soldiers had most likely thrown you into the old prison and that, if we went looking for you, we would land there too. On top of that, Graham had not returned home the previous night. Eric was sure he'd also been captured. As soon as we arrived here, we started planning your rescue."

He closed his eyes and shuddered. "We all knew the plan was risky, but we had to do something."

"But how did Eric know they were Gina's sold — ?"

Liam began answering before I had even finished the question. "They arrived at the fort shortly after we landed on Earth. Besides, where else could they have come from?"

Again, my attention moved to Harriet as she laid her hand over her brother's shoulder, a tear sliding down her cheek. As Jonas reached up and covered it with his, sorrow hit my chest for the anguish our siblings had endured during our imprisonment.

I moved over to them and Harriet flung her arms around me. "I told you I had a bad feeling. Why didn't you listen, Cass?"

Jonas shook his head. "You know that's not fair then, Harriet. You can't blame Cassidy for what happened."

"Of course, I know that!" Harriet said. "Still, you can't blame me for being worried about you guys."

Giving her a soft smile, I added, "Well, we're safe now, Harriet. I was so relieved when Eric told me that Liam had gotten you here."

As Liam walked over and laid his arm around my shoulder, we fell into silence.

The sweet aroma of fresh bread wafted through the air — and something else…mutton.

"It's weird. The shock wearing off has left me starving." I salivated, my stomach rumbling a loud gurgle, as if to confirm the point.

Liam gave my gut a leering glance and laughed — a laugh that soon became a body-rocking guffaw.

A second later, his laugh faded. His face grew dark. "That's really not the tiniest bit surprising." He tensed his arm around my shoulder and choked out, "I'm so glad you're back, Cass, and safe."

"Mm-m," I agreed. "I thought that was a bit of a hysterical reaction to a gurgling stomach."

He said nothing but clamped his lips closed, shaking his head slowly.

After a while, I stood, ambling to the edge of the lake, where I dropped to a large boulder. The water was mesmerizing — cathartic.

The sun was baking down on the rocks when Eric boulder-hopped toward me while balancing chunks of bread on the lips of two bowls.

Handing me one, he murmured, "Only eat what you can, Cassidy." He feathered the backs of his fingers over my cheek. "Might be better if you don't overdo it in the beginning. Give your body time to adapt."

Eric was right. I craved the nourishment, but weak and decimated as I was, my body rejected the rich food. I ate only a small amount before the effort exhausted me.

Setting my half-eaten bowl of food down, I lay back on the warm rock. When my T-shirt hitched up, Eric sucked in a sharp breath. "Cassidy!" He landed his steady gaze on mine, slowly shaking his head and speaking almost to himself. "It makes me real mad we didn't get to the fort sooner."

He smoothed his rough thumb over the yellowed bruises on my hip. I winced from the charge jolting through me. It wasn't pain that surged through my nerve fibers.

I met his eyes. "It's amazing you got there at all, Eric."

When he set his bowl on the rock beside mine, I sat up and lifted both of them. "Where do we do the cleaning?"

He wrested them from my grasp. "Not today, my — " He broke off and bit his lip then continued, "Today you rest." He chuckled. "Don't sweat it. Graham will drive you to the bone when you have your strength back." He dropped to a whisper. "Come with me."

I followed him a short distance into the cave entrance, where he laid the dishes on a stone ledge. Weaving his strong fingers through mine, he smiled a little cheekily. He led me along a broad path, which ran beside the cave's rocky outer wall—from the entrance toward the edge of the near-invisible Kaleidotonium shell. The bubble's doorway was like those of the habitats. But, like the outer shell of our smaller domes, this presented an interior with the environment vacant of life. The habitats, on the other hand, allowed onlookers to see through their mystifying exteriors. After heading through the trees of a recovering woods, we followed a winding path up a yellow straw-grassed slope. Eric plucked at a few long strands as we brushed past. My lips drew into a warm smile at the surfacing memory.

In his presence, a profound sense of safety washed over me. I dropped my guard. As it happened, that was a bad thing. The intensity of all those suppressed emotions seized me and my eyes filled with tears.

Eric stopped and gripped me against his chest, his bare skin warm against my cheek. I slid my arms around his waist, his comforting breath lightly brushing the top of my head.

"Hey, Cassidy." He pulled his head back, dropping his chin as he observed me. In a shaky voice, he murmured, "None of this ought to have happened. It never entered my mind that Gina would take the fort when I asked you to leave the craft. The danger I placed—" He broke off, his voice turning low, soothing. "It won't happen again. I swear it."

I pulled back and met his determined stare. "You can't say that, Eric. You can't protect me or even yourself or anybody out here." I waved my hand back toward the rocky beach. "And what about the others who need our help? Like Jaya? I know Liam would have told you about him and his people. And what if the younger slave women bear children? Can you imagine what Gina plans for those kids? Our safety is not guaranteed. No one's is." I almost doubled over as Gina's intentions slammed into my gut.

He closed his eyes, shaking his head. "You're right. Damn, I wish you'd never gotten involved."

My tension eased. "Now you sound like my mother." A soft smile stretched my lips, dampening my anger as her comment about Liam and me, before we had returned to Earth, replayed in my mind.

When he smiled, his dimples jolted my heart and my cheeks warmed.

While summiting the hill, we were exposed to all the surrounding lands. I cringed, glancing back toward the fort. Although I met only trees on the higher peak, I couldn't breathe away my heart's pounding.

Eric cocked his head, observing me. "They can't see us, Cassidy. You're safe here."

We descended into the valley and followed a path into a thick canopy of trees. Hidden behind a mass of rocks, a small pool bubbled clear, right down to the shimmering rocky base.

The only sounds tingeing the warm afternoon air were beetles chittering among the rocks, a few birds chirping in the surrounding trees and water trickling into the pool.

When my gaze fell to the edging rocks, I spun, wrapping my arms around Eric's neck. "How the...? You recovered our baggage."

He moved his hands around my waist and arched backward, meeting my smile with a gratified one of his own. "Well...technically, Liam recovered it."

He chuckled. "Like I told you, I was busy making friends with soldiers."

Not that I had brought many clothes on our trip, but the thought of my own toothbrush, shampoo, soap and clean clothes was like heaven.

Eric slipped around behind the boulders and leaned against them. The rock concealed most of his body, but his shoulder and hand protruded around the edge as he raised his hand toward his mouth and chewed at the long blade of straw still between his fingers. "You'll need privacy to bathe, but I'll be just around the corner," he murmured.

I lowered into the water then stopped. "Eric? Don't soldiers ever cross the ravine? On the train, I mean?"

"They have no need. They control the train from the fort." He gestured in the general direction of the far side of the lake. "The line ends just beyond the gorge." He growled. "She built that thing for one purpose only." He paused, his voice catching. "It wasn't possible to save the first group. The lake—" He broke off, then added, "It's insane what she's doing. More than insane."

A shiver shot through me, but hearing the agony in his voice, I couldn't press him for details.

He fell silent for a while. Then he spoke as if he were in the middle of a conversation. "It bothers us that they've already located this fort when you've barely been back here. Back on Earth, I mean. It makes us think they already knew about it." He snickered. "It's hard to get my head around that — to say, 'back on Earth'."

"Eric!" My interrupting shriek was all I managed as, sliding into the pool, was an enormous serpent. And it was swimming toward me.

Chapter Thirty-Five

In a flash, Eric launched into the pool. He landed, almost on top of the long animal, clutching it behind its head with one hand. He closed the other around its body. It twisted, writhed and looped its powerful coils, trying to escape. It opened its pale red mouth wider than I thought possible, dislocating its jaws as it twisted back — trying to make contact with Eric's skin. Eric heaved and panted, straining his muscles. He barely kept the serpent facing away from us — only just staying its inch-long fangs from finding their mark. The tips sparkled with venom.

"Cassidy…" He was panting, angling his hip toward me. "Reach into my pocket and get the knife out, will you?"

With every twist, the mighty snake got its mouth nearer and nearer to Eric's skin.

I thrust my hand into his pocket — forgetting about my exposed body as I groped for the knife.

The smooth handle slipped out with ease. "How are you going to hold it?"

"You're going to have to do that."

While I clung onto the flick-knife's handle, he fought and thrashed his way to the edging rock. In one final burst of power, he brought the snake's head down — smashing it hard against the rough stone.

The serpent went limp.

"Is it dead?" I hoped.

"Hah!" Eric snorted. "I very much doubt that."

I reached around him, his eyes not moving from the snake that was gripped in his hands.

He panted. "Press the button on the handle to flick the blade out. Then stab down…at the base of its head."

I flicked out the blade and stabbed the snake as instructed.

"Bushmaster," he muttered, heaving, his chest rising and falling in ragged gasps.

I peered around, uncertain if more dangerous creatures would accost me. None did. Finally, I moved back and re-submerged.

I didn't know much about snakes, but I was quite sure that a triangular head usually meant venomous — and a definite triangle terminated this enormous serpent's least-favored end. "Is it a poisonous one?"

In his waterlogged jeans, Eric turned to face me.

He snorted, shaking his head. "Very. Are you some kind of danger magnet?" Without waiting for a response to his rhetorical question, he continued, "People have been in here a hundred times,. Nothing like this has ever happened before. Clearly the indoor bathrooms would have been a better choice. I thought this would be nicer is all."

For a second, his eyes moved down. My cheeks warmed when I recalled the pond's clarity.

He noticed at the same time. "Um, I'm...uh, sorry," he stammered, his neck flushing as he turned his back to me, still clutching the snake.

He tossed it onto the rocks. I followed its trajectory until it landed with a resounding, wet thud.

He cleared his throat. "Anyway, Ethan will be happy about this."

I gasped. "Exactly what about a deadly viper could possibly make anyone happy?"

"He makes antivenom *and*" — he drew out the last word — "he's not opposed to coating the arrow tips in poison. He prefers the Coral Snake, though. Besides" — he shrugged — "snake stew doesn't taste half bad. They survived the meteor strike better than most animals, so we hardly feel guilty about killing them. There are more than enough of these creatures sliding around the caves."

"This is a very different world," I mused for the second time that day as Eric tensioned his arms and heaved himself from the pool. He did not move away as I continued washing, but sat cross-legged on the lip with his back to me.

After finishing my much-needed bath, I pulled myself from the pool then wrapped a towel around my body. My skin felt tingly fresh as I slipped a light, summer dress over my head and turbaned my hair in the towel.

"What were you discussing with Graham earlier?"

Eric slung my bags — and the now-dead viper — over his shoulder. "It's not fair, I know, but we were kind of angry with him for getting himself captured. He should have been more careful."

He flattened the snake's fangs and held the mouth closed with one hand.

"Are you always this crazy, Eric?"

He threw a deep laugh that rang with mock sarcasm. "If crazy is what keeps you alive, it stands to reason that I'd have to be."

As we meandered our way back along the path, a thousand questions still plagued me, but this one surfaced first. "Aren't you ever concerned about smoke or food aromas reaching the fort?"

"Hey, but you *are* a curious one." He smiled then answered anyway. "Apart from the Kaleidotonium bubble, breezes flow downriver through the valley. Air pretty much floats any smells away from the fort, so no, not really. Plus, we use electric stoves with extractor fans—so that helps." He chuckled. "In a day or two, I'll show you the farms. We don't slaughter, if we can help it, but we don't waste either—hence the mutton casserole today."

I shook my head slowly. "And all of that is inside the caves?"

"Yup." He nodded as a wry smile twisted his mouth.

When we emerged from the edging trees onto the rocky beach, a crowd instantly gathered—asking a million questions about the snake around Eric's neck.

Ethan got first shot and removed the entire triangular head, taking it with him into the caves.

Eric heaved the remainder of the massive reptile over his head and dropped it to the rocks.

* * * *

Much later that afternoon, Eric and I lay on a flat, sunbaked boulder at the lakes' edge. The warmth seeping through the blankets beneath us was somehow soothing.

The flaming red ball sank slowly toward the ridge. The afternoon shadows lengthened until finally, the peak claimed the last bright-red sliver of sunlight. As dusk drifted away, evening descended.

The quarter moon and sprinkling of stars lay scintillating against the black backdrop of the night skies. A pensive mood took hold of me.

Eric lay on his back with one hand behind his head, the other beneath my shoulders, holding me against him. "It's hard to believe you're here," he whispered, twisting toward me. A smile curled one lip while he squeezed me around the waist. "You're finally in my arms." He sighed.

"Me either," I whispered back as he touched his lips to my forehead.

Propping himself on his forearm, he rolled me onto my back and cushioned the blanket beneath my head — his aquamarine gaze shifting between my eyes.

The world melted away from us. Only Eric and I remained.

Stroking a loose strand of hair from my face, he slipped his arm around my waist and drew my body against his. As our eyes locked, he moved his tongue over his full lips then he lowered. My eyes slipped closed and our kiss fused. Deep longing swept through me as he parted my lips with his tongue then caressed mine, exploring my mouth gently yet urgently. His warmth reverberated through my body, the rhythm of our breathing wild and ragged. Too much electricity met too many uncontrollable feelings.

"Cassidy," Eric whispered hoarsely against my mouth.

He pulled away too soon. A deep moan escaped my lips as he drew upright and sat beside me, panting.

My breath heaved, my body arching upward, yearning for more.

He turned away and bit his lip. "Wow!" he murmured. "This is way better than before. It's hard to —"

When he broke off, I pondered possible endings to that sentence but came up blank. "Hard to what?"

He chuckled. "Stop."

Wry amusement flattened my mouth. "Mm-m."

It really had been better than before, though. Eric has been right about that. It was so much better than the holographic version, so much more intense. During the times when Eric had come to me on the craft, I had not considered that the remotest likelihood.

We slept on the rock that night, the sky our ceiling and stars our sentinels. Eric wrapped complete and perfect safety around my shoulders with his strong arms. At that moment, the warmth of home surrounded me. But my senses warned that some time might pass before we were indeed home or truly safe — if ever.

Chapter Thirty-Six

I woke the following morning to the fresh, pink glow of sunrise glinting over the peaks. Warmth spread through my chest as I absorbed the beauty of the planet.

Beside me, Eric stretched his arms high above his head and yawned, covering his mouth with a fist. He turned and again folded me into an embrace.

He was humming, almost purring, when Graham emerged from the cave entrance, sliding his hand through the crisp curls of his white-gray hair. He clapped his hands loudly, rousing those sleeping on boulders.

As all of us turned in his direction, Graham called out, "Rise and shine, you bunch of lazy louts. Your taskmaster has returned." With that, he broke into a deep laugh.

Eric faked a groan. "Argh. We start working for our keep again, I guess. It won't be as bad as harvest, so I shouldn't complain. Harvesters do most of that work."

I arched my body into a stretch and raised my hand to my mouth as a yawn forced its way out. "I want to contribute, Eric. Will you show me around?" I sat straight up and, extracting the blanket from beneath us, folded it.

"Patience, Cassidy. To tell the truth, normally I'm out there before dawn"—he gestured toward the cave—"but since we're already late, how about after breakfast we visit Zenobia?"

I liked that idea.

Middle-aged and paunchy, Chef flapped a white tablecloth before him, stretching it over a large, flat boulder just outside the cave entrance. Then Matt, his young, skinny, dark-haired assistant arranged a generous breakfast spread on it.

As much as my deflated appetite allowed, I tried the scrambled eggs, toast and coffee. It hit my stomach as a chunk of lead would.

No sooner had I finished than Eric grabbed my plate and mug. He set them, with his own dishes, into a large washbasin beside the breakfast boulder.

"Come," he murmured simply, holding his hand out to me.

I grasped his warm fingers and followed him through the cave entrance. As we entered the small frontal chamber, a strange sadness washed over me. This dark grotto had been Eric and Caleb's home for so many years.

For a second as he observed me, his brows knitted into a frown, but he appeared to understand my concern and half-smiled. "Don't worry... Only the entrance is like this."

He led me around a bend and into a long, broad, rock-walled tunnel.

At least five hundred empty canoe racks lined one wall.

I stopped. "Where are the canoes?"

As Eric glanced at the empty racks, he burst into a deep laugh. "In their racks, of course. They're made from Kaleidotonium, so they're super-tough. You already know that. Their tops seal…for camouflage. Obviously, we slide the canopies open for rowing. Roof's too low to sit upright on the benches when they're closed, so we sit on the base then."

I reached out to touch a boat, but my hand slid through vacant air. I rolled my eyes. "Good one. I was about to ask when you had the chance to use them."

Eric laughed again. "No, seriously, many racks still carry canoes, but those families who left took some. You wouldn't believe the most awesome boat races we had in the underground river, back when we were still holed up in here."

We moved on, pacing the worn rock floor. Above, a long, metal duct, running along the center of the roof, flooded the tunnel in bright, white light.

After half an hour of moving steadily downhill, an even more dazzling glow seeped in from ahead.

It grew brighter and yet brighter still before we stepped through an entrance into…the beautiful, sunny outdoors.

The crushing weight I had felt for Eric fell away from my chest and I threw him a wry glance.

He cocked his head in vague amusement. "We *are* still in the caves, Cassidy."

Waist-high wheat plants stretched away toward the distant cavern wall. I filled my lungs with sweet, crisp air as fragrant and fresh as any spring morning in Petriville.

My gaze shifted upward. I shot my hands to my eyes, shielding them from the brightness. High, high above the soil-filled base, puffy white clouds splashed the brightest blue sky. Surrounding the edges, distant, hazy mountains closed the farmlands into an apparent valley.

Neither the size nor the dazzling blue-and-white sky, nor even the distant mountains startled me because, to the far east of the cavern, the sun rose, bright and orange—arcing along the sky and bathing the plants beneath it in real, honest-to-goodness sunlight. I gasped. "That man is a genius! How did he do this?"

Eric laughed. "Government funding and impressive engineers. Sadly, most of the few officials who knew about this test facility were at a conference in Europe when the meteor struck. It came in so fast that nobody seemed to grasp that it was about to happen. The day before it hit, some who were here went to fetch their families. They never returned."

He flattened his lips and shook his head. "No one arrived, not after the strike. Everyone here was only in this place because of some or other strange, random coincidence. Fate, Graham calls it. Who knows? Maybe he's right."

Eric paused for a few beats. "Kaleidotonium lines every cavern, every tunnel and every space. In the larger caves like this one, the *sun*"—he emphasized—"and *moon* run between tracks along the center. Irrigation pipes run over the top of the Kaleidotonium shell and water droplets filter through then fall as raindrops. And the sky"—he gestured upward—"well, that's just the way the Kaleidotonium reflects light. It must be pretty similar in Petriville, I'm guessing. As for the clouds and the landscape, they are just amazing graphics displayed on the Kaleidotonium."

A path ran through the center of the cavern. We spent the next fifteen minutes crossing to the far side, where we entered another, much smaller cavern — only as bright as the inside of a house on a sunny day.

Brick-built stables lined the edge of the cave in a horseshoe pattern. A liver-chestnut face with a perfect white diamond pitched over a stable door.

"Zenobia!" I ran to her, rubbing her face as she pushed against my hand.

A warm laugh came from Eric, who was behind me. "They normally stay out. One of the kids brought her in, but she'll want to join her friends, I'm pretty sure."

I snapped a halter on her head and took her from the stable then followed Eric, who led us to a bright cavern on the far side. Green grass filled the gigantic paddock, as sun-lit and fresh as the wheat fields we had just crossed.

Loosening her halter, I released her into the long grass. Eric stepped closer behind me, wrapping his arms around my waist. With a twist and a buck, she galloped toward Boudicca, who stood with an unfamiliar big black horse. Both horses raised their heads, peering in her direction — while many others joined in the play.

"The big black is Warrior, my gelding," Eric murmured between kisses to my temple. "A whole lot more horses used to live here, but they left with their families."

* * * *

After dinner that night, while boulder-hopping the rocky beach toward Eric and me, Graham, with Ethan and Craig hot on his heels, hand-gestured his summons to Liam, Harriet and Jonas.

The old man's mouth widened in a warm smile as his rhythmic baritone flowed. "And so, our family grows."

He turned to Liam, fluttering Joshua's rolled digipar between his fingers. "Thank you, for this." He swallowed. "Joshua tells me that Gina plans for our demise, so for any communication through the pod, he's plotted a map of code words. It will be very useful, indeed."

After a pause, he continued, "We have had an eventful few weeks, though I fear that the excitement is just beginning... Off the subject, and though our circumstances were horrific, it was my great pleasure to acquaint myself with the young Cassidy and Jonas."

I grimaced, my cheeks warming. Graham had witnessed a bond between Jonas and me that Eric wouldn't understand.

Eric leaned forward and rested his toned forearms on his thighs, his eyes locked on the stone floor. For a moment, he raised them to meet mine. My heart jumped. But, clenching his jaw, he returned his attention to the ground.

Graham glanced at Jonas again then me. "Anyway, I knew that Eric would get us out." Graham smiled softly, gripping Eric's shoulder and sounding like a proud father. "This young man can accomplish anything he sets his mind to."

"I've noticed," Jonas muttered under his breath. I only heard him because I was eyeing him at the time.

My glance darted to Eric. His sour expression told me he had heard Jonas too. I squeezed my eyes shut.

"So, we have some decisions to make," Graham continued, unaware of the silent exchange between Jonas, Eric and me.

Graham went on, "Joshua mentions here that Gina apparently kept the landing codes in her head" — he tapped his skull — "so their lead collaborator could do nothing while you were out there."

Graham flashed his eyes between our startled expressions.

I spluttered on my words. "Lead collaborator? So much for our parents not keeping secrets from us anymore."

Harriet rolled her eyes. "I'm not surprised, Cassidy. With your hot head, you would have told Gina what you knew, just to see the shock on her face."

Liam nodded. "And they must have known that had they informed us, we wouldn't have kept the information from you."

Not wanting to further distract Graham from his engaging narration, we all nodded him on.

"Well, according to Joshua, they hope that banding together, we can perhaps overthrow Gina. Their main aim is to free Jaya's people and win our acceptance into their society, so we can face this new world together as one."

I pondered. How small-minded of me to think only of getting our parents out when Graham was concerned with the freedom of thousands.

Gina would — at best — enslave anyone she captured and set them to work with Jaya's people. Jonas, Graham and I had lived through some of the worst of her plans.

When Graham finished, Eric shifted his gaze between Liam and me. "Any chance of contacting your mother through the pod?" He raised his brows to the sky. "Now that the craft is not up there, I mean."

Liam sucked his upper lip between his teeth, shaking his head contemplatively. "It's very close. We might receive a signal, but Gina will be listening for sure." He rubbed his nose.

"That is not, perhaps, a terrible thing," Graham mused aloud, tapping an index finger to his lips. "We'll communicate a false message for Gina's benefit and use the code words to express our true intentions to your mother."

With that, having reached a semblance of an agreement, Graham adjourned the meeting.

Chapter Thirty-Seven

Taking Eric's hand, I turned to Jonas. "You seem better."

"…the courage to accept the things I cannot change." He light-heartedly clipped an old prayer while half glancing at Eric.

I puffed a soft laugh. "I'm glad to see you're back to your old self."

Jonas raised his brows then strolled toward the petite, dark-haired Olivia. She was the oldest of the four girls who had taken to shadowing him as though he was some kind of hero. On closer inspection, I'd observed that it was mostly Olivia who was stuck on Jonas. The three younger girls were more focused on Olivia's needs.

During our meeting, the evening sky had grown dark and overcast.

Eric faced me. Lifting both my hands in his, he cocked his head, his voice unusually strained. "What was that with Jonas earlier — that '*I've noticed*' thing?"

He didn't seem angry. It was worse than that. The way he frowned made him seem wounded. "While I'm not normally the jealous type, Cassidy, you're hardly making this easy on me. What *are* your feelings for Jonas?"

A flash of anger surged through me. "Please don't assume I reciprocate Jonas' feelings, Eric."

He returned my agitated response with one of his own. "I'm not assuming anything, just asking you a question is all."

I shook my head, some of my anger abating. "I'm sure what he thinks he feels is just the leftovers of a boyhood crush."

"That's *not* what it looks like to me."

"Well, he's my friend. Of course I care about him. I always will and would never lie to you about that." He still didn't look appeased, so I added, "Listen, Eric. I don't feel for him what I feel for you. I have never felt this way about anybody before."

As we stood on the boulder, my gaze drifted to the calm lake. Lit by the cave entrance, the large rocks reflected off the surface in a mesmerizing shimmer.

Eric blinked. "Much as I dislike how close the whole experience must have made you, it was good of him to nurse you back to health in there. To be honest, I'm not sure I could have done a better job." An impish smile stretched his lips. "Don't go repeating that, though. I'll just deny it."

I dropped a hip and tapped my toe. "So, you obviously haven't told Jonas that."

His expression confirmed my assumption, so I added in a serious tone, "You should, you know. He deserves some kindness for what he went through."

And I couldn't help but add a jibe. "Better that appreciation comes from you than from me."

He bit his lower lip then squared his stance. "Don't press it. Your defensiveness of him still irks me."

My mouth stretched into a smile as I looped my arms around his neck, pulling myself closer and coaxing his head down.

I placed my whispering lips against his ear. "I guarantee you it's not going to change. But I'm like that with all those I care about."

As I smile-pouted, he extracted his fingers then laid his hands on my waist.

When he slipped his arms around me and clasped me to him, I stretched up to meet his lips. The warmth of his skin seeped through his T-shirt, deep into me— his muscles taut against my body. I slid my hands up the nape of his neck, combing my fingers into his rough hairline. My lips parted to his soft, warm mouth, as I inhaled his smoky vanilla scent. We were breathing in ragged gasps, my body yearning for more of last night's long kiss.

Abruptly, it hit me. We were standing in the middle of the rocky beach. I bit my lip, gingerly stepping back as I glanced around. But those still out here didn't appear to concern themselves with our romantic endeavors.

Eric chuckled at my embarrassment. Did he know how his deep laughter, striking dimples and tropical ocean eyes all but caused me heart failure?

I gazed up and held my palm out to the first few large raindrops penetrating the bubble. As Eric followed my line of sight, he threaded his fingers through mine and led me into the cave. A moment later, a deluge started pelting the rocks outside.

For only a quarter of an hour this time, we moved down the same long passage. As we slipped into an offshoot, a fair-sized area opened before us.

Moon and stars sailed overhead. In full lilac blossom, jacaranda trees lined a paved walkway. And flowers, bursting into colorful bloom, fluttered in the evening breeze. The sense that we were walking in the open air of a star-lit night struck me hard.

I drew in a deep breath, filling my lungs with crisp, sweet air. "It's like we're not inside a cave at all, Eric."

The path ended at the doorway of a brick building. With a wry smile, Eric tugged open the large double doors and bowed me in. At least a hundred bedroom entrances led off each side of the corridor.

The first door stood ajar. My eyes fell on two young teenage girls, sitting against the headboard on the lower of two bunk beds. Almost dragging their eyes from the mancala board, they fluttered their fingers then shifted back again. Eric and I leaned against the doorway posts, observing their game. Deftly, they moved the smooth, colored pebbles along the two rows of small baskets that were gouged into the narrow marble palette.

Eric cocked his head. "Why don't you girls close the door?"

One of the girls answered for both. "We don't want to be alone."

"Me either, girls," Eric mused, "me either."

After watching their game for a few minutes, Eric pressed his fingers on mine. He gestured, with his brow, to the far end of the corridor.

A short distance farther along the passage, Eric opened a door on the same side. "This is Caleb's and my room." He bit his lip. "You can sleep here. I'll go next door." He gestured to an inside door with his brow. "Bathroom is in there."

I grinned. "You have en-suite bathrooms? Here I felt all sorry for you, thinking you were roughing it out here."

He chuckled. "There's a school and everything here. It's kind of like a small town."

Eric closed the door and, clasping his hands on my waist, he moved me back toward the foot of a single bed. He turned and sat, laying back and lowering me to his body in one fluid motion. Our lips parted as they touched and he slid his arms around my waist, gripping me to him. At first, Eric kissed me slowly, exploring my mouth, my tongue. But as his kiss grew in urgency and yearning, his mouth clamped down harder, heat pulsing between our bodies.

Abruptly he rolled me to his side and he sat up, shaking his head slowly. "We... I... The thing is..." He turned his pale aquamarines on my face, his brow low.

My stomach churned. *Is Eric getting cold feet? Why does he keep turning away from me?*

He was speaking again as if he hadn't paused. "The thing is," he blurted through gritted teeth, "you're driving me crazy, Cassidy. But you're only seventeen and I'm almost twenty-one. Plus, even if you were eighteen, Graham wasn't much thinking of birth control when he stocked this place."

"Oh... Oh, yes." I stumbled over the words.

The truth was that abandoning all moral traditions, Gina had made sure nothing would get in the way of her planned procreation. And since our fathers had been sterilized, nothing was available in Petriville either.

Eric lay back down and pulled me into his side. He didn't go next door that night, but neither did we give in to our urges. After some time, we slept.

* * * *

Dawn was breaking when I awoke.

Through Eric's large bedroom window, I drew in the sight of rain clouds drifting apart. The soft pinks of sunrise emerged against a pale blue sky, as though the inside of the cavern emulated the outside.

Although still asleep, Eric stirred when I unwound his arms from me.

I decided to seek out breakfast and strolled back along the corridor. My olfactory senses led me to a cavern on the far side of the cave entrance. I located the kitchen in a large rectangular room of white, plastered brick walls. Appliances and a breakfast spread second-to-none topped a long counter lining one wall, while electric stoves and fridges trimmed another.

Chef peered his balding head from the refrigeration chamber and grunted. "Top 'o the morning to you."

"Morning, Chef," I sang before entering a room lined with cupboards and Industrial dishwashers.

I took two plates, mugs and cutlery sets from the cupboard. Chef was still busy in the refrigeration chamber when I returned to the main area.

He called in a cheerful voice, "Help yourself, won't you, dearie?"

From a board on the counter, I selected slices of fruit and muffins then poured two cups of coffee. After laying the assortment on a white tray that was abstractly decorated with bright colors, I returned to Eric.

Nearing his bedroom, his voice reached me. I stopped and listened. Who was he talking to? No, he wasn't talking. Not exactly. He was versing a soft melody or chant, rhythmical.

If a song and the wind and the rain, tell six,
The ocean, a lake and the tree are nine,
Then where would you meet with your nearest and
dearest?
Why? Where the sun and the moon misalign.

"Oh...Cassidy. You snuck up on me." He half-raised onto his forearms as I entered his bedroom, his cheeks reddening and abdominal muscles pulling hard.

I ignored his embarrassment. "It's not fair to do that to me after our discussion last night," I complained, my lips tugging into a twisted smile.

After laying the tray on a study desk, I sat on the edge of his bed, combing my fingers through his hair.

"What?" he drawled, laughing as he laid his hand on my waist.

I added, "What was that, by the way? A rhyme? A riddle?"

He shrugged and smiled. "A bit of both and not much of either" — he chuckled — "more functional than poetic. My mom made Caleb and me repeat it over and over when we were kids. Like it was important — something to do with our home."

I cocked my head. "What does it mean?"

Half-laughing, he puffed a breath through his nose. "We never got to finding that part out."

His smile faded. "Cassidy, I'll be needing to go away for a couple of days. Then, I'll show you my favorite place in the whole world — nature's memorial to

Caleb—our favorite hang-out after Graham unsealed the exit."

A shiver crawled up my spine that Eric trusted me enough to bring his twin brother's memory to the surface. I absorbed the sadness in his eyes. A wave of deep sorrow washed over me for the agony he must have faced when Caleb had died. I wanted to ask him why he needed to go away and to where. But how could I ask now, with Caleb's death hanging in the air?

* * * *

For almost two days, Eric never returned. I grew frantic with fear, but Graham didn't show an ounce of worry—or perhaps he decided not to aggravate my concerns. "It's not unusual, young lady. He'll be back before you can pluck a chicken."

Not that I was ever going to pluck a chicken…

On the second day at lunchtime, Chef handed Harriet and me each a tray of sandwiches, not giving the option to refuse his request. "Take these outside, won't you, girls?"

As we lay them on the large, flat boulder just outside the cave, Harriet moved her eyes to the bubble entrance. "Well, look who the cat dragged in!"

My breath caught as I followed her line of sight, hardly daring to hope. Eric strolled toward us as if returning from a picnic, his expression impassive. But his shoulders were turned the tiniest bit down as if inwardly he was fraught with turbulence. As he passed Ethan and Craig, he tossed them his backpack. "Here. The soldiers' uniforms that Graham's been waiting for."

Then he grabbed my hand and a pile of cheese, cucumber and lettuce sandwiches from the boulder. After shoving almost half into my hands, he led me through the bubble exit.

We ate while we walked and took the winding pathway toward the rock pool. I broached the subject. "So, you were fraternizing with the enemy, Eric?"

As we descended the small slope to the pool I'd bathed in, he cocked his head toward me. "Things aren't always as black and white as you might hope, Cassidy. Graham needed more uniforms for when we go to the craft." He lowered to wash his hands, chuckling as he took in my dubious expression. "Seriously, Cassidy… Snakes are not waiting around just to ambush you."

Still, I was cautious as I bent to wash my hands.

With that done, he edged around the small pool and steered me up a sharp incline.

As we neared the tree line, Eric stopped. Light poured through from ahead.

He whispered, "Wait before we leave the forest." Then he pressed up behind me and covered my eyes with his hands. "Slowly," he murmured in a low voice, edging me forward up the last bit of the incline.

Dropping his hands from my eyes, he wrapped his arms around my waist—holding me against him. I gaspcd. Far, far below, a hazy panorama of trees and hills stretched away before my eyes. The river was a blue ribbon, snaking toward the ocean and reaching it right beside the craft. "This is incredible, Eric." I leaned my head back against his shoulder. "The whole world is laid out before us. I've only ever seen anything this beautiful in pictures."

"It sure is amazing." he whispered, turning me toward him, his arms around my waist as I slipped mine around his neck.

A mischievous tune entered his voice. His eyes glinted. "Do you trust me, Cassidy?

"I think so." I cocked my head, not sure I liked where this was heading — though the smile wouldn't leave my lips.

Eric edged me backward. The cliff fell away just behind me, sucking at my feet.

"Eric!" I drew out, my voice rising.

He tightened his arms around my waist, holding me against him. Still, he edged me slowly back. "Take a deep breath."

"No!" I shrieked. But the wind was already beneath my feet. For the second time in three days, I was freefalling.

Eric didn't release me as we plummeted together but he gripped me to his body with one powerful arm and my head to his chest with his other hand.

A second later, we hit the water, submerging into the deep. I gasped as I surfaced, still firm in Eric's arms. We had landed inside a small cave.

In reaction, I slapped hard at his face. He was too quick and chuckled, grabbing my wrist in mid-air before I struck.

Holding both my cuffs, he edged backward inside the cave and slid onto a low, smooth rock bank. As he moved his hands to my waist and lifted me from the water, his grin faded, his expression growing serious.

He folded me into his arms and slowly lay back, clasping me against his body, our clothes wet between us. I scanned his searching eyes, heavy brow and sharp jawline then reached for his lips, moist and hot. Again, his scent overwhelmed me. He flexed his arms, pressing against my back — gripping me against him. I moaned, combing my fingers through his hair. Eric gasped, reaching up and weaving his hands through mine. He clamped our lips together. Our breathing rasped through our bodies, passion surging. Eric broke.

"Cassidy," he groaned, rolling me to my back. He propped himself onto his forearm and gazed into my eyes, cupping his hand around my neck. Stroking my cheek with his thumb, he lowered to me once more. But his kiss was gentle this time — soft.

He pulled back, his beautiful aquamarines shifting between my eyes. "Cassidy," he whispered again as if about to say more.

I wanted him to, yearned for it.

But silently he rose then held his hand out to me. His whisper cracked, "Come."

I took his hand and followed him through a short tunnel then out onto a ledge. The view we had experienced from above — the vast expanse lying before us — seemed somehow amplified from here. I glanced upward to the ridge then to the rock pool beside us. Water flowed over its lip, falling to the vast expanse below. "So this is your favorite place in the whole world," I murmured.

"It is indeed" — he smiled — "and now it belongs to you too."

I shrugged one shoulder and the corner of my mouth twitched. I would never forget that Caleb's memory held true claim to this magnificent place. "That's not right, though, is it, Eric?"

Eric returned a soft, appreciative smile. "Well, you know what I mean."

I did. I knew that Eric would never have shared Caleb's memory with just anyone.

With our backs against the cliff wall and our legs dangling over the edge of the shelf, the hot afternoon sun soon dried our clothes.

"Eric." I grimaced, but I had come this far. I might as well come out with it. "Won't you tell me what happened to Caleb? Please… I want to know."

He fixed his gaze on the distant sun as it dipped below the horizon and splashed the clouds in a spectacular range of reds and oranges.

"He was so much better than me at pretty much everything—my better half in the truest sense. If you'd met Caleb, you wouldn't be sitting here with me now. You'd be off with him on some wild adventure for sure."

Eric held no jealousy or bitterness in his voice, only admiration and heartache.

He smiled to himself then continued, "He was seriously resilient—insanely so. When Jeff's men decided to go find out if those in Graham's nearest refuge had survived, Caleb just *had* to go with." He fell silent and coughed, his Adam's apple bouncing as he swallowed.

I shook my head. "Didn't Graham try to stop him?"

"Of course he did. He begged him not to go. But he was so damned stubborn."

"And you, Eric? What did you do?"

"I told him he was insane." A soft chuckle rose in his throat before his smile fell away. "Then I told him to stay with Graham and I'd go. But he somehow convinced me that Graham relied on me more."

"Maybe he was right, Eric. Maybe Graham did rely more on you."

He shrugged. "Maybe... I wouldn't know. But" — the rest of his sentence came out in a rush — "Graham needed us both."

He fell silent and I waited.

After side-glancing at me, Eric proceeded. "A month to the day after they had left, one of the crows returned with a message from Caleb. He said the others were dying from malaria and he himself was surely 'done for'. Those were his words, 'done for', like that explained anything. Then he tells me not to mourn him." He dropped his gaze. A single tear slipped from his eye as he choked, "And that he loved Graham and me."

My forehead stiffened. "What about sending a search party?"

Exasperation filled his thick voice, "You don't really think we just accepted that? Of course we searched for them, for two months. I headed the search party myself." His voice caught again. "We found pieces of bodies so scavenged and scattered that we couldn't identify anyone!"

We both fell quiet.

After some time, Eric turned toward me, threading his arm around my shoulder and pulling me to him. "Thank you for listening, Cassidy."

He kissed my forehead with so much tenderness. A hoarse whisper escaped his lips. "I've dreamed of bringing you here. Did you know?"

I bit my lip and, as if in silent consensus, we stood.

Glancing upward, I did not feel excited about the prospect of climbing the cliff. "How do we get back?"

"Through the cave." Eric chuckled. "I could have brought you that way, but where's the fun in that?"

I gave him a jesting jab in the ribs, and he grabbed my arm, reeling me into his side while we walked. As we emerged through a dense curtain of vines beside the warm bathing pool, we fell into easy laughter.

Chapter Thirty-Eight

For the following five weeks, we lived within the security of the refuge. Since potato-harvesting season had begun, machines excavated and washed enormous piles of the root vegetables. To earn our keep, we assisted with their bagging and refrigeration.

The food was better than good. Jonas and I quickly recovered from our fort ordeal.

Over that time, Graham assisted in preparing our coded communication for Mom. But, anticipating that Gina might have set a trap near the pod, we spent a large portion of free time brushing up on our MAC skills.

Well before the meteor strike, the world had revered the MAC Challenge. Graham had set a cavern aside for training.

He shrugged when we questioned him. "I figured that, if anything, these skills might turn out to be useful once our world recovered. Plus, we needed something to boost morale and remind us who we were."

Shortly after breakfast one morning, we rode through the caves and entered the enormous, grassed training ground. Everyone still in the refuge had arrived. Around a hundred men, women and children had climbed steep, rock-chiseled staircases to a high ledge cut into the cavern's rocky wall. Again, Kaleidotonium coated all exposed rock. The 'sun' rose across the eastern sky.

As we entered the cavern, a resounding cheer echoed. Smiling and waving in the way we had always greeted crowds in Petriville, we absorbed the small group's enthusiasm.

Graham announced in an amplified voice, "Since this exercise is to see that you kids haven't lost your touch, it is just for *practice.*" He emphasized the last word, then added, "So you may complete each task one at a time and we'll move onto the next as a group. You are *not* competing today. Do you understand? We need no injuries!"

The small crowd murmured a collective "Aww-w", which Graham ignored before asking, "Who wants the 'kick off'?"

Harriet thrust her bow into the air before anyone else could react. "I can't wait to try this place out." She nocked an arrow.

Harriet was about to undertake a small, non-competitive risk. Regardless, my stomach rolled as both Liam and Jonas gritted their teeth — always strangely protective over her.

"Very well," Graham called, oblivious to our distress. He raised a red flag. "I'm timing you in…three…two…one…GO!"

As Graham dropped the flag, Harriet burst her mare into a gallop. Barely aiming, she neared the first tall stake with a cluster of three red balloons floating loosely above its tip. Almost as soon as she released her arrow, a balloon in the cluster burst before her.

"One," Graham declared. The small crowd clapped and roared.

Harriet nocked a second arrow while galloping toward the next cluster. Here, her arrow pierced two balloons. When she neared the final cluster and let her arrow fly, again, one red balloon burst into a thousand ribbons.

"A total score of four balloons in thirty seconds," Graham yelled enthusiastically as Harriet slowed her mare then returned to us in an easy trot.

I went next and burst five balloons.

Liam shredded six during his turn, while Jonas transformed five into fluttering ribbons.

When Eric urged Warrior into a flat-out gallop, he sent three arrows flying true without a second's pause between. And again. And again.

My mouth dropped as Graham drew his words out in a bellow. "A perfect nine!"

Although Liam, Jonas, Harriet and I consistently hit the mark, it had never been at the speeds or accuracy that Eric achieved. Once, Liam had fired two arrows home in succession.

Finally, breathless, we drew our horses up.

Liam shook his head, bursting out a disbelieving laugh. "Hey dude, hope you don't ever plan on taking up the MAC Challenge in Petriville. You'll ruin our outstanding reputations."

Harriet high-fived Eric. "It's true. You're a lethal marksman. I, for one, wouldn't want to go up against you."

"We haven't reached the climbing or fighting part yet," Jonas muttered.

Eric was ready with a reply. "You're forgetting that my twin brother was a little insane. I had to keep my fighting skills honed just to keep up with him. To add to that, Tao, this brilliant Jujutsu and Kyūdō trainer, lived here with us. He insisted on daily cave wall climbing as part of our strength training." A smile warmed Eric's lips as if he were viewing a fond memory. "Put us through our MAC paces, Tao did. Fighting. Climbing. Archery. Riding. He demanded we perfect each discipline separately, before giving his permission to join them into one sport."

Graham called it, clapping his hands. "Okay, everybody, that's enough for one day. Back to work with you all."

With a half-hearted grumble, the crowd descended the steep staircases and moved back to their work areas in various sections of the caves.

* * * *

Shortly after sunrise the following day, with the newly coded message tucked in Eric's pocket, we readied the horses for our two-day mission.

It felt good to mount Zenobia, press my feet into the stirrup irons, close my legs around her sides, feed the leather reins up between my fingers and receive the soft pull of her mouth as she chewed at the bit. She pawed at the ground, as if anxious to get moving.

Graham had had a single packhorse loaded with one dome and a cage containing three crows, while we carried our food in backpacks.

With Eric leading the packhorse, we headed north to where the river escaped the lake then entered a broad, shallow crossing.

As Zenobia sank and squelched her way through the muddy, knee-high water, she bumped and bounced me around in the saddle.

Following the river, we meandered northwest until the raging torrent entered a narrow rock gorge. In a series of rapids and waterfalls, the water made its mountain descent to the forests and grassland valleys below.

Not much farther, a twisting ravine opened and, turning north into it, we snaked our way down the mountain. I strained my ears, listening for unwanted sounds—though the constant, whooshing river, plunging down the pass to the east, drowned out almost everything else.

Zenobia braced her hindquarters and hamstrings beneath me—straining to balance her body for the sharp descent. Although I leaned back, it didn't seem to help much. Her breathing continued to labor and white, frothy sweat broke out across her body.

Steep walls hemmed us in and unease quickened my pulse. I urged Zenobia up beside Warrior, shaking my head. "Eric, this is the perfect place for an ambush."

"It is," he agreed too quickly—as if he had already considered this, "It's also our only possible place of descent."

I was relieved when, in the early afternoon, we exited the ravine without incident and drifted beneath the sparse base forest.

Not long afterward, we neared the pod. Beside a stream, Eric dismounted Warrior. He stiffened, mounting unease almost palpable. "We'll set the dome up over the water and leave the horses inside then go forward on foot."

Even on foot, the forest ended too soon. The semi-submerged, octagonal monstrosity protruded before us. It jutted unnaturally from the landscape with ominous foreboding. I had only ever seen the inside before and that from the comfort of Mom's office.

"How did you summon the courage to go inside this thing?" Harriet gasped at Eric, seemingly bewildered by the idea.

He shrugged and half-cocked his head, his voice hoarse. "You have to understand. I'd recently lost my brother. And I kind of harbored a bit of a death wish." He shook his head then continued, "Hiding down there in the forest, I was thinking Caleb wouldn't hesitate. He'd just stand up and go in there." He floated his eyes to mine. "It worked out great that I took the chance."

For a time, he kept his focus on me. Then he sighed, blinked and re-centered on the dome. "Let's do this."

Without hesitation, he darted away and, a moment later, disappeared around the encircling rocky embankment. The rest of us sprang into moving. Intending to surround the pod, the others soon faded into the sparse brush.

I drew a breath, wiped my damp palms down my jeans and slipped over the lip. Barely missing its rotation, I ducked inside the camera's perimeter. Half-stumbling against the metal wall of the infamous PQ316T, gooseflesh washed over me. This very structure had been instrumental in my meeting Eric and a vast range of emotions stirred within my gut.

While edging along the outer wall, hairs on my nape bristled with the sense that someone might be observing our every move. I continued creeping along its boundary, my concern mounting. *Where are the others?* Their silence rippled through me.

A loud *thunk* cut that silence. I froze, catching my breath. Something or someone very substantial had fallen.

A moment later, emerging around the next bend, Eric came into view.

I kept my voice low. "What was that? Where are the others?"

He whispered too. "Keep your eyes open, Cassidy, but so far, we've seen only one guard. He's down. Liam's cuffing him. Harriet and Jonas haven't crossed my path. I'm going in, but I'll leave the door open so you can hear the conversation. Let's hope your mom is in her office."

A moment later, Jonas appeared behind me then Harriet joined us. We moved toward the entrance. There, we joined Liam, just as Eric slipped inside.

"Mrs. Jones?" he called. "Are you here?" I sighed with relief that Eric had not called my mother Emily, as according to the coded words, he needed to call her Mrs. Jones later. That mistake would surely have raised Gina's suspicions.

The second Mom stepped into view, I crumbled, but Liam caught me. "Don't, Cassidy." He pulled me against his chest. "Listen to what Mom says. You might hear something relevant only to you."

Mom's voice sounded strained. "Eric? I am so pleased to finally meet you." Since we stood outside the pod and not on the platform, we remained invisible to Mom. But her anguished image shone brightly through the open door.

Still wrapped in Liam's arms, I gulped and choked out a whisper. "I miss her so much."

Liam glanced down at me, mouthing, "I miss her too, sis."

Eric was speaking again. "As am I happy to make your acquaintance, Mrs. Jones. I trust that you and Mr. Jones are both well."

In the coded sentence structure, this one told Mom we were all safe. The relief that flooded her face was clearly evident. But she swallowed and quickly composed herself.

"We are coping, thank you, Eric. Well, no... That is not entirely true. Gina arrested Peter and Roger. She is holding them in the east prison wing."

This was the truth. She had inserted no coded words into that sentence. Now Liam's anguish threatened our concealment. "Hold it together, Li. Please," I begged. His face reddened as he clenched his fists and jaw against the anger straining to erupt.

Harriet had wrapped her arms around Jonas too. He frowned in utter helplessness, giving in to the pure anger gripping his posture.

Harriet arched her brow and softly uttered, "Are you telling me they built a prison now? And it's so big that it's split into wings?"

I bit my lip and squeezed Liam's hand, whispering, "We'll find a way to rescue them, Li."

Mom drew our attention back to her. "Eric, have you received news of our children? We have heard nothing at all. I considered a defect in the pod, but the signal seems fine. If you have not seen them, I cannot imagine where they may have ended up."

Mom added code words into her sentences, as would Eric. I took cognizance of each—this one conveying that Gina was watching, and they couldn't escape the craft.

She waited for him to answer.

"Graham hoped you'd heard something. We've seen neither hide nor hair of them out here. Not a whisper, nor a squeak—not in all this time," he responded on cue, telling Mom that we would have to rely on any forces they could gather as, from Graham's side, it would take several months to round up those who had relocated their families to their own surrounding farms.

She replied, "I searched every pod in the area for signs of them, but my searches revealed nothing, only a few guards and soldiers."

According to the code words, Mom believed they were not in danger, despite our fathers' imprisonment. I looked up at Liam, half mouthing, half whispering, "Why mention 'guards and soldiers'? Is she trying to warn us?"

Since Eric had communicated all the coded messages, he turned, but Mom stopped him. "Eric, if Cassidy reaches you—if you see her—please tell her how I miss our conversations outside my office. Tell her that I took the train to the zoo the other day, for memory's sake. We so enjoyed visiting the horses and the zoo together, her and I. I miss her and Liam so very much. If you see them please tell them all that we love them."

Eric had done it. Mom stepped from the platform. Although I knew to expect it, a gasp burst from my lips when she disappeared before my eyes. As Eric emerged from the pod, not attempting to avoid the outer camera—though we still did—the familiar access click of Mom's office door sent an icy river of chills through my veins.

More than one set of footsteps sounded through the open pod door. A moment later, the familiar voice made me shudder with loathing as Gina stated, "Mrs. Jones, please come with us."

No longer visible to us, Mom spoke for our benefit. "You will find nothing on me, Gina. You cannot hold me."

I launched toward the entrance, but Liam grabbed me around the waist before I reached it, whispering into my cheek while Eric quietly closed the pod door. "You going in there will only make things worse for Mom, Cass."

White-hot rage spread through my veins. "What was that?" I shrieked. "Will she arrest Mom now too? We've accomplished nothing by coming here. In fact, we've only made things worse. And what was she trying to tell us in her last sentence? I know it was something important."

Eric turned and faced me, taking my hands in his. "We have learned things, Cassidy. For one, Gina is back in Petriville. She was probably looking for an excuse to question your mom, anyway. Plus, you heard your mom. Gina can't hold her."

Liam interjected, "About the last sentence, Cass… Don't worry about it. When you're not trying to analyze her words, it will come to you."

Using a fist-sized rock, Eric made sure the unconscious guard would remain that way for some time. He removed the handcuffs and shoved them, along with the keys, into his jeans' pocket.

Finally, looking around, he muttered, "It's best we get out of here."

Chapter Thirty-Nine

Returning to the horses, we broke camp with uneasy tension gripping our small band. Eric scanned our surroundings while he mounted. "Soldiers will be raking this area by morning. We ought to bolt out of this place while there's enough light."

Our well-rested horses willingly trotted and cantered through the grasslands. As shadows lengthened, the nearing mountain pass glowed orange in the late afternoon sun.

But as we neared the snaking ravine, Harriet shot her eyes toward the summit. Her loud gasp ripped our attention to her. "What is that? Please don't—" She broke off in a whimper.

I followed her line of sight to the ravine's distant summit—to the ominous red dust-cloud floating above.

Eric nodded. "And judging by the size of that cloud, it looks like she's sent a pretty decent-sized mob."

He flashed a glance around. A moment later he decided, "We'll continue east."

Liam offered an additional suggestion. "The dome will conceal us if we move into the thicker brush. Anyway," he added, raising his eyes to the clouds rolling in on the eastern horizon, "it looks like it might rain later."

Jonas nodded vigorously. "You may be right, Liam, but just so you know, I'd sooner be dead than go back to that prison."

He threw a glance at me. I winced and blinked for a second but offered no verbal response.

Proceeding east, we met the same river Eric and I had eyed from above, the same snaking blue ribbon that emerged into the ocean beside the craft. We continued our journey beside it. All the while, black clouds drew nearer and nearer until thunder rumbled nearby, urging us to set up camp. We moved into the denser brush and stopped beside a small stream that was buried between two copses of trees. Dismounting, Harriet held Liam's mare while he erected the dome — with one edge skimming the top of the water.

As night and cloud blackened the skies, darkness shrouded the landscape.

Leading the horses through the entrance, we untacked them then piled their saddles, bridles, our luggage and the birdcage on a cluster of rocks.

Only minutes later, large raindrops started thudding against the dome's waterproof outer shield. I cowered from the loud crack and bright lightning that clawed across the dark sky. As the lightning eased, rain fell steadily harder.

After allowing the horses to digest their evening meal, Eric strapped head collars on Warrior and the packhorse. "It's not possible to take them the way we're going. It's best we release them now, while it's raining. If they meet the mob in the ravine, the men won't know which direction the horses came from."

Harriet complained, "But they'll track their hoofprints. And we'll be so slow without the horses that they'll easily catch us. Or worse, they'll follow them to Graham's camp."

"They won't keep up with the free horses, will they, Harri?" Jonas drawled. "And in this rain, we'll all but disappear as far as trackers are concerned."

Harriet shrugged. "Well, what do I know about the do's and don'ts of tracking?"

It was decided and, following Eric, we led our less-than-enthusiastic horses out into the pouring rain. Despite the wet weather — or because of it — the second we removed their halters, they took off in a gallop toward the ravine.

Back beneath the dome, while preparing one of Mom and Megan's dehydrated meals, a deep, shuddering breath grated through my chest. Before I could voice my anguished reflections, Harriet choked the same words that were souring my thoughts. "Our dads are in prison. Prison! How is that even possible?"

Jonas slammed his fist into a rock then shook it out — gritting his teeth. Liam tended to internalize his anger. His pupils had shrunk to pinheads of pure rage.

When Jonas continued flapping out his pained hand, I shook my head. "Let me look at that, you crazy human."

Eric's agitated voice reached me before Jonas responded, "I think he's quite fine, Cassidy."

I ignored him. "Are you okay, Jonas?"

"Of course I'm okay, Cass." With a scowling glance at Eric, he added, "It's obvious that self-inflicted injuries don't count."

My natural sensitivity for Jonas was making things uncomfortable for Eric, but none of this was Jonas' fault. Nothing had changed between him and me. But, when we laid our sleeping bags out for the night, Eric didn't set his beside mine. Instead, he allowed a large gap between us. My heart ached as I zipped myself in and settled back.

For a long while, Eric tossed and turned. His bag made irritating scratching noises—clearly audible above the rain pounding on the dome.

Just when my eyes fluttered toward sleep, a large shadow took form over me.

It produced a loud whisper. "Cassidy...Cassidy, are you awake?"

The sleeping-bag-clad figure took my startled movement as an answer. "What do you think about going back to the craft—"

I cut him off, frowning in horror, "Are you insane, Eric?"

He continued in the same soft tone, as if unaware of my anguish. "But what do you think about it? Let's get your dad out."

I never verbalized my response but took a minute to consider his proposal. Concluding that this was what I wanted more than anything, I looped my arms around his neck and pulled him down to me—reaching for his warm, soft lips.

* * * *

316

What seemed like a moment later, dawn spread its glowing thread across the horizon, drawing me back to consciousness.

Eric still lay beside me, his arm draped over my waist. I snuggled into his embrace and he tightened his grip, pressing his warm body against mine. Our late-night conversation replayed in my mind. I puckered my lips against the small smile forcing its way onto them. "Eric, did you mean what you said last night?"

He chuckled. "Why wouldn't I? Of course, we *should* help your dad escape that place."

After the others arose and while sitting on the grassy ground and enjoying a dried-fruit and nut breakfast, we presented the idea. They offered a few objections but were inclined to follow Eric's lead.

Using a digipar writer, Eric penned a message to Graham. Once the ink had faded, using the writers' back end, he selected Graham's seal. Stamping the old man's credentials into the digipar, Eric rolled and slipped the message inside a small metal ring.

While Liam ambled away to boil water for coffee, Harriet and Jonas drifted into their own conversation. Eric collected the birdcage, dangling it by its metal carrier ring. He lowered it to the ground and sat cross-legged to face me before opening the cage door. Sliding one hand inside, he gently wrapped it around a crow, which he extracted from the cage while using his forearm to block the others from attempting to escape. Then he coaxed the crow to expose its underside and clasped the small metal ring around its leg.

He repeated the procedure with the second and third crows, murmuring in answer to my unasked question, "It's the same message — in case some of the birds don't make it."

He never voiced the words he must have been thinking. They were foremost in my mind — *or if Gina's soldiers shoot any down.*

When he raised his eyes, I bit my lip. "Please tell me the messages are only accessible to Graham's touch."

Apparently distracted, he didn't answer immediately but urged the crow back into its cage then he stretched onto his side, propped himself on his forearm and crossed his feet.

When he finally spoke, he looked up and to the left — his mind still clearly far away. "The message is coded anyway. But yes, it will display only to Graham's fingerprint." Meeting my quizzical frown, he added, "Returning to when we visited the pod… What did your mom mean by adding those extra bits you mentioned?"

"I'm not sure, Eric." I sighed. "I haven't really thought it through yet. Or, at least, I can't work out what she meant."

"Would it help if we discussed the possibilities?" He plucked a long strand of grass then rolled it between his fingers.

I sighed again. "Maybe."

Liam returned with four mugs of coffee, handing us each one, while Harriet and Jonas drifted out of their conversation and turned their focus onto ours.

My gaze returned to Eric. "She mentioned the park outside her office and the train, but I can't begin to guess why she brought the zoo into the equation. We never even went there together."

"Cass" — Liam cocked his head to the side, considering — "Mom never referred to it as '*the park outside her office*', she just said '*outside her office*'. My point is that maybe her choice-of-phrase changes the meaning?" he shot with a questioning lilt.

We spent a while going through various possibilities but nothing helped. I could draw no rational conclusions.

"We've got time," Eric suggested. "It will come to you."

He stood, lifting the birdcage. "Best we release them now. Graham will need time to prepare."

"Prepare how, exactly? What did you tell him?"

"To prepare for battle. Craig will send crows to gather the farmers—a call to arms, if you will. Plus, Graham will need to send us boats and supplies. He and the others will come down later in small groups and meet us at the river mouth."

I scrunched my face in confusion. "But what if the boats go straight past us?"

Eric chuckled. "That wouldn't be great, would it? No, we chained off a section in this eddying pool, so the canoes collect in there—along with a multitude of other debris."

While he carried the cage, I took Eric's coffee mug and followed him outside the dome. Intrigued and bemused, I watched as Eric raised the open cage to the sky. In turn, the crows leaped onto the wire rim then opened their wings and, balancing against the breeze, launched into exuberant flight. They banked toward the south—toward the refuge.

Chapter Forty

We didn't leave camp that day. Besides Graham needing time to pack our canoes and send them downriver for us to retrieve, rain poured for most of it.

Sometime in the afternoon, while I leaned against Eric and he against a rock — both of us reading ancient paperbacks he had brought from the caves — it abruptly slammed into me.

I launched upright, dropping my novel.

Eric raised his eyes from his book and chuckled. "You've got it, haven't you?"

My mouth tugged into a beam. "I think so. My mother and I were on the sidewalk outside her office when I first mentioned the idea of tunnels beneath Petriville. We never went to the zoo together, so I got that part right. She probably threw that in to emphasize conveyor or sector four. That's the focal point. She's trying to tell us that the east prison wing is accessible from somewhere beneath or near the train station."

Hearing my explanation, the others bookmarked their own paperbacks and gathered around.

Liam cocked his head, looking upward as he dubiously contemplated my interpretation. Slowly, he nodded as if to himself. His expression brightened into one of acceptance then agreement.

As usual, he launched his words. "You're right, Cass. You've got it."

* * * *

The following morning, hot, sticky air engulfed us and shrouds of biting insects converged as water evaporated from the sodden ground and swirled with the heat of the scorching sun.

Leaving the tack, the now-empty birdcage and remains of our luggage inside the assembled dome, we tossed our backpacks over our shoulders.

As we exited the dome, I threw a single backward glance at the near-invisible structure. "I hope we'll be okay without its concealment."

Jonas raised his eyebrows. "It didn't prevent *us* from being caught, did it then?"

Considering his words, I gritted my teeth. Then I turned and boulder-hopped the short distance to the river. Still, I couldn't keep my eyes from darting toward every sound.

Eric caught my fearful glances and clasped my hand. "I'm pretty good at sounding out danger, Cassidy. Plus, the mob is so huge that we'd hear them approach."

He dropped my hand and moved north along the edging rocks.

I took in the gorge as it proceeded downstream, rising beside the river — or rather, the flow dropping between the walls. As I stood on the low bank of smooth boulders, the water looked inviting. I lay on my belly and thrust my hand into the cool swirl.

"Ouch!" I jumped up. The rock was cooking my skin. "Ouch," I squealed again, raising my T-shirt and looking down at my reddened stomach. "The water's nice though," I muttered to nobody in particular.

Eric had already jogged upstream along the river's edge and was paying no attention to my groans.

I called to him, "What are you doing, Eric?"

He raised his hand to shield his eyes from the light and peered first upstream then downstream without answering.

I tried again. "Are you looking for the boats? Will they be here already?"

His reply was dismissive at best and he wasn't referring to the boats when he answered, "Here it is!" He gestured to a gap between the rocks before a bend, slightly farther upriver.

Jonas and Liam caught up with him. The three men ran toward the opening. As I followed, Harriet joined me.

The bend was, in fact, a narrow channel that poured into an eddying pond on our side of the river. It filtered out between a gap and over some rocks, back into the main flow. A tree strained against the exit chain and its rock-embedded anchors.

A sizeable rocky mound concealed the grasslands from view. I sighed.

In an apparently practiced maneuver, Eric launched right into the middle of the swirling pool. Seconds later,

Liam and Jonas joined him. They tugged at the ropes, straining against some unseen weight.

Turning to meet Harriet's blank stare, I chuckled. "Graham had these canoes and their canopies built from Kaleidotonium."

"Huh? Wow!" Harriet was, for once, at a loss for words.

From the bank, Harriet and I pulled on the canoes' ropes, while the men shoved from below. It took all our strength, but finally, we managed to heave the laden boats from the water.

Eric reached for what he guessed was the middle of the canoe's canopy. Fiddling for a bit, he wedged his hands between the two sections and drew them apart. The smooth sliding noise seemed oddly out of place — like an audible mime.

Graham had secured several backpacks crammed with food against the hull.

Harriet gasped. "We'll feed an army with all this!" She paused then grimaced, adding, "Maybe that's his intention."

After filling the collapsible buckets with water, Harriet and I drained them over the rocks — impossibly hot to sit on otherwise.

Eric extracted the topmost bundle from one of the canoes then unwrapped and laid it out.

"Fresh bread," Harriet cooed as we sat down beside the bundle.

"An-nd chee-ese." I drew the words out, my mouth watering.

Jonas and Liam also tucked into the sandwiches, but Eric seemed preoccupied with the accompanying note. When I glanced over his shoulder, he didn't withdraw it from my view. I moved around and sat before him, laying my palms on his knees, listening as he read.

"We hope you're enjoying your breakfast. Chef baked the bread this morning. The food and goods you requested are in the backpacks. We will send the next group the day after tomorrow and stagger our parties after that."

The part that had made Eric draw his brows together and had glazed his eyes was what Graham had said next.

"Stay safe, my son. I love you."

He draped his forearms over his knees, lightly holding the digipar between two fingers.

"Eric"—I took his free hand in mine—"I know you're worried about Graham." It wasn't a question. His expression had already told me he was. "I wish I could give you some assurance that he'll be okay." I'd blundered my attempt to ease his concern so added, "Maybe he'll choose not to come."

Jonas chipped in, "Aren't we all worried about our parents then?"

I turned and snapped at him, "Yes, Jonas! Of course, we are. But *we* have not lost *everybody* close to us."

I urged Eric to his feet and led him away from the others. "Ignore him, Eric. Tell me what's going through your mind. Please."

He hesitated, threw a glance at Jonas then turned back to me. "Of course I'm worried, Cassidy. Graham isn't young anymore." He steeled his jaw and blinked a few times, extracting his hands and laying them on his hips.

"I get why you're helping us, Eric, but why must Graham come?"

"As far as he's concerned, this is his fight. Much as I wish he would, there's no way he'll sit back." He shook his head, then continued, "We must stop Gina. Graham wants to help make that happen. She had the knowledge, the time, the funding and the influence to save so many more lives. She could have warned them and helped prevent Earth's populations from such total decimation. She *chose* not to."

"Most of Petriville's citizens don't know what she's done, Eric. I only found any of this out after I met you. They're just going about their lives. They're innocent in this."

"Do you think I don't realize that, Cassidy?" He narrowed his eyes. "Do you think I don't know exactly who's to blame?" He took a breath, angling his face downward. He appeared to drift away, gritting his teeth and shaking his head as though a million thoughts were coursing through his mind. He again took my hand and squeezed softly, raising his aquamarine gaze to me.

In almost a whisper, he went on. "We're doing this for us too, Cassidy — for you and me and all those on the craft whose breeding instructions were laid out to them."

My breath caught at his words.

He glanced at the rocky mound. "It's best we get going. Our luck won't hold out forever."

Beneath the bright blue sky, we prepared for the next part of our journey, dragging the canoes into the river beyond the eddying pool.

"And so it begins," Harriet muttered then rolled her eyes. "Why are we doing this again?"

I was in no mood to engage in her undesired validation but puffed out a laugh anyway as Eric and I boarded our canoe. While waiting for the others to climb in, Eric held on to the edging rock. Together, we moved away. The water instantly gripped our canoes and tugged us out into the middle of the flow.

I thrilled, gripping the double oar in my hands and sliding the long blade into the water. I balanced the rolling motion of my body and flexed my abdomen against the pull. As I raised the oar from the river, water drops showered my head and body.

A definite upside of floating on the river was the cooling effect of the water — or the urge to *accidentally* shower Eric with water from my oar — a gesture that he generously returned.

We paddled only when necessary, more for steering out of the path of upcoming blockages than for propulsion. The fast-flowing current assisted with the hard labor and kept us mostly in the center.

Liam, Jonas and Harriet rode in the less-loaded canoe. Not that I was complaining... I hadn't been alone with Eric for days.

As we rounded a gentle curve, the water churned. "Get to the floor and seal the capsules," Eric sang like a ship's captain. "There's a small set of rapids ahead. It's not likely that we'll capsize, but the moisture will spoil the food if we do."

Dropping to the base, I slid the cover from the groove in one lip of the canoe while Liam did the same with theirs. Although they didn't have as much food in their canoe as Eric and I had, they did have some. Our canopy glided over and down, sucking into the opposite groove as it touched. The rapids were mild bumps and over too quickly for us to enjoy any alone time. Too soon, we reopened the cover and slid it back into its groove.

"You've been on this river before?" I phrased it as a question.

"Only once. Actually, it was just after the last time we spoke in the pod."

By mid-afternoon, the gorge became broader and steeper. Sheer cliffs of shiny black rock extended upward on either side.

The shimmering, smooth, increasing current tugged us forward, as if goading us toward our goal. I cocked my ear, listening. My stomach flipped and my hands shook. Every sound echoed through the cavernous space.

"Hey, Liam." Eric's voice reverberated through the silence, sounding way too relaxed, "Do you see that bend ahead?" He continued without waiting for Liam's reply, "When I say, 'keep to the left', it means, at all costs. A waterfall is just beyond it. It's a big one. Do. Not. Go. Over!" He emphasized each word, then muttered, "It will be the last thing you do."

I bolted upright and shrieked, "Waterfall? What waterfall?"

But Eric was still speaking. "Keep your canopy collapsed and row for your lives."

Chapter Forty-One

We reached the bend much faster than I had expected. The twisting sensation in my gut turned to sheer terror. Eric's strength outmatched mine. But as we edged around the bend, hugging the left cliff face, I pulled with every bit of power I could muster. Despite the cool drops of oared water as we battled the current's assault, sweat beads gathered on my brow. The thunder intensified, escalating into a deafening roar — an inescapable death trap. I poured all my strength into helping Eric keep our canoe against the silky, blackened cliff face.

But in the blink of an eye, the fast-flowing river wrenched Liam, Jonas and Harriet's boat from the edge. As we exited the bend, their canoe surged forward, right into the middle of the raging river. A V-shaped split divided the gorge in two — the calm water on the left and the disappearing river on the right. The waterfall lay *straight ahead* of their canoe.

"Pull!" Eric yelled at the same time that I shrieked, "No!"

Eric reacted in milliseconds. "Cassidy, hold us here."

He dropped his oar and lifted a coiled rope. Leaving me alone to battle the current, he lassoed it toward their canoe. The increased drag from the loss of Eric's strength instantly jerked at our boat.

Panic escaped my constricted throat as a hoarse choke. "How will they catch the rope?"

They were thrusting their oars into the water but gaining little ground.

"They have no free hands," I screeched, then "Liam!" burst through my lips.

I strained to keep our canoe in position—thoughts of the worst possible outcome repeating in my head. Liam, Jonas and Harriet were focused on rowing. Nobody caught Eric's lasso. It slid away from the canoe back into the dark water. Quickly hauling it in, Eric recoiled then tossed it again, calling out as he did. Harriet glanced up and dropped her oar to the bottom of their boat then clutched at the flying coils. They were losing ground against the strong pull of the waterfall. In frenzied haste, Harriet tied the rope to a crossbar then snatched up her oar and resumed rowing against the current. The weight and force behind their canoe jerked at ours—pulling it toward the faster flow.

"Eric"—I strained—"I can't...hold it...on my own."

"Just a moment more," he encouraged.

He tied our end down—tensioning it before he dropped to the bench, grabbed his oar and plunged it into the water. Their canoe was too near the waterfall's edge and gripped by the strong current. As hard as we pulled, the waterfall pulled harder. The absolute awareness struck me hard. It was now or never. Nobody had to tell us to row for our lives. Instinct and adrenaline took care of that. With renewed vigor, I heaved with every ounce of strength I possessed. Sweat poured from my body, my muscles screaming their protest and my energy waning.

For long, fretful minutes, we strained.

When their canoe finally sprang free of the strong current, the difference was as night was to day. It raced toward ours at an alarming speed. Eric and I almost overbalanced our canoe, but thankfully we only landed in a heap on the floor — with Eric on top.

"Well, that almost ended very badly," I mused aloud as I lay squashed beneath him.

He grimaced and scrambled off. "Sorry about that." He reached down and helped me up. "You okay?"

I raised my eyebrows and moved toward the bench, collapsing onto it. "Mm-m," I answered, non-committally. My mind wasn't on our tumble to the canoe base, though. Eric's familiar smoky vanilla scent had drawn it elsewhere.

"Sorry," he repeated.

The glossy black rock of the fork now separated us from the waterfall. The augite muffled the thundering rush of the continuously tumbling water.

Ahead, the inlet collided with a flat, pebbled area — a beach of sorts — and a blackened cliff-face backdrop. With one final burst of speed, we propelled the canoes at least part of the way out of the river.

Exhausted from the strenuous fight against the current, I dragged myself from the canoe and collapsed to my back — sprawling out over the small round pebbles. I was vaguely aware of Eric flopping down beside me, with Jonas, Harriet and Liam on my far side.

Eric laced his fingers through mine as I gazed up between the towering rock walls, still panting. A few higher clouds flitted over the gap, while puffy white ones floated lazily — starkly contrasting the bright blue backdrop. A hypnotic trance gripped my exhausted body and my eyelids drooped.

I was just drifting off when Jonas' voice startled me. Not his voice, exactly, but the fact that he spoke to Eric — asked him a question — used his name. "Hey, Eric… That split in the cliff face, back there. Does it lead anywhere then? Or do you know another way out of here?" In a way, he answered his own question. "The apparent alternatives are not at all appealing — over the waterfall or up the cliff." He chuckled at his joke.

I dropped Eric's hand and heaved myself into a seated position. Liam and Harriet, on the far side of Jonas, were sleeping, their chests rising and falling with every slow, heavy breath.

I pulled my legs to my chest and twisted, following Jonas' line of sight to a split in the back cliff face — about a quarter of its height.

Eric, still lying on his back, mumbled, "It does."

His stomach muscles contracted as he lifted to one forearm and twisted in Jonas' direction. But he said nothing, just leaned forward and plucked a blade of grass that peeked out from between the stones. Still giving no reply, he returned to resting and crossed one foot over the other, twirling the blade of grass between his fingers.

As Jonas waited for a more detailed explanation, he rolled his eyes at Eric's half-hearted lack of communication.

Eric was clearly not done. He was just taking his time. With his gaze on the water ahead of him, he continued working the grass between his fingers. "It cuts through the ridge and comes out on the other side, beside the waterfall. The descent on the far side is steep, so it's best we rest up tonight."

Was Eric's nonchalant response some masculine display of dominance? Jonas didn't deserve that.

I selected a few small pebbles and tossed them lightly onto Eric. He followed them with his eyes as they trickled off his rigid stomach muscles. He rotated his head toward me, with a semi-suppressed grin pursing his lips.

I cocked and eye and mouthed, "Not nice."

"Sorry," he soundlessly replied, though he didn't look very sorry at all—his vague attempt at hiding his smile was decidedly less than successful.

A moment later it fell away, and as he stared into the distance, he grimaced.

I stood. "Walk with me, Eric?"

Taking my hand, he clambered to his feet, but neither of us missed the twisted smile Jonas threw him.

Eric said nothing as he turned away and wrapped his arm around my shoulder, drawing me against his side. No smile made its way back onto his mouth as we walked, but he gripped me against his warm body. "Caleb and I used to rag each other in almost exactly the same way. It's strange that I make that connection with Jonas, of all people."

The thought brought a smile to my lips. "Maybe Jonas would like that, Eric. Would you mind if I tell him sometime?"

Eric gave a noncommittal shrug. "It's your choice."

As we continued to amble along the pebbled beach, our bond seemed somehow reinforced—strengthened—if that were even possible.

Chapter Forty-Two

Later that evening, barefoot and shirtless, Eric, Liam and Jonas dragged the canoes up the rocky beach and into the split in the back cliff face, which Eric had told us was a tunnel to the other side. Harriet and I heated stew from the stores then divided that and the remaining chunks of the morning's bread between the five plates.

Harriet and I ate while sitting on a rock near the fire. The men took their plates to the water's edge and sat on the pebbles — skimming stones across the smooth surface while they ate. Ringed ripples formed around each skipping pebble, taking my mind into a kind of mesmerized melancholy. They murmured and chuckled among themselves, Eric and Jonas even sharing a few light jokes. About to comment on their behavior, I turned to see Harriet widening her smile, her cheeks softly denting.

"I was just reminiscing about our first meeting. We were so young and innocent then." Her smile faded. "So much has changed."

"We were," I agreed. "And it has. Who knew you and Liam would end up together?"

Harriet gave me a warped smile and raised one eyebrow. "Really, Cassidy? You cannot tell me you never noticed."

I frowned. "You were like not even four years old."

As she threw her head back, a warm tinkling laugh burst from her lips. "What? Four-year-olds have crushes too."

I laughed. "Crushes don't last for almost fourteen years."

The smile dropped from her face. "Mine did."

For a moment, Liam stopped skimming pebbles and turned, biting his lip.

She fluttered her fingers in response. "Strange, I know. But it was always Liam, right from the get-go."

Liam abandoned his post and, still biting his lip, strolled toward Harriet, catching her in a one-armed hug. "Hey, babe" — he smiled mischievously — "let's get some shut-eye." And he half carried her through the cave entrance.

I joined Eric and Jonas at the water's edge, sitting with their arms looped around folded legs.

I stood between them, tired of being conscious of my proximity to Eric whenever Jonas was near, yet so much compassion flowed through me for my friend.

Eventually, I did the right thing and dropped beside Eric. "It's nice to see you two getting on."

Jonas turned his eyes on me. "Small talk is not getting on."

Eric gave a snigger. "M-mph!"

"Seriously, you two! This" — I gestured between them with my finger — "is not okay."

They both fixed their eyes on me.

I felt emboldened to continue. "Jonas, I know you think Eric is not good enough for me but you're wrong. And if you gave him a chance and got to know him a bit better, you'd see that too. Plus, I want to make something very clear. I find it insulting that you think me incapable of making decisions for my *own* life." I emphasized 'own'.

Jonas dropped his attention to the pebbles between his legs, but I continued, "Don't feel bad, Jonas. You know I love you with all my heart."

Now Eric stiffened.

Still, I continued, lowering my voice into a gentle murmur, "But you know how I feel about Eric."

As Eric relaxed, Jonas turned his gaze back on me. He gave a single, almost imperceptible nod.

With that, it did not become one of those evenings of skulking around trying to avoid Jonas, nor did it become a night of exuberantly flaunting our urges in front of him.

As I cuddled up to Eric, he laid his hand lightly on my knee. Together we watched the moonlight dancing across the water.

"Hey, Jonas," Eric murmured, "Sorry about before. You and Cassidy have something that takes time to build. It makes me a bit envious, I guess."

"I get it," Jonas muttered, his voice strained. "It's just—" He broke off and stood. "I'll be okay." He met my gape straight-on. "I won't get in the way of your happiness, Cassidy. And even if I trust your judgment, I still think he's hiding something."

Then he turned and strolled toward the cave entrance, leaving his words hanging in the air.

I rotated back toward Eric. A flash of dark anger pierced his eyes before he broke into an uncertain smile.

I ignored Jonas' jibe. He was probably concocting something from nothing. "Thanks for being kind to him, Eric."

Before answering, he shook his head and cleared his throat. "I can see how important he is to you. Not that I much like it..." he drawled, "but it appears I'll have to get used to it.

He smiled softly before lilting with surprise, "Cassidy, you're shivering. Come here."

In one quick motion, he lifted and moved me between his knees, wrapping his arms around me as I leaned back against his warm body. His stubble-dusted cheek scratched my skin. It was nice, as was his warm breath feathering the side of my neck.

"I'm just not used to Earth's fluctuating weather, Eric. Temperatures on the craft never changed that much from day to night." I paused. "Well, at least not while we were away from Earth."

As we drifted into silence, vague awareness seeped into me — the muffled waterfall, chirping night beetles, croaking toads, swirling river.

Eric whispered against my cheek, "My life hasn't been the same since I met you, Cassidy. From the first moment, I knew you would always be important to me — more than important. I'd go to any lengths to keep you safe. You know that, right?" He fell silent then asked softly, "Do you remember the day we met?"

"How could I ever forget, Eric?" I half-turned toward him. "My life hasn't been the same either. Not since then."

As he lay back on the pebbles, I twisted toward him. He lowered my body over his. My eyes slipped closed. He whispered against my forehead then touched the tip of my nose with his lips, his soft, moist, warmth reaching for my mouth.

The smooth pebbles ground together as they gave way beneath us. As he parted my lips with his tongue, his knee slipped between mine. I gasped. The sweet taste of his kiss sparked the familiar magnetic yearning. I wound my fingers into his thick hair as he smoothed the skin on my cheek with his thumb then traced the outline of my lips.

Heavy footsteps tramping over gravel alerted us. We both looked up the beach.

"Yo, you two! Are you going to spend the whole night out here?" It was Liam, being a typical brother.

I rolled my eyes. "I am almost eighteen, you know." I groaned. "Nearly the same age as Harriet." Both men laughed as Eric pulled me to my feet. Liam dropped his head — perhaps a little chagrined.

Chapter Forty-Three

"Are you sure we've come the right way, Eric?" I blinked as we emerged from the tunnel into the bright light of morning.

We stood on a narrow ledge, facing a precarious, overgrown slope. The unrelenting, thunderous boom of the waterfall coursed over the ebony-bouldered ridge. We couldn't go that way.

Neither could we go back the way we had come — dragging the heavy canoes from the beach alcove through the blackened rock tunnel. Only cliff faces remained — the one before us, a sheer descent, the one behind, an overhang that loomed above, shadowing us.

I stood above the precipice, uncertain — unable to discern a visible escape in any direction.

I should have known Eric wouldn't have made that mistake. As he observed my quizzical expression, a mischievous smile played at the corner of his mouth. It quickened my pulse into a rhythmic gallop.

He didn't exactly answer my question but called above the roaring water, "We'll lower the canoes to the river from up there." He gestured toward the summit of the ridge as he climbed, adding, "With the winches Graham sent."

Jonas followed Eric up the ridge. "Well, that answers the question about the boats." He growled. "But how are we supposed to get down there, then?"

I followed Eric's line of sight and grasped his intentions as Harriet threw her hands up. "I'm not climbing down there." She locked her eyes on the dreaded descent, her forehead furrowed. "It's seriously steep and much higher than anything we climbed in the MAC Challenge."

The prospect of descending the sharp gradient made my gut twist.

"It's not as difficult as it looks," Eric encouraged then continued musing. "We'll just need a solid anchor up here."

He skittered his eyes over the top of the ridge as he pushed at the boulders with his feet — testing for stability.

Liam had also followed Eric and Jonas up the rocky knoll and stood on a wet rock pinnacle — much closer to the edge than either Harriet or I were comfortable with.

"Liam!" Harriet begged. "Get down from there. Please."

"This one feels solid," Liam called out.

Not that Liam ignored her. He just didn't seem to comprehend or agree that he was in any danger. Eric was moving toward the hazardous wet rock with the winches and ropes.

After securing the device, they joined us at the tunnel's exit.

Tying a rope around a nearby tree, Eric tossed the other end far down the rocky face — over and between boulders, brush and trees.

"Use these to protect your hands against rope burn," he instructed, handing us strips of leather — as if that was all the information we needed to conquer the hazardous descent.

I wanted to protest — ask him to suggest a simpler alternative. Maybe, using the winches, he could lower us inside the canoes.

He was still giving instructions. "When you reach the bottom, go back to the river and find the first inlet. I'll slacken the lines until the canoes reach you."

Eric seemed quite confident about managing this colossal task, but he had clearly not considered everything. "How will you get down, once you've untied the ropes?" I frowned.

"Don't worry about me." He puffed out a chuckle. "I've done it before."

When my expression didn't change, he threw his sweaty arm around my shoulder and squeezed. "It's not that bad. You guys go ahead and abseil down the slope. In a bit, I'll be joining you."

He helped me wrap the leather strips around my hands. But as he was finishing, he lifted his gaze. "Now you be careful, Cassidy," he murmured, lifting my chin with his fingers. "Okay, babe?" My heart fluttered as he lowered and touched his soft lips to mine.

Nobody else's lightest touch had ever before caused such emotion to surge through me, had made my eyes prick with tears or had made my heart race when whispering my name.

"I'll be careful," I promised, "if you are too."

He turned, biting his lip as he tied the winch rope to the first of the canoes before bounding up the ridge.

Liam went down first, not precisely abseiling — we didn't have the equipment for that — but all things considered, he moved reasonably quickly down the steep slope. That gave me a small amount of confidence for my turn. Jonas helped Harriet to start, while Liam guided her from below. "Go safely." I winced as she lowered herself.

My stomach pitched and dove as I looped the rope around one bound hand and gripped it with the other.

"You'll be fine, "Jonas encouraged. "Just keep moving slowly."

"Thanks," I muttered through gritted teeth — not feeling so sure anymore.

I steadied my feet and found my balance. In moments, I was easing down the steep descent, passing trees and boulders — and slipping in the black mud...twice. By the time I reached the base, I was laughing, exhilarated by the adrenaline surge. My skin and clothes were all the same shade of black with barely any difference between them.

Liam clapped his hand on my shoulder. "You need a bath, sis." He looked no better himself.

Harriet was still grinning broadly. "How much fun was that?"

I turned to watch Jonas make the descent. "So super cool! I almost want to go again."

When Jonas reached us, a layer of the same black mud covered his clothes and skin.

Liam never hesitated. "Let's find the canoes."

He jogged off toward the edge of the river in search of the inlet.

The winch ropes bounced and jerked strangely above the water as the almost invisible, capsular canoes bucked and tugged against their lines — trying their utmost to follow the fast-flowing current.

We secured the canoes to boulders, using several ropes. Jonas signaled the all-clear to Eric.

My breath caught as our eyes met. Standing on the ridge beside the waterfall, he looked statuesque against the blackened cliffs. I shivered as a sense of dread overcame me. Would I lose him before the end of this? Lose him to Gina's treachery? As I contemplated the real possibility that Gina might kill him, I crumbled inside. My will, my strength, my everything dissolved into a thousand fragments.

Eric packed the winches and ropes into a backpack. While wrapping the leather strips around his hands, he boulder-hopped down the ridge toward the slope — as sure-footed as a mountain goat.

Distracted as I was, I turned to see Liam, Jonas and Harriet already striding back to the abseil base. I had to jog to catch up to them. When we reached it, I couldn't comprehend how Eric would conquer the steep descent.

I peered between the trees and boulders toward the top of the slope as Eric untied the rope we had used. Looping it around the tree, he wound the short end several times around one leather-bound hand. After wrapping the long piece once over the other hand, he backed down the slope, allowing its length to feed through while he glided past trees and boulders.

In no time, he was throwing his mud-covered arms around me, while Liam retracted and coiled the rope.

"See?" Eric smiled. "It was no problem at all."

We returned to the river and floated the canoes to a calmer pool — or at least, hanging onto the ropes, the boats dragged us along the rocky bank until we reached the quieter flow. Beneath us, the gorge grew higher, steeper and narrower, but Eric didn't seem discouraged.

Wasting no time, he tossed his backpack at Liam and yelled, "Hang onto that, won't you, bro."

He launched over the edge in a dive to the river—barely missing the canoes.

I gaped at his entry point, holding my breath as I waited. After what seemed like forever, his head popped through the surface. I expelled my air in a loud gasp.

In dog-like fashion, he shook the water from his head then raised an eyebrow at me, a wry smile twisting his lips. I threw him a half-facetious scowl.

After Eric secured the canoe ropes to rocks protruding from a broad lip at the water's edge, he clambered onto the shelf. Holding his hands up, he caught the backpack that Liam tossed.

Liam didn't wait long. He followed the bag after only seconds, with Jonas right behind him.

"You ready, Cass? Let's do this." Harriet grinned her dimpled smile.

As Liam and Jonas reached Eric on the rocky bank, I clasped her hand in mine and closed my eyes. "I'm sure this is not the last crazy stunt we'll perform. What do you think, Harri?"

She giggled. "And we'll get this mud off in the process."

Then, feet first, we leaped—sinking deep into the water.

Chapter Forty-Four

As the afternoon wore on and we drifted farther downriver, Eric often furrowed his brows and turned intense eyes skyward.

Dense, dark storm clouds roiled and rolled in the east, their volume increasing as they neared.

My stomach pitched. Until now, none of Earth's strange weather had made Eric worried.

Liam had observed Eric's concerned glances too. "Is this storm a threat to us on the water?"

More to himself than to Liam, Eric muttered, "The possibility of flash floods is concerning me."

He looked to the river's edge and apparently decided. Hand-gesturing for the others to follow, he oared toward the gorge wall and sided the canoe up against a broad ledge.

As the others pulled up behind us, Eric again drifted his gaze to the sky. "This one looks mean. Jonas, grab that hammer and the grappling hooks from under your seat — we'll secure the canoes to the gorge wall."

Jonas extracted a pouch and drawled, "So we're sleeping exactly where, then?"

Eric squished his brows at the obvious but answered anyway. "In the boats…use nooks on the ledge for ablutions, if need be." As Liam placed a grappling hook against the rock, Eric added, "You may want to set that higher. The top of that ledge should do. Water may rise and get rough tonight. A few solid anchors should keep us secure enough."

After making separate ablution escapes, we returned to the boats.

Just as we began our simple meal of dried fruit, nuts, cheese and crackers, the first large raindrops pelted the river.

Harriet threw me a sidelong grin as we prepared to seal the canoe capsule. "Aren't you two the lucky ones. A whole canoe to yourselves."

I rolled my eyes at her observation. "With you lot right beside us, I doubt we'll have much privacy."

Anyway, exhaustion gripped me and, lying on Eric's chest, I crashed into a deep sleep.

* * * *

We woke to a dawn without sun and heavy gray clouds hanging ominously low in the sky. Rain had poured for most of the night. The waterline now lapped over the ledge. After breakfast—an unidentifiable cereal mix, Eric prepared to extract the grappling hooks.

"Wait." Liam held up his hand, drawing Eric's attention. "This fog is so thick that we can barely see the other side of the gorge. If we get separated in this, we'll lose each other, for sure."

"Plus, we can't exactly call out. You never know who might hear," Harriet added without pause, completing his sentence.

Jonas attempted to flatten his puffy lips. "So, we join canoes then...*obviously*," he drawled the last word.

"But this couldn't be better." Harriet shot her head up. "Think about it. If we can't see anything, nothing can see us."

I rolled my eyes. "I don't know why that doesn't make me feel any better about traveling blind."

Nevertheless, after observing Jonas' suggestion of tethering the canoes, Eric and Jonas extracted the grappling hooks from the gorge wall.

The fog was so thick that while we floated downriver, at times the dense cloud shrouded both blackened cliffs and amplified every sound.

Something *was* out there.

"Listen!" I blurted, cocking my ear. "Is it only me or does anyone else hear that thump, thump?"

Harriet opened her bright blue eyes. "Yes! What is it?"

Slowly, our boats drifted onward. The noise grew louder then louder still until, on the far bank, an ominous shadow emerged through the heavy mist. My stomach tightened and I squinted to focus. How quickly my unease turned to anguish. A machine protruded through the fog with a large pipe descending into the water.

Alarm stung Eric's voice. "That's an antiquated irrigation pump."

Liam crimped his brow with curiosity more than concern. "But who the hell could be using it? We should stop and check it out."

"No!" Harriet and I chorused.

But Jonas nodded. "I agree with Liam. We probably should."

Eric stared contemplatively upward then murmured, "A family in the refuge mentioned their farm was along the river. Maybe it's them—come home. We could check it out tomorrow. It's best we set base first. That's not far from here."

Only half-heartedly attempting to cover the wry twisting of his lips, Eric winked at me. "In the meantime, we'll close the canopies against prying eyes."

Concealed, the low capsular roof forced us down to the thick canvas-covered base. Eric and I lay alone—without exhaustion forcing us into instant unconsciousness.

I rested my head on Eric's shoulder, the choppy water coaxing me into torpor as the canoe drifted with the current.

Seemingly a million miles from anybody, Eric bit his lip then whispered into my cheek, "Wow. Finally, I have you to myself."

"Hey, you guys"—Liam assumed his father-like voice again—"we can hear every word, you know?"

Eric burst into an unquenchable guffaw, though he tried to suppress it—or at least keep it soft.

"Shh," I whispered, "we don't know how sound carries out here. Plus, you're jiggling the entire canoe."

He was trying, shaking with the effort. Now Liam or Jonas' suppressed laughter arose from the other boat.

Eric's bouncing ribcage got me giggling—a giggle that soon augmented into a belly laugh. I hugged myself, curling up against the effort of suppressing my laughter.

"I think we have some hysteria going on here," Harriet sang in a cackling whisper. "Just saying."

"Mm-m," I agreed, and our laughter dwindled, though a warm ache had spread through my stomach.

Eric slid his arm around me, coaxing my head into the curve of his shoulder. He tucked my hair back, tracing the outline of my jaw with his thumb. I drew slightly back as he pulled his mouth into a line, neither soft, hard nor expressionless. He tilted his head and parted his lips. I met his serene eyes. He didn't say the words out loud or even in a whisper — knowing the others were listening, but I lip-read as he mouthed, "You, Cassidy Jones, I will love forever."

My chest crushed as if in a vise. Heat exploded through my body and I couldn't open my mouth to respond. Although I wanted to tell Eric that every part of me loved every part of him, no words came, only tears. They filled my eyes and ran down my cheeks.

Eric pulled back — observing me. Softly, he wiped at the wet drops with his thumb. He pressed his lips to my forehead then raised my chin with his fingers, his lips so warm, so gentle as he kissed the tears from my eyes.

Then his mouth was on mine, his kiss slow, deliberate. When I gasped, he pulled back. I reached up for more, touching my mouth to his as his tongue teased my lips apart. Our kiss flickered, swayed, leading us into a single, perfect moment in time.

"You're my world, my beautiful Cassidy," he whispered so softly that I could barely hear. As he pulled back, his voice caught. "It's still hard to believe you're in my arms. No matter how this turns out, I'll consider myself the luckiest man alive."

Although Liam might have heard that last comment, my big brother didn't respond. Perhaps he'd begun to understand — to comprehend how I felt about Eric and how Eric felt about me. This was not a fleeting moment for either of us.

I pondered our futures, not only Eric's and mine but everyone's prospects. What if Gina harmed this man who had become my reason for breathing? Life had already stolen so much from him that I couldn't bear it if she took more.

Eric cut into my thoughts. "They're very quiet out there." He propped onto his forearm and peered at the other canoe, his brows twitching. "They are still attached to us."

He called to them, "You guys okay?"

"We're still here," Harriet whispered back, lazily. "Not going anywhere."

Eric glanced around at our surroundings then slid the cover open. Liam followed suit as Eric moved to the bench and started rowing.

A few minutes later, Eric gestured to a ledge just above the waterline. Then he moved his hand upward to a second broad lip and farther to a fair-sized cavity that pierced the rock face.

"That's our home." Eric chuckled. "I knew the cave was around here."

After securing the canoes to the gorge wall, we scaled the short, steep cliff.

Liam arched a brow when he stood at the entrance. "This floor is so smooth that it almost looks machine-made."

Eric grinned. "Centuries of water run-off probably did that. It's a water chute — maybe even hundreds of thousands of years old. A little up north it exits right at the ocean."

The tunnel was large enough that Eric and I could easily stand upright and abreast.

The walls — at least up to mid-way — were as black and smooth as the floor.

From our many days of unrelenting toil, fatigue finally gripped me. I collapsed back against the wall and, sliding to the floor, gazed at a bright rainbow forming across the now-clearing afternoon sky.

Harriet dropped beside me and rolled her head along the wall to meet my distant expression. Saying nothing, she too turned toward the rainbow.

Liam clearly still had way too much energy and tossed a rope at us. "Make sure it's strong."

I glanced down at the coils, laying over our laps and side-muttered to Harriet, "At least this is a task we can accomplish sitting down."

As we began building the rope ladder, Eric, Liam and Jonas hauled the canoe stores into the cave — packing them out in one of the many offshoots from the main tunnel.

While Harriet coiled each rung separately, with a loop on both ends, I started on the main structure. Folding a second rope in half and leaving a gap in between, I knotted two loops at the top. Then I assisted Harriet with the rungs. Finally, we spaced and affixed each tread onto the main rope.

Scrutinizing our handiwork, Harriet commented, "Who would have thought? In one day we found two real-world uses for our MAC training?"

Securing the ladder with grappling hooks, we threw it out over the river.

I let out a "whoop, whoop," as it reached the bottom of two ledges — just above the waterline.

"Who wants first try?" I called to the men.

Without hesitation, Liam chuckled. "She who builds it, tests it."

Chapter Forty-Five

We had spent most of the previous day, the day after our arrival, planning a course of action. Since none of the men wanted Harriet and me alone together, we had finally agreed that Liam and Harriet would wait for the others. Eric, Jonas and I were to head to the river's edge and scout the outside of the craft for activity and to investigate the source of the irrigation pump.

Now, as we stood on the broad lip at the river's edge, Liam clenched his fists, his brows drawn.

I lifted his hand and loosened his fingers. "Don't look so worried, Li."

Liam slid his arm around my shoulders, and grimaced. "I really didn't want to leave you again, Cass. It's like my not being there is the worst kind of betrayal."

As he wrist-rubbed the bridge of his nose, I met his shimmering green eyes. "I can take care of myself."

It was the wrong thing to say.

He snapped, "Like the last time?" A deep sigh shuddered through his chest. "Look… I know you'll be more careful this time, but it doesn't make me feel any better." He paused, gritting his teeth as he whispered, "I can't lose you, Cass."

"What makes you think I won't worry about you, Li?" My eyes fell to the pebbles I rolled beneath my shoe. "Please don't get complacent." Again, I lifted to his gaze. "You never know who might use this river."

While Liam and Harriet held the boat steady against the bank, Jonas moved to the back seat, Eric to the middle and, balancing against the rocking motion, I dropped to the front.

I lifted the long, double-bladed oar and curled my fingers around the shaft, testing its weight.

Finally, I smiled up at Liam. "I'm ready for this, Li. I love you with all my heart."

My brother ground his teeth, shaking his head.

While Harriet kept the boat stationary, Liam attached one end of the coiled rope to the canoe and the other to an underwater grappling hook before dropping the coils beneath Jonas' seat.

As we moved away, I twisted back. Tears were trickling from Harriet's eyes. Liam pulled her against him, wrapping her in his arms as they watched.

The most acute sense of fear gripped my throat as we rounded the first bend — anguish worse than any I had ever experienced. So many people depended on us — most I had never met.

Ignoring the tears pricking my eyes, I focused on the double oar gripped in my hands — the resistance and release of the river as the blade entered or broke free of the surface.

Gently, we meandered toward the ocean. The rope coils unraveled, dropping into the water behind the canoe as if to hold a memory in place. Dark smudges rippled across the surface where the gorge ridge cast its shadows—a stark contrast to the glittering patches of the early morning sun, kissing the water. As it mingled with the ocean inflow, the current grew weaker.

No fog hid us today. As we drew nearer the beach, the gorge walls lost their protective height. Our strokes slowed as the menacing protrusion filtered through the soft morning mist. As the monstrosity of the craft grew into the foreground and stole all else from view, my stomach twisted. It towered above us, dominating everything around it. I didn't notice my pulse quickening—not until it thudded against my chest. Then the pounding was everywhere—in my ears, in my head, consuming my mind. Perspiration covered my skin, my body trembling.

Eric brought me from my daze. Sitting back on his heels behind me, he closed his arms around my waist and lifted me onto his thighs—pulling me against him.

"Hey babe," he whispered, his lips against my ear, his warm breath feathering my neck, "you're shaking so much."

"What are we doing, Eric?" I croaked. "We are so insignificant against this. How do we make headway against her...her tyranny?"

"We can do it, Cassidy. You're so much stronger than you know. Look at what you've already accomplished"—his voice quivered—"what you've already been through."

I turned, fixing on Jonas. He stared trancelike at the craft—impassively taking in the massive structure that swallowed the horizon from view.

"Let's stop here," Jonas choked, gesturing to a small overhang in the waning gorge.

Eric twisted back, compassion smoothing his voice. "Are you okay, bro?"

Jonas slowly swung his head from side to side. "I'm thinking about my and Cassidy's dads. It's a hell of a thing, this."

"That it sure is," Eric agreed.

The sound of crashing waves grew louder than the swirling river. Ahead, the gorge flattened and river broadened. Rock no longer built the banks, but reed-overrun earth created a bog-like edge. The reeds gave way to littered sea-sand, scattered with broken shells, seaweed, water-blackened twigs and even the occasional gray tree trunk. More than a few albatrosses swooped and dived into the ocean or glided in for beach landings. Brine and fish scented the air. I had not discerned this fragrance when we had left the craft.

I shook my head and turned away.

After securing the front and back ends of the canoe, we clambered up the low, rocky bank and lay flat. Jonas leaned over the edge and closed the canoe cover.

Again, the craft drew my attention. A third extended north past the lagoon—curling away so far from the beach that the northernmost point was a distant ocean haze. Where the arc neared the sand, the depth of its shadow grew, completely blocking the morning sun from view.

In the distant south, the craft extended over the beach and into the forest beyond. This was only one-quarter. It was as if an entire metallic planet had compacted and flattened to Earth.

"Jonas," Eric asked, "do you mind staying with the canoe? It's a good vantage point to signal from if you see something we don't."

"No problem." Jonas nodded amiably, appearing to really mean it. "Just make sure you stay in my line of sight."

Concealed from the craft, behind the dunes, Eric and I crept low over the grassy beach sand, sporadically glancing over our shoulders to return Jonas' 'okay' signals.

A quizzical frown made its way onto my forehead. "Eric, what if there are surveillance cameras?"

Eric shook his head. "If that's the case, she probably already has eyes on us. It's a chance we'll have to take."

When we reached the first of the sandy dunes and concealed ourselves among shrubbery, I turned for the umpteenth time, responding to Jonas' 'okay' signal.

Eric handed me the binoculars. "Can you see the elevator from here?"

Propping onto my elbows, I raised the binoculars to my eyes, scanning the perimeter of the craft. It was like an entire lifetime had elapsed since we had descended in that elevator. Less than a few months had passed, though.

"There it is!" I shoved the binoculars into Eric's hand. "Do you see it?" I gestured, directing his line of sight.

While Eric trained the binoculars on the elevator shaft, I turned back to Jonas for yet another practiced visual confirmation. There was nothing routine about this one. Jonas was gesticulating so wildly that he appeared to consider jumping up and running to us.

"Eric," I whispered sharply, shoving my hand toward Jonas.

He followed my gesturing hand with his gaze. We both tracked Jonas' crazed directing.

"Get over here," Eric whispered sharply, "over the ridge."

"But—" I hesitated.

"Yes," he whispered hoarsely. "It makes us visible from the craft. There's nothing for it now. Come quick!"

He jerked my hand, almost dragging me over the top of the ridge. We turned to face whatever onslaught approached.

If not for me seeing Jonas' warning and Eric's quick thinking and action, we would have been captured. As it was, we almost were. And we were not out of danger yet.

Dressed in full uniform, three large soldiers summited the ridge—only one back from where we lay. They talked and laughed so loudly among themselves that, were they not downwind of us, we would surely have heard them coming. After cresting the mound, they turned south.

I watched their self-satisfied indolence.

Disdain coursed through me. These men were slovenly at best. "Nothing to fight for over the past thirteen years has made them completely out of shape."

"Don't mistake them for pussycats, Cassidy"—Eric gestured to the rifles slung over their shoulders—"just because they're relaxed now. According to those *friends* I made, Gina mostly employs mercenaries." He paused then added, "The fact that these men are armed means Gina is anticipating conflict. Maybe she's under the impression that our force is larger than it is." He puffed out a snigger.

I turned to him. "Do you think they're moving between here and the fort?"

He glanced up and to the left. "It's possible...but unlikely. That railway only begins farther inland. We'll find out soon enough, I expect."

Eric peered over the tip of the dune and instantly dipped down again.

"Babe," he murmured, "we'll need to move again."

Although he tried to portray calmness, his stiffening features betrayed him. Gingerly, I peeked above the sand. I gasped.

Chapter Forty-Six

In the shortest time, the soldiers had changed direction. They were heading straight for us.

Eric grabbed my wrist. "Come, Cassidy," he urged.

I was moving too slowly. Eric had already gained cover in the long grass of the northern slope.

He threw his arm around my waist and jerked me toward him in a roll. Drawing and holding my breath, I followed his ease of motion.

As Eric propped on his forearms and covered me with his body, I gazed up into his beautiful face. Focusing on the ridge, he flashed his eyes down to mine then up again. When he lowered his head, his cheek warmed mine and his breath grazed my neck.

The soldiers summited the ridge so close to our heads that I could hear their footfalls hissing across the sand. After descending the dune, they turned south again — away from us. I released my breath in a gasp.

The soldiers trudged along the beach, angling toward the craft. Every sound floated back to us.

Eric darted his aquamarine eyes between mine as he whispered, "That was too close."

I rolled onto my stomach and raised my head. "Way too close."

"You going up?" one of the men asked, looking toward the top of the craft.

"Nah, going AWOL for a few hours."

The third man laughed. "Nothing ever happens, anyway. This woman is losing it — thinks there's some grand plot against her."

"Guess we're alive because of her," the second added.

"For what future?" asked the first. "I couldn't even save my own family."

The men fell silent and only spoke again once out of earshot.

As they headed toward the elevator, our eyes never left them. They did not enter it, though.

Just beyond the elevator, a triangular doorway almost magically appeared, penetrating the craft.

Snatching the binoculars from Eric's hand, I slammed them against my eyes. Immediately after they had passed through, three shark-fin shaped blades rotated from the outer rim toward the center of the triangular doorway — sealing it shut. Although it had already closed, I shoved the binoculars back into Eric's hand.

"Did you see that, Eric?" I rolled from my stomach onto my back again — gazing up at him. "Did you see?" I repeated, clasping my hands together. "Please tell me that Graham still has the uniforms that Liam brought."

"Of course, he does." He smiled down at my excitement, his dimples deepening. "And those that I acquired from my *friends*."

My mind ran wild. "Oh yes. Did anybody check for magnetic strips on the uniforms — maybe in the linings? Their access looked…automatic."

Eric gazed upward, recollecting. "Ethan never mentioned anything, but you can check for yourself. They'll surely be at the cave when we get back."

He cast his eyes up again. "Graham had our microchips removed and destroyed right after the strike. But if these guys still have theirs, that may be how they're gaining access."

I shrugged. "I doubt it, because ours were also removed."

Just then, Jonas slid over the edge of the ridge. "What's going on, then?" he whispered, observing our expressions. "Are we going in now?"

"No," I laughed sardonically, throwing a glance at Eric. I rolled out from beneath him. "I don't think so. Not yet, anyway. But I think we found the entrance Jaya mentioned."

"Well, that's a relief. I'd hate to go in there without telling Harriet. She was in a right state when we left this morning."

I nodded. "And if neither of you wants to make an enemy of Liam, it's probably a good idea not to let me go in there without his knowledge." An involuntary giggle broke through my lips.

Jonas' tone grew severe. "Listen, guys… We're very exposed to the top of the craft if somebody looks down. I've seen nobody so far, but we're sitting ducks here."

Eric, silent during our exchange, had kept his binoculars trained on the craft. A sharp jolt shot through him. "They're back!" he whispered, gesturing toward the exit.

The same three soldiers emerged from the triangular doorway. It was like a thousand insects were crawling over my skin. I froze. They had accumulated an extra four soldiers.

Although still around the curve of the ridge, we had nowhere else to go. If they veered just the tiniest bit to the north, they would catch us for sure.

The seven armed soldiers strode toward us, their boots shuffling through the sand. As they mounted the ridge and cleared the top, the ground beneath my head shifted. Then they were over.

I let out the breath I never knew I'd been holding, and as we edged to the front, I peered over the top.

Jonas scanned the sand-covered ridge, his voice hoarse, "How did you guys miss these bootprints when you first crawled up here then? They're everywhere."

Charged with adrenaline, I fired my reply, "There were none when we arrived!"

Although the obscene structure had claimed all our attention, I doubted the bootprints wouldn't have stolen some back. Not gunning for a silly 'he-said, she-said', I didn't tell Jonas that.

"What are these men up to? We ought to follow them." Eric whispered, once the soldiers had passed over the second ridge.

Jonas and I both nodded.

For the next few dunes, we flattened against each summit, taking turns as the lookout and giving the all-clear. Each time, before slipping to the other side, we listened for voices. My body throbbed to my every pounding heartbeat.

As the soldiers crested yet another ridge, it was my turn to check. From my position between Eric and Jonas, I raised my head and made a quick count.

Grabbing at their hands, a single word formed on my lips. "Stop!" In a soft, reedy gasp, I added, "Two are missing."

I raised my head again and re-tallied. Still, only five heads bobbed beyond the next ridge. I turned to Eric with my brows straining. "Where did they go?"

Eric raised his head, peered over then instantly dropped. As he gestured to a northern dip, Jonas and I followed his line of sight. Two soldiers were crouched over tufts of beach grass and, with the butts of their rifles, fidgeted in the sand.

The five heads on the far side of the dune halted. Two turned around and started bobbing back toward us.

"What's holding you guys up?" came a sharp voice. "We don't have time for this."

"Well, you might find something that interests you over here," one of the hunching men snapped back.

Giving a few grunts, the remaining three headed toward us too. As all five crested the ridge, they scanned their horizon.

I jerked down below the ridgeline and slammed my eyes shut, as if hiding behind my eyelids — figuratively burying my head in the sand.

"What was that?" one of the two men on the far ridge yelled.

Heavy boots ran toward us, the hissing of the sand growing into whishing as they climbed our ridge.

I again squeezed my eyes and held my breath, not wanting to face the man who would raise me to my feet. And worse — Eric and Jonas.

Unthinking, I closed my hand around a fist-sized rock.

The boot-falls stopped short.

A soldier yelled. Then three successive gunshots cracked the bright morning. Loud buzzing rang in my ears. The scream that broke through the ringing shattered the air and curdled my blood — a cry of sheer, unbridled terror. And it wasn't just one anguished scream or one more gunshot. Three more wails and three more shots erupted as the soldiers moved north between the two dunes. Every shot jolted through my body.

After what felt like forever, the soldiers moved off and disappeared over the dunes.

Eric and Jonas peered over the top of the dune, seeming to take in the devastation. Then Eric did a double take and gaped — really gaped at the bodies. After a moment he cupped his forehead in one hand and squeezed his temples. Jonas, though, just slowly shook his head, his eyes glazed.

Eric's voice cracked. "This is the family I mentioned — salt-of-the-earth farmers, the Cordovas are...*were*. We'd have called them back to the refuge had we known they were so close to the craft."

Jonas cocked his still-shaking head and swiped at a tear on his cheek. "It was their irrigation pump then, wasn't it?"

Eric nodded, seeming unable to answer in words.

I clutched Jonas' hand and laced my fingers through Eric's.

While Eric tightened his fingers around mine, Jonas' eyes dropped to our clasping hands — inspecting them like he was viewing a foreign object.

My voice emerged in a whimper. "We may not know why she's allowing it, but we must find a way to stop this...this... I can't even call her a *woman*!"

Absently, I wiped at my blurring eyes, gazing at the shimmering drop on my finger.

I sat back on my heels and took in the full scale of the horror beyond the dune. My blood raged, pulsed and burned inside my veins. "I've never truly hated anyone before," I rasped.

Jonas withdrew his hand and held it out, palm up, toward the bloodied bodies, shaking his head. "This is worse than anyone expected. Not even our parents considered her this cruel."

Eric finally spoke, his voice numb and flat. "They must have a funeral, a proper burial—a send-off into the afterlife."

"Yes," I agreed, "Liam can get the next group to fetch their bodies and take them to the cave."

This heaviness weighed down harder than anything I had ever experienced in all our time on the run, during our capture or in stories that we had heard at the refuge.

For the first time, it felt real—worse even than when Jonas returned from his beating and worse than hearing that Gina had imprisoned Dad, because I never thought he was in actual danger.

Now I wondered. Would Gina *seriously* threaten our parents?

* * * *

When we arrived at the canoe, it was as though I had not been present during our return trek. A dull fog had clutched my body and clouded my mind. I surveyed Eric and Jonas, absorbing how numb silence had gripped them too.

Chapter Forty-Seven

Dusk settled over the river, night beetles chirping a relentless foreboding chorus. But as we rounded the final bend and the hideout came into view, my eyes met several people, standing on the rock ledge. They bustled around eight additional tethered canoes, which bobbed lazily on the spot in the water.

The prospect of the new arrivals had excited me yesterday. But now, nothing could lift my spirits — the horror of today's events pervasively controlling my thoughts.

The rope ladder strained against the weight of the newcomers and the many packages they hauled into the cave. I half expected it to snap and drop its cargo into the river, but it held.

"Small mercies," I muttered to myself, metaphorically clutching onto any tiny shred of grace that could make our mission seem less asinine.

Liam and Harriet stood against the backdrop of the cave mouth. Silently, they watched our approach. But when meeting Liam's eyes, I couldn't help myself. A tear slid down my cheek.

His face fell slack, his brow knitting as my name formed on his lips. "Cassidy?"

He slowly shook his head then dropped to descend the makeshift ladder. Reaching the ledge before us, he grabbed the semi-submerged canoe rope in one hand. He reeled in the last remaining coil, grabbing it up with the others that Jonas had tugged and looped while Eric and I had oared home.

Liam pulled me from the boat, flashing a look at Eric and Jonas before gripping me to his chest. "Has something happened to Mom or Dad or Harriet's parents?"

Without looking up, I shook my head. Liam's chest deflated with his escaping sigh as he guided me to the rope ladder.

"What happened out there, baby sister?"

My lips wouldn't part to answer.

I gave one final glance at the rippling water before ascending the ladder. The new arrivals were sealing their canoe covers, camouflaging them with ours against the river water.

When Eric entered the cave behind Jonas, Liam again passed him an inquiring glance — not critical this time, just curious. He surely noticed that Eric and Jonas' over-wrought expressions mirrored my own.

"Come," Liam murmured. "Let's get you guys settled."

Darkness fell outside and the gloom in the tunnels deepened. Liam's headlamp illuminated our way through the inky blackness.

Mindlessly, we followed him into the tunnel's depths, where he led us into an offshoot and kindled a fire beneath a natural chimney.

As the tinder crackled to life, he shook his head. "I don't know what to say. You're all shivering, though it's not cold at all. The fire will help, but" — he concluded quietly — "I think you guys are in shock. What happened out there?" he asked for the second time.

Still, nobody answered, but I clamped my jaw against the threatening tears. Eric slid down the wall beside me, winding his arms around my body.

As I laid my head against his chest, the rhythmical beating of his heart lulled me into a deeper trance. When I glanced up at his impassive face, a single tear slipped down his cheek. He didn't move to wipe it away and, after a pause, another followed. Silently, he pulled me back to his chest.

I had not noticed Liam leaving, but he and Harriet returned with a pile of blankets, pillows and thin mattresses. Harriet crouched beside Jonas, encouraging him onto the soft futon. She sat and spread a blanket over them both, wrapping her arms around her brother's shoulders.

"What can we do?" Liam murmured as he handed us a broader mattress — his eyes soft with compassion and concern, "How can we help? Won't you tell us what happened? Please?" he begged quietly.

Lifting my gaze to his bright green eyes, I swallowed hard and found my voice. "It's so much worse than we expected, Li. So much. We're fooling ourselves if we think we can win this war. We don't have the numbers, the weapons, the training… We have nothing."

Eric squeezed my shoulder. "There's always a way, Cassidy babe. We have not come this far to give up. You know we won't sit back while Gina starves, tortures and kills these people. Plus, you're wrong. We do have some training—maybe not in military strategy, but we have a strong hunger to succeed and we will acquire the numbers and weapons, given time."

After a pause, Olivia and her three acolytes from the refuge appeared with bowls of hot pasta in a thick tomato sauce. They silently set them on the floor before us then backed away to the offshoot entrance.

"Thanks," Liam murmured. "Will you leave us to talk, please?"

While we picked at our food, Olivia and her girls lounged near the entrance.

Jonas extracted himself from his sister's arms and eyed the petite, dark-haired Olivia. Each time she caught his gaze, she shyly dropped her dark eyes to the floor. Through our dire circumstances, a smile found its way onto my lips. More than anyone I knew, Jonas deserved the love and admiration of this beautiful young girl.

Liam sat back on his heels, hands bridging his thighs, his voice soothing. "Listen, guys. We do need to know what happened out there, but you hardly seem in a state to give details right now. Rest tonight. We'll talk tomorrow."

"Aw," one of the younger girls complained, "we were hoping to hear an adventure tale."

Liam shot her a sharp look. "You do not want to hear these stories!" he exclaimed. "Now clear out of here. Let them rest."

Harriet caught my attention and in her gentlest possible tone, she whispered, "Let me take you to wash up, Cass."

Although hardly ready to venture out onto the open river, the value of not disappointing Harriet in her warm, tender moment surpassed and even raised me from my somber mood.

She didn't lead me to the exit, but into an offshoot farther down the tunnel.

The girls had fashioned a bathroom. They had placed a large central bowl with almost overflowing water-pitchers beside it. The chamber dipped toward a natural runoff in one corner, which drained discarded water into the vast unknown.

I scrubbed at my skin and hair, though no amount of soap or water could wash today's horror away. Despite that, I returned to the fire somewhat refreshed. Dropping to the mattress beside Eric, I laid my head on his shoulder. I drew in the fragrant shampoo from his damp hair as he slipped his arm beneath my head. "While we were bathing in the river, Jonas and I informed Liam about what happened to the Cordovas. He said he'd get someone to fetch their bodies in the morning."

While Eric smoothed my cheek with his thumb, I nodded. But without a word, I drifted away from the world.

The nightmares hit with wild ferocity—real and disturbing. Each time they assaulted, Eric brought my sweat-drenched body back with his soft voice.

At other times during the night, it was Eric who writhed and moaned. I crooned, holding him while I stroked his sweat-dampened head. This wasn't that uncommon with him though. He often called for Caleb in his sleep.

There was no escaping what we had seen, but we were lucky that we had each other.

I woke to dust particles drifting through the natural chimney, dancing in the soft light.

Eric sat against the tunnel wall with his knees up, fiddling with my wrist — or, more precisely, fidgeting with Great-Grandmother's bracelet.

I rubbed my eyes. "Does it interest you?"

Almost musing, he murmured, "Its design is so delicately intricate. At least a hundred tiny gold links make up the band." He shook his head, then added, "You were pretty restless last night."

"No worse than you" — I shrugged — "or Jonas, I'm sure."

When the scent of eggs wafted through the tunnel, Eric stood, stretching out his creaking joints. "Well, I'm going out there to see if those are eggs I'm smelling. I'm a bit curious as to how they survived rapids, being dragged through the tunnel, plus getting lowered over the cliffs at the waterfall." He laughed at his joke. "I'll keep some for you."

After a quick wash, I headed to the exit, passing Jonas on my way. Olivia and her entourage were on his tail. I smiled. "Have you already eaten?"

He rubbed his belly. "You can't tell, then?" Although sadness still tainted his eyes, he appeared almost back to his own cheerful self this morning. Perhaps it had something to do with Olivia, who moved a little closer to him.

"You'd better hurry if you want any." He guffawed. "Eric's attacking them like he's half starved."

"He'll keep some for me." I smiled—a smile that grew when Olivia slid her fingers into Jonas'.

He closed his fingers around hers, a little pointedly. "I wouldn't bet on that. At the rate he's going through them, there won't be any left to keep."

As he had promised, when I found Eric leaning against the tunnel's exit, he shoved a plate of eggs and a fork into my hand. "You don't mind cold eggs, do you?" He grinned, rolling a long strand of grass between his fingers.

I shrugged. "Cold is better than no eggs. Where's everyone else?"

"They've all spread themselves in offshoots along the tunnel. This place will get pretty crowded over the next few days."

A grimace tugged at my lips. "I hope nobody's taken it on themselves to inspect the craft."

"Relax, Cassidy," he drawled. "If you think we're paranoid, you should see this lot." He gestured over his shoulder into the caves with his thumb.

I rolled my eyes. "Prudence is hardly paranoia, Eric."

"True enough. But you ought not worry about trivialities. Save your energy for what matters."

Anxiety sent a wave of chills through me at the prospect of going into the craft at all. But I focused my mind. "Did they bring the soldiers' uniforms?"

He cocked his head and bit his lip, his dimples chasing my pulse into wild, rhythmical drumbeats as he reeled me in and kissed me lightly on the forehead. "Well, you know Craig trains the crows and Ethan works with weapons, right?"

I nodded and Eric continued, "Anyway, Craig was at breakfast. He says Ethan is coming with the next group. But back at the refuge, Ethan was thinking the same thing and scanned the uniforms. Guess what? You were right. He *did* find microchips in the jacket lapels."

I nodded. "So, all that remains is to see whether anyone has yet revoked their access."

"Yup, I guess," Eric agreed then added, "Craig and a few men collected the Cordovas' bodies early this morning. They took them to the far side of the tunnel — near the beach exit. We won't be able to wait until Graham reaches us — with no refrigeration chamber to keep them in. We'll hold a service once they've finished digging the graves. Beach sand is pretty soft, at least."

"Where — ?" I began, but Eric pre-empted my question.

"Don't you worry, Cassidy. The tunnel exits around a bend. It's not visible from the craft."

* * * *

It was with great sadness that, later that day, we bid farewell to the six Cordovas in a beach funeral. It was a traumatic send-off, even for those of us who'd never known them. The youngest boy had been nineteen — around our age.

Chapter Forty-Eight

When Graham arrived with his group a few days later, his eyes appeared sunken and drawn. They had brought an additional eight canoes, loads of food and sixteen more members. Our cave was now home to seventy people. More were still to come.

But our fathers were in prison. I feared their time was running out. The fire of revenge burned an uncontrollable, wildly blazing storm through my body, leaking into every beat of my heart. It constricted each breath I drew and consumed my every waking thought.

That evening after dinner, Graham handed Eric two small leather pouches. "Ethan said you might be running out of venom and antivenom." He shook his head slowly. "Do you know which is which?"

"Mm-m, maybe. I kind of hope so." But Eric broke into a pouting grin.

My eyes turned into saucers. "That's hardly very funny."

Eric raised his eyebrows and made a chuckling drawl. "Don't worry so much. Of course, I know which one contains the venom."

Graham shoved bolt cutters into Jonas' hands. They were not the ones we had used to cut our chains. Those surely lay at the bottom of the lake. Still, their presence sent shivers of numb dread through me. Although those had saved our lives, these now reminded me only of the sheer terror I had felt at the time. Perhaps this particular pair would leave us with more pleasant memories and help us rescue our fathers.

Finally, Graham tossed Eric, Jonas and me each a miniature can of blackout spray.

"In case they have cameras in the tunnels or prisons," he explained simply, as though our minds could sketch out the full details.

Liam shuffled beside me and laid his arm over my shoulder. "Please go over the plans with me, Cass. I need to know you have them down pat."

I raised my eyebrows and proceeded to satisfy his parental urge. "Graham, Harriet and you will wait for us at the canoes, keeping them safe until we return. In the meantime, Eric, Jonas and I will enter the tunnels through the triangular doorway, find the prisons and help Dad and Roger escape. After that, with Dad and Roger, we'll fetch our mothers and the Carter family from our homes. Then, we'll get the hell out of Dodge and meet you back at the canoes. Simple enough, right?"

He gritted his teeth and nodded. But when he moved his focus to Harriet, a shudder escaped me in a huge sigh.

For the remainder of the evening we bantered lightly. Still, when Eric and I finally retired for the night, our sleep was restless. In the morning, though, we were not the only ones who moved through the cave in silent contemplation, and after lunch, we reviewed our plans once more.

Finally, late in the afternoon, as we prepared to leave, Graham laid a hand on Craig's shoulder. "You know what to do."

Craig nodded, but Graham went on in his slow commanding voice anyway, "Send crows to gather as many from the farms as possible. Keep everyone here safe and away from the soldiers. But most importantly, do *not* go out there. Wait for us to return before you do anything, unless you have gathered ten thousand people willing to fight, which we all know is impossible."

The more we discussed our plans, the more its potential failure loomed over my head like a suspended dagger and the more terrified I became.

* * * *

After replicating our trek down the river and docking the boats beneath the overhang, we closed their covers. While creeping toward the ridge, my heart pounded in anticipation of a repeat performance. But, when we reached the path, the absolute vacancy of foot traffic stood out against the dusk shadows. The sky gradually darkened. My tension grew with the soft, eerie glow around the craft.

Despite wearing the uniform that Olivia had modified to fit me, I balked when I stood. Eric had removed his rank, but dressed in the close-fitting uniform, he radiated the air of an officer.

My heart thudded and, allowing my eyes to dip, I drew a breath to slow my pulse.

I pulled myself erect, attempting to portray the confidence of a soldier with every right to walk exactly where I was — heading with my fellow soldiers toward the craft.

Jonas almost choked from suppressing laughter when his eyes fell on my dramatized swagger. "Ease up on the overacting then, Cass. The exaggerated movements? They're not working."

In a feeble attempt to conceal my femininity, I had scratched my face with grit then rubbed dirt into the scratches. Now, after easing my swagger, I trudged forward, finding a more natural pace.

Still, I had to throw every bit of courage into remaining composed — not darting away at every sound. As stars blinked in the blackening sky, my chest filled with gratitude that, for now, the full moon kept her light hidden behind the craft. Through the deepening darkness, the eerie glow around the ship slowly brightened.

The entrance lay farther away than it had previously appeared, the elevator shaft larger than I recalled. As we neared, the intensity of my contracting gut threatened to double me over.

Drawing up, we ducked behind the elevator. Its jutting shaft concealed us from the small triangular doorway. Still, I dipped my head and pulled my cap low.

My stomach was so knotted that I wanted to vomit. Summoning my remaining courage, I sucked in a breath.

Then I stood — tall and confident — as Eric, Jonas and I rounded the edge of the elevator shaft.

Not even a dull light marked the outline of the triangular entrance.

Jonas blew out a sharp breath. "So the microchips don't work then?"

"Don't lose heart," Eric whispered, sensibly. "Maybe we need to get closer."

Before we had taken another step, a blue light burst along the triangle's border. It began to yawn—the series of overlapping shark-fin panels rotating outward. We ducked back around the elevator shaft as six armed soldiers emerged.

Chapter Forty-Nine

"It's now or never," Eric whispered, stepping out from behind the shaft. He was taller than any of these soldiers. His apparent confidence made me pull my own shoulders back, but my heart was thudding and I was sure everyone could hear it.

Drawing a deep breath, I mustered every bit of self-assurance I possessed. Together, we stepped from the shadows.

Intensely animated in conversation, they did not greet, acknowledge or even look in our direction.

We slipped past them and strolled through the triangular doorway. Seconds later, it rotated inward, sealing us away from the outside world.

Although I was sure that neither Eric nor Jonas needed the reminder, I said, "Don't forget about cameras." Perhaps I was reminding myself.

We stood for a moment in the belly of the craft — the outermost reaches of the ship. This was Jaya's world — beneath the apparent safety of Petriville.

I explained to Eric that we would pass beneath the grasslands, zoo, farmlands, stables and the entire town of Petriville. Only then would the innermost cavern open—the underbelly of Petriville's circular town square.

Eric slowly shook his head, his disbelief blatant as he took in the broad, shiny silver metal passage, the doors and tunnels breaking away at right angles.

He steeled his jaw with decided determination and strode the silver-floored perimeter tunnel of the ship.

When a group of men in track gear ran toward us, I dropped my head. But they too passed without pause.

"Take the first offshoot," I suggested then muttered under my breath. "Not that it matters, since they all lead to the same place."

"Yes!" Jonas threw a fist pump as we reached it. "Liam was right."

Dim, half-moon lights dotted the center of the ceiling, filling the tunnel with the dullest yellow glow. Even the lighting was on our side. But the part that had so excited Jonas was that, unlike those in the streets of Petriville, these dual conveyors extended all the way to the edge of the craft—to us.

Although the black matting was mobile, we stepped on. But it drew me back to when that consideration was repugnant to me.

Eric gave a soft chuckle, bringing me back as he whispered, "Maybe—just maybe—we'll escape this rat-hole before dawn."

We took up a slow jog, walking when shapes took form in the distant dull glow. But nobody gave a second glance as the conveyors crossed our paths.

Abruptly, the wind increased in the tunnel. Eric slowed then stopped—bristling.

Jonas drew up beside him and whispered, "The wind is probably coming from a cross-tunnel."

Eric nodded as if expecting that answer and started forward at a cautious walk.

A minute later, we breached the silver-floored junction and broke into a jog onto the next already-mobile conveyor.

My skin grew clammy beneath the hot uniform and weighty boots. But when I stopped for water, I wasn't the only one to half drain my hip flask.

The following conveyor and most beyond only came to life as we mounted.

At each intersection, Jonas or I listed off what lay above—farmlands, horses, domestic animals, ecological factories and Petriville's outskirts. Then, unsure exactly how many cross-street walkways were in town, our guesses blurred.

When we had crossed eleven intersections—having seen no soldiers since the second and no visible cameras at all—Eric panted, "How many to go?"

Just then, the wind grew, gusting much more powerfully than the cross-tunnel breezes. The conveyor ended. Eric stopped so abruptly that Jonas and I rammed into his back.

"Sorry," he whispered loudly, though I was sure it was Jonas and me who should have made the apology.

I walked forward gingerly and stepped onto the familiar grid. "It's as if a lifetime has passed since we stood here—at this precipice," I reminisced.

Eric gazed out over the edge of the abyss in stunned silence.

Far below, the stadium lay concealed within the massive drop and dim glow—a mere stone's throw over the solid silver guardrail.

I shuddered, my eyes following the curved railing around the edge of the grated platform, pausing at each of the twelve tunnel entrances beyond the grid. I scanned the enormous chamber's silver walls, shifting to the twelve upper tunnel entrances.

"Cassidy." Eric frowned, reaching for my hand. "Where do we go from here?"

This, Jonas' and my hometown, was unfamiliar to Eric. Yet he had re-gathered himself — was ready to move onto the next task — while we were still coming to grips with our surroundings.

"The tunnels are numbered. Do you remember that, Jonas?"

He nodded and I continued, "Let's hope the prisons are where we're expecting to find them — in the upper number four tunnel, near the train station."

Jonas agreed then turned to Eric.

Eric was running, circling the platform toward the neighboring tunnel. I followed a moment later.

No cage surrounded the ladder affixed to the metallic wall. A slip would send a climber plummeting over the lower railing into the abyss below. We had no time for those considerations now. Without hesitation, I darted up the rungs with Jonas and Eric hot on my heels. I peered into the tunnel, but still, no soldiers had appeared. Quickly, I clambered up the last few rungs with Jonas and Eric right behind. Inside the tunnel, we broke into a fast walk.

Eric extracted his can of blackout spray and I cocked an eyebrow at him. "That won't help, Eric. I didn't say anything to Graham, but any cameras down here will be too small for us to even see, let alone spray."

We continued our search for exits beneath the railway station. Then, the words 'East Wing' stood before us — etched into both walls. A single offshoot and two staircases flanked the tunnel — one ascending and one descending.

I turned to Jonas. "Which one?"

He had no more context than me and stared at me blankly.

While we pondered our decision, Eric folded his arms and arched both brows — clearly frustrated about feeling extraneous in this regard.

Making a snap decision anyway, he suggested, "We split."

Without pause, he launched toward the up-bound staircase.

I spun and bolted to the lower level, while Jonas slipped into the side tunnel.

The staircase ended in the center of a long gallery, with doors lining both sides from end to end.

I glanced around for cameras, but none were visible. Jogging down the long corridor, I zigzagged left and right — flashing glances through each small, eye-level window. *Prison cells for sure.* But empty.

My heart thumped, pounded — as if trying to escape the cavity of my chest. Dad could be so near.

A moment later, both Eric and Jonas leaped down the metal staircase, shaking their heads, after having completed the upper and middle-level checks.

I gestured to the doors lining the far side of the tunnel. They raced off, each choosing one side of the passage.

Already having checked at least half the cells in this section, my hope was fading. I peered into yet another cell, half-expecting my eyes to fall, yet again, on another empty bed. But I was wrong. Somebody *was* lying under the gray blanket. My breath caught and I dropped below the window line. How would I know if this was the right somebody, though?

Chapter Fifty

But I did. I knew immediately and looked again at the familiar form lying curled up under the single gray cot blanket, writhing in his sleep.

Tears pricked at the corners of my eyes but there was no time for sadness. Every part of me ached as I watched my tall, lean father in such wretched turmoil. But we had to move.

As if a switch flipped in my head, I shifted into high alert and knocked lightly on the window.

Dad stirred but didn't wake. I did not increase the intensity, though I knocked again.

Still, he didn't stir. I knocked again, not harder. And again. And again. One after the other, barely pausing between each.

Then, on my eighth knock,.3;0.Dad bolted upright, his eyes bulging as though uncertain whether he had been dreaming. He stood, facing the door and rubbing the sleep from his eyes.

I blinked furiously. "No time for tears, Cassidy," I whispered to myself as Dad stepped to the window and peered through.

As recognition set into his features, his mouth fell slack. He shook his head over and over, mouthing the words, "No, Cassidy. No, no."

I pointed at my left wrist. I would not leave now — leave Dad here. As he met my resolved stare, his shoulders slumped. He gestured upward to the air duct maintenance entrance.

My eyes followed then drifted to the ceiling in the passage — with a similar cover.

Eric, who, having observed my desperate attempts to get Dad's attention, sprinted toward us, bolt cutter in hand.

As he reached me, he lowered the tool to the floor, interlocked his fingers and cupped his hands. "Climb," he whispered.

Balancing on his shoulders, I stepped into his hands. He raised me toward the ceiling, steadying me as I lifted the duct opening and eased it backward. I braced my arms, thrusting myself inside. Eric didn't release me but kept pushing my feet until I was secure. He dipped down, picked up the bolt cutter and passed it through the opening. Without hesitation, I grabbed the handle then scrambled into the small inlet of Dad's cell. With the cumbersome implement, I snipped the padlock and eased the cover open. I turned to the passage entrance and fed the bolt cutters back to Eric.

Dad had piled pillows beneath the blanket and now stood on the corner of the cot. His own height, along with that added by the bedframe, made it easy for him to lift himself through the small opening. I edged away to create space.

When I dropped back to the floor of the main tunnel, Eric was no longer where I had left him. I didn't look to see where he had gone, but turned and peered through the cell window as Dad closed the cover from inside the duct.

Shortly afterward, he dropped down beside me and, wrapping his arm around my head, gripped me to his chest. "Cassidy, my daughter," he pleaded, "why did you do this? It could be a *setup*." He had gasped the last word.

"We were not about to let you rot in there, Dad."

As we turned toward the other end of the passage, Eric was stretching his arms upward — pushing Jonas' legs through the opening of another vent. On tiptoes, we ran toward them as Eric retrieved the bolt cutters from Jonas' protruding hand.

Eric switched the tool to his left hand and held his right out to Dad. "I'm very pleased to meet you, Peter."

Dad ignored his hand and gripped him in a man-hug. "Thank you for doing this, Eric, and for keeping my daughter safe. It's good to finally meet you."

Eric nodded but grimaced, flashing me a glance. "It's not as if I had much say in either this venture or Cassidy's safety. You know how stubborn she is."

Dad raised an eyebrow and nodded. For a moment, I was sure a smile touched his lips. But it slipped away before it had fully formed.

Roger also laid pillows beneath his gray blanket then clambered onto the bedframe. Wobbling unsteadily, he grabbed the edges of the hatch with both hands. Jonas wedged his feet against the side of the opening and helped heave his father's heavy-set frame through.

As soon as Roger and Jonas dropped to the ground, we took off in a tiptoed sprint through the passage, up the staircase and back toward the central chasm. At least our parents and the Carters all lived on the same block — halfway down conveyor two.

When we neared the ladder, I slowed then stopped. As I peered over the edge, my heart sank as shouts echoed through the tunnel.

"How did they get here so quickly?" I choked. "What chance do we have now?"

Another consideration steeled my resolve. "I'm not leaving without Mom."

Eric spun me around and laid his hands on my shoulders, meeting my eyes with a distracted stare. "Listen to the voices, Cassidy. Sounds to me like they aren't coming from behind us."

The shouts grew louder. A moment later, a group of soldiers raced across the grid beneath us, turning into another of the lower tunnels.

"What the — ?" I broke off in a choke.

A few seconds later, more soldiers crossed the grid, shouting for the first group to stop.

Jonas bunched his face. "Are those soldiers chasing other soldiers? What are the odds we may be witnessing dissent in Gina's ranks then?"

Eric puffed out a breath. "Sadly, that still doesn't mean they'll take up with our cause."

As the voices faded, we descended the silver ladder.

As my foot touched the grid, I wasted no time and raced lightly toward the homeward-bound tunnel. Without a backward glance, I launched up and escaped into the upper number two tunnel. Only then did I pause and wait.

A moment later, Dad popped his thinning blond head into view. Soon, all five of us stood in the tunnel. I turned and sprinted toward our homes, the silver floor somehow cushioning my footfalls as the others pounded softly behind.

It wasn't long before we reached the first airlock door. Jonas extracted the strange, angular device Aaron had given him all those months ago.

My heart pounded as Jonas slotted the device into the two aligning wedges while Eric twisted the airlock wheel.

Eric urged me through then piled in with the others.

The stairway leading up to the manhole was just as I remembered. I depressed the lever against the silver wall and the cover sprang open.

Jonas peeked his head out, whispering, "It looks quiet out here. But that's not really surprising, since it's the middle of the night."

Eric chuckled.

I threw him an exasperated glare, a considerable sigh flowing through my lips. "Seriously, do you guys have to make jokes at a time like this?"

It was like entering a memory when I stepped from the manhole onto the sidewalk. The brightly, animated twirling and dancing confectionary in Mama Candy's display window sent a thousand memories flooding my mind. I looked around. So many agonizing and conflicting emotions raged through me. Pain. Happiness. Good memories mixed in with bad — a single cesspool of joy and anguish. For Eric, I took a breath. For Dad, I forced myself to be calm. I took in the world I had grown up in. It seemed like so many lifetimes ago. But my memories — for the most part — had been good ones, hadn't they?

Eric froze as he emerged, his hands on his hips and mouth agape.

He shifted his eyes from Mama Candy's to the first of Petriville's lavish homes, to the beautiful lanterns lining the street, the perfectly manicured garden, the nearby adorned intersection bridge bathed in a soft lilac glow and the whoosh-whoosh of a sprinkler as it sprayed over the lawn. He rotated a full circle, taking in this small corner of Petriville. Slowly shaking his head, he gave a shocked wince.

I stepped around to face him, placed my palms on his cheeks and forced his tormented gaze away from our surroundings to my eyes. "I am sorry, Eric — so sorry. I don't even want to think about what's going through your mind right now. I know It's not fair, but please don't fall apart," I begged. "Graham needs your strength for just a short while longer and —" My voice caught. I dropped my chin. In the softest whisper, I uttered, "I need you, Eric." I looked up at him again and swallowed, knowing it was unfair of me from my protected life to ask anything of him. "I can't do this without you."

He closed his hands over and around mine, lowering them from his cheeks to his chest. His tropical-ocean eyes darkened. "It's fine, Cassidy. I'm okay, babe." He gritted his teeth. "Let's go. Let's finish this thing."

As I was about to step onto the homeward-bound conveyor, Dad squinted into the darkness. He widened his eyes as he grated, "What the — ?"

I followed his line of sight to the shadows behind Mama Candy's and gasped.

Dad dropped his eyes to the bright orange dart protruding from his arm. Eric slowed beside me, closing his hand around mine. He pulled me into his side, dropped my hand and wrapped his arms around me.

Surrounding me with as much of his body as possible, he whispered, "I'm so sorry, my Cassidy."

A cold shiver rocked me from head to toe. "I am sorry too, Eric. I never thought—" I broke off as the familiar sting slammed into my thigh. My eyes tensed.

I flashed a glance at Eric. "What are you sorry about, Eric?"

He never managed to answer before my balance teetered, my legs gave way and I crumpled to the floor.

Chapter Fifty-One

My eyelids fluttered. I clenched them against the bright light searing my throbbing head. But I couldn't move my hand to rub the pain away and I jerked at the shackles trapping my arms behind a thick pole. *Where am I?* My head wouldn't clear.

And where was...his name scorched its way through my throat, my voice echoing around me — a hundred times amplified. "Eric?"

The memories slammed into me — a hot stab in the chest. My eyes shot open and the full sun burned into them. I blinked and blinked again.

A fountain. Trees. Park benches. All were too familiar.

When robots glided into view, my gut screamed a thousand warnings. They carried a large, empty cage, which they then lowered to the cobbled paving near the fountain.

Throughout the square, crisp and clear, a slow, monotonous voice broke the silent morning. "Welcome home, Miss Jones." The familiar, hateful voice didn't sound in the least hospitable.

Petriville's multiple digital displays were alive with color—the bright orange 'Petrician Enterprises' crowned Gina's head, her face glowering down at her subjects.

My awareness sailed over the town square and landed on a figure clamped against the pole of one such bright screen.

I shook my head, my voice blaring through the speakers. "Liam! No! What are you doing here?"

Liam met my gaze, slowly shaking his head as he mouthed, "Sorry, baby sister."

I spat the words through my lips—a hiss through the speakers. "How? How did *she* know?"

Only my echo returned as Liam mutely squinted at me across the square. He glanced to his left—alerting me to his neighboring screen, then the next. I paused on each, tightening my forehead more and more.

I mouthed every name as a question. "Dad? Roger? Graham? Harriet? Jonas?" And slumped against his restraints on the nearest display was Eric, his eyes filled with sorrow.

A knot gripped my stomach as a savage range of emotions ripped through me. I yelled so loudly that feedback screeched through the square, "Tell me I'm wrong, Eric." Then I repeated more softly, "Please tell me I'm wrong."

The pained expression on Eric's features deepened as he met my eyes. "Don't you know I'd never betray you, Cassidy? But, however unknowingly, I *am* sorry I led us into this trap."

Gina cut him off, cackling. "Oh, spare us, Eric. Of course, he betrayed you, silly girl. It is, after all, his fault that you're here, on display for our fellow Petrivillians to witness our punishment of traitors."

Almost as an afterthought, she added, "Oh, young Mr. Jones. What kind of man allows his sister — a girl — to go in to rescue their father?"

Liam took a moment to respond, the screens zooming in on his face as his green eyes shimmered. "We didn't want the girls to stay out there on their own with your soldiers killing any people they came across."

Gina snorted, rolled her eyes and said, "Pfft," as though she didn't believe we were alone.

I scanned the area, but Gina's hateful visage was nowhere to be seen — only apparent on the huge screens. Instead, I raged at the crowd gathering along the town square perimeter, "What are you all staring at?"

Those eyeing us now cast their eyes down. Overall, they faced, not toward us, but were craning their necks and peering toward the top of the municipal building.

I followed their upturned faces to a balcony where, on catching my glare, Gina Petri waved a distant arm.

A deep glower crept its way onto my face.

The flag post rose up beside the municipal building wall, extending high above the balcony. In the light breeze, its bright orange flag hung downward — almost pointing at Gina's hard, stumpy outline.

As her silky, slow voice materialized, the screens broadcast her loathsome face across the town square and throughout all Petriville.

"Well, well… Now that I finally have your attention, Miss Jones, I dare say that you have become a trifle bothersome when, in fact, you ought to have been grateful for the incredible opportunity with which you were presented. I should most certainly have rejected your family had your true personality emerged during that early testing. Such a shame. So much promise." She shrugged. "Oh, well."

I scowled then dropped my eyes to yet another digital display as I opened my mouth to speak.

Eric beat me to it, growling up at her, his voice amplified as an echo across the square. "Why hold Cassidy or the others when we all know it's me you have a problem with?"

Gina rolled her eyes so dramatically that her entire head joined in the gesture, her voice ubiquitously piercing the air. "Ah, the infamous Eric Morgan." She pouted, tittering and turning her eyes to the crowd. "So chivalrous… I dare say that I was rather impressed that you managed to find your way into the fort. All that trouble, just to rescue the love of your life." Gina pitched her brows in mock-tenderness, an almost-giggle accompanying her words.

She threw her head back and gave a spine-tingling witch-like cackle. Mockingly, she moved her hand to her chest. "But such a racket you lot made when you left the pod after speaking to Emily… My men simply picked up your trail and *'encouraged'* you down the river. Of course, imprisoning your fathers was just a little…mm-m, what should I call it? A carrot? Yes, that's it…an incentive to entice you. They were good — my men. Subtle. I bet that none of you suspected a thing."

She paused and smiled then, loosely fisting her hand, raised an index finger to her lips. "And Graham Porter…such a romantic notion you had — save anyone and everyone. Bah! How did that work out for you?" Gina pouted again. "How many did you actually save?" She didn't wait for an answer but broke into a derisive chuckle, as though entertained by her ability to torment us.

In the same, mocking tone, she continued. "The world and its people were rather a disassociated, calamitous bunch before the meteor cleansed the planet. Murderers. Child abusers. Rapists. Besides" — she waved her arm over the crowd of Petrivillians — "this lot would have died anyway. I just had the foresight to save some of the...better of the species. Why do you think I had family interactions so closely monitored before selection? Twenty-four-hour surveillance" — she laughed sardonically — "and they had no idea. That is, after all, where the worst of humanity comes out — when they think that they are in the privacy of their own homes. Oh, you should have seen what I witnessed in some families."

She gave another contemptuous cackle. "Obviously, those vermin were not selected. You know... This behavior is often perpetuating, cyclically repeated by offspring." After a deep sighed she continued, "Sadly, dear Eric, you will not satisfy Cassidy's needs for long." She paused, allowing her words to hang in the air.

Eric took the bait and screamed up at her, "What the hell are you talking about, Gina?"

"I am talking about" — Gina giggled again — "the fact that Cassidy will outlive you by...mm-m...give or take, six hundred years." She pouted as though speaking to a sad five-year-old. "Surely you'd want her to be with somebody her own young age?"

I gritted my teeth, sensing she was about to declare her big revelation — make her true confession.

She directed her next statement at Eric. "Honestly, have you never noticed that Mr. Porter has barely aged in the, what, twenty-one years since you were born in his refuge?"

What *was* she talking about? Eric wasn't born in the refuge. And since the meteor stuck Earth only almost thirteen years ago…

I was about to run my logic by Eric — prove her lies — when Liam yelled above me, "It's another trick of hers, Eric. Don't listen. She's lying. Our life span is the same as yours. I don't look younger than my age, do I?"

Eric blinked, nodding slowly as if considering then agreeing with Liam's statement.

I looked back to the screen as Gina again threw her head back and roared, "Liam. Oh, Liam. So naive." She pouted again. "You received the airborne '*Longevity Elixir'* when the meteor struck Earth."

I frowned. "Our parents would never have allowed that, Gina."

Gina chuckled, "Well, that's because they received it too. Plus" — she raised her brows — "they were never told."

Harriet fired the words, her voice amplified. "You're lying! That's ridiculous. We'd only be like six or seven years old now."

Gina laughed again. "Not if we'd been in space for the past hundred and ten years."

I glanced at Dad, who gaped, his expression filled with horror. I frowned, bitterness acerbating my tongue.

Roger roared up at her in his strong Scots' accent, "This is a fiasco. You crazy bat! We can all work out that less than thirteen years of three hundred and sixty-five days does not equal a hundred and ten years. Stop feeding us this bunch of rubbish."

"Well, Mr. Winters," Gina went on, delighting in our confusion, "besides the past two years, every year-end at midnight, I fed you Petrivillian citizens a second airborne solution. Living in a dome has its uses after all." She chuckled then added, "It erased your memories for exactly three hundred and sixty-five days—three hundred and sixty-six on a leap year. Precise medical programming." She cackled. "It's a rather impressive technology. Needless to say, you received the solution nine out of every ten years. You retained muscle memory—which is why you kids got so damned good at the MAC Challenge—but everything else..." She trailed off, allowing her words to fully penetrate, before adding, "The solution only ran out a couple of years ago."

Abruptly, with two hand-waves, she dismissed the conversation. "Needless to say, I grow bored with this Q and A."

My blood curdled when she shifted her steel-gray eyes from Eric to me.

An even icier chill flattened her voice. "Oh, that reminds me, my dears. I have a gift for you."

As the crowd's collective stare adjusted, I didn't follow. Rather, I stayed locked on the large screen as the image on the digital display drifted down the flag post.

A rising swarm of tormented shrieks erupted, seeming to come from every corner of Petriville.

Chapter Fifty-Two

We didn't have to wait long to see the cause of their anguish. I should have known Gina would have made an example of me. My gut cramped as fear took hold — so much worse than the intensifying background wails.

Gina leaned over the balcony, smiling as her gaze drifted down the thick flag post.

Not only were banners rising, but sliding up the long pole was a square platform, no more than the width of one conveyor.

The intensity of the shock rocked me backward, slammed my spine against the digital display pole and turned my knees to jelly. On the small display platform stood a lone occupant. A short, thigh-high rail was the person's only protection from the vacant space beyond. And the familiar, long, elegant hands were cuffed together before her. I almost expected to see a noose around her neck — but there was none. I should have known Gina would make this more dramatic than a commonplace hanging.

Acidic tears burned my eyes as one name shrieked through my lips, cracking through the square. "Mom!"

Keys rattled behind me. I prepared to bolt.

Gina had pre-empted my reaction and snickered. "Now, now, Miss Jones. Before you do anything...rash, don't forget that I have your mother in a rather precarious position."

I slumped and didn't resist when the robot removed my cuffs or when it urged me toward the central cage.

Other robots forced Dad, Roger, Graham, Harriet, Jonas and Eric toward the barred enclosure. Some townsfolk gawped, some wearing masks of shocked bewilderment, yet others voicing mingled expletives.

"Gina!" I screamed—feedback squealing over the speakers. "What the hell do you want from us? And even if we give you that, who says you still won't harm my mother anyway?"

She clucked. "You're right, of course. Nothing says that I won't kill every one of you." She pouted, drawing her eyebrows together. "Yet still...you hope."

After ushering us inside, a robot closed and locked the cage door.

Eric reached for me and made an agonized frown before pulling me against his chest.

Jonas glared at Eric. "How did she know we were coming?"

Harriet rolled her eyes. "Seriously, Jonas! Didn't you listen to Gina? She all but herded us here. She knew we were coming even before we did."

Dad turned his eyes on Eric, not judging him, just pained. "How is it, Eric, that your coming to Petriville was the wiser choice when the result is that my beloved wife is standing up *there*?" His voice cracked on the last word as he gestured toward the high platform.

Eric set his jaw and dropped his gaze but said nothing as Dad moved to the edge of the enclosure — gripping the bars.

Just then, Megan Winters burst through the crowd, followed closely by Joshua and Caroline Carter. They raced toward the cage, gripping and rattling the bars like they could help in some way.

Roger held his huge palms up. "What are you doing here then, Megan? You should know you're safer at home."

Megan glared at him. "Now tell me, Roger, what good would that do when my entire family is in this cage?"

As he held his wife's fingers through the bars, Graham made his way to Joshua and Caroline as she murmured, "We're just pawns in her chess game. She's always had this power over us, even when we thought she didn't. Her bringing us into Petriville and leaving you out there... Even that was a tactic to show us her might."

My focus wasn't on any of them.

Even in Eric's arms, I couldn't tear my gaze from Mom, so isolated on the platform — her miniature stage.

Gina's slow, monotonous voice curled my lip into a snarl. "Well, Miss Jones. I am about to deliver a cause and effect demonstration, as it were, to help you grasp the meaning of consequences."

Liam yelled up at her, his voice cracking, "You *are* evil." It was as if he had only just comprehended this fact.

Gina merely cackled. "Whether your mother lives, Miss Jones, is your choice — yours alone. Agree now to never see nor speak to this *Eric Morgan* again and she lives. Refuse, and she dies. It's simple enough. I'll give you a moment to decide."

I clenched my teeth. "Why, Gina?" I screamed.

She threw out an exaggerated "Mm-mph!" Then she added, "Why do my reasons matter? Your mother's life is on the line because you refuse to see that I'm the one in control."

Eric folded me into his braced arms, bathing me in his perfect scent. We couldn't even conduct a candid conversation, because every word we whispered carried over the speakers. But Eric squeezed his eyes shut while a tear escaped mine.

Meeting my eyes, he murmured, "What I said in the canoe was the truth, Cassidy. Whatever happens for the rest of your life… Please don't forget that."

I nodded and swallowed what felt like a stone in my throat. Another tear slipped out.

Gina only gave us seconds before she sneered again over the speakers, "So what is the decision? I desire an answer."

We had had no need to speak — both knowing our answers. I met Eric's beautiful aquamarines one final time and gritted my teeth.

I stepped away, turned and fired, "I agree to your demands, Gina."

Dad moved away from the bars, wrapping his arm around my shoulders.

Gina's face appeared to droop. "Really? I heard no mention of that between you."

Before I had the chance, Eric almost growled at her. "It is not something we needed to discuss."

"Oh…" Gina admitted. "Oh, I am a little disappointed to hear that." She sighed. "Very well."

After that, everything happened too fast for us to have stopped it — or even to have been sure of the exact sequence of events.

The digital display moved from Gina's smiling mouth to her hand — to the remote clutched in her stumpy fingers. Raising it for all to see, she dramatically plunged a red central button on the remote. "Oops! I don't think I believe you."

Photography drones zoomed in on Mom, transmitting live feed as the cuffs fell from her hands. Terror gripped her features — blatant on the huge screen. She stared at the cage — at us. Ever so slowly, she shook her head.

Ice washed through my veins — sharp and dizzying. In the seconds it had taken for me to comprehend what was happening, everything slowed. My breathing faltered. My gaze stuck.

Sporadic spectator wails broke the numb silence that had fallen. The barrier before Mom retracted into the flag post. The platform beneath her feet dipped.

I wanted to tear my eyes away, but I couldn't. I couldn't scream. I couldn't breathe. Every part of me fixed on Mom as her body plummeted. Her terrified shrieks cut like a knife through the mid-morning air. She flailed her arms and legs, instinctively reaching out for a purchase that wasn't there. Her descending form and continual shrieking went on, and on, and on until I could no longer bear it. I rammed my fists over my ears, trying to block out the sound. Excruciating milliseconds ticked past. The cobbled paving rose up to meet my mother, smashing her body into a bloodied, broken horror.

A far off, primal shriek broke the silence. I took a moment to grasp that this noise, this irritation, had broken from my mouth, my chest.

I lost awareness of my surroundings, clinging to my father as we crumpled to the cold metal base. I was oblivious to the unwelcome onlookers and barely cognizant of Liam collapsing to his knees behind me, of his radiating warmth as his arms encircled my body or of Dad wrapping us both in his arms. Vaguely, Liam's soft sounds of grief reached me.

Eric's far-off choke sounded muted, as if not intended for my ears. "This is my fault, Graham. It's like you said in the beginning—I should have stayed away from that damned pod."

Eric's words came through a thick haze. Because as, from behind, Harriet threw her arms around Liam, his guttural howl wrenched my heart through my chest. I heaved, twisting my head to the side. Acidic vomit clawed up through my throat, out onto the cobbled paving.

Tears streamed down my cheeks, falling to the ground. "Why, Gina?" I pleaded to the display board. "Why did you do this?"

Her face grew dark. "Really, Miss Jones? Do you truly have no idea to what lengths I will go to get what I want? Surely you grasp that you did this to yourself?"

Dad dropped his arms away and drifted to the cage bars, locking his eyes on the screen—back on Mom's broken, bloodied body. Tears flowed in unrelenting rivers down his cheeks.

Through the numb fog, I gazed on as medical robots, dressed in white scrubs, raced onto the scene.

"No," Dad begged, rattling the bars as they placed Mom on a stretcher. His voice cracked. "Don't take her away. Please. Let us say goodbye."

Without the slightest acknowledgment, they ran off in their near-glide—Mom on the stretcher between them.

The drones again focused on Gina, her arms folded, a smug smile flattening her lips.

Behind her, an elevator door opened. A woman stepped out—a younger version of Gina with the same stumpy body and hooked nose, walking with the same choppy footsteps.

Susan Petri drew her dark brow down. She summoned Gina, holding up an ultra-thin silver tablet. As Gina inspected the screen's contents, her face darkened. Then both women retreated into the elevator and the doors slid shut.

Chapter Fifty-Three

Liam stood in a daze and helped me up. Then he twisted toward Harriet and lifted her to her feet. As he wrapped her in his arms, she again flung hers around him, her head against his shaking chest.

Megan wailed from outside the cage. "Is everybody okay with homicide now? Gina just murdered an innocent woman!"

She clutched at her throat as if struggling to breathe. "Em-m-mil-l-y-y!" she repeated, in a long lament.

Roger gripped his wife's hands then reached for Jonas, reeling him in too.

The live feed switched between our cage and random images of Petrivillian citizens. Everyone was gathered either along the edge of the town square or spread over Petriville's many sidewalks and walkways—all eyes fixed on the screens.

I gaped on as though watching a movie.

Mom was dead. Nothing could change that. Not now, not ever.

Eric skirted my stomach contents, worried lines etched down his face. Slowly, he pulled my numb body against his chest.

When I met his gaze, he shook his head, tears filling his eyes as he rasped, "I didn't know what wheels started turning when I entered that pod."

He quickly palmed away the moisture from his eyes.

A broken whisper escaped my lips. "Neither did I, Eric. Not back then."

His voice emerged as a croak. "That's on me."

"No, Eric," I said. "No, it isn't. I'm starting to think that this is exactly what Gina wants, for us to blame ourselves and ultimately each other. *Please*. Let's not fall into her trap."

Liam stepped up beside me, hands on his hips and teeth, gritted. "I am really...*really* having a hard time not blaming you both for this!"

He shoved Eric. "Why'd you have to have my sister? Why not take somebody from the refuge? You had more than enough willing girls to choose from."

Eric didn't resist and, stepping back a few paces, he fell to the ground.

"Why take it out on Eric, Liam?" I snapped. "I'm as much to blame."

Eric got to his feet and met Liam's glare with soft acquiescence in his eyes then laid his hand on my shoulder. "It's okay, Cassidy. I get it."

He glanced away, blinking the shimmer from his eyes.

"I don't," I yelled, almost *needing* Liam to hurt me. I deserved it. I had just as well killed my mother.

Eric bit his lip and turned his eyes back on my brother. "Of all people, Liam, you know that when you meet the *one*, no substitute will suffice."

Dad cocked his head toward us then turned and stepped away from the bars, drying his eyes with his palms.

He squared up to both Eric and Liam, his voice calm. "Please stop. You can't do this. Not now. Fighting will not bring Mom back."

Eric gave a slight nod, his expression complaisant. "I never meant for anyone to —"

Roger cut him off. "Hold on a sec, won't you then, Eric?"

Seeming suddenly unsure where to direct his wrath, he yelled up at the nearest screen, "Will you not allow these people to grieve in peace, then?"

The displays had broadcast every word we had uttered across Petriville.

For a while, I thought Gina had acceded to Roger's demand as the image faded into black and our voices stopped returning to us.

Silence fell for several minutes after which, a butler-type robot walk-glided down the municipal building stairs toward the cage.

Drawing near, it announced in the most pompous tone, "Good morning, ladies and gentlemen. Would a Miss Cassidy Jones care to accompany me for a consultation with Ms. Gina and Miss Susan Petri?"

For a moment, we all glared at the robot, which, unable to read our mute conveyances, waited for an audible response.

I was about to refuse, but my need for answers got the better of me.

Dad read my internal dialogue and gripped my wrist. "No, Cassidy. Do *not* go out there."

Eric, sensing that my mind was made, shook his head. "No, babe. No!"

I met his agonized stare. "I need to ask her why, Eric. Surely you see that."

He stepped to the door and blocked my way. "Not if it means losing you too."

The others moved to block the exit, but I met their pained expressions head-on. "I'm not a child you need to take care of. If Gina wants to see me, I want to know why."

Liam threw his arms around me, gulping. "I'm sorry for what I said, Cassidy. I don't blame you or Eric. But please don't do this."

I gently withdrew his arms. "It's not about that, Li. But I *am* doing this. You would too."

Ignoring their bewildered expressions, I pushed my way past them and stepped up to the exit gate. "I am Cassidy Jones."

The 'butler' didn't hesitate but opened the cage door and allowed me to exit, while adeptly blocking off any possible escape to everyone else.

Eric cleared his throat loudly and, encircling his wrist with one hand, scratched his jawline with the other. I met his pursed expression.

My brows pulled together. So did his. He shook his head—fortifying his grip around the wrist.

He shouted, not to me, but to Gina—who was evidently still listening.

His voice rang thick across the square. "Gina! If you can hear me, you'd best think twice before harming Cassidy. Because if you hurt her and I somehow get out of here, you'll be watching your back for the rest of your pathetic life."

The robot didn't hold on to me. There was no need. Gina knew I would never abandon those I loved.

I followed the 'butler' toward the municipal building, flinching when we neared the place where Mom had lain. But, forcing confidence into my gait, I strode the broad stairway and gained the summit well ahead of the robot's almost floating stride. Then I stepped into the only open elevator. It didn't close until the robot had entered, but in a short while, we were gliding upward.

Chapter Fifty-Four

When the doors opened, the robot waved me ahead. I stepped onto a thick, lavish, patterned office carpet. A large photograph of Gina and Susan took the focal point of one grandly decorated wall. Surrounding that, were many photos of Gina's grandchildren, Gregory and Amanda—mostly taken during some-or-other minor league MAC event. A kingly, dark-wood desk stood at one end, with huge bay windows behind. Plush, brown leather one- and two-seater couches made up the remainder of the large furniture. Tall, opulent wooden lamps stood around the room—the placing appearing more decorative than functional.

Side-by-side, the squat bodies and hook-nosed faces of Gina and Susan Petri leaned against the desk with their arms folded.

I sneered. "What do you want now?"

Gina cocked her head for a moment. "What I *want*"—she emphasized the last word then went on—

"is for you to know that you cannot defy me" — she paused and added — "and to have a little chat."

I spat my response. "*Seriously*? I have nothing to say to you, Gina. But I want *answers*! Why did you kill my mother?"

She ignored my outburst and continued, "Well, while you were...uh...sleeping, we tested your friend's DNA. Susan just brought me the results. As it turns out, we had a match. He is not that young, after all. My mistake. I assumed he had been born in the refuge — an ancestor of Graham's original lot. While he is, in fact, quite a specimen. His family may well have been selected had his twin been a female. Yes, yes. I know Caleb. Where is he, by the way? Their parents were...mm...rather revolutionary scientists, if you may. Coincidentally, we had some dealings. Sadly, their children never met our male and female sibling criteria. I expect Graham invited them down here intending to draw them into his scheme. They studied with Joshua Carter under Graham's tuition."

I did not answer her question. I would *not* tell her that Caleb had died. But my jaw slackened as I formed the connections in my mind. Graham saving Eric and Caleb was no coincidence after all.

Gina wedged her horn-rimmed spectacles into the crook of her hooked nose and drew her mouth into a smug sneer, her tone condescending. "You didn't know any of that, did you?"

She paused for a moment then stood taller, trying, unsuccessfully, to level her eyes with mine. Then she walked toward and began circling me. "But that is not why I called you up here. I wonder, Miss Jones, whether by casting acerbity over your and Mr. Morgan's relationship — the way it has soured my taste — will affect how you view each other in the future. Maybe you won't be able to see past the fact that he caused your mother's death. Perhaps he'll no longer be able to look you in the eye and find solace in another's arms — Amanda, perhaps."

A cynical laugh burst through my lips before I thought to stop it. "Eric will never be with your granddaughter."

My mind drifted to all the moments when I had fallen asleep in Eric's arms or woken to him touching me. It wafted to his words in the canoe, waking in the tunnels with him stroking my wrist... *No, not stroking, fidgeting...with my great-grandmother's — !*

His last gesture as I had left the cage with the robot hit me like a gut punch. Abruptly, I knew what he had meant in circling his wrist. He had injected the lethal coral snake venom into the pen's long-empty ink tube and had been replacing it when I awoke that morning.

Without looking down at my arm, I loosened Great-Grandmother's wrap-around bracelet. But, at that moment, Gina moved away. Taking a breath, I let it retake its hold around my wrist.

Gina's voice drifted to me again. "There's no reason that Mr. Morgan wouldn't choose Amanda — beauty as she is. Or maybe his brother, Caleb, has better taste than he does."

A deep desire burned in me to figuratively ram Amanda's unremarkable disposition and plain countenance down Gina's throat. But it wasn't Amanda's fault that Mom had died. I gritted my teeth. "Is this why you summoned me, Gina — to torture me even more?"

Again, Gina neared. Once more, I tried retracting Great-Grandmother's bracelet. But for the second time, she withdrew as she continued. "No, in fact, there is something else that you may find of interest." She paused for many long seconds then arched her brows and proceeded. "When I received word that the leader of the rebellion was a woman, I knew that it could only be your mother—what with your attitude and her desperate need to protect you. Oh, but when I put the puzzle together, everything made sense—the communications between her and the technicians, having video feed deleted. Yes, I knew of that."

She sneered her next word. "*Charismatic* as she was, and being in my central office, she had access to all the right people and, therefore, information. It could only have been her. Of course, she denied it…pathetic woman."

I seethed. "My mother was anything but pathetic. She was kind and sympathetic, a loving and supportive wife and mother." Gina was too far away. While speaking, I allowed the bracelet to re-envelop my wrist.

Suddenly, Gina moved so near that her breath on my face made my skin crawl.

She lifted my chin with her stumpy fingers. "Pathetic—just like your mother," she taunted as Great-Grandmother's bracelet came free in my hand.

I stepped just the tiniest bit back to gain leverage. Then I thrust the nib as hard as I could into Gina's upper arm, twisting it deeper and deeper as she howled.

A pang of guilt struck. I cringed, withdrawing the pen as the final sparkling drops of venom trickled off its end.

Susan shrieked, backing away behind the desk as if she were my next target. She reached beneath the wooden lip and pressed a button, wailing, "Mother! Mother! What have you done, Miss Jones?"

As Gina collapsed to the floor, guilt again surged through me.

Ignoring my conscience, I cocked my head at Susan, my brows reaching for my hairline. "Why would you even ask that, Susan? Are you as insane as Gina? She killed my mother and her soldiers killed an entire family on the beach. Plus, what about those she's imprisoned and tortured? Like Jaya and who knows how many others — including Jonas and me."

Susan remained calm, ignoring my outburst. "How much time does Mother have?"

My voice matched Susan's flat tone. "Not enough time for the medic robots to save her."

Although Petriville's medical facility was in the municipal building, I didn't expect help to arrive before Gina succumbed to the coral snake venom.

I was wrong. A moment later, the elevator pinged. Two medic robots emerged, holding a stretcher between them.

Behind them strode the same gorilla-like soldier who had followed me on the train. I reflexively cringed away. The gorilla burst past me, dropping to Gina's side.

Gina wailed and snarled, as though in disbelief, "This girl...this evil thing tried to kill me!"

The gorilla, who I was sure was here to make my arrest, continued ignoring me and gently lifted Gina onto the stretcher.

The medic robots turned and, with Gina's suddenly vulnerable body on the stretcher between them, retreated into the elevator, taking the hateful woman from our presence.

I didn't follow their exit but fixed my eyes on the younger Petri woman, whose steel-gray stare was on the soldier.

Still, the gorilla didn't acknowledge or even glance at me. Instead, he walked toward Susan.

Chapter Fifty-Five

As the gorilla fed his fingers through Susan's, her eyes looked soft — unusual for the too-familiar steel-grays that I loathed.

In a quiet tone, she inquired, "What poison was it?"

I grimaced. "How did you know it was poison?"

She sighed as though growing weary of my questions. "Because you didn't go for the jugular. Also," she drawled, lifting Eric's pouch of poisons and antivenoms from her desk and slowly jiggling it, "this little recovery may have assisted in directing me to that conclusion."

Guilty as I felt, I didn't concede and threw my own question back at her. "Why should I tell you?" At the same time, a new thought struck. "It was *you*! You were the female rebellion leader Gina mentioned. You let my mother die in your stead," I screamed.

Susan lowered her gaze. "I did not *allow* her to die in my stead. A courageous woman, your mother was."

Susan stepped around the table and handed me a rolled digipar. "Its contents will be unveiled at the touch of Peter, Liam or yourself."

I glanced down at the rolled letter with Mom's familiar, rounded scrawl. My throat constricted — but it would be Dad's to open.

Susan continued. "When Mother took Emily into custody, I went to see her. Your mother was in sector ten's cellblock and wrote this letter while I sat at her side. I wanted to give myself up, but Emily insisted that it was only me who could see this rebellion through to the end. I already had more than half the military on my side." She paused, flashed a glance at the soldier beside her then went on. "Emily made me swear to finish what we'd started."

Susan dropped her eyes to the floor. "I am so, so sorry for your loss. Your mother was one of the bravest women I knew."

By the time she had concluded, I was hugging my sides, groaning. Rivers streamed down my cheeks. Never again would I see my mother. Never again would I rest in the warmth of her loving embrace.

Susan's words had not made sense.

I choked out my outrage, raw and ragged. "Why was *he* following me then?" I threw a gesture at the gorilla who was standing beside Susan.

Susan sighed, shaking her head slowly. "Miss Jones, meet Austin. You really are quite naïve. Austin was protecting you from Mother's men. You didn't see the one following you on the train, did you? In the train station, that man was about to break into the bathroom where you'd hid. Who knows what he would have done to you if he'd succeeded? Let's just say that Austin taught him the error of his ways."

My mouth fell agape. "That's rubbish. Then why would *Austin* have reprimanded the soldiers in the fields about the slaves?"

"Yes," Susan agreed, "he told them to make sure the slaves ate enough food."

The words flew through my lips. "It didn't sound like he was protecting them."

"Cover, Miss Jones. Don't you see that? How far do you think we would have gotten if Austin went in there all soft and cuddly?"

"I still don't believe you, Susan. He was shooting at us in the tunnels."

"Was he really, Miss Jones? Did you actually see him shooting at you?"

I cocked my head, my words slow, considering. "I saw him draw his weapon. Then we ran. We dived into the tunnel and I heard footsteps, more than one set. We kept running along the conveyor until Jaya pulled us into the side tunnel."

"Yes," Susan murmured, "that sounds about right. Austin drew his weapon and shot at the men coming from the other direction. He was keeping them away from you."

"Why would Gina order our murders? We were kids!"

"A hundred-and-ten-plus-year-old kids," Susan reminded me. "Mother decided that you had become a liability."

As silence fell, Susan lifted the flat, silver tablet from the desk and tapped out a few words. After a pause, she looked up. "It seems the medics established the poison as coral snake venom and have administered the antivenom."

My mouth dropped at her next sentence. "So, you will not be arrested for murder today. As for attempted murder, I think we can grant temporary insanity on that account."

Susan was not going to lump me with that label. "I am not insane, Susan. I knew exactly what I was doing."

"Yes," Susan agreed, "you may well have, but let's just say you were unreasonably provoked."

At that moment, the elevator pinged. The door glided open and Gina stepped out, glaring at me. I glanced at her arm, where I had stabbed her with the venom-filled pen no more than ten minutes before. Not even a tiny blemish remained.

Susan didn't rush to her side but murmured, "I am glad that you're better, Mother."

Gina still glowered at me. "Why has this girl not yet been arrested?"

Susan sighed, "Now, Mother, be rational. Miss Jones watched you kill Emily. But everyone is okay, so no harm, no foul." She paused.

When Gina continued scowling, Susan added, "*Right?*"

Gina didn't concede. "She deserves to be punished."

Susan didn't relent. "I think she has faced punishment enough, don't you?"

The elevator pinged again. When two more soldiers entered the plush office, I was sure my arrest was moments away. They walked not to me but to either side of Gina.

Susan glanced at me then back at her mother.

She proceeded in a slow, measured tone. "Mother, I hoped we could do this privately, but I am placing you under arrest."

As the soldiers took Gina's arms, she screeched and wrenched at them. "How dare you? I am in charge here. You cannot arrest *me*!"

She had said the last word with such force and emphasis that the soldiers' features darkened as doubt washed over them. They appeared to loosen their hold on Gina. But as she attempted to rip her arms away, they again hardened their grip, their eyes on Susan, who dispassionately observed the scene—quiet and resolute.

Gina wrenched her face into a pained expression. "Susan? Why? I have done everything for you, given you all you desired."

Susan didn't waver. "Since we're back on Earth, Mother, you can no longer hang the return codes, which you kept locked in your own mind, like a noose over my head. But it is time that you face retribution for your actions."

Gina dissolved her hurt expression. "This is mutiny! Revolt! You cannot command my soldiers."

"Oh, but I can, Mother." She held up the gorilla's adjoined hand before continuing, "As you see, these men are in agreement with me. All these years they have witnessed the conditions under which you have kept the slaves. Did you never stop to think that that might come back to bite you?"

Gina spat her response. "So you saved my life only to arrest me?"

Susan didn't hesitate. "I do not want you to die. You're my mother. But you have done wrong. And now that you have murdered Emily Jones, I can't in all good conscience allow you to continue your rule." She paused then added, "Then there's the matter of *why* you deserted the scientists who developed the '*Longevity Elix*' — " She broke off.

Gina snarled, "As though you're so innocent, Susan!"

Curiosity ripped at my stomach. I wanted confirmation of what it screamed at me.

I ground my teeth and snarled back, "Why *did* you abandon those scientists, Gina? Who were they?"

Her words sickened me as she raised her chin and cackled, "Ha-ha. Why, Miss Jones, I do believe you already know the answer. They were, of course, Mr. and Mrs. Morgan."

Susan held her gaze steady when meeting mine, as if to ward me off her mother — stay my intense desire to attack the insane woman with all the wild ferocity that was coursing through my veins.

She shifted her eyes back to her mother and continued, "So, Mother, you're being placed under arrest for murder and crimes against humanity, since I cannot hold you on abandoning the Morgans or, for that matter, Mr. Porter."

Gina thrust her shoulders back. "Don't think that you've heard the last of me, my oh-so-perfect daughter."

The soldiers led Gina, now resolute, into the elevator.

"Are you going to release my dad, Liam and our friends now?" I stated flatly. "I'd like to go home."

Susan gave one curt nod and gestured to the elevator. "That's already arranged."

With that, I pulled my shoulders back, turned and strode — rolled digipar in hand — toward the elevator.

A moment later, the familiar ping sounded as the doors opened.

I slumped during my descent into what world I faced without Mom. A few seconds later, the elevator halted and opened to that world. I again straightened and stepped from the elevator. But before I left the building, a ping sounded at the opposite elevator bank and the doors drifted open.

Chapter Fifty-Six

I gaped at the two emaciated figures emerging from the elevator ahead of two soldiers. But I did a double take. These men were aiding rather than forcing the weakened people forward.

I shook my head in an attempt to clear it. "Jaya? Aaron?"

Aaron lifted one hand in a slight wave, a cheeky smile making its way to his lips. "Told you that you wouldn't forget us — memorable as we are." He ended with an easy laugh — a laugh that faded as he took in my tear-stained face and swollen eyes. He phrased his sentence, tentatively. "It was *your* mother Gina murdered?"

Jaya raised the familiar pale-blue eyes, contrasting dark pupils analyzing, and offered a pained nod. The rasping cough escaped with no laugh this time. "That woman knows no bounds. Sick! I tell you. Sick psychopath. There is no other word for her condition.

You're in for tough times ahead, young lady. You tell us when we can help. Anytime. Do you hear me?"

Not that Jaya was in any position to help anybody, I nodded.

Jaya proceeded. "Tell that brother of yours that I knew we mattered to him. Kept me going, that did. And look... This bunch is taking us to the hospital. Now, be sure to visit when they settle me in my new home. Young Miss Petri is signing a deal with us and building houses in town to accommodate every slave down there. There's something else... She will exchange credits for our work."

Another rasping cough rattled the frail body. A soldier made to steady Jaya, but Jaya pushed his arm away, wheezing. "When I need your help, you can be sure I'll ask for it."

I met Jaya's eyes. "That is happy news, Jaya. But you get your health sorted out before you think about helping anybody."

Somehow, a smile found its way onto my lips. As the soldiers ushered them toward the hospital wing, Jaya's rasping voice faded. "Be sure to tell your handsome brother."

I blinked against the sunlight when emerging atop the municipal building's wide staircase. Those in the square stared — as if observing the newly resurrected. None celebrated the victory of my return. There was nothing to celebrate. Although the speakers were still muted, the screens had again come to life. While I descended the municipal building stairs, tiny drones skimmed around me, focusing on my wretched face and broadcasting the live feed to the huge screens. In silent homage, the onlookers bowed their heads. I sought only the barred enclosure beside the fountain and found a robot unlocking and opening the door.

Eric and Liam sprinted at me across the square, with Jonas and Harriet just behind. Dad appeared in a daze while Roger, Megan, Joshua, Caroline and Graham nurtured him from the cage.

Reaching me first, Eric flung his arms around me, a single gasping word escaping his lips. "Cassidy!" For a brief moment he drew me against him, surrounding me with his body as if he'd never let me go.

Eric ceded his grasp to Liam when he spun me away, pulling me into his arms and against his chest.

"Liam," I choked out. "What happened out there? Why did you get caught?"

"I'm so sorry, Cass," he apologized as if it had been his fault. "The soldiers trapped us. They knew we were coming. That's when we realized Gina had led us into a trap."

He pulled back, his forehead furrowing. "When you went in there"—he gestured to the municipal building, his voice trembling—"I didn't know if we'd see you again." He paused, his voice cracking. "Why did she kill Mom?"

I met his anguished eyes, my own again overflowing with tears. "Please, can we do this at home, Li? I can't bear it right now."

Harriet stepped into view with tears cascading down her cheeks. She slapped me on the shoulder. "Damnit, Cassidy. You can be so stupidly stubborn sometimes. Don't you ever do that to us again." Then she threw her small arms around both Liam and me. Her voice turned so tender as she whispered, "I am so sorry about your mom, Cass." For the first time, I noticed that Harriet's skin had the look of someone older than the nineteen years she was supposed to appear. Perhaps the physical and emotional exhaustion had got to her.

I swallowed the lump in my throat and extricated myself from their arms, ceding Liam to Harriet's embrace.

I met Liam's bright green shimmering eyes. He rubbed the bridge of his nose then wiped at his cheek.

Jonas appeared before me, wrapping his arms around my shoulders. "I don't know what to say, Cass. I wish things were different. If you need anything—" He broke off.

Silently, I laid my head on his shoulder.

Eric's eyes filled with tears as he embraced Graham with all the love afforded a true father. He cupped the old man's nape in his hand, his thumb tipping the crisp curls of the white-gray hair, his free arm encircling Graham's ribcage.

Graham's body shook. His whispered sobs barely reached my ears. "It is finally over, my son. Finally, over," he repeated softly.

Eric dipped his eyes, his posture rigid with emotion as he whispered, "Is it true we're over a hundred and ten years old?"

Gratitude appeared to touch Graham's soft eyes that he and his beloved son had reached this point. "It gets rather more complicated than that, Eric." He shook his head and pulled away from Eric. "I'm afraid I have some explaining to do." Tears slipped from his eyes. "In the refuge, I did the same as Gina did here. I'm no better than her. Every year, I filtered the annual wipe solution to you all. But it was your parents... They couldn't emphasize enough how devastating the psychological effects could be from an unnaturally long life."

Eric frowned in confusion, stepping back from Graham half a pace, his words gushing out. "What the hell do my parents have to do with this?"

Graham threw a glance at me as though asking for help, but everyone, having overheard the first part of his expletive, had now gathered around — even Dad, though I doubted he would take in a word.

I didn't know everything, so I shook my head. Graham continued, "I knew your parents. Very well, in fact. Too well," he added quietly, his eyes slipping closed. When Graham again met Eric's aquamarines, the old eyes shimmered. "Your parents were the most brilliant scientists I had ever had the pleasure of working with. Together, they developed *Ellie*, their endearment for the *Longevity Elixir*." He swallowed. "To counteract *Ellie*, they also developed a neutralizer, called *Ellen*. I was to administer this on our return to Earth. That would have, in essence, *reset* the biological clock, to age naturally from that day forward. Sadly, my containment got destroyed when a cave-in crushed the storage freezer. It took weeks to dig it out. And I couldn't tell anybody what we were digging for. By the time we reached it, the freezer door had been broken and the neutralizer compromised. It was with some luck that the freezer holding the annual memory-wipe solutions were elsewhere."

I grasped the thread. "Well, Gina will still have her supply, unless she's already administered it — which, judging by her earlier comment, she has not."

Graham sighed. "Gina told them she would destroy *Ellen*, so there was no antagonist to her *perfect specimens* producing as many offspring as possible within their lifetimes. They left it with her anyway. Their consciences were clear."

Liam interjected, "Wouldn't that cause an inbreeding problem, though?"

Graham shook his head. "Unlikely, according to the calculations."

Eric's mind was still on his parents, his eyes shining bright. "Why didn't you tell us, Graham—Caleb and me—that you knew them?"

Graham sighed as if more than just his lungs were deflating. "They made me swear not to. Even now, I am reluctant to break their trust—amazing people as they were. You were not vacationing here by accident. Apparently, your uncle, who was away in Europe, wouldn't hear what your dad had to say about the asteroid. Your parents came down here to entrust you and Caleb to my custody, but I failed them. I lost Caleb."

Dad patted Graham's shoulder in solace, but Eric withdrew another half a pace as Graham continued. "Your parents were ill. They had been exposed to a lethal dose of radiation during an experiment. They had weeks to live and didn't want you and Caleb to see them die that way. We concocted the story of the accident to protect you—make it final for you and Caleb without you having to witness them suffer."

Guilt dragged a horror-filled sob from Graham, but still, Eric never neared to comfort him. "No matter what you promised them, you should have told us. We were tougher than you think."

Graham met Eric's stare dead-on. "You're right. I've repeatedly questioned myself about that decision. But those were your parents' final wishes. Who was I to deny them that?"

Eric stepped nearer Graham, laying his hands on the old man's shoulders. "Graham, you're the father I've known for most of my life — the father I adore. Just give me time to process this. Please."

Eric twisted to me, drawing me away from Jonas and into his arms. "How will you ever forgive me, my Cassidy?" he whispered.

I shook my head. "None of this was your fault, Eric. I think Gina is a sociopath."

My heart was crushing in on itself. I had to lighten this heavy load.

I threw Eric a jibe. "So what do you know? You're not just a plebeian, after all."

Giving me a slanted eye and resting his chin on my head, he reciprocated with his own, "Like I said before, danger magnet."

My laugh flowed more easily than I expected. Eric gave the softest chuckle.

Then Eric and I turned away and ambled, hand in hand, toward conveyor number two.

The crowd parted for us, murmuring words of condolences as we traipsed onto the familiar black conveyor street.

But, passing by the animated Mama Candy's and beneath yet another digital display, my eyes drifted up. The live feed had ended. No longer did Gina's face fill the space beneath the bright orange 'Petrician Enterprises', but Susan's.

For a moment, a cold shiver ran down my spine, and I closed my hand more firmly around Mom's rolled digipar. *Surely Susan wouldn't have given it to me if she hadn't told me the truth?* I shook the thought from my mind and met Eric's beautiful eyes as he bit his lip, flashing his dimples at me.

Easing into the semblance of a smile, I squeezed Eric's fingers — the fingers of the man who Harriet had once assured me was a figment of my imagination but who I knew was a real man — the one who owned my heart.

Want to see more like this?
Here's a taster for you to enjoy!

The Pathfinders: Abomination
Jane Dougherty

Excerpt

Tully raked his fingers through his thick black hair, an expression of disgust on his face. Even his head was sweating! The window blinds stuck out like stubby black wings, keeping off the glare, but doing nothing to prevent the scorching heat radiating up from the bare asphalt outside the building. The air throbbed with the same rhythm as the whirring fan on the teacher's desk. Teacher? Yeah, right, he was in school. He almost remembered it was a physics class, but it was too tiring to drag out the information, so he let it fall back into the pit of magma that the heat had made of his brain.

A crash and the sound of brittle laughter from the building site of the new sports complex nudged at his attention. Men in hardhats wiped streams of sweat from their faces and glared up at the searing brilliance of the sky before scuttling into the relative cool of their portacabins for lunch. The crane operator had already knocked off, and the metal monster was still, steel against pewter, pulsing in the dull heat.

Tully shifted in his chair as an oppressive feeling formed and squirmed in the pit of his stomach. Had he forgotten something important? Homework? Had he locked one of the cats in his room? Couldn't remember—too damn hot. His unease focused on the silent metallic struts of the crane that hung practically overhead, like a giant predator, waiting.

The interminable lesson ended, and Tully rocked back in his chair, stretching arms and legs. A pen jabbed him in the back. He winced and turned his head. Carla grinned at him from the desk behind, and the nagging unease in his gut curled up and went to sleep.

"You are awake then. I couldn't decide if you were asleep or you'd had a stroke."

"Whose warped brain did it come out of anyway, the idea to have classes on a Saturday morning?" he asked, stifling a yawn.

"Somebody-or-other Stalin," Carla replied. "Benito, I think."

Together they walked out onto the quadrangle, the rather pretentious name given to the tree-bordered lawn that formed the geographical center of the school. The heat hit them like a blast from a baker's oven as soon as the doors slid open.

Tully cringed. "We could stay inside."

Carla raised her eyebrows. "It's traditional."

"Traditionally, it's not like the Gobi Desert out here," Tully muttered, wiping sweat from his forehead with the back of his hand. "Honestly, though, this weather is getting weirder. Don't you think?" He looked at Carla. "It isn't just me, is it? I mean, you remember summers that were just sorta normal hot, don't you? There's something funny going on. Something they're not telling us."

Carla raised an amused eyebrow again. "They? Is this one of your conspiracy theories?"

"Yeah, how about this one—all those billions of Chinese leaping about for the New Year celebrations have knocked the world off its axis, and we're falling into the sun?"

"It could just be a global conspiracy of soda manufacturers to boost sales," Carla said brightly.

Tully grinned back. Carla was probably right. She usually was. Usually.

* * * *

The lawn of the quadrangle was as brown and dry as a Middle Eastern hillside after a tribe of desert nomads had pastured their goats on it. Groups of students picnicked in the shade of the wilted plane trees that cast welcome shadows and shed a faint leafy odor that was almost healthy, unlike the less attractive city smells of car exhaust and junk food.

Sitting with his back resting more or less comfortably against a mottled tree trunk, Tully unwrapped his lunch. He spread the greaseproof paper package on the grass and, with a soft sigh that was mainly affection and only a tiny bit exasperation, picked up the large wedge of leek quiche. As he flicked his dark hair out of his eyes, he caught Carla looking at him. She grinned. She was always grinning. Tully had never met anyone else of such unflappable good humor.

"What's so funny?"

Carla laughed. "Are you sure that's your lunch you picked up and not something your dad was planning to fix the bathroom ceiling with?"

Tully pretended to inspect the quiche suspiciously. "Now you mention it, I think it might be part of his relief model of the Paris Basin," he said sarcastically. "But what the hell? I'm hungry enough to eat his Taj Mahal made out of matchsticks or his life size reconstruction of Champion the Wonder Horse." He took a large bite — too large — and chewed energetically.

"I'm sorry." Carla touched his hand contritely, and Tully forgave the grin she couldn't quite suppress. "I know you don't like people poking fun at your dad. I love him too. He's one of the best. But even you can't pretend he can cook, and don't be so spiky."

Carla had put on her most beguiling expression. Her whole face, chestnut hair, golden skin, teeth and bright eyes glowed. Tully could almost hear her purring.

"Prickly."

"Prickly then. If you give me a piece of that quiche, I'll share this focaccia with you. Gabriella made a ton of it yesterday in a fit of homesickness, and she'll be mortally offended if there's any left by the weekend."

"As long as you've got a good dentist." Tully broke off a chunk of pastry, and rounds of undercooked leek detached themselves and dropped into the grass. "I think a couple of my premolars have come loose. Sausages he can manage, but Dad's pastry is the ultimate deterrent. "

They both laughed, thinking of Jack, Tully's big, easygoing father, who never wore anything smarter than his best jeans and a clean T-shirt, with his massive hands and farm worker's arms, his bright blue eyes and dark hair, grizzled at the temples. He imagined him in the untidy kitchen, throwing flour and butter about, searching for the salt, swearing when there weren't enough eggs.

Tully's house, four stone walls and red tiled roof, forgotten by time and the developers, sat in a patch of wasteland between industrial estates and sterile farmland. The center of a ramshackle assembly of barns and outhouses, it was the heart of the Community.

Tully didn't remember life before the Community, like he didn't remember his mother except as a fuzzy warm presence. When she'd died, his dad hadn't been able to bear the constant reminders of her—in the house, the walks they took together, the shops, the town, even the language. When a lorry driver friend had told him about this community of Hairies outside Paris, unreconstructed hippies living on a vacant lot with their own generator, their goats and their allotments, Tully's dad was all ears. These were people who spoke a language his Molly had never uttered, in a country they had never visited, living a life on the edges of everything they had known together.

It didn't take long for him to pack up little Tully and everything useful, stick it in a van and leave Liverpool, England, and the ghost of Molly behind. A farm worker's cottage with a roof that was still intact became Tully's home. In winter, there was a fire in the hearth and icicles on the bedroom windows. In summer the doors stood open, and cats and the hot breeze drifted in and out.

Tully was going to his fancy international school to learn how to be a Very Important Person and save the planet. Jack was doing his bit in the Community to at least destroy as little of it as possible, to make himself as innocuous and discreet as a squirrel, or a cricket, or a barn owl.

And barn owls make lousy pastry cooks.

Tully could have made that last observation aloud and Carla would have understood, like she understood Euclid and German. She understood him so well. Tully only felt complete when he had his arms around her, her head nestled in the crook of his arm, her hair tickling his chin. In his dad's favorite cinema that smelled of stale popcorn, feet and a century of dust, she made him feel like the strong, silent hero in old Gary Cooper films. With her slender, almost angular, frame and elfin features, she seemed fragile, vulnerable, but like the wasp-waisted cowgirls, she was really tough as old boots.

"Fancy the cinema this afternoon? The Champo's showing Casablanca. Again."

Carla grimaced. "Not in this heat. I don't know why the owners of that place think you can't watch an old film without the authentic atmosphere too — sweaty armpits and hair lacquer."

Tully sighed. "I'm not going around the shops."

"Let's just go for a walk in the woods."

FINCH
B O O K S

Sign up for our newsletter and find out about all our romance book releases, eBook sales and promotions, sneak peeks and FREE romance books!

About the Author

Carryn W. Kerr is a young adult fiction author. She has a deep love for all things relating to the English language and considers stories as the rainbows of a sometimes cruel world. Rather than creating characters, she believes they always existed. Hers was the privilege of meeting them. When writing their stories, words flow through her fingertips like a gushing stream. She finds pleasure in escaping to fictitious realms as they develop and grow in her imagination.

Carryn began the adventure of life in a small South African village in the province of Kwa-Zulu Natal. When she isn't writing, she can be found working out in the gym, running, or trying not to fall off her horse as they train and compete in dressage.

For many years she worked in IT. Carryn lives with her husband and son in Johannesburg, South Africa. Her married daughter is on the beautiful island of Zanzibar.

Carryn loves to hear from readers. You can find her contact information, website details and author profile page at https://www.finch-books.com